ALSO BY B. CELESTE

Underneath the Sycamore Tree

LINDON U
Dare You to Hate Me
Beg You to Trust Me
Lose You to Find Me

PAST THE
Broken Bridges

B. CELESTE

Bloom *books*

Published by Bloom Books, an imprint of Sourcebooks
P.O. Box 4410, Naperville, Illinois 60567-4410
(630) 961-3900
sourcebooks.com

Cataloging-in-Publication data is on file with the Library of Congress.

Printed and bound in the United States of America.
KP 10 9 8 7 6 5 4 3 2 1

To my father.

CONTENT WARNING

This story contains themes of physical abuse, alcoholism, drug addiction, terminal illness, gun violence, and death. Please read with care.

PLAYLIST

"What Was I Made For?"—Billie Eilish

"loml"—Taylor Swift

"Something in the Orange"—Zach Bryan

"Always Remember Us This Way"—Lady Gaga

"What a Time"—Julia Michaels ft Niall Horan

"Beautiful Things"—Benson Boone

"Better Off Without Me"—Kyle Hume

"Drive"—Halsey

"Without You"—The Chicks

"Missing You"—Lauren Weintraub

Prologue

SAWYER

2005

THE SLOW TRICKLE OF running water is how I know I'm close. Just past the two big crape myrtles blooming with pretty pink blossoms and through the magnolia bushes that always scratch my arms is a little wooden walking bridge over the tiniest stream. I tried following it once to see where the water went, but the shrubs that surround the area are too thick to get through.

Mom hates it when I explore because I always wind up coming home with stains and rips on my clothes, but Daddy says there's a reason my name is Sawyer—I was born to explore. And since I'm brave like he is, nothing about the humid air, wild animals, or chance of getting lost scares me. I always find a way home.

Pushing past one of the shrubs that separates me from my favorite place, which is the area of streams and gardens outside the big houses I want to live in someday, I stop short when I spot a little boy leaning against one of the mossy oaks shading the area.

A startled noise escapes me, and I step back onto a twig until it snaps under the weight of my rain boot, causing me to fall backward onto the damp ground. I frown when I lift my hand and see the mud caked onto my palm.

Mom is gonna be mad again.

The shrubs part with a different set of small hands, bringing my eyes up to the boy standing in front of me on the other side. Doesn't he know this is *my* secret place? I found it months ago and never had to share it with anybody. Not even Mom or Daddy when they ask me where it is I go on my bike in the middle of the day.

I squint past the sun to get a better look at his dark-brown hair that's similar to Daddy's and then down to his eyes that remind me of the muddy Mississippi. I don't know many other kids outside my new school, but he looks about the same size as the boys in my class.

He's watching me curiously through a pair of black glasses when he finally asks, "Why are you on the ground?"

I lift my hand to show him the mess. "I fell."

"Why'd you fall?"

I was told not to talk to strangers, which is exactly what I tell him. He smiles at that and reaches down like he's offering to help me up, but I don't take his hand. I push myself off the ground and wipe my hands down the front of my jeans, leaving streaks of mud on the denim.

"This is my bridge," I tell him, crossing my arms over my chest.

He looks behind him and then back at me, pushing those glasses up his nose and smiling. "You built it?"

I blink. How could he think I built that thing when I'm only eight? "No, but it's mine."

His smile grows. "If you didn't build it, isn't it anybody's bridge? Your name isn't on it."

I stand confidently. "Yes, it is."

He watches me. "Are you SH?"

The third time I came here, I snuck one of Mom's butter knives to carve my initials into the side of the wood. But as soon as I did it, I thought I'd get caught, so I packed up my things and biked home as fast as I could pedal before the police came after me.

"What's that stand for?" he asks.

I press my lips together.

He looks down and kicks his sneakers, caked with dirt, on the ground. Quietly, he says, "I'm Paxton if it makes you feel any better. That way we're not strangers."

My parents told me to be really careful whom I trust, but they always talked about adults being the dangerous ones. Daddy sat me down and said to never go into somebody else's vehicle or accept candy from anyone I didn't know. But Paxton is too young to drive, and he hasn't offered me any candy. So he can't be so bad, right?

The girls I go to school with only ever want to play dolls and dress-up, which are boring. Maybe having a boy friend would be better.

"I'm Sawyer."

The name has him looking back up.

"Like *Tom Sawyer*," I add. "It's a book."

"I haven't heard of it."

Shrugging, I look behind him at my happy place. "Can I come in? I have fruit snacks."

When he sees me lift the small backpack, his muddy-brown eyes light up. "What kind?"

That night, I tell my parents about my new friend

Paxton, who's nine and goes to a neighboring school. His dad isn't in the Navy like mine, but he teaches about grass or something at the big college in Baton Rouge. Paxton knows a lot about plants because of his dad, just like how I know about boats from mine.

And the next week, he's at the same spot by the mossy oak, waiting for me like he said he'd be. He tells me that his friends at school only like playing video games, and I tell him mine only like playing with makeup and girly things. I sneak two bags of chips and some fruit cups into my bag, and we share them on the little bridge, swinging our legs above the flowing water.

"You never talk about your family besides your dad being a teacher," I say, crushing up little pieces of potato chips and holding out my hand to the birds chirping on the oak branch above us.

Paxton watches me curiously. "They won't come to you."

I stay still, watching as the robins tilt their heads and creep closer to examine the offerings in my palm, squawking in indecision.

Eventually, the bigger one swoops down and lands on the heel of my hand, pecking at the bigger pieces of the salty snack. I smile at him.

"They're robins," I tell the boy staring in disbelief. "See how this one is darker than the other one? That means it's a male."

The robin brings back pieces to the female waiting for his return, their rusty bellies moving as they swallow the chips.

Paxton pushes up his glasses. "How did you do that?"

"They know I won't hurt them," I answer, brushing the crumbs off my hands. "So how come you don't talk about your family much?"

4

He frowns, staring at the birds watching us and waiting for more food. "I don't know. They fight a lot."

"About what?"

Paxton stays quiet, ripping up blades of grass from the ground and watching the breeze blow them out of his palm. "About everything."

I hug my knees to my chest. "My mom gets angry at my dad all the time. I think it's an adult thing. That's why I don't want to get old. They seem mad a lot."

He lifts his shoulders silently.

"Do you want to try feeding the birds? Robins are docile. I'm sure they'll come up to you too."

Paxton looks over to the last chip before plucking it from my hand. "How do you know so much about birds?"

"My dad bought me books on animals, and there's one all about different species of birds," I explain, watching as he crushes the chip and lifts his arm like I did.

We wait for a few minutes before the same bird flies down and takes the offering.

"See?" I ask happily, noticing the small smile return to his face. "Do you feel better now?"

He leans back and watches the birds. "Yeah. Maybe a little."

The week after that, he brings us snacks and tells me that his parents are getting a divorce. I tell him I'm sorry even though I don't know what that means. When I ask my parents, they tell me it's when two people fall out of love and decide to live separately. I ask them if they're going to get one since Daddy is deployed a lot, but they promise me they won't.

A month goes by, and I see Paxton every single week. I tell him that my mom is going to have a baby, so I'll have to share their attention, but that I'm excited. Especially if it's a boy. He asks how I'd feel if it's a girl, and I guess I'd be okay with it as long as Daddy teaches her the same stuff he taught me so she's not boring.

"I think she caught cooties," I tell Paxton, trying to teach him how to skip rocks in the streams. "Daddy told me that girls can catch cooties from boys, so that must be how she got the baby."

Paxton thinks about it, mimicking what I did as he tosses the rock only to see it sink. "Maybe. Someone at my school tried telling me that a stork brings it, but I don't think I believe that."

I make a face. "A stork?" I ask thoughtfully, searching for another rock to throw. "I don't remember reading about that in my bird book."

Paxton just shrugs.

After almost two months of our afternoon meetups, I find a bruise on his arm that sort of looks like the one I got when I fell trying to climb the tree in my backyard. "What happened?"

He winces when I poke it, jerking his arm away and rubbing it. "I don't know," he says, tugging on the sleeve of his T-shirt to cover it. When it bounces up, I see three more just like it.

"Mom says I bruise like an apple," I tell him, lifting my pant leg to show him the three tiny ones on my shin. I'm always covered in them, but these have been taking forever to heal. "See? I got this one from tripping up the stairs, this one from our dog Maggie, and this one from our evil cat, Moon. I don't like her."

"Why not?"

"She's evil," I repeat. Then I tell him how she hisses all the time. Maybe she knows I prefer Maggie and gets jealous of the easygoing golden retriever.

The rest of the afternoon, we watch the clouds roll in, knowing our time is coming to an end for the day. I turn to him, crossing my legs under me. "Do you think the storm they're talking about is going to be really bad? Daddy had to go into work, but he told Mom that she should take me to my grandma's house for a few days just in case."

I haven't seen Daddy worried before, but whenever I ask if everything is going to be okay, he and Mom tell me it'll be fine. Then I see them watch the TV and look at each other the way they did when I had to be rushed to the hospital after falling from that tree.

Paxton frowns, looking up to the sky. "I don't know. It doesn't seem like it hit Florida that hard, but my parents are thinking about going too."

"Where?"

He lifts his shoulders. "Probably just inland. We've got some family in northern Louisiana that are far enough from the water that it should be fine. It's not like hurricanes haven't happened here before, right?"

I nod, eyes moving back to the sky. "Right."

We sit in silence again, watching the sun completely vanish behind the fluffy gray clouds.

"Maybe it won't be so bad and we can meet here next weekend," he suggests, resting his chin on his knees. "It's nice having a friend."

I smile cheekily. "I'm your friend?"

His cheeks turn pink. "Unless you don't want to be?"

I pull out the last pack of fruit snacks I brought with me and pass it to him. "I don't just share my snacks with anybody, Paxton."

He grins, dumping half of the gummies into his hand and giving me the other half. "What about the cooties?"

Giggling, I pop a fruit snack into my mouth and nudge him with my foot. "I'm willing to risk it for you. Just don't give me a baby, okay?"

He holds out his hand. "Deal."

We shake and then sit there until the first raindrop falls, only parting ways when the sky opens up around us.

If I'd known that was the last time I'd be walking away from my happy place and the brown-haired boy with my favorite muddy eyes, I probably would have tried staying longer. Learned his last name. His favorite color.

Anything.

But three days later, on August 29, 2005, I found out why Daddy looked so worried about Hurricane Katrina.

And even though he sent us to my grandparents' house in North Carolina and we heard from Daddy as much as we could while he was out on rescue efforts, I was sad. Sad because I knew the chances of me ever seeing Paxton again were low. Sad because Mom was sad. Sad because Daddy told us he'd be away for a long time to help the people who couldn't get out.

When I watched the news on the TV with my aunt Taylor and grandma, I learned a new word from the anchor. Devastation.

Maybe sadness didn't cover what I felt.

I guess I was devastated.

For me and my family and the state I hoped Daddy's job wouldn't take us from this time, like it had from New York and Florida and Virginia.

But I guess the storm did that for him.

And months later, when I'm still thinking about the place I'm told I can't go back to, I swear to myself that one day when I'm a grown-up, I will.

Chapter One

SAWYER

2018

Tick tock. Tick tock. *Tick tock.* They say bad things happen in threes, but I don't want to believe that. Because the more you worry about when the other shoe is going to drop, the less you let yourself live. And if there's anything I've learned over the past five years, it's that life is too precious to be wasted on fear.

Nurse Katherine beams as she caps off the last test tube and sets it back in the holder, breaking my focus from the ugly round clock on the wall that tells me I'm minutes away from well-deserved freedom. "So what now, Sawyer?"

I look from the middle-aged woman I've come to consider a friend over the last six months to the woman I got my red hair and baby blue eyes from, who's sitting quietly in the chair by the examination table. She looks nervous because we've had this conversation plenty of times over the last year, but she's never discouraged me from what I want to do.

Not after the long battle I faced.

Turning from my mom to Katherine, my favorite nurse in the oncology unit, I smile. "I'm going to college. An *actual* college."

Katherine's eyes brighten at the news I've only told a few close family members. Dad is proud of me. Bentley, my little brother, told me he wanted my room when I left, and Aunt Taylor insisted on hosting a going-away party. If my grandparents were still alive, I'm sure they would be as happy for me as Katherine. Or maybe as nervous as the look on my mother's soft face. "I think that's wonderful! You've taken online courses for credits, right?"

Giddiness takes over, making it hard to sit still. I've told her about the courses I didn't find challenging enough and how badly I wanted to go on campus somewhere. For obvious reasons, namely my lack of immune system thanks to the chemicals being pumped through my body, I had to push those dreams away. Temporarily. "Yes, and I already double-checked to see that they transfer to the college I'm attending so I won't start as a twenty-one-year-old freshman like some weirdo."

Katherine pats my knee and peels her gloves off, tossing them into the trash bin by the sink and turning on the faucet. "Where did you enroll?"

Licking my chapped lips, I peek at Mom again. Her eyes glisten with concern and pride. I know she's happy for me, but it's not easy for her when we spent so long together bonding over something so tragic. "I got accepted at Louisiana State."

Katherine's eyes dart to my mother before coming back to me, as if doing the mental math of the distance between New York and Louisiana. "LSU, huh?"

She's a mom, so I'm sure she sympathizes. It isn't like mine can come with me to school, and I doubt she'd want to even if she could. I've missed the Bayou State since we left it thirteen years ago, but I know she feels differently. They lost everything when the levees failed after Katrina.

I only lost Paxton.

Despite Mom's hesitancy toward my determination to move down south and escape New York's cold weather, she says, "We're very proud of Sawyer. She's worked so hard for this."

Katherine must know how difficult that is for her to admit, so after she dries her hands, she brushes Mom's arm. "If there's anybody who can handle college, it's our girl. Isn't that right?" She turns to me with a wink and grabs the tube holder off the counter. "By the way, I'm loving the blond. Are you going to keep it or try something fresh for your new adventure?"

Touching the ends of the wispy hair tickling my shoulders, I smile at the woman I've grown so close to. "I'm not sure yet. I kind of miss the red."

Mom laughs at the statement that I've made plenty of times before in my head. "You used to hate your natural color. Remember how you'd beg me to let you dye it? You wanted the most God-awful colors too."

Okay, the black I wanted would have been a terrible choice against my pale skin. I probably would've resembled one of those creepy porcelain dolls they make horror movies about. "We all had an emo phase, Mom," is my grumbled defense.

That phase also included thick eyeliner that I still don't know how to apply correctly, plus My Chemical Romance—and Avril Lavigne–inspired punk-rock outfits. I'd like to think I pulled it off.

Sometimes.

The thin pieces of hair around my finger don't compare to what my desired red locks, not quite orange but a mixture of dark red and copper, were years ago. I'm glad Mom didn't let me destroy the healthy strands. They used to be so thick that hairdressers had a field day layering them during haircuts and telling me how pretty they were. I'd hear the same thing every time I sat down in the spinning chair and got the cape draped over me: *Be lucky to have what some women pay hundreds of dollars to get.*

My lips twitch downward.

Haircuts used to be so mundane—just something I did every six weeks with my mother and grandmother in North Carolina. Maintenance cuts, really. Mom would complain about how expensive it was but would fight Grandma Claudette whenever she'd try to pay for each of us. I miss those days.

I miss having people play with my hair and massage my scalp. I miss the ego stroke that came with the unique color people said made my eyes pop.

I miss life before I was sick. Before all the treatments and tears and hard days, when all I had to worry about was eating my vegetables so I could go outside and play.

That life feels like it was ages ago, and I don't even remember who I was before the cancer. Who knew one little trip to the doctor's office for what we all thought was a cold could change so much?

Whenever I start feeling sad about the things I can't change, I think of what Mom always told me when I'd look into the mirror at my bald head and start crying.

Better your hair than your life.

And she's right. So right.

"Sawyer?" I hear, snapping my eyes up to where Katherine is standing by the open door.

Releasing the hair and dropping my hands into my lap, I sit straighter. "Sorry, what?"

"I said good luck with everything," she repeats with the same warm smile that's made me feel at home since the day I walked into the treatment center for yet another round of chemo. "And as much as I adore you, I hope I never see you again."

I laugh. "Back at you, Kitty Kat."

She waves us off and walks out.

I barely have time to climb off the table when Mom asks, "What were you thinking about?"

I hate that she knows I was lost in my head, but I don't want to dwell on any of it anymore. It doesn't matter. After five years of off-again, on-again remission and treatments, I'm done.

Done-done.

It was hard enough going from being on the rise of popularity at fifteen to a social pariah nobody wanted to talk to. Like my cancer was contagious—like *I w*as. Switching to homeschooling wasn't what I wanted to do, but it was the only way I could keep my sanity during a period of time that was already difficult to navigate.

I don't want to keep hiding, and I don't want to keep letting the cancer win.

I turn to my mother, who's extending my winter coat out to me. "I was thinking that we should get chicken nuggets," I say. "I promise I'll save some for Bentley this time even though he's a total dweeb."

The woman who's been through hell and back with me stands with suspicious eyes as I shove my arms into the sleeves of my coat. I'm sure she knows that isn't what I zoned out thinking about, but she doesn't pressure me into the truth. "Do you mean that this time, or are you going to tell your brother that you got him nuggets and then feed them to Maggie in front of him?"

I giggle, walking out the door with a newfound sense of freedom, knowing it's time to move on to bigger and better things. "I can't do the same thing twice or he'll expect it. Duh."

Mom sighs.

I grin. "He deserved it after eating the last Pop-Tart that he knew I was saving."

"You two are something else," she mutters.

"But you love us."

She kisses my temple. "More than life, baby girl. More than life."

I look back at the clock in the lobby when we get my final set of paperwork from the clerk.

Tick tock. Tick tock. Tick tock.

My skin buzzes with anticipation, excited to see the sun. To feel it on my too-pale skin that Mom makes me slather in layers of sunscreen in the summer and lotion in the winter.

And at the end of the day, I share my chicken nuggets with my little brother, watch his favorite dorky movie about rings and hobbits, and endure his gross habit of dipping his popcorn in pickle juice.

Because I know our time together is limited.

Swiping at the foggy mirror until a blurry image of my face appears, I readjust the soft coral towel around my torso to make sure it's covering all the essentials.

14

When I was diagnosed with an aggressive form of non-Hodgkin's lymphoma at sixteen, treatment was brutal. The only good news was that the type of diffuse large B-cell lymphoma I had tended to respond well to chemotherapy. *Usually*.

The first treatment was six months. After the first two infusions, the hair on my scalp felt so tight that it was too uncomfortable to keep. I'd asked Mom to cut it, but she'd been too emotional. So I went into Dad's closet, found his old hair clippers, and took as much as I could off myself until she came into the bathroom and gasped at the mess of hair on the floor.

"Baby, what did you do?"

I pass her the clippers and whisper, "Please?"

It was hard for both of us, but she held back her tears and helped me finish until there was nothing left but skin. And when we looked at the floor and saw the scattered pieces of what made us look so much like each other, we both cried until our blue eyes were rimmed with red.

A few days later, Mom surprised me with my first wig. Red. Not quite like our natural color, but close. The highlights were prettier than the copper ones we had, and it helped us pretend that things were okay. At least for a little while.

Dad told me I was beautiful either way when we video-chatted from his naval base in Louisiana, where he'd stayed after Katrina, but it took me a long time to feel that way and believe it.

Touching the fuzzy hair slowly growing in haphazardly, I fight a frown at the prickles that tickle my fingertips. "I look like a chia pet," I mumble to myself under my breath.

My fingers graze down the sides of my face, tracing the

sunken cheekbones that have given my normally round face a chiseled look that I don't love or hate. A pair of rough, chapped lips meet the pad of my thumb, reminding me that I need to buy more lip balm before I go anywhere. Then my fingers go downward, the smooth skin of my neck allowing for a sullen breath to escape, until my fingertips touch the raised skin of the old port in my chest where all of my medications used to go.

Goose bumps cover my arms when I drag my finger pads over the sensitive lump, where a long, pink scar remains. As much as I hate looking at it, it's a reminder of what I faced. I'm stronger because of the tribulations that came with the sickness. Each time it came back, I fought harder.

Knew what to expect.

Handled it.

For me and my future.

For Mom.

For Dad.

For Bentley.

I'd like to think I'm better for it now because I'm not nearly as scared as I used to be about where life could take me. Now it's about taking it by the horns and choosing where to go from here.

Standing taller, I give my lean frame, hidden mostly by the bulky towel, one last look before walking into my attached bedroom, where it looks like a tornado tore through. I've never liked packing, so I always wait until the last minute to do it.

Because no matter how excited I am to go back to a place where seafood, pastries, and jazz music greet you on every corner, I know this time will be different.

And as I look around the robin's-egg-blue room I picked

out when we moved into the house, I'm hit with nostalgia. Because I don't know when the next time I'll see it will be.

Three hours later, in my cotton pajamas covered in ninja ducks that Aunt Taylor bought me for Christmas, I click the last two locks into place on my suitcase and study the empty closet behind me.

Mom walks in and wraps her arm around my waist, her hold gentle but firm at the same time. "Are you positive about this?"

Stay, she's asking.

I look at her and nod. "I'm sure."

I can't is what I really tell her.

Her hand reaches out and caresses the side of my face, her eyes lifting to my patchy scalp. I see her throat bob and her eyes glaze before she takes a deep breath.

She knows I need to do this.

For the first time in what feels like forever, I'm finally going to *live*.

Chapter Two

SAWYER

Bentley tries escaping the noogie I'm giving him in front of the passenger drop-off section at the airport, but the thirteen-year-old is even weaker than I am, so he can't fight me off. "Admit it, dork. You're going to miss me."

He eventually wiggles his way out, darting under my arm with a laugh. Unlike Mom and me, he's got Dad's brown hair. Dark, like the Hershey chocolate he constantly steals from my room. I put an unopened bag in my desk drawer for him that I'm sure won't take him long to find.

As he tries flattening his hair back down, he rolls the blue eyes that we share. "How could I miss your bad music blasting through your door and your mood swings when it's that time of…?" His face blossoms with heat as he stops himself from finishing the sentence.

"When it's what?" I pry, knowing the teen can't say it.

He loses his courage. "*You know.* When you, uh…"

"Bentley," Mom chides, trying to fight the amusement that clearly wants to curl her lips. "Menstrual cycles are completely natural. It's fine to say the word 'period' without being embarrassed by it. I got them. Your sister gets them. Your future wife will get them."

I snicker when he turns a deeper shade of red.

"Yeah, yeah," he mumbles. "Whatever. Let's stop talking about *that* in public."

"Let's hope you get a growth spurt soon, or that attitude is going to get you pushed into some lockers," I tell the five-foot-three rat.

"Sawyer!" Mom scolds, shooting me a look.

My brother and I both laugh, causing her to squeeze the bridge of her nose. They're going to miss me as much as I'm going to miss them. Even if we get on each other's nerves sometimes.

As excited as I am to land someplace where I don't need my fluffy down jacket, sadness sweeps over me.

"I should get going," I tell them, fighting a frown. Most of my things are being shipped to the tiny apartment Dad has outside New Orleans. He has a rental truck waiting to pack it all up and bring it over to the apartment building that my parents helped me secure near the LSU campus. "I have a couple hours before takeoff, but I want to call Dad and make sure he'll get there on time."

Mom walks over and gives me the tightest hug I've gotten from her in a long time. It reminds me of the one she gave me after we found out about my cancer. I come from a family of huggers, but I'd never been held the way she did that afternoon at the hospital. "Behave yourself down there."

"I will," I tell her.

At least I'll try.

She pulls back, her hands going to my face. I can tell

she's going to cry, which I made her promise not to do. "And if you need *anything*—"

Her voice cracks, making me groan. I put my hands on top of hers. "I'll let you know if I need something, but I'll be okay. It's college. I've got plenty of resources." When that doesn't seem to appease her, I add, "Dad isn't that far from me, and I know you're a phone call away too."

The reminder has her gently patting my cheeks before letting go and pushing Bentley over to hug me goodbye.

"Be good for Mom, dork face," I tell the lanky boy, who reluctantly wraps his noodle arms around me. I'm tempted to mess up his hair again, but I'm nice this time. Pulling away, I eye him. "If I hear you're bad, I'll cancel my Netflix subscription so you can't watch your anime shows anymore."

He snorts. "I can get my own."

"With what money?" Mom and I ask simultaneously.

My brother blinks at the response before grumbling, "Fine, I'll be good. Just go already."

Mom swats him on the arm at his response, but she rolls her eyes and gives me one more hug before I pick up my carry-on. "Call me as soon as you land, Sawyer. I mean it."

I'm about to remind her that she can track my location, but I decide against it. I had to show her how to comment on an online post three different times in the last month. Reminding her how to track me isn't going to be any easier. "I will. Promise. You better head out before the parking police come back and yell at you again."

She looks to where the man wearing a neon vest is walking over to us. Shoulders dropping, she squeezes my hand and then lets go. I wave to her and my brother, grab my belongings, and head inside, knowing I have to be the one who walks away first.

Mom never will.

That's why I love her so much.

And the first whiff of the airport smells like a mixture of freedom and anxiety that I'm more than willing to take on if it means doing it my own way this time.

I pull out the crumpled piece of paper from my pocket that I've been working on for the past three months. The second I opened my acceptance letter to Louisiana State, I started this list. It's torn, wrinkled, and smudged, but I can't help but smile when I strike my pen through the first two items.

~~Go back to Louisiana~~
~~Attend college~~

Nibbling my lip, I carefully fold the paper back up and tuck it into the side pocket of my backpack just in time for the boarding process to begin.

I stand, a newfound giddiness dancing in the pit of my stomach as I line up with the others in my boarding group.

My eyes go to the clock on the TV screen underneath the boarding details.

Tick tock. Tick tock.

Under my breath, I whisper, "Here I come."

Chapter Three

BANKS

"YO, BANKS!" SOMEONE YELLS, nearly pelting me in the head with a basketball.

I catch it at the last second, glaring at my dipshit best friend as he jogs over to me. "What the hell, dude? You could have broken my glasses. Again."

Dawson Gable takes the ball back with a slick grin, tucking it under his arm. "It's a good thing your dad has good vision insurance, huh?"

I'm not sure my father would say the same. At least, that's not what he said the last time I came home with broken lenses that needed to be replaced thanks to my friend of ten years.

"Speaking of your old man," he remarks, matching my pace as we walk to where my four-door pickup truck is parked in the back lot of our apartment building. "He almost failed me last semester. You believe that shit? Man acts like he didn't feed me over the past decade. You'd think that'd earn me a little something in class."

That's Dawson's problem. He expects the upper hand from everybody. What he doesn't see is the side of my dad that I do. He only thinks my father is a typical hard-ass—he doesn't realize how far that goes. "You know he's not like that," I tell him, opening the creaky door and tossing my bag onto the bench seat. "It doesn't matter if you're my friend, he's going to treat you like any other student."

"What about as star of the basketball team?"

I deadpan, wondering if he's serious or if he's playing. "You sit on the bench ninety percent of the time, dude."

His hand flies to his chest as he stumbles back dramatically. "Shots fired." When he stabilizes himself, he leans against the hood of my father's old Ford. Dad had been in a good mood when he'd agreed to let me drive it after getting my license. I'd been more than surprised when he passed me the keys, given his mood is typically unpredictable.

"I thought we were friends, but I guess I was wrong," Dawson continues. "If there's one thing I learned from watching *The Mighty Ducks,* it's that there's always a chance."

We used to play the hell out of that movie. I'm pretty sure one of our moms had to buy us a new VHS when the other one shit the bed. That is, before both our mothers left us with our fathers. At least his dad is decent. I don't know why he always wanted to spend time at my house when I could have used an escape too.

"Too bad you didn't sign up for hockey then," I say. "Maybe you'd see play time."

"Brutal," Dawson says, rubbing under his nose and sniffling. I eye the movement, trying not to think too much into it. "You need a Snickers or something. You're not you when you're hungry."

I finally stop examining him and chuckle.

"Where are you going, anyway?" he asks.

Where else? There are only two places I tend to go willingly besides my apartment, and I'm not scheduled to work at the campus store today, which is a small miracle. "The Botanic Gardens."

My best friend shakes his head, probably thinking I'm as pathetic as I feel sometimes. "I should have known. I don't suppose I can change your mind? The guys were going into the city to celebrate our last day of freedom before classes start."

"Let me guess. Bourbon Street?"

His eyebrows wiggle. "As if there's any other choice," he remarks knowingly.

I check my watch, frowning when I realize the old Citizen my grandpa gave me stopped working at some point. "I think I'll rain check. I told my pops I'd stop by for dinner tonight."

"Damn. No invite for me?"

I raise my brows. "Would you rather be spending the night with my dad and me or your friends at the bars?"

As nervous as I get when Dawson goes out these days, I know I have to trust him to handle himself. That was part of his program.

He snaps his fingers and points at me with his index one. "Fair point, my friend. You have fun with that. Tell your dad I'll see him in class. I'm sure he misses me."

My dad has nothing bad to say about Dawson as a person. But as a student… "Sure will, bud. I'll talk to you later."

He shifts as a small U-Haul turns into the lot, parking near the front doors. "Fresh meat," he says to me with mischievous eyes. "Maybe it's a hot chick. Haven't had one of those here in a while. We're starting to get outnumbered by all the jockstraps and computer nerds."

I watch as an older man gets out of the front seat. A dad, probably. There's a bush in the way of whoever climbs out of the passenger side, but I can see a pair of flip-flops and lean bare legs that probably don't belong to a dude.

Peeling my gaze away from the new girl, I slide into my truck. "Try not harassing her too much and maybe you'll actually get laid this year. You've been on a dry streak for a while."

He throws up his middle finger. "Not all of us are tall, dark, and nerdy like you, Banks. Maybe if you left a few women for the rest of us, we'd have a chance."

I snort, even if guilt nudges the pit of my stomach. It's not exactly like I sleep around. Much. I focus on school and myself. If I'm bored or a little too drunk, sometimes I let loose. But that's rare these days. And it isn't like Dawson is unattractive. By society's standards, he's technically better looking than me. At six-six, the man towers over me by almost four whole inches and is built like a pro baller would be. You'd think as a Luke Kennard look-alike with nearly the height to match the NBA player, he'd be a catch with the ladies.

Maybe this year will be his year. I sure as hell don't plan on getting in his way the way I stupidly did when it came to the last girl we were both interested in.

I slip the key into the ignition, eyes going back to the U-Haul. My neck tingles with a familiar feeling as a streak of blond appears past the bushes, a box in the girl's hands. Clearing my throat, I shoot my friend a grin. "I'll do my best to let you have a few this year, man." Nodding my chin, I start the truck and pull out of my spot.

When I see Dawson walking toward the U-Haul, I roll my eyes. Hopefully he doesn't bother whoever the poor girl is. I don't have the energy to ensure that he doesn't make a fool of himself because all of my energy will have to go toward surviving the heavy family dinner that I've been dreading since I woke up this morning.

Pushing open the wrought-iron gate leading to the yellow, two-story, raised center-hall cottage a few hours later, I stop as soon as the creaky door closes behind me to stare at the house I've called home for the past twenty-two years. The two-hundred-and-fifteen-year-old home is styled after French colonial plantations. It's aged and beautiful and well kept compared to some of the others in the Garden District here in New Orleans.

My father's love for architecture and landscaping is the reason I'm in my last two years at LSU's architectural program. I don't have a lot in common with the man who raised me, but my degree is the common ground we need. The intense five-year program has been brutal, but I don't regret it for a second because it makes me appreciate everything I've had growing up.

Like this house, with its open porches along both levels that are supported by white columns and have a beautiful view of the surrounding double-gallery homes and American-style townhouses. Each house is stacked with brick, iron, ivy, and Spanish moss lining the gates, along with oaks and willows surrounding the properties.

My city doesn't compare to any other. It's the best, and I don't feel guilty being biased about it.

When I finally walk through the front door, the strong scent of Cuban cigars hits me. Teeth grinding, I veer right until I'm greeted with a plume of smoke in the living room.

"I thought you were quitting after the doc told you that your lungs needed a break," I grumble, opening a window.

Dad taps the end against his ash tray on the end table. "Why don't you sit and have one with me instead of bitching? I got one of those Liga 5 ones you like."

Once in a while, I entertain the old man and smoke a stogie with him, but I've never liked the nasty bastards. They were always his thing. I remember Mom complaining about the smoke and how expensive they were getting when he'd spend a good chunk of his paycheck on packages of them. It was one of the reasons she left him, left *us*. Maybe that's why I never developed a taste for the pricey tobacco.

Dropping into the armchair across from him, I drape a foot onto the edge of the coffee table and see the old Western he's watching on TV. "I'll pass this time. Is this John Wayne?"

"Clint Eastwood," he corrects, grabbing the remote and turning the television off. My lips twitch at the only distraction I had. "How are you feeling about classes this semester? You've got Delvey *and* Laramie, don't you?"

Here we go. "Yeah. I've got Laramie's Architectural Design course and—"

"Honors?" he questions, cutting me off.

I blink, swiping my tongue along my dry lips, and use the time to take a deep breath. "Yes, it's the honors class."

My father dips his chin in praise. "Good."

The leg still resting on the ground bounces when we fall to silence. I've always been a damn good student. Honor roll. Principal's list. President's list. Top three of my high school class until senior year, when I managed to snatch the salutatorian spot. But Dad wasn't as proud as I thought he'd be because the guy I stole the spot from lost it because of some marijuana scandal that got him expelled.

Point is, I'm smart. Always have been. In part thanks to the man smoking a few feet away. He taught me a lot of what I know and motivated me to learn the rest.

Too bad that's not always good enough.

"What elective are you doing?" is his next question, pulling my attention up from the carpet, where an old cigar burn is left from one of his benders.

Rubbing the heel of my hand against my jean-clad thigh, I lean back in the chair, knowing he won't like my answer. "Creative writing."

His brows shoot up as expected, his tone thoroughly unimpressed. "A writing class?"

"I've exhausted a lot of my other options over the past couple of years," I tell him.

Secretly, I'm tired of science, history, and math classes. I took a few art courses here and there that were decent, but not my favorite. I figured English was a good route to go. "It'll be a nice breather from all my usual stuff. Shit, maybe it'll inspire me."

Dad used to say that you could draw inspiration from everyday life and incorporate it into your sketches. When I was a kid, he'd take me to his favorite parks and sketch the landscaping in the pad that he eventually gave to me when I officially enrolled at LSU. His original pictures are still in there—every bush, tree, and flower drawn to perfection in pencil or charcoal. He always told me that life itself was an experience that you could build your craft on, so I don't see how literature and the fictional world are any different.

"Don't you think your focus is better spent on things that'll advance your career?" he asks.

"It still counts toward my degree, Dad. I'm not wasting my time by taking this. There's a reason why schools make electives part of their requirements. They don't want to burn us out. Plus, it fits into my schedule better. It's only once a week on Wednesdays. I can work more hours at the store and focus on my homework."

The thoughtful noise coming from him doesn't bode well for the outcome of this conversation. It's the same story, different day. Just when I think I've done something to impress the tenured professor, he makes it seem like a wanting effort.

By the grace of whatever God exists out there, he drops it. "Have you heard from your mother recently?"

It's moments like these when I wish Dad and I had more than architecture in common. Like sports. Then I could distract him with the latest NCAA March Madness predictions or talk about who we think could make it to this year's Super Bowl. Because there's one other topic outside school I dread talking about with him—Mom.

Yanking on the collar of my shirt as I absently stare at the blank TV screen, I say, "She called the other day wishing me good luck at school this semester."

We only talk a few times a year, so I don't know why he bothers asking. She'll call before school starts, on my birthday, and on Christmas to let me know when to expect my present. She lives two hours away, but I haven't seen her in years. Maybe because she knows nothing will change with us.

I've accepted her absence as much as she has mine. I guess she assumes we're both better off.

She couldn't be more fucking wrong.

When Dad is silent, I look in his direction. He's taking another puff of his cigar, letting the smoke out slowly in front of him. I focus on that instead of the pinched expression across his face. "She still with the plumber?"

Jaw ticking at the same question he's asked me for the past ten years, I answer, "Yeah. She's still with Joe."

"Joe," he grumbles, shaking his head.

That's all he says, but I can see the way his eyes darken with a swarm of emotions that I know aren't good. It's all in his brown eyes that shift to a hazy black.

People used to say we looked just like each other when I was a kid. But that stopped a long time ago. Now, the man barely looks like himself.

I get up, not wanting to be on the other end of his bad mood. "Want a beer?" I ask, heading into the kitchen for the only thing I can hope will help him not explode.

Before he can answer, I'm pushing one of the canned IPAs into his hand and sitting back down with my own. I crack mine first, figuring I'll have one with him. Although, knowing him, one will turn into six. All I can hope for is that he winds up being a happy drunk today, or else I'm going to really regret turning down Dawson's offer to join him on his pub crawl. I'd rather be getting shit-faced there than dealing with the borderline alcoholic sitting next to me.

To keep the peace, I bring up the one thing I know my father can talk for hours about without getting angry. "I think I know what I want my senior design to be for my capstone."

"Don't think I'm letting go of your ridiculous decision to take a writing class, Paxton. I'd like to think I'm not contributing to your education only to see you waste both our time."

Paxton. I fucking hate that name.

Because he only uses it when he's pissed.

But I let it go and tell him about my project design, hoping it's good enough to appease him.

Hoping, for once, that *I'm* good enough.

And when he finishes one beer, I get him another because it's the only way to keep him busy enough to stay seated.

He never says a word as he empties can after can.

In the back of my head, a voice hisses, *You will always be an enabler.*

Chapter Four

SAWYER

I'D FORGOTTEN HOW MUCH I missed Dad's hugs until his arms are squeezing me against him in goodbye eight hours after helping me move in. He'd done the same thing at the airport when he picked me up, except he lifted me off the ground and spun us around as if I were five instead of twenty-one. But I didn't mind. I laughed and hugged him back, not caring about the people who watched us and probably judged.

"I'm so damn proud of the woman you've become," Dad tells me again, making it hard to fight the fresh glaze of tears that come with his compliment. My whole life, I've always wanted to make him proud because he's the best person I know. He's strong and brave and selfless. Who wouldn't want to be just like him? He was even recognized in a newspaper article for the lives he saved after Katrina, which Mom has framed in the living room at their house in New York.

I playfully push his shoulder. "Don't get all mushy on me. Mom already did that."

His low chuckle brightens his brown eyes, making him look a lot younger than fifty. The speckles of silver in his dark hair are the only reminder that my father is getting older. Not that it stops him. As a senior chief petty officer in the Navy, the man keeps in shape. He says he needs to if he's going to match the new recruits' energy. "You know this is hard for your mother. She worries about you. We both do."

There's a lot left unsaid about why they're so worried, but the concern melded into his expression is hard to misinterpret.

I nod in understanding. "I get that, but I'll be fine. And look—" I gesture toward the one-bedroom apartment he helped me set up today. "I live in a great place. The area is safe, you said so yourself. I know Mom did research almost every night when I told you I didn't want to live on campus."

My father eyes me, and I know what the look is for. He's not concerned about the apartment or the crime rate. At least, that's not his main concern. He sees past the pretty blond wig and light makeup coverage that hide the truth. "You have been through so much, baby girl. It's hard to not worry with this next step."

Swallowing down the emotion from his thick response, I take a deep breath. "Isn't this next step better than the alternative?"

For once, he's quiet.

Somber.

I don't mean to hurt him or Mom or Bentley. The only goal I have in life is to finally live it, and that's what I'm doing. It's why I didn't want to waste time living in a dorm room, sharing a bathroom with strangers and wondering if I'd get along with my roommate. Mom liked the idea of me being near the campus health clinic, where I could be monitored more quickly, but I had to remind her that there were certain things campus staff probably weren't trained for. They only agreed to this apartment because of how close it was to the hospital and Dad's base where his housing unit is.

I try reasoning with him the best I can. "If I need something, you won't be that far away. Plus, I promised I'd call Mom all the time."

They both understand that things can change. Haven't the past five years proven that there's no guarantee in life? That's why I'm here, so I can be a normal twenty-something-year-old. Maybe I'll go to a party. Maybe I'll drink. The possibilities are endless.

My parents aren't stupid. They're just my parents. Neither of them wants to see me go through any more than I already have. But I'd rather have the normal experiences than the ones that have aged me.

Dad lets go of a soft breath. "I really am proud of you, kiddo."

I blush, looking down at the hardwood floor. *My* hardwood floor. Even though I never liked my feet being cold, I'm excited to step on it in the mornings when I drag myself from the queen bed in the back bedroom into the kitchen in the front for a survivalist drink. Aka caffeine.

He checks his watch and stands taller. "I've got to get going. Thank you for entertaining your old man for the day. Make sure to eat those leftovers in the fridge before they go bad. Seafood shouldn't be left for long, even if it's cooked."

Rolling my eyes at the information that certainly isn't new, I say, "I know, Dad. Just because we're in the Big Easy doesn't mean I haven't had shrimp before."

His smile matches my own—Mom has said so herself. *That smile reminds me so much of your daddy,* she'd tell me on the days we both missed him. "All right, all right. I'll get out of your hair." He cringes at the term, caressing said hair, before pressing a kiss to the top of my head and reminding me, for the third time, to lock the door behind him.

Which I do.

And then I turn around and study the small space with a big smile. There isn't much on the walls, save for the photo Mom took over the summer of me and our elderly golden retriever Maggie, who's way more gray than yellow in the face anymore, and one of my favorite pictures of my parents from their twentieth-anniversary dinner that I swiped from their mantle. They were laughing because Bentley and I were making dumb faces to get Dad to smile since he's spent too long being told not to for his military photos. The couch is a Salvation Army special that my father only paid fifty dollars for, the coffee table was an old one from his apartment, and the rug underneath it is a cheap clearance find from when Mom and I went shopping a few weeks ago.

Nothing matches, yet I love all the mismatched woods and colors and patterns. The unique look is utterly chaotic, just like me.

Sitting down on the edge of the brown couch, I cross my legs under me. "Big things are coming," I tell myself. Wiggling into the firm cushions, I settle in and stare up at the ceiling.

A tickle forms in my throat. "Big things," I repeat, coughing into the crook of my arm and ignoring the tug in my chest.

It's half past eleven when I finally hear footsteps coming

down the hall. Stomach growling and irritated by how late my food is, I whip the door open and step out to give the delivery person a piece of my mind.

Maybe if I wasn't hangry, I'd find the tall, dark-haired boy wearing thick black glasses attractive. Hot, even. Katherine would say he's the H-A-W-T kind of hot that she used to call the new oncologist whenever he'd walk in. Her face would get all pink, and she'd stammer her words at the silver fox.

Except the lanky person in a dark sweatshirt and jeans is eating *my* cheesy gordita crunch wrap from Taco Bell— literally eating it right in front of me! And since anyone who knows me knows that I don't tolerate my food being stolen without some level of She-Hulk anger that could scare a bear, I can't in good faith consider him even the slightest bit cute.

"You're the worst delivery person ever," I tell him in awed disgruntlement. I mean, seriously? You'd think if he was going to eat a customer's order, he wouldn't carry the bag all the way inside. "I tipped you and everything."

The boy stumbles when he hears me, his shoulder bumping into the wall and bouncing off it. Is he drunk? Who lets these people DoorDash? You'd think there'd be some sort of screening process.

Half of my gordita crunch falls from his hand, splattering in a ground-beef-and-cheese mess on the hallway floor. May it rest in peace. "You're not from around here," he slurs, using the wall for balance.

I blink. That's all he has to say? "Who says?"

His eyes, hidden behind the square glasses that make him look like Clark Kent, roam over the front of me. My toes curl into my slippers, making me hyperaware that I came out

36

here in nothing but a thin pair of pajama shorts with Tweety Bird on them that barely cover my goods and a baggy LSU sweatshirt. I'm slim but definitely love pasta—and tacos— with a chest that's small enough to go braless under most shirts but big enough to have *something* to look at, and he must like what he sees because he keeps staring.

Or maybe he's just had a lot to drink. Because seriously. Who eats somebody else's tacos? That's just messed up.

He puts what's left of the food back into the bag. "Your accent says so." Wiping the back of his hand along his mouth, he drops the bag onto the ground between us. "And the fact you're in Baton Rouge and still chose Taco Bell to order this late when you had other options. You're in Louisiana. We're the second-biggest distributor for seafood next to Alaska, Birdie. You could have done better than tacos."

Birdie? My eyes drop to the shorts that he's focusing on again. I tug on the hem of them to try covering a little more of my thighs, to no avail. "So you decided to teach me a lesson by eating the food I paid for?"

Half of his lips turn up at the corners as he dips his chin down. "Nah. Was hungry. Saw the food sitting outside and figured someone forgot they ordered it."

He kicks it toward me with his work boot that looks well worn—scratched-up and muddy. Weirdly, I've always found that attractive. It reminds me of hard work and adventures. But then again, this man stole my food. I can't just let that slide. He's definitely getting a one-star review. With words. Very carefully selected ones.

Wait. "You *found* the food?"

He hums. "It's cold," he tells me, stumbling toward the end of the hall and sliding his palm against the drywall for balance.

My eyes go down to the discarded bag of half-eaten food before they move back up to the stranger reaching for his pocket. "So you aren't my DoorDash driver?"

He pulls out a set of keys. "Nope," he calls over his shoulder, struggling to fit one into the lock. Eventually, he gets it and pushes the door open, nearly toppling over when he puts too much of his weight on the swinging door.

That's when it hits me that the cute, food-stealing boy is my neighbor. And before I can tell him he owes me ten dollars, he disappears into his apartment and closes the door behind him—or more like slams it with his dirty boot—without another word.

"What the hell?" I repeat, frowning at the food I'd been craving for the last few hours. Leaving the bag where my rude neighbor dropped it, I go inside and head to the fridge, where I see a note taped to the leftover container of shrimp reminding me to eat it instead of ordering takeout.

I snort at my father's handwriting, crumpling the paper and picking at the seafood since my other plans were dashed.

Closing the refrigerator, I run my hands over the list I taped to the front after he left earlier. Sighing to myself, I curl up on the couch and dig into the food.

That night, when I'm tucked into bed with my silk headwrap on that matches my pj's, I can't help but wonder about the boy across the hall.

And he's the last thing I think about when I fall asleep.

Chapter Five

SAWYER

IF THERE'S ONE THING I quickly learned the second I stepped onto LSU's campus, it's that the movies got it wrong. Girls don't get dolled up to go to classes. There's barely any makeup on their faces or hair styled to careful perfection. Most of them are wearing leggings and their college garb, which makes my skinny jeans and long-sleeved shirt look overdressed.

At least I didn't go all out with my hair. The sandy-blond color I chose to start the semester with is braided back and resting carefully over one shoulder. Casual but cute. I touch the tips of the braid as I walk out of the Journalism Building, blocking the beaming sun with my free hand and already feeling the slightest trickle of sweat under the expensive heat-friendly wig that my mother bought for me. She'd gotten me three different kinds of the same shade so I could play with lengths, and I know she spent a fortune on them because they're real hair. I learned the hard way that synthetic wigs don't last nearly as long and, after a few failed trial runs with a straightener, that they aren't meant to be styled with heat.

It's a comfortable sixty-nine degrees today, but with the sun out, it feels like I'm baking in my clothes since I've been used to thirty-degree days in upstate New York. Most people are bundled up in layers, but this is nothing compared to northern weather in January. As soon as it hits fifty at home, everybody is in T-shirts and shorts.

"Stop being a baby," I murmur to myself, wishing I'd put on a wig cap. I'd been running late, sleeping through my first alarm and accidentally hitting snooze twice after that. I used to be a morning person, but that changed over the years. Now I'm lucky if I can interact with people before nine, which makes eight a.m. classes a near impossibility unless I'm heavily caffeinated.

Pulling out my printed schedule that I color-coded with the highlighters Bentley got me as a going-away present, I double-check the building and room number for my last class of the day. I memorized most of it, but I had a bad dream last night that I got lost and walked in ten minutes late. Everybody stared. *Everybody.*

It was worse than the time I had a dream where I went to school and the wind knocked my wig off in front of everyone standing outside. From that day on, I've been adamant on the best wig fasteners *just in case.*

I'm walking toward Field House Drive when somebody taller than me jogs over and stops beside me at the crosswalk, shading me from the sun. "Hey," he greets, a big grin stretched across his scruffy face with familiarity.

I offer a timid smile at the stranger. "Hi." It takes me a minute to recognize him. He came over and introduced himself to Dad and me when we were moving in. I remember it was the first time I ever saw somebody taller than my father, who stands at almost six foot five. "You're Dawson, right?"

His grin widens. "And you're Sawyer. You look different today though."

I look down at myself, wondering what could possibly be different. I skipped shorts for my favorite pair of skinny jeans, and the shirt I opted for isn't the stained one I wore when I first met the boy in front of me. "Put together?" I ask, half-jokingly.

His eyes roam down the front of me again in appraisal. "I *did* like your shorts. A lot."

What is it with boys and shorts? It's like they've never seen legs before. "You and my neighbor across the hall," I murmur, more to myself than him as I look both ways and wait idly for the cars to pass.

Dawson hears me anyway, brows furrowing at the comment. "What number is your apartment again?"

I think back to that stranger-danger conversation I had with my parents as a kid, but my gut isn't telling me to run. Self-preservation be damned, I say, "Four D."

A twisted look weighs the corners of his lips down for the briefest moment. "Ah. Gotcha."

His less-than-stellar reaction piques my interest. "Friend of yours?" I guess. After the last car passes, I start walking, Dawson following right next to me.

"Something like that."

I'm not sure what that's supposed to mean, so I don't push. It's none of my business, even if the guy is my neighbor. "Well, tell him he owes me a taco after he stole mine."

Dawson gives me a funny look. "He stole your taco?"

"My delivery," I correct, still peeved that I never got my

crunch wrap. I haven't heard the door across the hall open or close since the incident. I'm pretty sure he's alive, but I've heard drunk people can choke on their vomit if they're passed out. When would I start smelling something to be alarmed over?

Realizing my train of thought is getting dark, I push it away. "Who just takes somebody's food if they didn't order it?"

Dawson shrugs. "Broke college kids?" he guesses, making a thoughtful face. "Pretty sure I stole a whole pizza at a party once. I was hammered. Don't think it stayed in my stomach long once I downed half of it."

I wince at the mental image. "Most guys wait to divulge those kinds of gross stories to keep a good image of themselves."

"I am who I am, baby."

I try holding back the face I make at the pet name.

"Where you headed?" he asks rather than continuing to flirt, looking at the schedule still gripped in my hands.

I show him, relieved he isn't going to make this weird. "Allen Hall."

"I'm headed that way," he says, offering me a boyish smile that's more friendly than charming. "I'll show you."

I don't tell him that I already Googled it and memorized which route to take. It's a two-minute walk. Easy. Instead of admitting what a dork I am, I say, "Thanks."

What's the harm in letting a cute boy be my tour guide? The senior who showed me around during my short orientation two days ago was moody and rude, so I'd take a smiling face any day.

Dawson grips the strap of his backpack as he looks around us, nodding at a few guys who pass by and fist-bumping one of them. "What's your major? Pretty sure I saw you over at

Doran, but that doesn't make sense. You don't seem like an ag kinda girl."

What does an ag girl look like? *What even is ag?* I make a mental reminder to Google that later when I get home. "What kind of girl am I?"

"Hot," he answers automatically.

I stop walking, taken aback by his bluntness.

His cheeks turn a light shade of pink, the same color as his bloodshot eyes, as he swipes one of those massive palms through his short blond hair, stopping beside me. "Er, sorry. Too much? My buddies say I can be."

I've never been called hot before. The closest I got was being called pretty by a boy I used to go to school with. That was before the cancer and the chemo. Once I lost my hair...well, those kinds of compliments stopped. People saw past the wigs and fake smiles. I guess once they know you're different, there's no changing their perception of you.

I was the sick girl, which made me untouchable. Vulnerable. I'm determined to never be that girl again. Not here. Not ever.

Clearing my throat, I absentmindedly touch my hair again. "Maybe a little. But..." I lose my voice, shrugging instead of finishing my sentence. It's nice to hear an attractive boy call me hot. It makes me feel normal for once.

We keep walking. I wonder if he realizes that he's not guiding me anywhere. He clears his throat. "So what's your major?"

"Communication," I say after realizing I never answered the first time. "I haven't focused in on a medium, but I was thinking journalism. I like to write."

"What do you want to write about?"

I say the first thing that comes to mind without any hesitation. "Life."

43

His brows rise. "Deep."

Is it? I should ask him what he's majoring in, but we approach the building I need. "Thanks for walking with me," I say, stepping ahead of where he stops in front of Allen Hall. Unsure of what to do, I stare at the ground.

"If you ever need a ride to campus, let me know. Like I said yesterday, I live right downstairs from you." Rubbing the back of his neck, he lifts his shoulder. "It's not a bad walk here, but we get a lot of rain this time of year."

Did he see me walking this morning? It was too beautiful to get a ride, not that I would tell my parents I opted to walk. The doctors told me exercise was good as long as I wasn't overexerting myself.

Dawson already offered to give me lifts when he talked to Dad and me, and Dad thanked him before I could. I think that was his way of saying *thanks but no thanks* on my behalf. "I'll keep that in mind. It was nice seeing you again."

This dismissal makes him chuckle. "Yeah. It was nice seeing you too. I guess I'll see you around." He starts backing up, narrowly dodging a few students walking behind him. "If you ever want to hang out, I know a few good bars around. Doesn't have to be just us. We could get a group together."

I've never been the best at making friends. I used to think I was charming enough to draw people in, but after I started homeschooling, my social skills were only ever used in the oncology unit with women and men much older than me.

I think about my list.

Make new friends.

"I'd like that," I say, rubbing my arm. "I'll take you up on it."

That big, doofy grin is back. "You do that."

His tone is flirty again. Or, at least, I think it is. I've

only had one boyfriend in my life, and that was in eighth grade. Brady Tompkins didn't exactly have any game, but what thirteen-year-old would? And, technically, we only dated for a couple of days because I was worried my parents would somehow find out and ground me. Dad always told me I couldn't date until I was thirty, and I thought he was serious back then.

When I open the door to my classroom a few minutes later, I find that I'm not the only person who likes arriving early. There's a boy near the middle with his back turned to me, and a funny feeling buzzes under my skin.

Brushing it off, I study the space to find the perfect seat. Not in the front where the teacher's pet sits, but not directly in the back either, where the professors probably write you off as the screw-off. The dark-haired boy has it right.

That tingling sensation moves up my spine, causing prickles in the back of my head when it settles into the edge of my skull. Warm. Calming.

When I drop my bag onto my chosen desk, the boy turns in my direction.

I gape when we lock eyes—his brown, a pretty color that seems familiar trapped behind a black pair of glasses.

I glare at him and say the first thing that comes to mind. "You owe me a taco."

Chapter Six

BANKS

THE HANGOVER IS STRONG, but not enough to forget that I dickishly stole this chick's food. Though it *was* outside in the cold, so I figured it was fair game. If I didn't get it, the racoons probably would have.

As I give her a once-over, I realize Dawson got his wish. This girl is hot. Short, petite, with a good face. Even scowling at me. I've always had a weakness for blonds.

Rubbing my eyes, I lean back in my seat and stretch my legs out. I could pretend I don't remember, but then I'd be a bigger asshole than I already have been. "You couldn't have wanted it that bad if you forgot you ordered it."

The way she stares at me is comical. She pushes a piece of her blond hair away from where it fell in front of her ocean-blue eyes. Another weakness of mine. It's almost not fair. "I didn't *forget*. They never said it was delivered. The app must have messed up or something."

All I say is "Unfortunate."

Turning forward, I open my ratty notebook and start

doodling in the corner of a fresh page. I think she'll give up and sit down in her chair a few rows over, but she decides that we're not done talking.

Her things drop directly beside me before she noisily pulls the chair out. The legs scrape against the floors, making me cringe at the horrid sound. The Motrin I took this morning did very little for the headache pounding in my ears, and she's certainly not helping. If I didn't think my father would somehow find out about my absence so early in the semester, I wouldn't have come at all.

Unapologetically, she sits down.

I don't pay her much attention despite the obvious way she's gawking at me. Dawson basically called dibs on her the day she moved in. He even texted me about it. Didn't say her name. Barely said anything other than she was blond, cute, and "totally into him," which I have a feeling he exaggerated.

It doesn't matter that she's my type. I wouldn't do that to my best friend. Especially after the unfortunate situation last time. "You going to take a picture, Birdie? It'll last longer."

Her cheeks turn pink. "That's not my name."

I look back to my doodles, trying not to remember the way her bare legs looked in those shorts. I'm a leg dude, and she's got the kind I want wrapped around my waist. But that's the last thing I want to think about right now.

Because of Dawson. And because I don't need a distraction and something tells me the girl beside me would be exactly that.

My silence doesn't deter her. "What are you drawing?"

"Nothing."

"Looks like a flower to me," she replies, leaning closer. She smells like lilac and cherry wood. Lotion? Shampoo? I try tuning it out even though it wraps around me, taunting me to look her way.

Sighing, I close my notebook. "Do you believe in personal space?"

"Do you believe in manners?" she shoots back. Her voice isn't sharp or witty but casual and firm. Challenging.

"My mom would like to say yes," I reply easily, lifting a shoulder. "She would have whooped my ass otherwise."

When other people start trickling in, she turns forward and says, "Could've fooled me."

And the surprising answer has me laughing lightly under my breath. "I'm Banks," I tell her, staring at the whiteboard at the front of the room.

"Is that a first or last name?" she presses.

"Just Banks," I inform her, sinking into my chair. The only person who calls me by my first name these days is the reason I feel like garbage.

I feel her eyes on me. "I'm Sawyer."

Eyes turning to the blue-eyed beauty, I study her facial features. I used to like that name because it reminded me of when things were easier. Back before it felt like I had nobody, when I had a quiet spot to hide away and a redheaded girl who was always up for an adventure.

I've known three girls named Sawyer in my short twenty-two years, but only one ever piqued my interest, thanks to her constant curiosity. I don't know what ever happened to her after Katrina hit—if her family made it out or lost everything. Weeks after the storm brutalized Louisiana, I'd made my way back to the small clearing to find it nearly destroyed.

And no Sawyer.

I went back every single week for two months, hoping

she'd be waiting there with a backpack full of snacks and more random facts about birds.

She was never there.

Eventually, I realized she wasn't coming back.

My eyes go to this girl's light hair before flicking back down to her eyes. I've never tried picturing what my Sawyer would look like when she was older because I didn't want to get my hopes up.

The girl beside me watches me with furrowed brows, probably wondering why I'm staring at her like a creep.

Cracking my neck, I turn away again. "It's not a flower," I tell her, shading in my image with a pen to give it a better shape. "It's a magnolia tree."

A noise rises from her throat, but she doesn't say anything. When I glance at her from the corner of my eye, her chin is resting on her palm as she watches me draw. I usually don't let anybody look at my drawings, but this is mindless work until our class begins.

"Do you draw other things or are flowers"—she stops when I shoot her a look—"*magnolia trees*," she corrects, "it?"

"I don't take requests."

"I wasn't asking you to."

I look at her, studying her soft features. "Is Sawyer your first name or last?"

"It's *just* Sawyer," she replies, grinning cheekily at me.

Touché. "I draw a lot of things" is the only reply she gets from me before I go back to the current sketch in front of me.

"I hope you didn't drive," Sawyer says a few minutes later.

My pen pauses over the paper. "What?"

"Last night," she elaborates. "I hope you didn't drive. You were wasted."

"I was fine," I grumble. I know the roads around here like the back of my hand.

Was it smart to get behind the wheel when I'd had one too many? No. But I wasn't about to crash at my father's place or waste money on an Uber when the college store barely pays minimum wage. One ride from the Garden District to here would be half my paycheck.

The girl beside me deadpans, "You could barely walk straight, Just Banks."

I eye her humorlessly. "It's Banks."

That subtle grin tilts her lips again, showing straight white teeth. A pretty smile is a dangerous one.

Chuckling under my breath despite myself, I go back to my drawing and let her watch. Silently.

Thankfully, it doesn't take long after that for the white-haired professor to walk in wearing a purple button-down and bright-pink bowtie that matches his suspenders. He stops at the podium, dropping his belongings onto it. "Welcome to creative writing," he greets us with a clap of his hands. "I hope you all have vivid imaginations and a love for the written word because you're going to need both in this course."

Sawyer perks up, her attention fully on the man in charge and away from me. It gives me time to look at her profile, noting her feminine features that look delicate somehow. Innocent. Her excitement over the introduction of class is... cute.

I do my best to ignore her the rest of class, not wanting the drama that would come with even the mildest of interest in the girl from across the hall.

Chapter Seven

SAWYER

"ARE YOU USING THAT face wash I bought you?" I ask Bentley over video chat as he shovels food into his mouth. "Looks like you could use it."

From the background, I hear, "Be nice to your brother, Sawyer."

Snickering at my mother's chiding, I say, "If I can't pick on him from fifteen hundred miles away, what's the fun in being his older sister?"

Bentley grins, a piece of lettuce stuck between his front teeth that I point out. "It smells girly," he tells me, picking at the spot with his finger.

"I got it from the men's section," I tell the little shit. It took me thirty minutes to find one I was sure he'd use that *didn't* look or smell feminine because I knew he'd do this. "It's supposed to smell like the woods or some manly bullcrap like that."

Mom yells out, "Language."

She acts like Bentley doesn't know any curse words, but

I've heard him play *Fortnite* with his friends. Their conversations are more colorful over their stupid video game than mine are with people in real life. "I said bullcrap!" I defend, laughing. "Sorry. I'd hate to corrupt his virgin ears."

Bentley snorts as Mom comes into the frame with a disapproving expression on her face. She takes the phone and starts walking to the kitchen with it. It looks like she's stress cleaning again—something she's always done to quiet her anxious mind. Once after my first week of chemo when I'd been so violently sick I couldn't keep anything down, I found her on her hands and knees using a toothbrush to scrub between the kitchen floor tiles.

"Speaking of virgins," she says, "are you taking your birth control pills?"

My brother gags in the background, and I turn pink, grateful I have an entire apartment to myself to be embarrassed by my mother on a different coast. I can't imagine what I'd do if I had a roommate who overheard her. "Geez, Mom. *Yes.* Although I don't know why you think I've been hoeing around when I've only been here for a couple days."

"First of all," Mom says, using that tone of voice you don't want to argue with, "sleeping around doesn't make a woman a 'ho.' That term should have died and stayed in the past. There's nothing wrong with being sexually active as long as you're being safe."

"Oh God," I groan, burying my face into one of the couch pillows. "Can we not talk about this? There isn't even anything to talk about."

"All I'm saying is that I want you to be safe," she reiterates, unfazed by the embarrassment she's causing me as she sprays a cleaner onto the countertop out of frame. "That's why I asked about the pills. I know your father wasn't totally on board, but it was a smart move now that you're in college and surrounded by opportunities."

Oh my God. Did she really just imply opportunities with men are like campus jobs I'm trying to apply for? "Well, I am," I squeak out, clearing my throat. "Taking them, I mean. So you don't have to worry."

I can tell she's amused by my tone. "Oh, honey. I say it because I care. But I'll let it go. Are you taking your other medications? The vitamins that the doctor prescribed? What about—"

"Mom," I cut her off. "I've got it covered. I'm taking everything I need to like I promised I would."

I look at the pill bottles all stacked by the toaster. Every morning, they're some of the first things that greet me. I make sure to pour each one out and take them with my coffee. Not only to appease my mother, but to make sure I can make the most of my time here. Anything can happen when you least expect it, but I'll be damned if I give life a reason to screw me over again.

"Fine, fine," the woman who raised me relents with another solemn sigh. "Tell me about your day. I want to hear everything. How were classes? Have you met anybody yet? Friends? Boys? Girls?"

Settling into the couch, I hug the pillow to my chest and rest my chin on the edge. Truthfully, the last two days have been lackluster. The only thing we went over in my classes was the syllabus, and a few professors made us go around and share a fun fact like we're in middle school, but that was it.

The most exciting thing that happened was the way bantering with *Just* Banks made me feel. Girlish. Dumb. Carefree. I could tell I annoyed him, which made it way more fun. I haven't seen him in the building or on campus to try poking at him some more, which has only been a little disappointing.

But I don't tell my mother any of that. She already gave me the safe sex talk once, and I don't need her thinking that because I find a boy cute, it means there's going to be an engagement anytime soon. Especially since the *opportunity* to see him is mere feet away from my front door.

"It's been a good week," I opt for, choosing my words carefully. "I met a few people who I could become friends with."

I spoke to a few girls I have history class with, not that our conversations were long. One of them I only said hi to, another I tried talking to about our majors—she was undecided and uninterested in telling me much more—and I told a different one that I liked her sandals because she'd caught me staring at her missing toe. Not my best first impression, even though I wasn't judging her. I'd been half tempted to share my battle scars and ask what happened. Considering she bolted before I could say much else, I didn't consider it a win. But it was progress all the same.

My eyes go to my door, where I hear footsteps outside. Banks clearly isn't interested in being my friend, but that only makes me more determined to get him to like me. Being easy on the eyes is simply a bonus.

The floor outside my apartment creaks, which I know is from the floorboards directly in front of my door. I almost wonder if Banks is going to knock, holding my breath with anticipation as if that'll help me hear better. But my chest deflates when I hear the steps fleeing and then the door across the hall opening and closing.

I don't have time to be disappointed because Mom breaks me from my thought with "…your father that it's perfectly okay if you're exploring the dating world since you're a grown woman now. I swear, he wants you to join a convent."

How'd we get back to this?

"He'll always see you as his little girl," she continues, not realizing I tuned her out. "We both will. But we also hope that one day you're going to meet somebody who will make you see how much life is worth living."

Hugging my legs together, I let out a tiny breath before sitting up. "Mom…" I pause, closing my eyes and rubbing my head where an ache has settled into my temples. It's been a long day, and my appetite was limited, which never helps the headaches I'm prone to. "Can we not do this right now?"

She grows quiet, and I feel bad for raining on her parade. But "one day"… Well, I don't want to think about "one day." I'd rather she not either.

For a lot of reasons.

"Okay, honey. If that's what you want."

Lips pressing together, I stand up and walk toward my door, where curiosity gets the better of me. Undoing the deadbolt and flicking the lock, I crack the door open to see a ten-dollar bill taped to it and a coupon for Taco Bell directly underneath.

Smiling at the unexpected gift, I yank the items down and hip-bump my door closed. "Maybe you're right though," I offer, staring at the coupon in my hand.

"We just want you to be happy," Mom says softly, her voice warm and motherly.

I set the money and coupon onto the counter by my pills. "I know you do," I answer, grabbing one of the multi-vitamins and toying with the label that's peeling off it. "I am happy though. Being back here…"

55

They know I missed it, but they'll never understand the yearning I felt in my soul when they told me we couldn't go back. I loved being in North Carolina with my grandparents, and I liked New York when my parents found a new place upstate near my aunt Taylor. But nothing ever compared to Louisiana.

"Being back here is what I need," I finish, nodding in certainty.

My eyes scan over what my neighbor left me.

I hope she understands that I'll always need my family too, but I need *this* more.

From the background, I hear Bentley yell out, "Did she find it? Ask if she found it."

Mom laughs lightly. "Your brother wants to know if you found what he tucked into the back pocket of your carry-on."

Brows pinching, I walk into my bedroom and dig around my closet until I find the bag he's talking about. When I reach into the back, I hear the familiar crinkle of wrapping that's music to my ears.

I grin when I pull out a package of my favorite chocolate fudge Pop-Tarts, and whatever sadness I felt settle into my chest a moment ago is suddenly gone. "Tell the dweeb I said thank you."

Mom doesn't scold me for name-calling. Instead, she looks at me with a wavering smile and says, "Try to get some sleep. You look tired, baby girl."

And when I look at myself in the mirror as I take my wig off for the night, I realize how right she is. I touch the bags under my eyes, tracing the outlines with my fingertips and a relenting sigh, not letting my eyes wander to the patchy pieces of hair scattered along my scalp.

That night, I do what my mother always hated. I eat my Pop-Tarts in bed, uncaring of the crumbs they leave behind, until I drift off to a dreamless slumber.

The tray of food comes out of nowhere, painting the front of my camo cargo pants with warm, thick liquid. Gaping, I stare down at the mess. Is that...? I sniff. Jambalaya?

"I'm sorry, I'm sorry, I'm sorry," the short-haired brunette says, one of her hands cupping her mouth as she stares at my outfit. Her free hand is still holding onto the now-empty tray. "Oh my God, I'm so sorry."

Frowning, I move away from the scattered food, shaking a piece of sausage off my white sneakers. They're new but should be easy to wash since they're fake leather. Mom used to put Bentley's and my shoes in the washer whenever we'd get them caked with mud when we'd go outside on adventures. Or, more like, when I dragged my little brother outside. He preferred video games to exploring.

"It's okay," I tell her, grateful it wasn't scalding coffee that got dumped on me. "I guess this was a sign that today's outfit wasn't it."

I felt cute in a tomboyish kind of way. The long-sleeved black shirt is keeping me warm with the temperature drop and hugs my narrow torso and the slight curve of my chest. My B-cups are nothing to look at, but they're about the only curves I have thanks to chemo. I lost a lot of weight that I was never able to gain back over the years. I'm pretty sure one of the only reasons Mom was okay with me coming here was because she thought I'd get fattened up by good Southern food.

"I'm so sorry," the brunette says again, dropping the tray onto the table beside her and quickly using one of her napkins to try cleaning off my pants.

I laugh, ignoring the people watching us in the dining hall. It's crowded because lunch hours are almost over, so I'm not surprised we have a large audience. "Seriously, it's okay. The stain sort of blends with the pattern anyway. See? You may want to go get something else before they start closing down the grill."

She looks up from where she's squatting in front of me, pausing with her cleanup. "You're really not mad?"

I shrug. "Unless you're about to tell me you did it on purpose, then no. It was an accident. And clothes wash, so I'm not worried about it." I could tell her about the hundreds of times Bentley spilled stuff on me, and some of those were *definitely* not accidents, even if he told Mom they were. I never got mad at him. Much.

The girl finally stands, and I realize how short she is compared to my five-five. She barely comes eye level to my boobs. Her face is hot when she notices the attention we've garnered, and she winces and hides behind the pieces of dark hair framing her face. "I feel bad. I tripped on my shoelace."

I glance down at her untied shoe, which she sighs and kneels to fix. "They're cute," I compliment her red Chucks because apparently complimenting women's shoes is the only method I have for making friends.

She points at mine. "Yours are too. Even with sauce on them."

I snort, examining them. "They'll wash." I offer her a hand, which she takes to stand. "I'm Sawyer, by the way."

"Dixie." She drops her hand and blushes deeper when a janitor comes over with a mop bucket and starts cleaning up. "My parents were obsessed with the country band Dixie Chicks when they had me."

It's been a long time since I've listened to their music. My mom wasn't a big music person, and Bentley prefers indie rock or screamo that's barely tolerable to my ears. "That sucks since they changed their name."

"Yeah, they weren't happy."

I gesture toward the line of kids still waiting for their lunches. "Come on. We should probably get something. I saw their grab-and-go section today, and it was lacking, unless you want a soggy BLT wrap."

Dixie's mossy-green eyes drop back down to my ruined pants. "You're going to stay?"

My stomach rumbles. "I'm hungry. I've learned the hard way I get cranky when I don't eat. Nobody wants to deal with me when I go She-Hulk on their asses."

She laughs in surprise. "Well, it's on me since mine is on you," she offers, following me to one of the lines.

All the food here smells delicious, so Mom will probably get her wish. Instead of the freshman fifteen, I'll gain the junior twenty. And I'm sure my parents would think I looked better for it.

After we gather our things and Dixie pays, we head to an empty table in the corner. "You really didn't have to pay for my stuff," I tell her again, even though I appreciate it. Everything here is cheaper than what I'm used to in New York, but I'm all for saving money when I can because it's my parents' money that they transfer into an account for me, as if they haven't almost gone bankrupt to care for me in the past.

She waves it off. "It's the least I can do."

Before I can answer, an arm drops around my shoulders,

tugging me into a muscled chest and startling me. "I thought that was you," a familiar voice says.

Dixie squeaks, her eyes wide when she sees Dawson draped over me.

I nudge him with my shoulder playfully. If he moves just right, he'll probably feel where my port used to be just under my collarbone. I've managed to hide it well so far, which hasn't been hard. It'll be more difficult when the weather gets hotter and my summer wardrobe comes out.

"Hi, Dawson," I greet, offering a small smile and noticing how red his eyes look today. Mom used to have bad allergies and take medicine for it when the seasons changed. But hers never looked this bad.

Dixie looks between us, awe in her gaping lips. Does she know him? It seems like there's familiarity carved into her arched brows.

"This is Dixie," I tell him when he finally moves his arm and takes the seat beside me. "We just met. Dixie, this is Dawson. We live in the same building."

Slowly, her head bobs. "H-Hi." Licking her lips, she blurts, "I know you. We have history. Er, I mean we had history together. Last year. With Goodwin."

Based on her darkening cheeks, I'd say she more than knows him. I've been a girl with a crush before, so I know what it looks like.

Dawson doesn't seem to recognize her, even though he says, "Oh yeah. Dixie. Right."

Totally clueless. I scoot my chair out to try giving her a minute alone with him. "I need a drink. Dixie, do you want one?"

She's still looking at Dawson as she shakes her head slowly.

Internally, I giggle.

When Dawson notices my pants, his brows go up. "Whoa. Very...Picasso of you."

I'm not sure that's an accurate artist for the scattered stains on my camo, but I let it go. "Life happens. You want anything to drink?"

He smirks. "Nah. But the offer is still open for me to get you one. Preferably together."

My eyes go to my new friend Dixie. "In a group, right?"

Dawson glances at Dixie before those red-rimmed brown eyes come back to me. "Yeah, if that's what you want."

I smile at the boy who I'm fairly sure is stoned right now. I used to go to chemo with a boy not much older than him, and he definitely enjoyed his medical marijuana. "Maybe Dixie and I can join you and some others then. It could be fun."

Dixie makes another noise before I eye her and subtly gesture toward Dawson, but when I leave them alone to get water, I see Dixie silently sitting there and fidgeting with her hands while staring at her food. It takes Dawson a few minutes to say something to her, laughing, and then he waves her off and walks away.

When I get back, I ask, "Where did he go?"

Her face is still red. "He had class. How do you know Dawson Gable?"

A full name. She does have it bad. "Like I said, we live in the same building. That's only, like, the third time we've ever spoken."

She blinks in disbelief, shaking her head and playing with her new bowl of jambalaya. "He seemed very...touchy with you."

"I think he's like that with everybody," I theorize, not

that I can be sure. I've seen him on campus with his arms around different girls and messing around with a couple guys who dish it back to him. "If it matters, I don't like him or anything. I mean, he seems nice. But he's all yours."

Her green eyes snap up to me.

"So," I press, leaning my arms against the edge of the table. "What do you think about going out for drinks with him?"

She licks her lips. "That's Dawson Gable…"

Amusement lifts my lips. "I know."

"He didn't recognize me," she mumbles, shoulders dropping in defeat.

Okay, true. "He knows you now. So…?"

She watches me, nibbling her bottom lip. "I guess one drink couldn't hurt. If you think it's a good idea."

I perk up. "I think it's a great idea. I'll let him know the next time I see him. We can dress up, and you can get his full attention. He'd be dumb not to remember you then."

She looks skeptical but still agrees. "Want to meet at my dorm the day we go? I haven't gone out in a while and could use the help getting ready. I live in a single on campus."

I grin, grabbing my apple. "By the time we're done with you, Dawson Gable will be panting."

Dixie shifts in her seat, but I can see the ghost of a hopeful smile on the bottom half of her face as she stares down at her lunch again.

When I get home that night, I cross another item off my list.

~~Make new friends~~

Chapter Eight

BANKS

DAWSON SLAMS THE XBOX controller down on the coffee table and stands up. "What a fucking dick. Can you believe that?"

I look at the screen, where his character was killed by whomever he's up against. He's never been the best at any video game we played, so I *can* believe it.

Right before he peels off the headphones, he says, "Don't talk about my mom like that!"

He tosses the expensive gaming equipment onto the couch, ears red when he catches me gaping at him. "Dude," I say slowly. "You realize you're probably fighting with a twelve-year-old boy, right?"

Dawson turns the TV off. "Whatever. He cheated. I'm sure of it."

Unlikely, but I go with it. "So what are your plans for the night? You said something about drinks, but then you got distracted by like a squirrel or something."

He helps himself to a bottled Coca-Cola in my fridge,

using the edge of the counter to pry off the cap, and ignores where it lands on the floor. "I'm taking our new neighbor and one of her friends to Lafitte's over in New Orleans."

Why is he taking them all the way there when there are bars nearby? "Wouldn't it make more sense to take them somewhere around here? We both know how you get when you drink. I don't think taking anybody to the city is the best idea if you're going to indulge."

He guzzles half the bottle before belching, smacking his chest. "Lafitte's has the coolest vibe though. It'll be funny to see if the ghost messes with them."

Lafitte's is said to be one of the most haunted bars in the French Quarter of New Orleans. The building used to be a blacksmith shop where the Lafitte brothers did illegal smuggling and are said to have hidden some of their treasure. Once in a while, people claim the piano will start playing when nobody is near it, and others say they get touched when nobody is around. It's a running joke that Jean Lafitte is just a horny ghost who likes attention from women and men.

An equal opportunist, I guess.

Dawson's eyebrows wiggle suggestively. "Plus, they've got Queen Voodoos."

What exactly is his plan? Those purple drinks are strong. I can usually handle my alcohol well, but those fuckers knock me on my ass. "Not even the locals can handle them." The drinks don't taste like alcohol, which makes them danger-ous. I've seen tourists get screwed up so bad, their buddies have to help them walk out of the bars before they're even done with one. "I doubt you have to get them drunk to sleep with you if that's your plan."

The thought makes me feel like a jackass. I don't know

our neighbor or her friend, but I do know college girls. Usually, it doesn't take much more than some charm and a flashy smile to get them where you want them. I'm enough of a dick to admit I've used the combo a time or two to get girls to warm my bed for a few hours.

Offense takes over his face. "The fuck, man? I can get laid without the help of alcohol."

I hold up my palms. "I wasn't saying you can't, but *they* don't know that. These chicks don't know you at all. Maybe take it easy on them the first time you go out."

I can tell I pissed him off, but one of us needs to be smart. His track record with partying is more infamous than his stats on the basketball team. I don't want him going down a path he can't come back from when he's worked so hard to get where he is now. Especially not with Sawyer in a city she's not familiar with.

Scratching the back of my neck, I lean against the counter and cross my arms. "Are you going to be good tonight? I know it's been a year, but I want—"

"I've been good," he cuts me off, mouth twitching to fight a scowl. "A few drinks won't hurt me."

How many times did he say that last time? A few drinks turned into a six-pack, which turned into a twelve-pack, which turned into him agreeing to a lot of other dumb shit that involved rolled-up dollar bills and white powder.

"Marco is gone anyway," he mumbles, guessing what I'm thinking. "He's not around to influence things anymore. The frat has a new pres who's trying to clean up his mess."

We both know that there are plenty of people still around whom Marco probably talks to. His father and uncles were all presidents of the same fraternity, making Marco a legacy. I'm sure they probably donate to events when they need funding to keep their doors open after Marco was arrested for possession and distribution last year and expelled.

Dawson got wrapped up in that mess when he was rushing the frat, doing whatever Marco wanted him to. I've seen him do a lot of stupid stuff in our years of friendship, but he went down a dark path the second he started using what he was supposed to be selling.

I won't pretend like I haven't seen the way he scratches his nose or rubs his eyes or zones out in the middle of the day like before. I learned to read the signs, to keep an eye out. That's why I went to a few of the meetings with him after shit hit the fan and Marco was kicked out for good.

Dawson stares down at the Coke before setting it down on the counter. "Come with. That way you can keep me on my best behavior. It can be like a double date. Plus, Sawyer said you owe her a taco. We can stop on the way back and absorb some of the alcohol."

"She told you about that?" I ask, wondering if that's why he got all weird about if I'd met her yet. It was hard not to run into her in the hall, but I tried. Because I felt her eyes on me whenever we did cross paths—felt the way my skin buzzed from the attention I didn't ask for whenever she was around. I couldn't explain it and didn't want to try because I knew Dawson wouldn't get it.

He smacks my arm, whatever irritation he was feeling gone. "Seriously. When was the last time you went out? You rain-checked me before to hang out with your dad like a loser. Make it up to me. Sawyer's friend is pretty cute. You might like her."

He's never missed an opportunity to shoot his shot. I respect him all the more for it, even though nine times out of ten it winds up in rejection.

I've never cared much to do the same, especially not on setups. But I don't have anything going on tonight, so I don't have an excuse *not* to go. And, oddly, I want to see what Sawyer is like outside class. Is she as fiery? Or reserved?

"Fine, but I still think we should take them to The Station," I say. "It has live entertainment on Fridays, and it's close by. If you don't scare them away, then we can take them into New Orleans."

We. I don't want to get his hopes up or plan things too far in advance, but I also don't want to be the buzzkill who brings everybody down.

His sigh is heavy, but I can tell he's going to give in. "Deal. But since you changed the plans, you get to be the DD."

My eye twitches. "How considerate," I reply dryly.

He winks. "Considerate is my middle name."

Sawyer and her friend Dixie are elbow in elbow as they walk ahead of us into the bar, whispering and giggling about whatever girl talk they're having. Dawson is staring at both of their asses, his gaze locked specifically on Dixie's because of the short leather skirt she's wearing. I can't blame the guy since I'm doing the same to Sawyer in the tight pair of jeans that hugs her lean legs.

Dawson nudges me. "They look good, huh?"

The girls are opposites—light and dark. Sawyer is taller than Dixie by a few inches, paler than the tan on her friend, with blond hair reaching her mid-back unlike the dark-brown curls that barely touch Dixie's shoulders. Sawyer is louder, more abrasive. I can tell by how she carries herself that she has the type of confidence I've always found attractive.

Dixie is quieter, shy, only talking to Sawyer the entire drive to the bar.

Apparently, Dawson got both the girls' phone numbers through Dixie yesterday. I don't know what game he's playing, but only one of them has been looking at him doe-eyed, and it's not the blond who lives across from me. Yet he was texting Sawyer all afternoon when he was supposed to be doing homework for my dad's class. She told him that she and Dixie would be waiting for us at her apartment at eight o'clock.

When Sawyer opened the door, my brows had gone up at the outfits they were in. Hers is much more casual than her friend's—a tight pair of denim and an equally tight top that hugs the petite body I could wrap an arm around—and Dixie is in a miniskirt and a top that shows off a sliver of toned, tanned skin underneath. They're both cute girls, but my eyes always find their way over to those tight jeans and the girl in them.

"Yeah," I agree, shrugging. "They do."

He tips his chin to Dixie before elbowing my rib cage. "She seems sweet. Your type. Maybe we both can get some tonight? I'm not the only one who's had a dry spell lately."

I don't know why, but my eyes go to Sawyer when he says that. Jaw ticking, I pry my eyes away from her ass and hold the door open for Dawson and me. "Maybe."

But I have no intention of sleeping with Dixie. Or Sawyer, for that matter. Still, I can't help but feel a weight in my stomach knowing what *he's* going to try tonight, and it pisses me off that I'm even thinking about it.

What he doesn't know is that I went home with some random chick I met at the campus store two nights ago. After a tense phone call with my father about my creative writing class, I'd been pent up and needed to relieve some tension. The girl, whose name I can't even remember, was happily willing to provide that.

Thirty minutes later, the four of us are at a table in the back with drinks in our hands. While I'm nursing my one and only beer of the night, Dawson is already half done with his second one, and the girls have barely touched their fruity concoctions that look like punch.

While Dawson has been talking Sawyer's ear off about how her classes have been, I notice the way her friend Dixie watches them in silence. She looks uncomfortable, and I wonder if she was as reluctant to come tonight as I was. Maybe we do have a lot in common. And she *does* resemble the last girl I brought home.

"What are you majoring in?" I ask over the loud music playing, having no idea what conversation to have with her.

When she realizes I'm talking to her, she peels her eyes away from the other two. They're green. Pretty. "What?"

I lean over the table so she can hear me better, trying not to crowd her personal space too much. "I asked what you're majoring in."

"Oh." She grabs her drink and nervously stirs the straw around. "Music. I haven't narrowed down a concentration, but I've always loved jazz and experimental media."

Sawyer breaks apart from the conversation she's having with Dawson and wraps an arm around Dixie's shoulders. "This girl can play one hell of a violin. And don't get me started on the piano. I could barely play the recorder in third grade, so I don't know how she does it."

Even in the poor lighting, I can see Dixie's face turn red from the attention. "You haven't even seen me play."

"I Googled you after you told me earlier," Sawyer admits, causing my brows to go up.

"You can be Googled?" I ask, impressed.

Dixie clears her throat, using the drink as a way to stall.

Sawyer answers for her. "Yes. If you look up Dixie Milano, you can find her performance at Carnegie Hall. Carnegie frigging Hall!"

I've heard of it before but can't say I know its significance. Based on her tone, I'd say it's a big deal. So I offer Dixie a casual, "Congrats."

Sawyer rolls her eyes. "I used to live in New York, so I guess I'm more impressed than most people would be."

I tuck that tidbit of information about Sawyer away for another day. New York. I wonder if her face lit up the same way there as it does here. Or is that why she left?

Dixie cuts in. "It's not a huge deal. I was young—"

"Which makes it a bigger deal," Sawyer argues firmly.

Dawson must feel left out because he chirps in despite not having any clue what we're talking about. "That is a huge deal."

I snort, knowing damn well he didn't hear what it is he's agreeing with. My focus goes back to the tomato-faced brunette across the table from me, who's still toying with her drink. "Well, if jazz is what you want to study, there's no better place to be than Louisiana."

Her smile is warm with appreciation as she tucks a piece of hair behind her ear. "That's what I was hoping."

Dawson stands, tapping Sawyer's shoulder to regain her attention when he realizes he's lost it to Dixie and me. "I'm getting another drink. Sawyer, you want to come with me and grab some food?"

The blond looks from him to her friend and then at me. With raised brows, she asks, "Dixie, did you want to go with him? You told me you were hungry before we left."

Dixie's eyes go to Dawson before she sinks into her seat with a gentle head shake. "I guess it passed," she murmurs.

I see the way Sawyer frowns, but she regains the smile when she sees Dawson still waiting for her.

Interesting.

"We'll be right back," she tells us, scooting her chair out and following Dawson over to the counter across the room, where people are ordering baskets of basic, greasy bar food.

When it's just Dixie and I, I lean back. "You don't want to be here."

Dixie goes to say something but stops herself. Rubbing her lips together, she moves another strand of hair behind her ear and glances back down at her drink. "I wouldn't say that exactly."

Which means yes.

"If it makes you feel any better, I didn't want to come out either. But I gotta make sure that guy"—I gesture toward my friend, who's laughing with Sawyer over something—"behaves himself."

Her eyes go over to them, her teeth nibbling her bottom lip. "How long have you known Dawson?"

"A long time. Since we were preteens."

She turns to me. "And you went to college together too? That's pretty cool. I didn't like anybody enough in high school to do the college thing with them."

I shrug. I've always known I'd go to LSU because of my dad. If I went anywhere else, I'd be paying a hell of a lot more money than what I do here. Having a parent as a professor has its perks, even on the bad days.

"What about you and Sawyer?" I ask. "How long have you two known each other?"

Dixie takes another drink. "We actually just met. I dumped my lunch on her. She never got mad once."

Huh. Most women would freak out if that happened to them. I've seen it. "Sounds like a fast friendship."

We fall to silence as her eyes go back to the two people we came with. Except I don't think her focus is on the blond girl like mine is but the boy beside her.

Clearing her throat, she toys with her drink straw. "He seems very...friendly," she says of Dawson, her eyes trailing in his direction briefly and then moving away before she's caught.

He's playfully pushing Sawyer, who doesn't touch him back. I note that. But does Dixie? "I know for a fact he can be a flirt. Always has been. He usually bombs it anyway. I wouldn't put much stock into that."

"Into what?"

I tip my chin in his direction. "Look at Sawyer. She's putting space between them. He's the one moving in, not her. Plus, she gave you the opportunity to take her place and go with him."

I'm not sure if I point that out for her benefit or mine, but it makes the tension in my squared shoulders ease in the slightest way.

Dixie watches them for a moment longer before turning her body away. "I didn't realize..." She frowns, stopping herself and shaking her head. "It doesn't matter."

I offer the only advice I can. "Give him time. Dawson is a dude. We're not the smartest when it comes to chicks being into us."

The way she worries her lip makes me wonder what's on her mind. "I heard some things about him last year from some of the sorority girls at Kappa Kappa Gamma. Is it... Are those things true?"

She doesn't need to elaborate on what the rumors are if she heard them at a sorority. Greek life talks more than local gossips. I knew word got around when Marco Hastings got arrested for drug distribution, but I didn't know where that left Dawson on the social ladder on campus. He got to stay in the frat, but he was put on probation. One wrong move, and he wouldn't have just gotten kicked out of Greek life; he would have been expelled like his former president was.

As far as I'm concerned, he got lucky.

"Dawson is…complicated." It's the last word I'd use to describe my friend to his face, but it's the perfect one for the situation. "He got tangled up in the wrong people and made some mistakes. But he's a good person."

She quickly shakes her head again. "I didn't mean to imply that he wasn't, I—"

"Dixie," I laugh, stopping her. "My point is that he's in a better place now than he was last year. Like I said. Give him time. He'll come around as long as you don't let all that shit from last year get to you."

Hell, maybe a girlfriend is what he needs. It'll take up his time and keep him from spending it with the wrong crowd.

I remind myself of that when I think about which girl he might want to settle down with, making my leg bounce under the table.

Thankfully, Dawson and Sawyer get back with a few different appetizers for the table a minute later, ending the conversation.

Dixie offers me a silent thank-you before falling into conversation with Sawyer about something school related.

It becomes obvious over the course of the next few hours that Dawson is oblivious to Dixie's interest because he's doing everything in his power to get Sawyer to laugh at what he says. I'm tempted to ask Dixie if she wants to leave when I see the way she watches her friend with a shade of green on her shoulder similar to the color of her eyes, but I think better of it when I count the number of beers Dawson had to drink.

By nearly eleven o'clock, Dixie and Sawyer are both tipsy. Only then does the brunette seem to let loose, her frown slipping into a smile as her friend convinces her to dance to the live band that came in a couple hours ago.

Dawson elbows me as we watch them circle each other around the dance floor. "You feeling Dixie?"

She's a nice girl. Pretty. Easy to talk to. I have no reason *not* to be into her, but I've never liked being pushed in one direction. Plus, she's here for him, whether he realizes it or not. And I have no idea where Sawyer is at because half the time, she's entertaining the conversations that Dawson starts with her, and the other half, she's trying her hardest to nudge Dixie to take her place.

"She's cool," I tell him.

"Cool," he repeats in amusement. "This bar is cool. The music is cool. You either need better glasses or more alcohol."

"If you're feeling her, then you do something about it," I return, pushing my frames up my nose. It wouldn't hurt my feelings, considering my indifference to her. "She's your type, isn't she?"

Dawson laughs. "Every woman is my type. But my sights are locked and loaded. And do you see Sawyer? She's all over me. My game is strong tonight."

I wouldn't say she's "all over him," but I don't burst his bubble. Most girls wouldn't stick around this long if there wasn't any interest, so I don't know her motivation. Is it for her or Dixie? Or is it something else?

"You going to do something about it?" I ask curiously, watching the girls hug and laugh.

Dawson leans against me, draping a heavy arm over my shoulder. His breath reeks of beer when he says, "You know damn well I am."

"Dawson…"

He stumbles toward them before I can say anything, dropping an arm around both girls' shoulders. Whether they let him stay that way because they're drunk and having fun or because they're appeasing him, I'm not sure.

Only one of the three looks back though, searching the room until her eyes land on me.

I lift my glass of water to Sawyer, and she smiles. And I'd be lying if I said that smile didn't do something to my chest that I don't like.

But do I look away?

No.

We spend the rest of the night watching each other instead of the two friends we brought along.

The tingling in my neck returns.

It's getting harder to ignore.

Chapter Nine

SAWYER

Saturday morning, I'm grateful for three things—the cool tile floor in my bathroom, the toilet, and the aspirin that my neighbor made me take when he walked Dixie and me inside after dropping off a very drunk Dawson at his place downstairs.

Groaning, I peel my sweaty body off the floor and lean my back against the tub of the shower. I smell awful and feel worse. And I barely make it halfway to standing when I lurch forward, nearly missing the toilet when my stomach empties for what feels like the fiftieth time, getting puke in the ends of my hair that, thankfully, survived the night without the nightmarish outcomes that the dream version of me was terrified of.

It's been a while since I vomited this violently. Since the first week of my last round of chemo, maybe? The nurses hook you up with the best drugs to make sure you aren't throwing up your vital organs, but I guess colleges don't pass those kinds of things out at the campus store.

"I'm never drinking again," I moan, eyes blurring as I flush the toilet. I rinse out my mouth and brush my teeth, freezing when I see the blood I spit out with the toothpaste. I watch as the red-and-white foamy mixture swirls around the drain before disappearing altogether. Swallowing my panic, I put my toothbrush away and rinse again until everything comes back clear.

I cringe at how horrible I look in the mirror when I finally dare to lift my gaze. My wig has slipped, and the strands are so staticky that it definitely looks like I slept on the bathroom floor all night. My mascara is smeared under my bloodshot eyes, and my cheeks have little lines on them like they used to when I'd get sick during treatment. After washing off my makeup, I give myself one more once-over and realize it's not going to get better than this.

Sighing, I peel my gaze away from the mirror and try pushing my sensitive gums to the back of my mind.

When I walk out of the bathroom, I see Dixie sitting cross-legged on the couch holding a Styrofoam cup in her hands. "Oh my God, is that coffee?" I ask.

She points to a to-go container on the table with a second cup resting in the holder. "Banks dropped them off a little while ago. It should still be warm. He'd said we'd need them. And these."

Out of nowhere, she produces a bottle of Advil. Banks did that? "That was nice of him," I murmur in surprise, catching the bottle and dumping two pills into my palm. When he stood outside the door last night with Dawson, my heart did a little tap dance in my chest. I'd already looked forward to going out, but I was more than happy to learn he was coming with us. Especially since he's like a ghost around here; the only sounds I hear are his footsteps in the night.

"How do you look so good?" I ask the girl who looks like she's been awake for hours. I'm pretty sure she had more than me when Dawson suggested tequila shots. Banks and I said no, so they did two each. I could tell Banks wasn't happy, but I chalked it up to having to DD three drunken idiots home when he only had one beer, a soda, and some water the whole night. "Did you switch to water last night and not tell me? I feel like trash, and you look fine."

Dixie wiggles her cup. "It's not my first rodeo. My freshman year was a little wild since it was my first taste of freedom away from my family, so I built up a tolerance. Plus, I'm running on a high. You know how I got Dawson's number the other day? He texted me this morning saying he had a lot of fun last night."

I perk up. "I told you he wouldn't be able to resist when he saw your legs in that skirt. You should keep it, by the way. It looks better on you than on my chicken legs."

I don't remember when I bought it, but it was long before I shed the weight my last round of treatment took from me. Most of my wardrobe didn't fit after, leaving me in leggings, tees, and a few odds and ends that didn't make it look like I was wearing a potato sack. Mom took me on a shopping spree for new clothes before coming here so I could use the going-away money the women at the cancer ward raised for me. It was a substantial amount for people who had their own families to feed. I tucked some of it away and spent a lot of it on things that made me feel confident in my skin again.

The leather skirt was the only thing left hanging from the old version of me, and I decided to shove it into my overfull suitcase last minute and bring it with me just in case I wanted to dress up here. It feels right to give it to someone who could use it more.

"I'm pretty sure Banks and I had to pry you two off the dance floor when they were doing last call," I tease, pushing my thoughts away.

She bites her lip to try hiding her smile, but I see it. "I'm glad you convinced me to go. I had more fun than I thought I would. And Banks seems nice."

Nice. When I told her about the taco incident, she thought it was funny. Maybe if he hadn't paid me back for the stolen goods, I wouldn't have seen him as anything other than a prick. But I already used my ten-percent-off coupon to get a replacement wrap, thinking about how Banks all but called me a Yankee for choosing Taco Bell over the local restaurants.

"I guess so," I answer half-heartedly, although it's too soon to tell if that's really the truth.

Dixie watches me carefully. "Do you two not get along? He seemed okay with you last night. Most guys don't help people when they're drunk if they don't at least tolerate them."

I have no reason not to like him. In fact, I don't dislike him. "We don't really talk. I was surprised that he even came."

"But you're neighbors."

"He probably has a girlfriend who occupies his time because I don't see him around much" is my reasoning, hoping the shrug emphasizes that I wouldn't care either way.

Dixie hums, sipping her coffee.

"Is it obvious I don't drink often?" I ask, grabbing the coffee in the holder and sitting on the opposite end of the couch. It smells delicious, easing the slight pounding sensation in my temples but not necessarily settling my achy stomach.

"I've seen people get so bad they needed their stomachs

pumped, so I'd say you did all right," she reassures, letting go of Banks. "The first party I ever went to, I was surrounded by people snorting cocaine. The cops ended up coming and breaking it up, and a ton of people got busted with fake IDs and hard drugs. I was lucky enough to sneak out the back before they found me and the girls I came with."

Cocaine? "Dang. And my mom was worried I'd smoke weed," I mused, getting Dixie to laugh again. "I've never even been to a college party."

I went to a high school party once. I was a fifteen-year-old sophomore. It was the first boy-girl party I'd been invited to, the first time I drank, the first time I ever kissed a boy, and the only time I ever had sex. Well, sort of. I'd like to think the interaction between me and the random senior I hooked up with that night didn't count, since he barely lasted ten seconds by the time we got things rolling. I counted each painful second and was grateful when it ended, wondering if anyone could see the difference in me that I thought I would when I'd agreed to do it.

I was stupid and drunk and left feeling guilty that I'd lied to my parents about staying at a friend's house when we'd actually gone to the party instead. The next morning, I woke up so sick that I thought it was karma for lying. I puked so much my voice was raw and raspy. I couldn't eat anything without turning green. I spent a week sleeping on and off and praying that the punishment would end.

If only I'd known it was just beginning.

"Not your thing?" Dixie guesses, sipping her drink and settling into the couch cushion. "It's not really mine either. I've only been to a couple with some girls I had class with. They were trying to get me to join their sorority. I think they were glad I didn't after that. We were...different."

That's one thing I've never been interested in, not that there's anything wrong with joining Greek life. I've heard good things about some organizations. But most of the ones I saw around campus wanted the kind of rah-rah spirit that I just didn't possess.

"I've never had the opportunity," I admit. We haven't exactly gotten to know each other well, and the whole "cancer" topic isn't one I like to break the ice with. Frankly, it's not on my list to tell anybody unless I absolutely have to. When Dixie asked to come over and raid my closet for our night out, I hadn't even wanted her to see my apartment in case she discovered the wigs I'd shoved carefully in boxes on the top shelf of my closet or the cabinet full of medicines that made me look like some sort of addict. The entire time she was here, I worried she would find out and see me the same way my former classmates did before I opted to homeschool.

Instead of divulging too much, I tell her what I'm comfortable with. "I went to school online for the first two years because life was a little…hectic. This is basically my freshman year even though I have the credits I need to be a junior. Everything is new to me."

I'm not embarrassed by it. In fact, I'm proud. I think my history makes me unique. I've gone through hell and back and still managed to find a way here. I'd say that's impressive. It takes a lot of willpower to live when you have little to live for. I wanted to give myself a reason to.

Dixie doesn't judge me. "I debated going to school online, but I need discipline. Plus, if I'd stayed in Pennsylvania, my parents would have driven me crazy. They wanted me to keep playing music since I was getting offered paying gigs. I love them, but I wanted to do my own thing for a little while. You know, take a break and explore other options in the industry."

I know from previous conversations that her childhood consisted of piano lessons, violin lessons, and singing lessons when her parents weren't schmoozing with important people at country clubs. They both knew how to play at least one instrument, her mother used to sing in their local church choir, and her father taught guitar lessons. Their constant pushing got her to win three talent shows at the elementary school she went to, where she earned free tuition into some ritzy music summer camp. While I was getting mud under my nails and learning how to climb trees, she was keeping hers short to learn piano keys and strings.

I'm grateful my parents never tried pushing Bentley or me to do anything we didn't want to. Maybe I should be glad there were no special talents that any of us had. We couldn't play sports. None of us knew how to read music, much less play an instrument. I've only heard my father sing, making up lyrics as he goes when he doesn't know the actual words. And I vaguely remember Mom singing along to an eighties pop song in the car on the way to school. Bentley told her to stop because "she wasn't good like the singer." He was four, but he was right. It was borderline painful.

"I guess I'm lucky," I say. "My parents both support me being here and doing what I need to."

She smiles. "Tell me about them."

Wetting my lips, I hold the warm coffee cup closer to me and loosen a soft breath thinking about my childhood. Where do I even begin? My family is tight-knit, something you need when you grow up in the military. I learned that firsthand seeing the village it took to raise me, and eventually Bentley, when Dad was away.

If Mom didn't have Grandma and Grandpa Parish in North Carolina, I'm not sure what would have happened when we had to leave New Orleans before Katrina hit. Aunt Taylor in New York was another big asset when I got sick. My grandparents were too old to take care of Bentley when all the doctor appointments began for me, so we moved to upstate New York to be closer to Mom's sister. I guess it all worked out because the kind of medical attention I needed went beyond what the small urgent care we had near my grandparents could handle.

Fate, Dad called it.

Even though it took us farther away from him, being in New York meant the best treatment options for me. Something we didn't know we needed until the doctor came in wearing a bright-yellow shirt with a tie covered in farm animals to deliver the bad news. I remember thinking the colors of his shirt were far too happy to be worn by someone telling us such sad things.

"We caught it in time," he tells us, scooting the rolling stool over to where my mother sits beside me. "Cancer is a scary thing, but this form is very treatable. You'll be up and running around again before you know it."

It was Aunt Taylor who comforted Mom when she cried that night—the first of many times. They never knew that I snuck downstairs when they thought I was in bed to hear how bad it was for them, but I eavesdropped on them talking over wine in the kitchen.

Looking back, I wish the doctor hadn't been so optimistic. Maybe then my mother and I wouldn't have gotten our hopes up. Because one round of chemo became two, and two became three, and the remission only lasted about a year before I had to go back in for round four.

Touching the damp ends of my hair that I tried washing in the sink after this morning's excursions, I hide my frown when I realize how long it's been since I've touched my own hair. During the first year of remission, my hair got long enough to cover my head and tickle my ears. I styled it into a cute pixie with the help of YouTube but never found the confidence to wear it outside the house. I wish I had because it didn't take long before the next round of helpful poison made what little I had fall out and leave me back at square one.

I cried alone in my room, not wanting to ask my mother to shave my head again. So I did it myself. It was patchy. I cut myself and bled for far longer than I should have. Bentley found me a few hours later in the bathroom and helped me clean up. He never said a word about it, but I could tell my little brother was horrified. I did that to him, and secretly, I never forgave myself for putting him through it.

Instead of telling Dixie the long, drawn-out sob story of the past five years of my life, I opt for a condensed version. I don't consider it lying, simply censoring the truth. Slightly.

I tell her all about my father's naval career, the moves we had to make because of it, how Hurricane Katrina uprooted us from my favorite state, and how I swore I'd come back someday. It feels good to say that, sitting in a one-bedroom apartment furnished with all my secondhand necessities, exactly where I said I'd be when I wasn't sure I'd get the chance to.

She hears about my annoying little brother who's nearly nine years younger than me, my mother's embarrassing safe sex talks, and all the ways I miss their overbearingness.

"But here I am," I conclude, studying the quaint space. It's nothing extravagant. The decorations are minimal, the furniture cheap. But it's mine and only mine. I had to share hospital rooms plenty of times whenever I stayed for monitoring. If I was going away, I wanted a space of my own that I didn't have to share with anybody at all.

"Here you are," Dixie repeats, her eyes following mine as she takes in the apartment. "So what are you going to do with the newfound freedom? Have parties here? Invite cute neighbors over?"

"Cute neighbors, huh?" I muse, taking a long sip of my drink to hide my growing smile as one specific Clark Kent lookalike comes to mind.

I let the caffeine work its magic and stare at the list I made that's still taped to the fridge.

Turning to her, I set my cup down. "Want to see what I plan to do with it?"

One thing I notice over the course of the next few weeks is that my neighbor is avoiding me. I'm not entirely sure why. I'm starting to wonder if I did something dumb the night we all went out together. I even asked Dixie, who had no clue why he'd be keeping his distance when he always says hi to her when they see one another on campus.

I was going to ask him in class, since we have creative writing once a week. We usually sit next to one another when he doesn't show up late and occupy one of the seats in the back near the door. I always smile and wave, sometimes even trying to make friendly conversation, but his replies are too lackluster to give me the courage to ask if I did something. So I chicken out and focus on the workshops Professor Grey gives us to do with other people, never bothering to pair up with the boy whose familiar brown eyes find mine at least once during the three-hour course.

During lunch the day after I tried and failed again at speaking to Banks, I spot Dawson sitting with a group of boys who I've since learned are on the basketball team with him. Apparently, Dixie is an avid fan. She even convinced me to go to an upcoming home game with her next week.

When he sees me, he pushes off the table and ignores the guys hooting at him for ditching them. "Hey, pretty lady," he greets, giving me the same one-armed hug I've grown accustomed to. He keeps the arm around my shoulder as we walk to a nearby table that's half empty.

"You didn't have to leave your friends," I tell him, looking over at where the guys are wiggling their fingers at us and laughing.

Dawson turns his back to them and flips them off before making himself comfortable across from me. "You're my friend too."

My brows go up as I doctor my sandwich. I can't say I'm particularly hungry today, and I don't know if that has to do with the low mark I got on my last journalism assignment for not getting a second interview for the article I was assigned or if the heaviness in my stomach is something else completely. I don't remember the last time I felt well enough to try crossing things off my list because it's always something bogging me down. "I am?"

He chuckles. "Damn. Way to hurt a guy's feelings," he muses. He's clearly fine, so I don't bother with an apology.

"Speaking of," I lead in, smacking the top roll back onto the meat. "Did I do something to Banks? You're friends, right? If he said something, I'd rather know about it."

Confusion furrows his brows. "Not that I know of. Why?"

I shrug, trying to seem unfazed by the fact that Banks doesn't put in an effort to talk to me. In hindsight, he barely did the night at The Station either because Dawson talked most of the night for all of us, but it feels personal. "I don't know. Maybe he's just quiet, but I get the feeling I did something that annoyed him."

Dawson watches me for a minute, curiosity marring his face as he scratches his chin and the small amount of stubble there. "Nah, I doubt it. It takes a lot for Banks to get pissy with people. Trust me. I've tested those waters a time or two."

I'll have to take his word for it because I have no reason to dwell. "Okay. I just wanted to make sure since we're neighbors. I was always told it's important to have good relationships with the people you live near. You never know what could happen."

He stretches his long legs out so they're in the aisle between tables. "I'm sure he wouldn't leave you in the building if it were on fire, if that's what you're worried about," he jokes, although there's something off about his demeanor. "But even if he does, I'll save you."

I ignore his flirty wink. "Good to know." Spooning out some of the soup of the day, I blow on the steam billowing from my spoon. "So Dixie and I will be at your home game next week."

He perks up. "You will?"

I nod, carefully setting the utensil down and dipping my roll into the broth. I would have thought she'd tell him, but maybe it was meant to be a surprise. "She got us tickets. She's really excited."

"And what about you?" he pries.

"I've never been a sports girl," I admit. I watched football with Dad once, but I didn't understand anything that was going on. "But I'm looking forward to it. I think Dixie even got us matching jerseys."

His dark eyes sparkle. "Hopefully with my number on them. Gotta represent the best player."

I smile because I wouldn't be shocked if Dixie *does* have his jersey. "I guess you'll have to wait and see."

Dawson leans back, drumming his fingers along the edge of the table. "Wish you would've told me sooner. I probably could have gotten you the tickets for free and saved you two some money. Players get a certain amount a year to give to friends and family."

"Does your family not come?"

He shakes his head, watching me eat. "They're divorced and don't live around here. But it's fine. They went to almost all of my games in high school even after they split. Can't expect them to follow me around forever."

I suppose that's true. "Well, we'll keep it in mind for next time. I'm sure she already has other games planned out."

His lips kick up at the corners. "Good."

I debate how to stay on the topic of Dixie without giving too much away. "She told me you majored in history."

He pulls out his phone, his brows pinching as he murmurs, "Did she?"

I'm not sure what's captured his attention, but it doesn't seem good. "Yeah…" I do my best not to glance at his screen even though my curiosity is getting the better of me as one of his knees starts bouncing. "She's taking some sort of musical history class. You should ask her about it. I bet you two have a lot in common."

Dawson pales when he sees whatever is flashing on the screen. "Shit," he murmurs, scraping the chair back. "I gotta go. I'll see you two Tuesday though?"

"We'll be there," I call out, watching him walk away and put the phone to his ear.

Weird.

After only being able to take two bites of food, I dump the rest into the trash bin by the door as I fight the nausea creeping into the back of my throat. As I walk toward the exit, I see Banks stroll in with his notebook tucked under his arm. He looks lost in his own little world, but the second he glances to his right and sees me, he straightens.

I lift my hand to wave, about to walk over when his gaze dips and he walks into the food hall without so much as a nod in my direction.

"Guess that answers that," I murmur to myself, debating following him in. Glancing at the time on my phone, I say screw it and head to the grill section Banks is browsing.

As if my suspicions weren't enough, the way he stiffens as soon as I stop beside him cements it for me. "You're avoiding me," I declare, getting the attention of the line cook behind the counter.

Banks grabs one of the wrapped paninis. "I'm not avoiding you," he replies, focusing solely on the food displayed in front of him.

His lack of eye contact says otherwise. "Are you sure? Because it sure seems like you're being weird right now."

From his profile, I see his jaw tick. "Maybe it's because you're harassing me in the middle of a lunch line while I'm trying to get food," he snaps back, voice cool enough to make me frown.

Okay, I get that. I should have probably just walked out and gone to class early. "I wanted to clear the air, that's all," I tell him quietly.

I wait for him to say something else. When a few awkward

89

moments go by in silence, I peek at the employee still watching the two of us before backing down.

"Sorry for bothering you," I tell Banks, flushing at the rejection. All I want is to be friends. Or friend*ly*. That's not too much to ask for. Is it?

I hear a deep sigh as I'm walking away. "You caught me in a bad mood," he admits.

When I turn, I suck in a breath as I see his split lip. It looks like mine when Bentley and I were playing with a wiffle ball bat and things got a little carried away. "What happened?"

His chin dips, trying to hide what I already saw. "It's nothing. An accident."

He doesn't seem like a fighter, but I don't know him well at all. "Are you okay? Make sure you keep that cleaned. Once, I got a cut and it got infected."

He takes his things and heads to the fountain drinks to get a plastic cup. Naturally, I follow close behind. "I'll be fine."

Pressing him will only make him angry, so I don't. "Well, if you need anything…" I rub my lips together, watching as he pours himself Dr. Pepper. "You know where I live. I've gotten good at cleaning wounds."

The comment finally catches his attention, his eyes drifting to mine with silent curiosity. He doesn't ask what I mean, and I don't elaborate. I didn't even mean to let that slip. I bruised easily as a child, got cut during my many adventures outdoors, and broke a few bones climbing things I shouldn't have long before I ever got sick. I guess it was all practice for when life kicked me while I was down.

I can't explain it, but his eyes pierce mine in ways that see right through me. Stomach tightening, I try figuring out the feeling that settles into my gut. It goes beyond the nausea. Familiarity? Something else?

"I'll keep that in mind, Birdie," he says, his low tone making goose bumps pebble my arms.

It almost makes me forget I don't feel well.

Almost.

I have to run out of class halfway through to empty what little is in my stomach. There's a tinge of red that I choose to ignore as I wipe my mouth off, take a deep breath, and meet my eyes in the mirror.

The girl staring back is a stranger.

Hollow.

Tired.

I close my eyes, rinse out my mouth, and walk away without having to look at her again.

Chapter Ten

BANKS

THE LONG TREK THROUGH Julian T. White Hall is one I've done countless times over the years—long before I was a student here. I can get to room 316 on the third floor four different ways with my eyes closed and know at least five different ways to get out quickly if needed.

Anxiety bubbles the closer I get to the cracked door, my eyes roaming over the brown nameplate on the wall beside it.

Terry Banks, PhD.

Rapping my knuckles against the wood, I push the door open wider to see my father standing by the bookcase near the window, which is full of books and guides on landscaping and architecture. A few textbooks from previous classes are thrown in, including some he's made me read during the summer so I don't "dry out" and "waste my time off rotting brain cells" like he always says video games do.

He turns, pulling his glasses off when he sees me standing at the doorjamb.

"Dad," I greet, stepping in and closing the door behind me.

His eyes immediately go to my lip, his mouth curling downward before returning a book to the shelf. "Paxton. How's your day been?"

Casual conversation. I can handle that. "It's been good. Submitted my project for approval to Laramie."

He walks over to his chair and sits, setting his glasses down beside his keyboard. "When are you going to hear back about it? He's known to make his students do revisions. Some don't get the approval until weeks before it's due."

I've heard as much, and I'd be lying if I said that didn't make me nervous. But I'm proud of the concept I came up with. More so because of the idea behind it, which I can share during presentation week. But every time I've tried telling Dad the inspiration, he's always found a way to cut me off with topics he cares more about, so I gave up. "I'm confident he'll like what I've got. We're supposed to get feedback next week."

My father hums, his eyes still focused on the fat lip that hurts like a bitch. "Did you ice it?" he asks.

Swallowing, I wrap my fingers along the edge of the armchair. Squeezing until there's a bite of pain in my finger-tips, I nod once. "I did."

He keeps staring. I don't know what's on his mind because the man is stone-faced as ever. Then he says the last thing I expect. "I'm sorry. For..." He shakes his head, clearing his throat when his eyes dip to my lip again and then move away quickly to something on the wall.

"It was an accident," I murmur.

And it was. This time. If I hadn't startled him trying to wake him up when I found him drunk and slumped over in his armchair at the house, he wouldn't have swung at me.

He's done a lot of intentional things in life, especially after Mom left us, but this was different. I can forgive him a lot easier for this.

"I just..." His words trail off, and for a moment I don't think he's going to finish the thought. "I've changed."

My body freezes, save for my fingers twitching along the arm of the chair. Instead of answering, I stare at his desk. It's organized—each file, paper, and folder all in a specific place. I've always found that funny. His life here is nothing like the one at home, where the real mess is. Where it has been for most of my life.

"I'm so sorry," he says, hovering over me where I'm lying on the floor. "It was an accident. I've changed. Tell your mother I changed."

That's all he cared about.

What she thinks.

Even after she left.

Pride is a bitch like that.

He looks at my notebook, clearly as ready to move on from this conversation as I am. "How's that other class treating you? The one where you're writing fairy tales or whatever it is they're making you do. Ready to drop it for something more tantalizing?"

And here we go. At least I know he's back to himself because hearing him apologize was a little too weird for me. "So far I like creative writing. It's a new type of challenge. Works the brain in other ways."

The huff coming from him is in obvious disbelief, but I choose to ignore it. "Hopefully you realize what a waste of time it is before the drop period is over."

There's a lot I could say to him, but I've learned to be smart over the years. The less I say, the better. The safer. "I should probably get going soon. I told Dawson I'd meet him at the library before my shift at the store this afternoon."

My father turns to the computer, waking it up and signing in. "Speaking of, I highly suggest you tell him to start showing up if he expects to pass. There's no reason for him to be missing my noon course."

He hasn't been showing up? He told me the other day he actually liked the material this semester when I asked him how it was going. "Yeah," I say slowly. "I'll let him know."

Dawson has been acting strange lately, but it's not unusual for him. I figured it had something to do with Sawyer or Dixie. I swear, every time I see him on campus, he's all over one of them, and whenever we're hanging out, he likes to bring Sawyer up in some form. It digs at me, and I wonder if he knows it.

I like Dawson, and I want him to be happy. But I also want to get to know the firecracker who confronts people head-on even if it's uncomfortable. Like yesterday. The last thing I wanted was to talk to her, or anybody for that matter, but she didn't give me another choice.

I respect it. Maybe it's exactly what Dawson needs in his life—somebody who won't kiss his ass but tell him how it is.

Swiping at my jaw, I stand. "Was there anything else you wanted to tell me?"

It was his idea to meet, not mine. I figured it was better here when I could use class or something else on campus as an out rather than agreeing to come home later. Dawson has been AWOL for a couple days, so the chances of actually seeing him are unlikely. If he doesn't answer my texts again later, I'll have to go to his apartment and make sure we don't have a repeat of last year when I found him unconscious on the bathroom floor.

I've changed, Dad said.

I want to believe it. Like I want to believe Dawson has. But the last time Dad told me that, he got blackout drunk and started yelling so loudly the neighbors called the cops to make sure everything was okay. He didn't lay a hand on me, but if the officers didn't knock that night, I have a feeling he would have done more than leave me with a split lip.

Dad's gaze moves from his computer screen to me, eyes darting to my lip and then back up again. "That was all. I wanted to make sure that we were okay."

Not that I was okay. That *we* were okay. God forbid he thought I would badmouth him to the wrong people on campus.

At the end of the day, he's still my father. I love him. No matter the battles we go through. And even if it's hard for me to believe, he has gotten better in a lot of ways. I'm not sure I'd stick around if he hadn't. Even if it meant giving up my free tuition.

"We're good," I reassure, grabbing my notebook because I have nothing more to say.

Enabler.

His shoulders ease from their stiff, squared position. "Good." There's a pause where he looks at what I'm holding. "And reconsider your little writing class. Your time is here valuable. There are other electives that could use more of your brain cells than what you're being taught there."

Replying would be pointless, so I salute him sarcastically and leave before he can comment on it. Halfway down the hall, I remind myself that he means well.

Most of the time.

Nothing he could say would make me drop the class. If I'm being honest with myself, a large part of that is because it's the one time a week I get to know Sawyer a little better without feeling guilty about it. Sure, I don't exactly play Mr. Nice Guy and converse with her unless she starts it, but being the wallflower gets results too. You learn a lot about people when you observe them.

Like how she touches her hair when she's nervous or overthinking. Or how she's friendly with everybody, always complimenting somebody for something she finds in their stories or the prompts Professor Grey gives us. And she indulges people with the smallest details of her life to relate to those she owes nothing to. Like when she brought up the golden retriever she misses back home. Or her little brother, whom she pretends she doesn't miss as much but must based on all the stories she shares with a smile on her face.

I pick up the smallest mannerisms, which only tugs at the interest already anchored in my gut. She uses her hair to hide on the days it's down, fidgets with her hands when someone is reading her work as if she's not confident in it, and is always watching her surroundings the same way I am. I know because she's caught me almost as much as I've caught her glancing in my direction.

I don't feel guilty about knowing any of that. After all, I'm not seeking her out if we share a class together, which means I'm not imposing on Dawson's dibs.

At least, that's what I tell myself to feel better about my decision to stay.

———————————

After the start of semester hustle slows down, the campus store is always painfully boring. Kids already have their books and supplies and rarely need to come in for anything else.

"Three people," Lucy groans, banging her head on the counter until her bright-blue-dyed hair falls out of its bun. "We've had three people all day. Why do they do this to us?"

"Better be careful what you say," I remark, still working on the inventory list our manager gave me to do before he left. "They always cut back on hours after the first month or two."

Lucy sits up and spins on the stool, her hair whipping around her. "Good, let them. I don't know how you do it."

Simple. I like having the peace that I don't get elsewhere. "It gives me time to work on assignments without much interruption."

"You live by yourself," she points out. A fact she knows because she's been to my apartment on a few occasions long before she got a boyfriend.

I'm grateful we can still be friends. If that's what you want to call it. Otherwise, work would be awkward. The punk-rock chick was fun when we spent time together off campus, but I think we both knew it wasn't a long-term situation. That probably helped salvage civility. "Dawson spends more time at my place than he does his."

Lucy leans her elbows against the edge of the counter, one of her eyebrow rings catching the light as she arches the brow in inquisition. "I'm surprised he got over the Desiree thing so quickly. He swore up and down he wasn't going to forgive you for that."

I try to forget about the girl in question, and it's safe to assume Dawson has too since his focus has been on other women. "It's been over a year."

"And then with Marco..."

I eye my former fling, feeling defensive over my friend. "Is there a point to this?"

She holds up her hands in surrender. "I think it's nice

that you two are close. It's obvious after everything that he needs somebody. And you..."

My eyes narrow in warning.

Lucy sighs, standing up. "I obviously never got to know you that well, but I think you could use somebody too. Everybody needs at least one person in their corner."

Guilt curls itself into a ball in my chest. I like Lucy. I liked her when we first started hooking up, and I like her now. But I never allow myself to get close to somebody because I never want them to know the version of me that I barely get along with.

"You're a good person, Luce," I tell her.

The compliment makes her roll her eyes. "I know. That's why Sean smartened up and did something about it. Somebody had to."

Had she been waiting for me to? I always thought she was fine with casual. "So you two are good?"

Her smile warms. "We're great." Jabbing her thumb toward the back, she says, "I'm going to finish breaking down the boxes if you need me. But Banks?"

I look at her.

That smile remains, making me feel like an even bigger tool for not giving her a real shot when I had one. She cares about people, about me, but never pushes the way most people tend to. She asked me about my lip, accepted the bullshit answer whether she believed it or not, and let it go. It made being around her easier. She was always easier.

"You're a good person too," she says. "I hope you let yourself believe that one day."

Gaping at her as she disappears into the back room, I lean back in my stool. Swiping at my jaw, I look down at the inventory sheet and sigh.

After a couple of hours pass by, the sliding doors open, and a familiar face walks in, beelining right for the snack section.

When Sawyer sees Lucy organizing the chips, the girls laugh at something like old friends. I watch them from the counter, ignoring the sketch pad in my lap that I've spent the last forty minutes working on when I see how they lean into one another and giggle in low voices.

One of my brows draws up when Lucy points in my direction, causing Sawyer to turn. When she sees me sitting behind the register, she straightens. I don't know why her smile disappears or how I notice that it's only gone for a millisecond before reappearing.

She grabs something from the shelf and walks over. "Long time, no see, Just Banks. I didn't know you worked here. I've only ever seen Lucy and some skinny guy who looks like he hates the world and everybody in it."

Lucy snorts at the description of Teddy, which is oddly fitting. "That's our manager. Can you blame the guy when this is his full-time job?"

Sawyer giggles again, the sound stirring something in my chest. "Poor guy."

I pick up the Pop-Tart and scan it. "I didn't know people still ate this cardboard."

She passes me the cash for it, down to the cent, and grabs the snack that I barely tolerated as a child. "At least the cardboard has frosting. They're a guilty pleasure of mine. Don't you have a comfort food?"

Lucy chimes in. "She's the one who's been selling us out of that flavor."

Sawyer shrugs, unashamed. "The vending machines around campus only have the ones with strawberry filling. It's gross.

I prefer chocolate fudge. When the peanut butter ones came out, those were my favorite. Then they stopped making them."

My coworker beams. "I used to go for the s'mores. Although the chocolate fudge is a close second. And if you toast them, they're like an orgasm in your mouth."

The last thing I want to hear from two attractive women, especially one whose body I'm familiar with and another I might like to get familiar with, is anything having to do with orgasms. Or their mouths.

Gazing between the two of them, I can't help but ask, "Do you two know each other?"

It's my neighbor who shakes her head. "Not really. She's the one who usually sells me these."

"Some of us are actually personable enough to make friends easily," Lucy teases. She turns to Sawyer. "Sorry. Banks is the broody type. He'd prefer sitting here in silence, as horrible as that sounds."

Sawyer smiles at me, her eyes dipping down to the sketch pad beside me. "Are you really broody, or is it the tortured artist in you?"

It takes everything in me not to smirk. "Who says I'm tortured, Birdie?"

Her answer is quick. Smooth. "Your eyes."

One of my brows raises again at the response.

Lucy stares between us curiously. "Do *you* two know each other?"

Sawyer tucks her Pop-Tart into the back pocket of her jeans and smiles at Lucy. "I moved in across the hall from him."

My coworker's eyes land on me, but I choose to ignore them. "Interesting," she says, a secretive smile tilting her lips.

I roll my eyes at them. "Not really." Going back to my sketch pad, I say, "Enjoy your flavored cardboard."

Sawyer laughs. "I will." Before she leaves, she notices the open package of fruit snacks on the counter by my set of pencils. Her smile is small, amused. "Guess you do have a comfort food after all."

I glance down at the food I've been picking at, which tastes like my childhood. "Who doesn't like fruit snacks?"

She shrugs. "Heathens, probably."

I chuckle.

Sawyer waves me off. "Bye, Lucy," she calls out.

I can feel Lucy's eyes on me when it's just us. "What?" I ask.

"She says it reminds her of home."

I look up. "What does?"

"The Pop-Tarts."

I blink.

Lucy looks at the closed doors. "I can't tell if that's sweet or sad if that's all she has to remind her."

Thinking about it, I follow her gaze to where the blond disappears down the sidewalk. "Sweet," I go with before returning to my project.

If something as small as a childhood treat can make her think of home, she must have a lot of love that she left behind.

I can't think of one thing I miss that I'd want to keep around to remember.

It's hard to ignore my former fling's gaze. "Is there a reason you're staring?" I ask, still focusing on my sketch.

Lucy waits a moment, her eyes going to my lip before moving away. "No. No reason."

I don't call bullshit because once I see that grin on her face, I decide I don't want to know what she's thinking.

She starts humming, going back to the project she was working on before Sawyer sauntered in.

I can't help but glance at the door and then at the empty box of Pop-Tarts Lucy tosses on the floor to be thrown away.

Before she can catch me staring at them, I force my eyes back to my work with nothing but Lucy's humming filling the silence.

Chapter Eleven

BANKS

WHEN WEDNESDAY ROLLS AROUND, there's a notable absence in class that has me staring at the empty seat Sawyer usually occupies. When ten minutes pass by after the professor starts his lecture on proper grammar, I realize the girl who's usually more punctual than me isn't coming.

I check the time on my phone every few minutes, my eyes going to the door in between the doodles I draw in my notebook. I shouldn't care. *I don't*, I tell myself. But…a nagging feeling nips at my stomach.

The first hour of class goes by quickly, learning about shit we should have known since elementary school pertaining to sentence structure and punctuation. But the way people seem to be taking notes on it all makes me question America's education system.

When we get our twenty-minute break before the last hour of class, which focuses on workshopping our four-page short stories, I pull out my phone and debate shooting

Dawson a text to see if he's with her. I'm not sure how I'd feel if he was. *It's none of your business,* I remind myself.

So why the hell does it feel like someone punched me in the stomach when I keep glancing over at the empty spot?

Tapping my pen against my open notebook as my class-mates start pouring back into the room, I glance at the clock on the wall.

A minute goes by as I contemplate my next move. Another thirty seconds crawls. Then another.

It's none of your business, I tell myself again, hoping it'll stick.

It doesn't.

Before Professor Grey can come back, I slide out of my seat and grab my things. Nobody looks twice when I leave the room, not that I'm shocked. I haven't exactly become buddy-buddy with anybody since the semester started, so very few people pay me any mind.

Except for the girl whose apartment door I'm knocking on twenty minutes later.

I hear distant rustling coming from inside, but nobody comes to the door. Brows furrowing, I wait a few minutes before knocking again. I'm not sure why I'm here. People skip class all the time. But Sawyer doesn't seem like the type.

Tucking my hands into my front pockets, I step back and listen to the little noises inside. *This is stupid. You don't care,* the voice tries to convince me.

I'm about to listen to it and walk away when the deadbolt clicks and the knob turns before I see Sawyer in the cracked opening. My eyes narrow when I see the bright-red tissue she's holding to her nose.

Without thinking, I push the door open, forcing her

back. Eyes narrowing, I stand to full height and ask, "Who did that to you?"

Her eyes widen at my tone. "What? Nobody."

I close the door behind me using my boot, not caring that I'm being rude and inviting myself in. She told me she was good at cleaning up wounds, which sat the wrong way with me since the day she said it. "If somebody did this—"

"Nobody did this to me, Banks," she promises, voice muffled from the way she's holding her nose.

I guide her over to the couch and sit her down, tilting her chin up. "Keep your head back," I direct. Her apartment is set up the same way mine is, with the exception of the rooms being on the opposite sides, so it's easy to navigate.

Going over to the kitchen, I search the cabinets for a washcloth, wet one with warm water, and then grab fresh tissues from the box on the counter.

She accepts the Kleenex and watches as I sit on the edge of the coffee table in front of her.

Has she always been this pale? The only color on her is the blood smeared between her nose and lip. "How long has this been going on?"

Sawyer blows out a raspberry, leaning back on the couch. "It started right before class. I thought it was finished after a few minutes, but it came back. It's been off and on since."

Christ. She's been bleeding for the past hour?

"Is this normal?"

When she doesn't answer right away, I can't help but examine her exposed skin for anything else. Cuts. Bruises. I'm well versed in what to look for when somebody lays a hand on a person.

Besides a tiny bruise on her arm that can't be from

anything like a hand, she's clean. Only then am I able to relax my shoulders.

"Sometimes it is," she answers, sighing. "It's been a while since this has happened. I used to get them a lot during the winter because of the air. The house my mom bought had a wood stove, so it was hot and dry. A humidifier helped."

"You got one of those here?"

She shakes her head. "Like I said, it's been a while since this has happened."

I take the moment of silence to look around her place. It's almost as bare as mine, but there are a lot more decorations littering the living room. Colorful pillows on the couch. A throw blanket that looks handmade. Pictures of a golden retriever on the wall that must be the one she talks about a lot.

"You're supposed to be in class," she points out, breaking me from my nosiness.

I shrug, taking note of the take-out containers piled in the kitchen garbage. "You weren't there. Wanted to make sure you weren't dead. I hear that's what friendly neighbors do."

Her laugh is featherlight, perking my ears up. It almost makes me smile. Almost. "Touché," she muses. "I wasn't avoiding you. Just slowly bleeding out. No big deal."

The attempt at humor doesn't sit well with me, even though it's something I'd usually appreciate. "You'll be fine. People get nosebleeds all the time. Let me look."

She cringes but pulls the tissue back. It looks like the bleeding has stopped, so I give her the warm cloth to wipe off the stained blood on her skin.

"Did I get it?" she asks, wiggling her nose.

I take the cloth from her and gently wipe at the one spot that she missed. Her lips are pressed together and her cheeks pinken, and I don't know if that's because of me or because she isn't feeling well.

Clearing my throat, I set the cloth down. "Got it," I murmur.

We stare at one another before her eyes dip down to the blood-stained items. She gets up, swaying slightly on her feet. I grab her arm until she stabilizes herself, the pink in her cheeks darkening as she pulls her arm back. "I'm fine. I got up too quickly."

I stand, watching as she throws out the dirty tissues and tosses the bloody washcloth into one of the back rooms.

When she comes out, she crosses her arms across her chest. She's wearing the same baggy college sweatshirt as the first time I saw her, but instead of the shorts that showcased her nice legs, she's in matching college sweatpants that do little for her body.

It's probably better that way.

Dibs, I remind myself, thinking of Dawson.

The last thing I need is a repeat of Desiree.

Rubbing the back of my neck, I grab the silver-wrapped snack from my back pocket that I almost forgot about. "Got you this." I don't make eye contact as I pass her the Pop-Tart. Chocolate fudge. "Probably broke it when I sat down, but it should taste the same."

She slowly takes the gift like I pass her a check for a million dollars, her mouth curving upward as she stares at the treat. "You didn't have to make up an excuse to see me, you know."

"I didn't," I lie. I totally did.

Why else would I justify buying frosting-covered cardboard? Lucy giggled the whole time she cashed me out at the store, only laughing harder when I told her to shut up.

"Does this mean we're friends?" she asks, not calling me out on the way my eyes lazily drag down the front of her.

"Do you want to be?"

She licks her lips, the tip of her tongue darting out the side for a moment in contemplation. "I don't see why not. Not many people are willing to clean up a random person's bloody nose. Or buy them snacks."

My eyes go to the part of her in question to make sure it hasn't started bleeding again. "You going to be good?"

She nods, waving the food I gave her. "Now that I have this, I've never been better."

We're silent again.

Sawyer moves her weight from one foot to the other. "So…?"

Huffing out a laugh, I stand from the coffee table and walk toward the door. "Yes, Birdie. We're friends."

My eyes catch a piece of paper taped to the refrigerator as I walk past it, but I don't see what the handwriting says before Sawyer moves in front of it.

"Thank you for the Pop-Tart," she tells me with a soft smile. "*Friend.*"

Her blue eyes glimmer with playfulness, making me grin in amusement. "Anytime, *pal.*"

Professor Grey pairs us up in teams of two the following week to work on a new set of prompts for the last hour. Since Sawyer and I were absent from the last class, we get partnered.

I've seen her a total of two times at our building since I came to her apartment. Once, when I was coming home from another mundane shift at the store, and another time when Sawyer was walking out in a pair of workout pants and matching top that left very little to the imagination. I asked if she was going for a run.

She laughed. Loudly. And then she produced a Pop-Tart out of thin air and bit into the top as she walked away, still giggling at the question with a shake of her head.

Another tidbit of information I tucked away.

Not a runner.

"These are dumb," she grumbles now, reading over the prompt selections. We're supposed to pick one sentence a week from the options Professor Grey prints out and turn it into a story. We get twenty minutes to come up with something and then another twenty to share with our partners before spending the final twenty minutes of class having a few people share with the group.

My eyes rake over the choices, realizing they all have to do with love. "It's Valentine's Day this week," I tell her when I see the theme.

She makes a face, her lips twisting down as she taps her pen against the paper. A quiet "Oh" is all I get in response.

I lean back, stretching my legs out. "Not a fan of the commercialized holiday? I thought women loved that shit. You guys get chocolate and flowers and all that other lovey-dovey crap they push on us."

Her bottom lip tucks into her mouth, trapped by her top two teeth digging into it. She stays like that, contempla-tive as she circles one of the prompts and says, "I've never had a Valentine before. Unless you count elementary school when they used to make everybody bring in those stupid Valentine's Day cards for their classmates."

I don't count that since it was obligatory. Plus, there

were always some parents who went all out with the fancy ones that had candy they probably spent a fortune on. I was lucky if my parents even remembered to get the dollar store versions amid all their other issues.

"You've never gotten chocolates from a boyfriend?" I ask.

There's another moment of hesitation where she plays with the ends of her hair loosely hanging past her shoulders. "No."

"Huh." I watch her a little more closely, but the only thing she's focusing on is the assignment. She only looks up at me when I say, "They're idiots then."

Her tongue slowly drags across her bottom lip before her teeth dig into it again. The faintest dots of pink coat her cheeks. "I've never... I didn't really date before."

The response takes me off guard. "How old are you?"

"Does that really matter?" she snaps, embarrassment in her tone.

I think about it before dismissing it. "I guess not. I'm just trying to figure out how any guy could be dumb enough not to shoot his shot with you."

Maybe she's as oblivious as Dawson when it comes to people being interested in her. Sometimes, naivety can be cute. Especially with a face like hers.

Sawyer starts writing in her notebook, only getting a sentence down before bringing the pen to her mouth and staring at the words for a long, silent moment. "Have you dated a lot?"

I could lie to her, but I have nothing to hide or be ashamed of. "Depends on what you consider dating. I had a girlfriend in high school. Two, actually. Last one broke up with me before graduation. It was for the best."

We were going to two separate schools on opposite sides

111

of the country. It was never going to work, so we called it. She still reaches out sometimes to see how I am. Half the time, I forget to reply.

"And since then?" she presses.

"Tit for tat," I offer in compromise. "I tell you something, and you have to do the same."

She thinks about it, her teeth coming down on the pen again, before nodding.

"I've never dated seriously in college," I answer. "I found it too distracting."

"But dating casually isn't?" she doubts.

I grin. "It's my turn." The nervousness on her face has me amused, but I keep it simple. "How old are you?"

Her shoulders relax. "Twenty-one. So is casually dating not as distracting?"

"It's certainly more fun when there's less pressure," I tell her honestly. "We're college students. We have our whole lives to find significant others. I never came here expecting to meet mine."

Sawyer looks away, studying the other people writing and talking among themselves. There's a distance to her eyes that make them look like the stormy waters of the Gulf Coast during hurricane season—moody and dark.

I expect her to ask me another question, but she simply goes back to writing her story without so much as another peep.

"Was that all?" I doubt, wondering why she shut down so quickly.

"You don't have much longer to write your prompt," she answers quietly, her pen scribbling along the lines of her notebook paper.

I try figuring out what I said to upset her. It wouldn't

be the first time I've opened my mouth and said something dumb. I'm sure it won't even be the last. "There's nothing wrong with coming here looking for love."

Her daggered eyes have the potential to be lethal if looks could kill. "I'm not here for that either."

I've touched a nerve, and it intrigues me. "I guess we have that in common. So why exactly are you here then, Sawyer?"

"What are any of us here for?" she counters, her eyes on her paper instead of me. "I'm here hoping to figure myself out. Before..." She stops herself, shaking her head.

"Before what?"

Clearing her throat, she asks, "Is Banks your first name or your last name?"

"Last."

"What's your first name?"

I cross my arms over my chest. "My turn. Why put a time limit on figuring out who you are? That comes with life. We're always changing. Evolving. Adapting. Who you are in college won't be who you are five years from now. Or ten."

She offers a thoughtful head bob, and for a moment, I don't think she'll give me an answer at all. "Not all of us have the same timeline, Just Banks. Time is relative that way. Same as how we spend it."

I hum, unsure of what else to say. It seems like she's thought about this before, and I wonder why.

Eventually, Professor Grey says, "Time's up! Go ahead and exchange your stories with each other and we'll have three new people share theirs with the class."

I look at my empty paper.

Sawyer looks at the paragraph on hers.

When she looks up, I smile. Then I reach over and use the pad of my thumb to smooth her bottom lip. "Ink," I murmur.

A little breath from her caresses my thumb, and I watch as her throat moves with a thick swallow. "Oh." She touches her lip. "Thanks."

"Of course."

Except there was no ink.

Sorry, Dawson.

Chapter Twelve

BANKS

I'VE ALWAYS THOUGHT VALENTINE'S Day was a scam—a consumer's holiday. If you don't bother spending money buying people gifts on any random Friday, do you really love them?

As far as I'm concerned, it's a get-out-of-jail-free card. You get a bouquet of flowers, maybe a box of cheap chocolates from the store, and lay on your thickest charm. Women go nuts for it.

I'd know because I'm just as guilty of doing it in the past, except I never really cared that deeply about the girls I showered with half-assed presents—like the stuffed animals with those stupid mushy sayings on them or boxes of those pharmacy fifty-percent-off chocolates they keep on the endcaps for people like me who don't want to think too hard or spend too much.

Which is why I find it so ironic that I'm standing in front of the candy display at work, looking at the Valentine's Day–themed chocolates that come out once a year. Most of them are sold out—students buying them for their significant other last minute to say they got them something, the way I used to.

Lucy shows up beside me, knocking her elbow into my rib cage. "Are you shopping for a special someone?"

Peeling my focus away from the assorted candy, I give her an unserious look. "Are you forgetting who you're talking to?"

She snorts, walking over to the counter and hopping onto it. "On the contrary. I know exactly who I'm talking to, Mr. I'm Too Damaged for Relationships but Still Do My Best to Make Them Happy."

The glower I give her doesn't stop her from teasing. "Whatever," I grumble, walking away from the display and fixing a few of the shirt hangers off to the side.

"It's not a bad thing," she appeases. "I think if you find the right person, you won't be so closed off. But word of advice?"

I don't know why I look at her like I actually care what she has to say about the topic. It only supports her suspicions, which are hardly accurate.

Lucy's lips waver into a knowing smile as she leans back. "Get her something she'll actually like. Not some random candy bar from the college store. You can do better than that."

I play nonchalant. "That would imply there's a 'she' to begin with."

Her eyes sparkle with mischief. "Stupid isn't a good look on you, my friend. We both know that there's a 'she' with blond hair who has a hankering for sweets. If it's not her buying us out of those fudge Pop-Tarts, it's you. And I know you don't eat them."

My silence says nothing and everything all at once,

giving her an answer I don't verbalize. I should have known she'd bring that up, but I was hoping she wouldn't.

She taps her temple. "I have eyes, Banksy. I know a crush when I see one. I don't buy people their favorite snacks just because."

"You used to bring me my favorite pretzels," I remind her, thinking about all the times she'd show up at my apartment with the honey mustard–dusted pretzel bites.

She snorts. "That's because I had a crush, dummy. It wasn't out of innocence. I get paid way too little to be buying things for people who don't mean something to me."

Huh. "I didn't know."

"We were sleeping together," she muses with a roll of her eyes.

"I—" I stop myself. I don't know what to say. Am I that oblivious?

She must read my mind. "Boys are so dumb."

Can't argue with her there. "Pop-Tarts don't have to mean anything."

Lucy's smile grows. "Keep telling yourself that. Maybe one day you'll believe it."

My eyes involuntarily go to the snack display where the Pop-Tarts usually are. The only flavor laid out is the strawberry-filled ones, making my lips twitch.

Unfortunately, Lucy is still watching. "Banks and Sawyer, sitting in a tree. K-I-S-S-I-N—"

"Stop," I cut her off with a glare. "Don't go starting that shit. I don't have a crush."

"You totally do."

There's one relatively big problem with that theory that I let her in on. "Dawson likes Sawyer," I mumble, putting the sizes of the sweatshirts we sell back in order on the rack.

Lucy is quiet for a second. "Oh."

I wait a minute before glancing in her direction. Her feet have stopped swinging on the counter as she studies me.

Her brows are arched on her forehead. "So is this a Desiree situation or...?"

Desiree. The name makes my eye twitch as old memories resurface of the raven-haired girl coming on to me at a party. I liked her. I liked the way she watched me. The way she flirted. If I was honest with myself, I liked how forward she was without being overbearing.

But Dawson liked her too.

And he liked her first.

And after a night of drinking at a party we'd both been at, when Dawson was off doing God only knew what for Marco, Desiree made a move. In the back of my mind, I knew it was a dumb decision to let things progress.

But I did.

And when Dawson found out...

Well, things got bad. Fast.

I swore to myself I'd never hurt him that way again, especially not when he's vulnerable. One wrong move would send him over the edge, and that's what I'm trying to avoid.

"No," I decide, looking over at the snack display again briefly before clearing my throat. "It isn't like that."

I can feel her eyes on me, but I opt to get back to work and ignore her for the rest of her shift.

Before she leaves for the day, she says, "In case you want to do stock, we just got a new shipment of food in. I left some of them out to go on the shelves."

She knows stock is the one thing I hate doing, but I nod anyway and tell her to have a good night.

Twenty minutes before closing when I'm bored and

118

trying to kill time, I go to the back and find the box she was talking about. She left it out in the middle of the room with a note taped to the top.

Just in case there ever becomes a special someone in your life.

Sighing, I grab the box of Pop-Tarts and take it to the front to scan. When I clock out, I'm carrying the whole box with me and trying to ignore Lucy's taunts echoing in my head.

The panicked look on Dawson's face when I pull into the driveway has me on alert as I park my truck in its usual spot.

"What's wrong?" I ask, closing the rusty door behind me as he walks over, rubbing the back of his neck.

His eyes go down to the Pop-Tarts, forgetting whatever is on his mind. "Since when do you eat those?"

He knows I've never had much of a sweet tooth. "The mood struck," I reply, not willing to bring up the real reason and make him think twice about it.

Dibs.

Not that it matters.

"It's Valentine's Day," he says, lifting his red-rimmed eyes to me. I try not making a face when the wind blows and I get a whiff of marijuana. I knew he liked dabbling in pot, but I thought he was going to try giving it up when his sponsor said the California sober tactic rarely worked.

"What about it?" I ask, frowning when he scratches his nose.

He looks behind him before his shoulders slouch. "I sort

of suggested getting dinner with Dixie tonight, but I didn't know what day it was."

Dixie? I don't know whether to be confused or relieved. "I thought you called dibs on Sawyer. Isn't going after the best friend a little cliché?"

"You would know, wouldn't you?" he replies coolly, eyes narrowing in accusation.

I hold up my hands in surrender because I'm not in the mood to do this with him. "It was an honest question. You've been all about Sawyer since she moved in. I didn't know you were even interested in Dixie, since you were pushing me on her at the bar."

Defense takes over his face. "Maybe I like them both. You've never had an issue playing people, so why can't I?"

What the hell? "I've never intentionally played anyone, and you're hardly the type to."

"And why is that? Because I can't get anybody I want like you can?"

I drop my head back and take a deep breath to calm myself before answering. "No. Because you're a good guy."

He's quiet, cringing when he realizes what a dick he sounds like.

"Are you okay?" I ask, studying him. "You don't look like you've been sleeping, and you smell like pot."

Dawson shifts. "So?"

"If you want to go to a meeting, I can go with you. Screw Valentine's Day. It's a pointless holiday anyway."

"I don't need to go to a meeting," he snaps. "I told Dixie I'd take her out, so that's what I'm going to do."

Since I can't force him, I let it go. "Fine. I still don't see why you're taking Dixie, but I hope you two have fun."

I start walking around him when he grabs my arm to stop me. "Shit. Wait. I'm sorry. You're right. I haven't been sleeping."

He sounds genuine, so I brush off my irritation.

"I tried asking Sawyer if she wanted to hang out, but she said she wasn't feeling good," he explains. "And then Dixie and I were talking, and it somehow led to us making dinner plans. I didn't even think twice about it being Valentine's Day, and I can't back out on her."

My mind wraps around one thing. "What's wrong with Sawyer?"

He eyes me in exasperation. "I don't know, dude. Focus on the real problem. I basically agreed to take a chick out on a Valentine's date, and I'm not prepared at all."

I remind myself to check on Sawyer later when Dawson is gone. "What do you expect me to do about it?"

"I…" He frowns. "I don't know. You've always been better when it comes to this shit. Girls are all over you all the time. For once, I want that to be me. Is that so bad?"

He honestly thinks I have it that easy? "Look, the only advice I can give you is to figure out what you want. And *who*. Because I think we both know that two friends involved with the same person can get messy. You don't want to hurt anybody like that."

The way you were, is what I don't say.

Dawson sighs, scratching the column of his throat. "What if I don't know what I want?"

"Then you'll have to figure it out."

He's silent, looking back at the building. "Maybe you can find out what Sawyer's deal is for me," he remarks, perking up.

Is he out of his mind? I'm willing to do a lot for the guy,

but not that. "What exactly do you want me to do, pass her a note that says, 'Do you like-like Dawson Gable; check yes or no?' I'm not doing that."

"You live across the hall. You can tell me if she's bringing somebody home so I'm not wasting my time."

He wants me to spy on Sawyer? "You're literally doing the same thing. With her friend."

"Come on. You owe me."

I *owe* him? "When are you going to decide enough is enough? I've done a lot for you over the past year. Or have you forgotten?"

He doesn't meet my eyes when he quietly murmurs, "I haven't."

I may not be particularly close with Dixie, but I don't like knowing she's some sort of consolation prize to him. We are all a part of other people's choices in life—they either want you or don't, which inevitably determines if you find the person who does. But there's something in the tremor of his eyes that are still bloodshot from who knows what that tells me he's not exactly of sound mind. I don't want either of these girls being mixed up in something that I know from personal experience is mentally taxing.

"Just tell me if you see anything," he says.

I relent, not that I ever plan to do that. Mostly because I don't think he'll give up first. "Fine. But this is the last time you tell me I owe you."

"*I'll* owe *you* if you can help me figure out what to get Dixie before tonight," he bargains. "I'm short on cash, and the stores are probably picked through."

I happen to know both of his parents put a significant amount of money into his checking account for rent and food every month. There's no reason he can't afford a

122

ten-dollar box of assorted candy. "Where did the money your parents gave you go?"

"Had to buy textbooks."

Books for classes aren't cheap, but I highly doubt that's where his money went.

"Don't look at me like that," he says before I can question him. "They haven't been giving me as much since last year because they don't want me spending it on the wrong shit."

That might be the first smart thing I've heard them do. I reached out to them for help when I first found out he'd been using, but they didn't believe me until they got a call from the hospital after he was given Narcan from overdosing.

I glance down at the Pop-Tarts. If they stay in my apartment, they'll go stale until I eventually throw them away. But if I give them to Sawyer, then Dawson could find out.

I could do a lot of things right now.

Help him or not.

Either choice would be a selfish one.

If I stick to my original plan, it's to gain something from Sawyer. But if I help Dawson win over Dixie, it's to keep him away from the girl across the hall who's long since piqued my interest.

Wetting my lips, I gesture toward the building and start walking. "Come on," I call out, making my choice. "I've got an idea. It's cheesy, but it'll work."

Dawson follows blindly, and I only feel a little bad that he doesn't question my intentions.

Maybe that makes me a shit friend.

But when I dig out my mother's old cookie-cutter set and find the heart-shaped ones, I don't feel nearly as guilty when I tell Dawson to cut into the Pop-Tarts.

I'm doing him a favor, I tell myself.

An hour later, he's out the door with a paper plate full of Saran-Wrapped snacks, and I'm left staring at the few I snatched up.

I take the leftovers over to Sawyer's, hesitating to knock. Instead, I place the plate of heart-shaped Pop-Tarts on the floor with a Post-it note saying I hope she feels better, knock twice, and walk back to my apartment.

I hear the door open.

Then silence.

I debate looking out the peephole but decide against it.

It's a few minutes later when I hear the door across the hall close.

Only then do I glance out the peephole and see the missing plate.

I tell myself it's an innocent gesture—that everybody needs a Valentine at least once in their life.

The next day, the empty plate is back in front of my door with a new Post-it note attached. When I pick it up, I realize there's a package of fruit snacks underneath the paper.

All that's written on it is a phone number.

I don't use the number.

And I stare at the fruit snacks until that fuzzy feeling creeps up the back of my neck again.

Chapter Thirteen

SAWYER

THE HEADACHE THAT'S BEEN pulsing in my temples for the last few days finally subsides enough to let me leave my apartment without wanting to cry. I blame myself. Without my mother's constant nagging about drinking water and taking my medication, it was easy to forget until it physically hurt too much to do anything. Every time I got a text, it took everything in me to answer it until I couldn't look at the screen anymore without feeling like I was going to vomit.

My mother was the only person I texted back within minutes. If I didn't, she'd make Dad come check on me or book a flight to do it herself. I didn't need that, no matter how much I missed her.

Dropping my phone to the bed after watching an old video uploaded online of Dixie playing a Led Zeppelin song on the piano, I flop onto my back and shake my head in disbelief.

"Insane," I tell her, propping my feet up against the wall and wiggling my freshly painted nails, which Dixie made purple. "I thought piano players only did stuffy music. Like that deaf guy, Mozart."

Dixie is upside down from the angle I'm looking at her at, but she slowly turns to me from her desk chair. "Beethoven was deaf, not Mozart."

I think about it. "Oh. Which one had a dog named after him?"

She blinks. "Beethoven."

All I say is "Huh."

Dixie moves on. "Classical is what most of us are trained in. It's what my parents wanted me to play. But I won more competitions playing AC/DC and Def Leppard mashups. You should have seen their faces when I got onstage and started playing Bon Jovi."

From what she said, her parents are the ritzy country club types who go golfing every week and attend charity galas. I've never seen photos, but I picture them wearing matching cashmere sweaters and khaki pants while drinking tea at the club with their pinkies up. Not that there's anything wrong with that, I guess. But it seems like they're all about their image, and Dixie playing what she wants and coming here ruins that for them.

The girl whose shoulder-length hair I put into a French braid twirls in her chair mindlessly. "My parents both come from old money, so it isn't like they depended on what I earned from my performances to get by. That would have been way too much pressure."

I could imagine. My parents had the misfortune of getting a daughter who cost them more money than I earned them.

She props her elbow on her desk and rests her chin on her palm. "I think it was a pride thing. They liked bragging to their friends that I played at Carnegie. When I told them I wasn't applying to Juilliard, my mother about had a conniption."

I roll my head to get a better look at the subtle frown on her face. On the outside, the girl who owns more cardigans than I can keep count of looks like she's too soft for life. Her features are doe-like and fragile, she's quiet, and she barely goes after what she wants. Like Dawson Gable, who she talks about relentlessly, especially after he brought her Pop-Tart-shaped hearts that looked suspiciously identical to the ones at my door on Valentine's Day. Except I know it wasn't Dawson who dropped them off because he doesn't know my secret obsession with the childhood treats. And I also know for a fact Dixie doesn't even like overly sweet things like I do. She's a savory type of person, and anyone who hangs around her knows that if they pay enough attention.

Which begs the question—why did Dawson give those to Dixie? And whose idea was it?

It was easy not getting in my head about it when my brain felt like it was going to explode, but now that I'm better, I can't stop wondering what the motive was. And that always leads to thinking about the boy next door. And the fact he never used my number I left for him.

I'm secretly dreading class on Wednesday, hoping he doesn't feel awkward about it.

Forcing the thoughts away, I ask, "Are you close with your parents?"

I can tell Dixie loves her family, and sometimes they're the hardest people to stand up to when it comes to what you want.

Even though I know my mother and father would do anything for me, it wasn't easy telling them what I wanted to do. With all the money they spent on me over the years and all the worrying they did, I knew asking to leave was risky. Selfish, even. Thankfully, they understood.

"I need to do this," I tell my mother after Bentley goes to bed. "For me. Please."

Dixie leans her elbows on her bent knees. "Not as close as we used to be, but we talk still. They clearly accepted my decision to come here, even if they didn't like it. I think they're letting me live my life and spend time figuring myself out."

Figuring herself out. Sounds familiar. "That's good then." As far as I'm concerned, that's what all parents should want for their kids. If they want to spend college learning who they are, they should be encouraged for it rather than questioned. Like *some* people tend to.

She nods in agreement, a faraway look about her as she starts spinning in the chair again.

When we get quiet, I decide to break the silence. "You never went into detail about how your date went. Have you heard from Dawson since you guys went out?"

She hasn't said much about the bubbly boy who joins us a few times a week for lunch. He typically sits by me, save for the few times I've made up excuses to leave early to give them some one-on-one time. Dixie always texts me asking what to talk about as soon as I'm gone, which I conveniently miss seeing so she can figure it out.

Dixie's head tilts back, groaning. "No. I saw him on campus last night with a group of people, but I don't think he saw me."

"Why didn't you go up to him?"

Her expression turns dumbfounded. "Do I look like the type to go up to a cute boy and strike up a conversation?" She gestures to herself with a frown, flicking her cardigan. It's a blue one today. Yesterday, it was beige. The day before, white. The day we went through her closet to find something to go out in, I understood why she wanted to raid my wardrobe. Apparently, you can take the girl out of the country club, but not the country club out of the girl. "Plus, he was talking to another girl. So…"

Oh. *Oh.* "Maybe they're friends?" I offer weakly.

Doubt clouds her features. "Maybe."

Dawson seems like a flirt, but he doesn't seem like a serious relationship guy. "I don't think you have anything to worry about."

She makes a face. "That's what Banks said."

When did she ask Banks about Dawson? "I didn't know you two talked."

Dixie's lips grow into a tiny smile. "The night we all went out. Sometimes he'll sit with me at lunch if I'm alone and you're at class."

How come I didn't know that? And why does that make me… I don't know. "Mad" isn't the right word. "Jealous" would probably fit better, and I hate that the little green monster stirs to life simply because Dixie gets attention from Banks.

"That's nice of him," I offer, hoping my voice doesn't sound as off as I feel. "You should suggest doing something with Dawson again if you want to see him."

She gapes. "Like another date?"

"Or just a casual hangout to feel him out."

Her nose scrunches, making it hard not to snort. I can see she thinks that's a terrible idea. "I don't think I can do that."

I point out the obvious. "You didn't think you could suggest dinner out either, but you did. And he took you out on Valentine's Day. But it was only a suggestion if you don't think you can do it again…"

129

Dixie's eyes flicker into a mischievous grin. "Is that what *you're* going to do with Banks? Suggest 'casual hangout time' to feel him out?"

Dixie thought it was cute that he came over to help me with my bloody nose because he was worried about me not showing up for class. I'm glad I didn't tell her about what he brought me, or she would have wondered the same thing about Dawson's gift as I did.

Eventually, I shrug. "Maybe I will."

After all, he prefers *casual*. And maybe...maybe that's what's best for me too. Nothing too serious. Nothing that could hurt feelings. If he's willing to offer it, who's to say it's a bad idea for me to accept?

"I wish I had your confidence."

I watch her, biting the inside of my cheek. "It isn't confidence," I reply quietly.

Her brows furrow. "Then what is it?"

How could I possibly explain to her what it is when there's so much she doesn't know? When you've lived as little as I have, you make up for the lost moments. "I guess it's about figuring out what you have to gain when you have nothing left to lose."

Dixie stares, a frown sweeping over her features. It dims her eyes that remind me of the fuzzy moss I used to love leaning against when I was a kid. "That's a sad way to look at life."

"Or it's a smart one," I counter, sitting up and crossing my legs under me. Not wanting to be a Debbie Downer, I change the subject. "Let's cross some things off my list together! I was looking into doing something this weekend, actually. Living it up. You could invite Dawson along if you want."

She's seen the extensive list, so I'm not surprised to see a wary look on her face. "Which item are you looking into exactly?"

I grin. "Wanna see some alligators up close?"

Dixie pales. "Uh…"

"Dawson could play protector," I reason, trying to sweeten the deal. "You could suggest the swamp tour to him."

Her top teeth dig into her bottom lip. There's reluctance on her face, but I'm guessing she relents when she sees the excitement on mine. "I suppose I have nothing to lose. Except maybe a limb…"

I beam, picking up my phone. "I promise all of your limbs will be accounted for by the end of the tour. I'll buy the tickets."

———————

I lower the phone after reading the message and frown as a bite of wind hits me. Zipping up my jacket all the way, I tuck one of my hands in a pocket while the other reopens the text as if it'll change somehow.

Dixie: I'm sorry. Don't be mad

I wish she'd told me she didn't want to go when I suggested the Cajun Swamp Tour because these tickets weren't cheap. But what can I do? I'd never make somebody do something they're uncomfortable with.

Her name flashes on the screen when I don't reply after a couple of minutes. As soon as I swipe to answer, she repeats, "Don't be mad."

My shoulders are heavy as the twinge of disappointment burrows itself in. "I'm not, Dixie. Why didn't you tell me you didn't want to go earlier this week? You could have been honest."

Her tone has a mixture of embarrassment and guilt in it. "Have you ever seen *CSI: Miami*? My dad used to love that show, and it scarred me as a kid. They were always finding body parts in the swamps or inside gators' bodies. It freaks me out to be up close and personal with one."

"That's just a TV show," I remind her. "And I looked it up. Only four percent of alligator attacks are even fatal. That's practically nothing. Plus, it's crocodiles you have to worry about anyway. Alligators are like the black bears of the marshes. Harmless. Usually."

The noise she makes isn't one that sounds like she believes me. "Dawson couldn't go anyway. He said he had plans with the basketball team after practice. I didn't want to seem clingy since I'm the one who suggested we hang out last time too."

"Are you sure you don't want to have a girls' day with me anyway?"

Dixie is quiet for a second. "No offense, but I think our versions of girls' days are different. If you wanted to get your nails or hair done, I'm totally down. Maybe even shopping, since you think I own too many cardigans."

I do think that, but I would never make her change something she loves. And the thought of going anywhere to get my hair done is laughable. What would I do? Take my wig off and ask them to shampoo it? I plan on taking my fake hair with me to the grave.

Literally.

"I'm sorry," she says again when I don't respond immediately.

Instead of pushing her on a girls' day, I try to reassure her it's fine. "Don't worry about it. By the way, I saw Dawson when I was heading out of my apartment, and he said there was a party on Greek Row tomorrow night that we should go to. Maybe we can do that together instead."

Dixie doesn't answer right away. "Who is 'we' exactly? Because I don't know if I want to be a third wheel."

What? "What do you mean by that?"

"It's just..." She sighs. "He never said anything to me about a party when I asked him to hang out. But then he sees you and invites you to one. Don't you think that's weird?"

Okay, I see her point. "Maybe he found out about it after you talked. It's not like that with me and Dawson anyway. You know that."

"But does *he*?"

Frowning, I stare at the ground. I've never done anything to make Dawson think otherwise.

But you've also never done anything to make him think there's not a chance.

"I..." Guilt crests in my chest. Maybe, secretly, there's a part of me that enjoys the possibility of someone giving me attention because I've never gotten it before. Being flirted with is a new experience—one I like. So, no. I guess I haven't turned Dawson down anytime he's gotten that way. I let it go.

And that's not fair to Dixie. "I don't know," I admit sadly.

I'm met with silence.

Then she says, "I just remembered I have to do some homework. I'll talk to you later, okay?"

"If you want, I can skip this," I offer weakly.

"No," she insists. "I really do have homework. You go and have fun."

133

I pull the phone back to check the time. "I have to call an Uber to get to the meeting place for this tour then. Say you'll come to the party! I've always wanted to go to one, and we don't even have to think about boys. I'll even let you raid my closet again to find something cute."

"Sawyer..."

"Please?" I beg, drawing out the word until it's borderline annoying. "It'll be fun."

"I'll think about it," she relents, pausing. Her voice is softer. "Be careful on the tour."

"I'll text updates to let you know I'm alive and avoid sending you any pictures of the scary animals I see."

That seems to appease her. "You can send turtle photos. And I'm really—"

"Stop saying you're sorry," I tell her, ears perking up when I hear the apartment door open behind me. I turn to see Banks walking out, so I wave at him. "I'll talk to you later."

Banks stops beside me. "Who shouldn't be sorry?" he asks curiously.

He still never used my number, which makes me regret ever giving it to him. And since he hasn't mentioned it, I don't either. The few times we've been around each other, he's made it a point to acknowledge me whenever he sees me. Usually with a greeting that ends in "pal" or "buddy" to prove some sort of point.

I just don't know if it's a point he's making to me or himself.

I tell myself being friends is a good thing, so I accept the small victories. During last Wednesday's class, he doodled me a picture of Tweety Bird when Professor Grey was lecturing. The day before that, he offered to give me half his shrimp po' boy to finally have a taste of Louisiana cuisine. They're baby steps in the right direction.

"Dixie is bailing on the Cajun Swamp Tour that I booked for today," I tell him.

His brows pinch. "You actually want to go see the wildlife?"

I find an odd sense of pride that he's surprised. "One thing you should know about me if we're going to be friends is that I love adventures. And I've never seen an alligator up close. I hear there are wild boars too, and I always thought they were cute in an ugly kind of way."

He doesn't seem to know what to say, but he slowly starts shaking his head. "You're something else."

"I'll take that as a compliment." I power up the Uber app and start searching for a ride.

"Are you going alone?"

"Don't worry," I tell him, thumbing through the rideshare app. "I already promised Dixie that I wouldn't get eaten by anything while I'm out there."

"Wasn't worried about that."

I'm not sure if that's a good thing or not. Friends should be worried about other friends being harmed by things with pointy teeth.

After a moment, I hear his keys rattle. "Come on," he says, gesturing toward the truck I've seen him get in and out of plenty of times when I may or may not have been watching out the window. "I know where they meet."

"You don't have—"

"We're friends," he cuts me off. "Right?"

That stops me from arguing. We joke that we are, but it isn't like we talk that often. "Well…right. I guess."

He nods and starts walking to the pickup, not waiting for

me to follow. It takes me a few seconds, but I finally catch up in time for him to open the passenger door for me.

Nobody has opened a car door for me besides my mom and dad, and that was usually only when I was weak and drooling on myself from treatment. It's hard to fight the smile as I climb in, ignoring the way he watches me.

"What?" he asks.

I shake my head. "Nothing."

We stare at one another for a moment longer.

He eventually breaks eye contact, shuts the door, and rounds the front of his truck. With one hand casually draped on top of the wheel, he says, "So when does our tour leave?"

Our? "You want to come with me?"

Banks doesn't bother looking at me as he backs out of his parking spot. "Unless you don't want me to. But it sounds like you've got an extra ticket, and I've got the know-how to get there. Beats doing homework today."

It probably isn't flattering that he's only coming with me because his other alternative is school assignments, but I'll take it.

Because I think Banks likes me more than he wants to admit.

Friends.

I settle into the seat and watch the passing surroundings with a big smile on my face. And the silence between us doesn't feel awkward at all. It's comfortable. Calming.

Friends.

As we're driving, I see a large bird swoop down in front of the truck, pulling me from my thoughts. "Look," I exclaim, pointing in the direction of the large, feathered bird making circles around us. "I think that was a red-tailed hawk."

Banks's eyes go to the direction I'm pointing before he

looks at me with a skeptical gaze. "You know a lot about birds?"

I watch as the bird in question swoops down like it found its prey, its pretty red tail the reason for its name. "Not really." Not like I used to, anyway.

A lot of the pointless bird facts I used to retain went away after the first few rounds of chemo. Banks doesn't need to know that though.

"When I looked up the Cajun tour, it mentioned possibly seeing hawks on it because they hunt snakes and small reptiles. The swamps are good hunting grounds for them."

I can feel his eyes on me for a moment longer before he eventually focuses back on the road.

All I hear is a quiet "Huh."

When I look back over at him, his fingers are wrapped tightly around the steering wheel.

He must not like birds.

Chapter Fourteen

BANKS

THERE'S FEARLESSNESS IN THE girl beside me as she leans closer to the railing of the boat that separates her and the reptiles she's hoping to see, her smile big as her eyes roam the murky waters.

Captain Pat is going on about how the cold weather will impact which animals we'll see, which I can tell disappoints my neighbor. "If we see an alligator up close, you'll be able to see the ridges on its back. Those are called scoops, and they regulate their body temperature. If their body temperature goes below seventy-five degrees, they're at risk of food sitting in their stomachs and rotting."

A few of the other people on the tour with us scrunch their noses and make noises of disgust, but not Sawyer. "So their back is basically a solar panel," she comments to the captain.

The elderly man in charge of our tour smiles at her. "Exactly. That's why you'll see a lot of them lying on logs. They're warming their bodies. And since today is a cooler day without a lot of sunshine, a lot of them are going to be trying to keep warm by burying themselves in the mud. I'm sure we'll come across a few along the way, which I'll point out, but it won't be the same number as if it were eighty out."

For the first forty-five minutes, I watch Sawyer more than I do the water. She happily tosses some of the food we were given into the water, watching as a few smaller alligators come to accept the offerings. When she's happy, her whole face brightens. Once in a while, she'll look at me, and those blue eyes get me feeling some kind of way. My chest swells with a ridiculous amount of pride that she's paying attention to me. Like a goddamn schoolboy. She doesn't say a word, just smiles and quickly turns back to the turtles to take a few pictures for Dixie.

I think back to Dawson's favor. Spying on Sawyer is the last thing I want to do. Because I'm not sure how I'd feel if there *were* somebody else in her life. And realizing that reminds me of all the reasons I shouldn't be here at all.

I'm glad Dixie bailed though. It gives me time to see Sawyer's face light up over facts most people wouldn't think twice about or spew a few of her own that I'm not sure how she knows.

Like how she could tell the giant bird I would have assumed was a bald eagle was actually a red-tailed hawk.

My eyes go to her hair again, trying to picture it red. I wonder what my Sawyer would look like and if she'd like this one.

"The cypress trees are gorgeous," Sawyer says to me, nudging my knee with hers and pointing until I lose my train of thought. "Look."

I'm impressed she knows what they are. "Did you know

they're the state tree?" I ask. "It's one of the most sought after around here because the wood is impervious to rot. You can't cut it down, but it's fair game if it falls. People make good money on it if they can get some."

"You're into landscape, huh?" She leans back, tucking her hands into her pockets to protect them from the chill. "You doodle a lot of plants in your notebook during class."

I've never been a note taker, but if I draw, I can almost always remember the material we're taught based on the picture I'm drawing while the lecture happens. "My father teaches at the college. His specialty is in landscape, so it's something I grew up around."

She watches me with arched brows, her head tilting as she studies me. "That's kind of cool. Most people I know have parents who are in banking or something boring."

"Is that what your parents do?"

Her face softens at the topic, her gaze drifting back over the water. "My dad is in the Navy actually." There's pride in her voice when she talks about him. "He's stationed here in Louisiana right now, but he's been thinking about retiring and moving to be with my mom and little brother in New York."

Thanks to the bases around, I grew up with a lot of military kids. I used to feel bad when their parents had to go away, until I was old enough to wish mine would do the same.

I keep staring at her, remembering that my Sawyer's father was in the Navy too.

My eyes graze over her blond hair.

A coincidence.

There are a lot of military families stationed in Louisiana. Sawyer's family wasn't the first or the last.

Wishful thinking, I decide.

"What about your mom?" I ask, letting the curiosity go.

Her tongue dips out as she turns to look at the trees lining the swamps again. "She's a stay-at-home mother."

It seems like there's more to the story, but she doesn't elaborate. "You miss her," I note, seeing the way her lips waver downward.

When she looks at me again, she lets her shoulders drop a fraction. There's a shine in her eyes that wasn't there before. "Yeah. Is that silly?"

"Doesn't matter how old we get, we're always going to miss our parents. Just means we love them no matter the circumstances." I'd know better than anybody. "What's silly about that?" I finish.

Her knee bumps into mine again in appreciation, but it stays there this time. The warmth from her leg is making it very hard to pay attention to whatever Captain Pat is saying about the swamp.

I should move my leg.

For Dawson and whatever feelings he may have for the girl next to me.

But I don't.

I put my hand on her knee.

The next time she looks my way, her gaze roams over my face. "Your eyes," she says quietly, watching me watch her. "They remind me of the muddy river."

Her head tilts thoughtfully, slowly shaking as if thinking of something that she doesn't share.

Then she glances down at my hand still on her knee, bites her lip, and turns back to the water.

Giggling as she hops out of my truck, Sawyer rounds the front where I'm waiting for her. "You're really trying to tell me that modern country is better than the classic kind?"

If only my dad were with us to hear somebody finally agree with him. He loves everything circa Alabama, Merle Haggard, and George Jones. His version of "modern country" is Reba McEntire, George Straight, and Garth Brooks. The man has been stuck in the nineties for as long as I can remember.

He doesn't like many people, but even a man as miserable as him wouldn't be able to fight Sawyer's easygoing wit.

"There's variety nowadays," I reply, after we spent the last twenty minutes arguing over what to listen to as we found somewhere to eat.

Unlike her Taco Bell excursion, I plan on feeding her true Louisiana cuisine—and not the kind we get served at school. So I pulled up to a new creole seafood joint that opened right outside New Orleans and ignored her rant on how modern country is more crossover than anything when I turned the radio to a preprogrammed station.

"It's not the same old dry shit you always hear. Old country is depressing." She makes a noise of disgruntlement at my statement. "Those artists followed a formula to the point where every song was the same."

"I'm not sure I agree," she tells me, her eyes scanning the big chalkboard menu placed outside the ordering counter before turning to me. "Look at Garth Brooks. His music made waves when he came onto the scene, and he got a lot of shit for how different it was, but now he's respected for bringing his flare to country music, and it's inspired a lot of contemporary artists. Same as Shania Twain. Even the legendary Dolly Parton shifted her music tone after a while.

All of those people are who grew the kind of music you like today. They made it okay. So can you really put a formula on creative expression?"

I can't say I've ever thought too deeply on any music genre. I've only ever used it as background noise to drown out life. "I think there's a formula on what sells," I counter easily. "Music labels see what works in a market and produce similar products. I won't argue and say those artists didn't make an impact. All I'm saying is that I prefer today's music."

She shakes her head, blowing out an exasperated sigh. "Fine, I'll let it go even though I think it's a disservice that you could disrespect such legendary people who helped form your favorite music."

I snort at her dramatics. "Speaking of music, how's Dixie, the prodigy?"

Sawyer's smile falters for the briefest second, her eyes going back to the menu as we get closer to the front of the line. "She's fine. I'm sure she would have enjoyed herself today since we barely saw any gators."

Does she wish her friend was here instead of me? Because I can't relate. "She missed out," I reply, stepping forward when the line moves.

"She likes Dawson," Sawyer admits, as if I couldn't tell from the few hours we spent at the bar together. "He invited us to some party tomorrow, and she got all weird about being a third wheel."

I shouldn't butt into business that isn't mine, but I'm interested in how she gauges the situation. For Dawson, of course. "*Would* she be a third wheel?"

Sawyer frowns. "No. Why?"

I lift a shoulder. "Curious, is all."

Her eyes narrow, but I look at the menu and avoid the

way her gaze pierces into the side of my face. "Seems like more than that."

It's finally our turn. "Order whatever you want. It's on me."

"You don't have to—"

"You bought the tour tickets," I say dismissively. "I'll get lunch. But you have to at least try the crawfish. Deal?"

She doesn't fight me on it. "Okay."

Once I pass the cashier my card, we wait off to the side for our order. "Dawson is a good guy," I tell her when we fall to silence. "I said the same thing to Dixie when it was obvious she had a thing for him."

"She mentioned as much." A pause. "And I know he is."

"But he's…" How do I put this nicely? "I love the guy, but Dawson is a little aloof. Your friend likes him. He likes you. I'm pretty sure he likes her too. I don't think he sees what we both do though, when it comes to how invested she is. So where does that leave *you* in this?"

She blinks up at me. I don't know what's going through her mind, if she's contemplating an honest answer or a bullshit one. I hope she'll give it to me straight, but she doesn't owe me that.

Toying with the ends of her hair, she glances at the people collecting their food and walking to the nearby picnic tables. "I'm not playing games with anybody, if that's what you're wondering. I want Dixie to be happy, and I want Dawson to be happy. That's why I keep suggesting they hang out together."

"And you?"

When she finally meets my eyes, there's a distance to the blue tone, making them look more like dark denim than the crystal color they usually are. "What I want doesn't matter."

How could she think that? "That's a sad way to live if you're putting everybody else's happiness before your own."

Her tongue darts out again, wetting her bottom lip, and I track each little movement until it rests in the corner in thoughtful contemplation. "Happiness is subjective," she replies, walking to the counter when they call our number. I follow her. "If my friends are happy, so am I. It doesn't have to be a sacrifice."

I help her, taking the big tray and gesturing for her to grab our drinks. "That still doesn't answer my question."

We walk over to an unoccupied table. She puts her lemonade down across from my sweet tea and sits. "Why are you pressing me about this? You couldn't have cared less about me weeks ago. What changed?"

On the contrary. I was far too interested and had way too much going on. Between Dad and Dawson, giving any heed to what my dick wanted was only going to add more trouble into my life. "I care about my friends. Dawson is my oldest one. I'm looking out for him."

He spent a hell of a lot more time with me over the years than he did at his house, and I appreciated it. Dad was on his best behavior when he was around. It was for after Dawson left that he saved the drinking and other shit. I owe Dawson a lot for things he'll never know. Things I swore I'd take to the grave before telling a soul. It was my burden to bear, not his. Especially not when he had his own shit to get through.

Sawyer takes one of the shrimp, carefully studying it before peeling the tail off. "Life is already a game as it is, Banks. The last thing I plan on doing with mine is playing with people to make it more complicated than it needs to be. I'm here to be twenty-one and experience college and the culture. I'm here to live and be happy. That includes making friends."

She seems defensive. "You're upset."

"I'm not."

"You are."

Her eyes stay on her food. "I told you before, I never dated. I never..." She stops herself, processing as she plays with the fries in her basket. "I'm not used to the attention, and I like it when I get it. Does that make me a bad person?"

If she's a bad person, then we all are. "No, I don't think so. We're human. We like feeling wanted."

"Dawson has always been nice to me," she says quietly. "I guess I soaked that in a little more than I should is all."

"He's easy to get along with," I reason.

All she does is nod, and I can tell she's shutting down.

I pick up a crawfish. "A deal is a deal," I tell her, wiggling it.

She looks from the offering up to me and then back down again before accepting it. "You're something else, Banks."

I lean back. "Sounds familiar."

We stare at one another before clinking our shellfish together in cheers and digging in.

"Dawson doesn't always make his mind up easily," I offer after a stretch of silence while we eat. I wipe my hands off as she pauses what she's doing to peer at me through her lashes. Swiping a napkin across my lips, I set it down on the table with an easy shrug. "Sometimes you have to help make it for him."

She sets down her food. "And what decision is it you want me to help him make?"

The question is a challenge.

Not a hard one.

A test.

"Whatever you want," I answer.

Be with him or let him down gently.

I know which one I'd prefer.

For a moment, she doesn't say anything at all. Then a thoughtful noise rises from her throat as she digs back into the food. No words. No indication as to what her choice will be.

It's not mine to make. Or influence.

An hour and a half later, listening to classic country instead of the modern station I usually opt for, I'm pulling into my usual spot behind our apartment building and cutting the engine.

"Are you going to the party tomorrow?" she asks, unbuckling. "The one Dawson brought up. He said it was at one of the frats."

That doesn't narrow it down any. "I'm not sure what I've got going on."

Lies. I never have plans on the weekends.

She nods, glancing out the window before turning her body toward me. "Think about it" is all she says, leaning in and pecking me on the cheek. I turn just enough to feel her lips graze the corner of my mouth, causing her to suck in a startled breath.

Sawyer pulls back a fraction, our mouths so close I can feel her small, exhaled breaths. They're warm. Inviting.

My eyes focus on her lips, a hunger rising from my stomach.

When she leans forward, her mouth brushes over mine in the barest kiss that I'm not even sure happened by the time I can process it. It feels like a middle school move—one you want to make but aren't sure of. But she did it.

And I'd be lying if I said I didn't want her to do it again.

"That should answer your question from before," she tells me, her hand touching mine before she grabs the door handle and climbs out of the truck. "Good night, Banks."

She shuts the door before I can reply, waving through the window as she disappears into the building.

All while I sit dumbly behind the wheel, still buckled in and still thinking about that kiss.

That should answer your question.

She's wrong.

Because now I have a hell of a lot more.

From the rearview mirror, I see another figure too tall to be Sawyer disappear into the building.

Chapter Fifteen

SAWYER

DESPITE WAKING UP ON Saturday morning groggy and fighting the bone-deep exhaustion that coffee barely touches, I force myself out of the apartment to try crossing another item off my list. The wet February weather has been putting a damper on my chance to look around and cross one of the most important items on my list off, thanks to the flooded roads and hiking trails, so I'm determined not to let another sunny day go to waste, no matter how tired I am or how desperately my body begs me to rest.

Adjusting my sunglasses to fight the beaming sun baking my skin, I glance at my phone's GPS and follow its route to a nearby park in the Garden District.

I'm not sure if it's Katrina, the chemo, or a combination of the two that makes everything look so different than it did when I was eight. I thought the world was so much bigger when I was little, but it's changed. Now things are much smaller—more fragile. Like at any time, they can be taken away.

They can be, a voice whispers inside my head.

I ignore it.

There are little pieces of my memory that are still strong, like the beautiful architecture that the levees didn't destroy after the storm ripped apart the state or the cultured atmosphere around every block that's full of every kind of art and music you could think of. I remember the hope that filled the air when I was a kid and can see how much it blossomed when the nation backed the state when it was underwater.

Other memories remain fuzzy from the years I've been away. The smells. The food. I couldn't tell you which house we used to live in without my parents' help or even where the street is, but I remember the yellow bedroom that always made me happy when I woke up to it filled with sunlight peeking through the white curtains.

But one memory is clearer than ever.

The bridge.

My bridge, with the oak that shaded it and the myrtles and magnolias that encased it like a security blanket—a hidden world just for me and Paxton. Those few summer months were some of my favorite days because I finally had someone to share them with who wasn't my mom or dad or one of the boring kids I went to school with. It was hard making friends when we always moved, so I didn't even bother until the boy with thick glasses and a sense of adventure.

I thought about him a lot after we left, wondered if he still lived here. If he moved away. If his parents ever worked out their problems the way I hoped they would for him.

Eventually, my curiosity faded, and so did he.

Because I had other things to focus on.

When I pull my list out of my pocket, I run the pad of my thumb over the item that I put stars next to.

Find my happy place

I may not know exactly where it is, but I have a vivid memory of using a dull butter knife to mark it with my initials. I remember the myrtles. The sound of the running water from the little stream under the wood. The second I pushed those bushes out of the way to get to the quiet place that was ours and ours alone, I was calm.

I'd like to think that, after all this time, it's still there. Maybe Paxton still goes there.

Or maybe that's my wild imagination. Mom told me it was a useless venture because most of the area was wiped out after Katrina thanks to the failed levees, but my gut tells me I'll find it.

Broken or not. It's there.

Looking back, I wish I hadn't snuck out to go to the bridge on my own because then I'd have a fighting chance at finding it with my parents' memories. They always asked, always told me not to stray too far, but still let me go alone. I think they knew I would anyway. And looking back, I'm glad I had that independence while I could.

Despite the frustration of not knowing, not remembering, it's all part of the adventure.

And after one Uber ride full of silence and tense driving on a crowded interstate, I'm at my second possible location. I spent the last week Googling all the different trails, hoping I'd see pictures of the familiar sights, but nothing came up. I'm pretty sure the bridge wasn't too far from the house my family rented because it never took that long to ride my bike or walk there, but most of the time, my feet were tired and hurting by the time I got there. I used muscle memory back then. Unfortunately, a lot of that is gone after six rounds of chemotherapy and one round of radiation that left me lucky if I remembered to wear underwear.

The Garden District is one of the prettiest neighborhoods in New Orleans as far as I'm concerned and the best option I have for finding the bridge. Surrounded by old architecture and well-kept landscapes, I take in the aged willows covered in moss that line the roads and the streetcars passing by on St. Charles Avenue full of daily passengers.

In hindsight, I probably could have saved some money by getting a ride into New Orleans and taking the streetcar into the Garden District like I read online, but oh well.

Hiking the small backpack higher onto my shoulders, I study the map on my phone before clicking off the screen and walking.

I didn't have a phone when I was eight, so I don't need one now.

Except twenty-five minutes later, I'm on a street that looks a little less pretty than the rest of the area, my body aches from the exercise it's not used to getting these days, save for my treks around campus or to the nearest fast-food chain, and my feet hurt. There are a few people lingering outside the homes that don't look as cared for as the bigger ones on the main drag, all staring at me and saying God knows what, which produces the kind of laughter that makes goose bumps cover my arms. I look to the dogs chained and barking, ready to protect their owners and property, and decide to turn around before one of them breaks away.

Hurrying back in the direction I came from, I join a few other people who look like tourists sightseeing. Aimlessly, I follow them until they disappear into a bookshop, pointing at a window display of books about local history that are apparently signed by the author.

A headache starts tapping my temple, making my shoulders slump in disappointment.

Maybe my sense of adventure has dimmed since I was a kid because this always seemed a lot more fun when I was younger. Then again, it was the only freedom I had. The rest of the day, when I wasn't at school, I was told to do my homework, eat my vegetables, and take Maggie out for a walk. Going out was my escape from the responsibilities that annoyed me as a child.

If you only knew how good you had it.

Now I regret ever complaining about the days when I had to do the bare minimum. And I also regret my choice of Converse, jeans, and a sweatshirt today because I'm achy, sweaty, and cranky.

Just as I'm about walk into the store—that's hopefully got its air-conditioning on high—my phone starts ringing in my back pocket. I smile when I see Mom's name, feeling a little comfort hearing her voice.

"Hi, pumpkin," she greets. "I hope I'm not bothering you, but I wanted to check in since we haven't spoken all week."

I step off to the side to let a few people pass by me on the sidewalk. I have been putting off our phone call because I've felt like crap for days. I knew the second she heard my voice, she'd freak out and assume the worst. "You're not. I'm out looking around right now."

"By yourself?"

"Yes, by myself. I'm safe."

"Do you have your pepper spray?"

I frown, forgetting that they even got me that. Dad also bought me a purple stun gun. After showing me how to use it, charge it, and store it, he made sure I put it somewhere

I'd have it at all times. Which is in my apartment, probably next to my pepper spray.

Whoops.

Hesitantly, I say, "Yes?"

Mom sighs. "Sawyer..."

"I forgot," I admit. "I was excited to get out and enjoy the sunshine, but I promise I'm being safe. I'm sticking to the main roads where there are lots of people."

"What happened to your friend? I thought she was going to go out with you. And make sure you wear sunscreen! You don't want to get—"

"Skin cancer?" I snort, half amused. "I think I'll be fine, Mom. And Dixie and I are hanging out tonight. We're going to a party. And yes. There will be alcohol. No, I won't be dumb."

Probably.

She's not stupid. She and Dad know I'm going to drink. I got drunk at the first party I attended in high school. I embarrassingly drunk dialed my mom and she showed up with Bentley in tow and all but dragged me out.

Too bad it hadn't happened before I lost my virginity in the back of car and then got sick in front of everybody. Mom definitely wasn't keen on letting me do much on my own after that. Not that it mattered. Life changed quickly not long after, putting a damper on my social life. The only people I was partying with for the years following were the doctors and nurses pumping me with cocktails of expensive medications.

Instead of lecturing me, she says, "Be careful."

I smile, grateful she's not telling me to stay home or going on about the effects of alcohol. "I will. How are things at home?"

Over the next few minutes, she tells me that Bentley tried out for the ski team, which is laughable. My brother plays video games and can barely walk in a straight line without hurting himself.

"It's for a girl, right?" I guess. Why else would he sign up for something like that? "Because he always came home complaining about what the gym teacher used to make them do. Like run two laps."

Mom laughs because she knows I'm right. "I didn't ask him why he wanted to join. But if it is for a girl, or a boy, then maybe it'll help him get out of his bubble. That kid is far too concerned with his games."

Leaning against the side of the building, I watch a few dogs sniffing each other across the street. "And Maggie?"

"She misses you." A pause. "We all do."

Swallowing, I nod. "I miss you guys too. Have you heard from Dad? We talked the other day, but he had to go because there was some issue with one of the new recruits."

Mom tells me about their last conversation, which mostly had to do with me. "He was going to ask if you wanted to meet up for lunch sometime. I think he wants to check in on you now that you're closer."

Most people would probably hate having their parents so close, but I spent most of my life hearing my father's voice through a phone or video. Having him nearby is a nice change. "I'll have to see when he's free. There are a few things I have coming up on the weekends, but otherwise I should be around."

Mom is quiet for a second. "What kind of plans do you have?"

She already knows there are things I want to do in my time here, but I never went into specifics. Who wants to talk about going to parties and hooking up with people to their parents? Nobody. Plus, it's sad to admit that I'm planning on having sex. That sort of thing should probably be spontaneous, not something to cross off a to-do list.

But the longer I stay in my head, the more I want to go through with it. Casual. Easy. College is full of guys who are more than willing to be both, and my lips still tingle from the boy who I want nothing more than to be the one to help me.

I don't tell her about that. "Oh, you know. Random stuff. Dixie and I are going to a few basketball games, and she wants me to go to some jazz museum with her."

It's not my scene, but it's only fair that I do things she likes since I'm dragging her out with me.

"You at a basketball game?" The humor in her tone makes me smile. "I think I want a picture of that. Since when are my children into sports?"

"Isn't college about trying new things?"

"It is, you're right. Just remember," she says, using her mom voice. "Be easy on yourself. I'm not only talking about at the party, but in general. I know how much you love being out, but you need to listen to your body."

It's like she knows I'm not at my best today. She used to call it momstincts—mom instincts.

You'll understand when you become one, she'd tell me, brushing hair out of my face.

But we both knew that was merely optimism talking, not logic.

Lips twitching, I nod as if she can see me. "I know."

I never told her about the nosebleed, or she would have freaked out. Like, "bought a plane ticket and shown up at my apartment" freaked out. I also haven't told her that I wake up more times than not coughing up a lung. There's a laundry list of things I've kept to myself and written off. I'm not going to do that to her.

I can make a million reasons why I keep getting nosebleeds and a million and one more excuses about everything else. It's all the same.

Some people would call it denial.

I call it blissful ignorance.

"I mean it, Sawyer."

Oh, God. I can hear the tone of her voice. "I know, Mom. I've been careful."

"And you'll let me know if you're not?"

Swallowing, guilt seeps into my conscience. "I will," I say, cringing at the lie that tastes bitter in my mouth.

After we say goodbye, I stare at the black screen before tucking my phone back into my pocket.

"Sounds like a serious conversation," a familiar voice says.

My head bolts up, eyes locking on Banks. We haven't seen each other since I kissed him yesterday, and I figured he was avoiding me again. Not the best reaction, but that was the risk I took by doing it.

Surprise has me straightening. "What are you doing here?"

Banks doesn't look any different than he does when I see him on campus. Faded jeans that seem a little stained. A black sweatshirt. Dirty work boots. His brown hair is tousled, like he's run his hand through it a few times. "My father lives nearby."

"The professor?" I recall.

He nods, sticking his hand into the front pocket of his jeans. "What about you?" It's a casual question. No awkwardness from what transpired between us. His eyes go to the store. "Getting a book?"

"I got a little turned around," I admit. "I wasn't planning on stopping here, but…"

He looks around and then checks his watch. It looks expensive. Old. Sentimental, maybe? My father loves watches and has the kind of collection that most men would be jealous of.

"Is there somewhere you're trying to get?" Banks asks.

Not wanting to explain the sentimentality of my bridge out of embarrassment, I shake my head. "I'm just looking around. Being a tourist for a day. I thought about doing a hike or something."

I've been out once before trying and failing to find my happy place. Banks saw me in my outfit and assumed I was going for a run, and I didn't correct him then, either. I was too invested in how his eyes had gone down the length of me in heated appraisal until my toes had curled in my shoes.

His eyes go back to his wrist, looking at the time before scratching the back of his neck. "I've got some time."

Is he offering to show me around? "I don't have a game plan. I was going to wander."

"You shouldn't," he says. "Walking around here isn't as bad as it could be in the French Quarter, but it's still safer to be with somebody. There are areas nobody should be by themselves."

My mom would like him.

Whoa. Scratch that. If I'm smart, Mom won't know about him. Because then she'd have hope, and I'd hate to dash it.

"Do you have plans?" I ask. "I don't want to keep you

from anything, especially since you already hung out with me yesterday."

His eyes flash, as if he's reminded of how our night ended. "I'm not complaining about yesterday."

It's a cautious statement that says a lot without saying too much at all.

Confidence and maybe a little relief that I didn't botch our budding friendship have me smiling. "Okay then."

"No Dixie or Dawson today?"

I shake my head. Dixie was supposed to meet Dawson at the library. Since I haven't heard from her all day, I'm assuming they're there. "Nope. Just me."

Once again, his eyes lazily study our surroundings before they drop to his watch. He must have somewhere to be, but before I can tell him I'll be fine on my own, he says, "I've got time. If you'll have me."

If you'll have me.

As if I'm going to tell him no.

And as he gestures for us to walk down the sidewalk, I wonder if he remembers what I told him last night. *That should answer your question.*

I guess only time will tell.

An hour into our impromptu walking tour, I say, "It must have been nice growing up here. You're surrounded by beautiful buildings and history."

It's practically my dream. The house my parents rented on the outskirts of New Orleans all those years ago wasn't nearly as pretty as the ones we've passed today.

Banks doesn't seem that impressed though. "I like how

quiet it is," he agrees. "It's a peaceful area for the most part. Which makes me wonder why you're here. Most college kids gravitate toward the French Quarter. Ever heard of Bourbon Street?"

Of course I've heard of the party area. Who hasn't? "What's wrong with liking a little peace and quiet? You're here."

"I grew up here."

"I grew up near the city," I tell him. "There isn't nearly as much peace there."

"New York, right?"

All I do is nod as I examine the ivy lining the gates we pass.

"You must be close with your dad," I comment after a while, looking around and wishing I'd brought my polaroid camera. It was a Christmas gift from my parents. Right before I left, my mom bought me a photo album to put all the pictures I took in. *A book of memories,* she called it.

I haven't touched it because every time I look at the box, I wonder if Mom will be okay with the memories I collect.

Don't think about it, I tell myself.

Banks doesn't answer right away, making me glance in his direction. "We get along fine" is the answer he settles with.

I can't tell if that's a man answer or if there's more to it. "Is it hard having him at the school?"

My neighbor, who has only pointed out a few buildings and celebrities' homes along the way, shakes his head with his eyes facing forward. "We don't cross paths much, so it's not bad. It helps me pay for college, so I can't complain."

That must be nice. "My parents took out a loan for me to come here," I admit. I still feel bad about it, considering how much debt I caused them. If it weren't for Dad's military benefits, we probably wouldn't have made it out from under all the hospital bills. "The online university I went to wasn't hard, but I didn't exactly leave an A student. Scholarships were limited when I transferred my credits."

Mom tried getting me to write an essay about my experience with lymphoma to help pay for school, but I refused. I'd felt like a walking sob story for long enough. Medical students would come and go during my time at the hospital, using me like a test dummy—hands-on experience for their own education. I didn't want to use my plight for my own benefit.

So, much to her dismay, I opted for student loans. Which they inevitably took out for me because they didn't want me struggling in the future.

I may be off treatment now, but I know I'm not out of the woods. I've spent years reading my body, knowing what symptoms mean I have to see a doctor again. My parents want a future for me that isn't riddled with medical debt and unhappiness, but deep down, they know it's almost impossible.

Denial.

My future and theirs are different, but I'll let them live in their fantasy land for a little while longer because they're letting me do the same. It's the only way they can truly be happy, and I won't take that away from them.

Not yet.

Lips tugging downward at the thought of what they'll be like five years from now, I force myself to shake it off. I don't expect either of them to understand my choices, just to accept them. And they have, reluctantly.

And what do they get in return?

I bump into Banks and bounce back, stumbling until his hand snakes around my arm for stabilization. "Whoa. You good?"

Cheeks heating when I realize I hadn't paid attention to him stopping, I nod. "Sorry."

"What were you thinking about?"

I try blowing it off. "Nothing. So where's a good place to eat around here?"

"You're avoiding the question."

"I'm hungry," I counter.

Banks doesn't stand down. "My mom's eyes used to glaze over when she was sad. I saw it enough times before she left to know when somebody isn't okay."

I walk over to one of the iron fences and run my hands along each railing as we start moving again. "I was thinking about all the things my parents have done for me."

He doesn't say anything.

Biting down on the inside of my cheek, I loosen a tired sigh. "They're going to be riddled with debt because I wanted to come here."

"You can pay them back over time. It's not the end of the world. A lot of loan offices have repayment plans that students use to work toward their loans. It isn't like they're going to be in debt forever."

My shoulders tense. "Right," I murmur, knowing that won't be the case. "So your mom—"

"I don't want to talk about my mom," he cuts me off.

Wetting my lips, I nod once at his tense posture. "Okay."

We keep walking until we get to a blue building that smells like seafood and stop right outside the doors.

"You kissed me last night," Banks says.

I rub my arm and glance at the people walking across

the street. "I thought you were going to pretend that didn't happen."

A thoughtful noise rises from him. "I should."

I peek at him nervously, not sure if I should be hurt by that. Why would he want to pretend it never happened?

"But there's no way in hell that's going to happen," he concludes, eyes dipping to my mouth.

A spark of victory has me standing straighter at his admission, and I'm *this* close to asking him the biggest favor ever. "Good to know."

He watches me for a little while longer before ducking his chin. "Commanders is my favorite in the Garden District. Let's go."

I'm still standing right where he left me when he turns into the front entrance of the restaurant.

And I swear I see a small smirk that tells me he knows exactly what he's doing by teasing me.

Prick.

But I take the out and follow him in, not arguing when he chooses to order for us and pays.

It feels like a date.

Except we don't put a label on it.

I think...I think that's for the best.

Casual, I remind my heart.

Chapter Sixteen

BANKS

THE SECOND I SEE Dawson stumbling around the frat's kitchen, I know something is up. It takes two minutes of watching him struggling to open a bag of pretzels to realize what.

I grab the bag from him and open it, voice lowering so nobody in the hall overhears. "I thought you were done with that shit. You promised."

He stumbles, catching himself on the kitchen counter and shaking my helping hand off. "Funny," he slurs, sniffling as he snatches the bag from me. "So did you. But you never keep your word. You haven't since sophomore year."

Dawson convinced me to rush a few fraternities our sophomore year. It didn't take long for me to bounce because of the shit they had some of the new kids doing. Sure, I'd promised to do it together, but I wasn't going to be part of their little hazing projects just to get the upperclassmen's approval.

Dawson was a different story. He knew exactly which

Greek house he wanted to join and was willing to do anything to be initiated. Legal or not. It didn't matter that I told him we should both bail because his mind was set.

As bad as it was for his mentor, Marco, to be caught with twelve ounces of cocaine last year, it was worse for Dawson because he became addicted to the product Marco was making him distribute. If the new president and I hadn't found him, I don't know if he'd be here now. And the thought... Christ. It fucks with me. Makes me feel like I was partly responsible because we'd gotten into a rift over Desiree. He'd been mad. Understandably so. Avoided me. Told me I was a horrible friend for going after his girlfriend. I didn't know they were actually serious since he'd never been serious about anything in his life.

But I knew better than to get involved at all. That's on me.

If I'd known how deep he was into his use, I would have tried stepping in sooner instead of turning the other way.

"I don't know what you're talking about," I tell him.

"I don't know what *you're* talking about," he snaps, scooping out a handful of pretzels. He drops more than he keeps, stepping on a few that are scattered on the floor with his Jordans because he can't stand straight.

"Come on, man. Don't lie to me. Remember what happened last time?"

He glares with bloodshot eyes, which are a dead giveaway as to how bad it's gotten. Pot used to take off the edge for him. But the way his face has gone gaunt tells me it's beyond that point again. "That was an accident."

An accident. I let myself believe it before because I didn't want to think about the repercussions of his continual use. I wanted to believe he had a handle on it. I don't know when it stopped being fun for him, when he decided he needed more; all I know is that it was too late to convince him to stop when he was found. He hadn't liked me being at the hospital with him and even tried kicking me out after I told him I called his parents, but I stayed. Whether he liked it or not, we were friends.

I won't let him do something detrimental to himself again.

"Yeah, well, that accident could have ended your life," I point out, stepping toward him. "You said you were done. That Marco was gone for good. What happened?"

He took the steps. Got the help. Went to the programs and made his peace. Moving off campus helped. He didn't want to be roommates but was open to renting the empty space downstairs when it became available. Away from temptation and close to friends. That's what his counselor said he needed most, and he listened. I thought getting out of the frat helped too. Maybe I was wrong.

Dawson looks down at the mess he made before his eyes go to the hallway, where loud music is thumping from the living room. "It's nothing I can't handle. A little unfinished business."

We both know that's not true. During one of the counseling sessions he invited me to, he admitted to the group he'd almost gotten knifed by somebody who was in withdrawal and needed another hit. Did he really want to risk his life like that again? "You got a second chance, man. Why risk it for somebody else's gain?"

When he doesn't answer, I know it has to do with Marco or one of the goons who still help Marco out even after his expulsion.

"Daws—"

He walks past me, bumping my shoulder forcefully until I stumble back. "Don't worry about it. Why don't you go hang out with *Sawyer* and get off my back?"

Sawyer? "What is that supposed to mean?"

He rubs his nose, sniffing who knows what. Now I'm wondering why I let him disappear for more than ten minutes when he got here and said he had to piss. It never takes him that long, even at parties. If the line is too long, he goes outside and finds a spot.

"I saw you two," he tells me. "Last night."

The back of my neck burns when I think about the figure I saw outside the building when Sawyer got out of my truck. "I don't know what it is you think you saw, but—"

"Don't do that. Don't gaslight me." He shoves the bag into my chest, but I don't catch it in time before it falls to the floor. Pretzels go everywhere, making me cuss. "You two were practically making out in your truck. It's like Desiree all over again. I asked you to figure out if she liked anybody, and you went in for the kill like you always do. It pisses you off that I have women who like me more than you because you've always been jealous of what I have."

He honestly thinks that? Maybe there was a time when I was jealous of his home life. How his parents, even though divorced, are amicable. Maybe I have wanted what he's had a time or two before. But not now. "No offense, buddy, but you've got too many problems for me to want to jump on the Dawson Gable train."

His glare is ice-cold.

"For the record, we never made out. *She* kissed *me*. Just like Desiree did. Hit me if that's what's going to make you feel better, but don't go back to using because you're pissed.

This isn't like before. It's not worth losing all the work you put in to get sober."

I don't know how he got back in contact with the people who put him in that position to begin with, but I'd like to think it has nothing to do with me.

"You're really going to act like this isn't history repeating itself?" he asks, dumbfounded. "I know you slept with her."

"I never slept with Sawyer."

"With *Desiree*." He shoves a finger into my shoulder. "Try to tell me you didn't. Go ahead. I fucking dare you. You never change."

"I already apologized for that. This is nothing like with Desiree. She made her decision about *both* of us. She's gone. Let's not forget that. I thought we moved on."

He grabs one of the liquor bottles that somebody left on the counter and uncaps it, taking a swig of the cheap vodka. "I thought we did too until I saw you drooling over Sawyer."

I try taking the bottle from him, but he whips it away, almost falling over. "Last I heard, you've been spending a lot of time with her friend, so how much do you really care about her? Be honest with yourself, dude. You have no fucking idea what you want these days."

Dawson's face grows red. "Did you ever think that maybe it's nice to have options for once? You wouldn't know what it's like because you've always gotten what you wanted whenever the hell you wanted it."

A laugh bursts past my lips, bitter and cold. If that's what he thinks, he doesn't know me well at all. He's never tried to see past the mask that I wear every goddamn day of my life. "That's ridiculous. Look, I don't want to do this. You're not in your right mind. Let's talk about this tomorrow. Maybe cut out early. We can get the girls and head back to—"

"Speak of the devil," he announces loudly, pushing off the counter and walking toward the doorway, where Sawyer is standing and looking between us with skepticism on her face. "It's our girl, Banks. Sawyer, do me a favor."

Her eyes widen when she sees how drunk he is, smile wavering when he stumbles toward her. He's got at least a foot on her, so trying to catch him is pointless, but she puts her hands on his arms all the same.

"Are you okay?" she asks him.

Anger bubbles under my skin as he invades her personal space, and I know he's doing this on purpose to get to me.

Dawson nearly drops the glass bottle when he loops one arm around her waist and says, "Do me a favor and let me know which one of us is a better kisser."

I see the frazzled look that widens her eyes right before his mouth is crushing hers.

It takes me a microsecond to go over and rip him off her, causing them both to stagger backward. I let Dawson go and manage to stabilize Sawyer before she hits the table set up behind her.

What I don't expect is for my best friend to grab me and swing his fist as hard as he can until it connects with the side of my face. It's a solid hit, made stronger by whatever is coursing through his veins right now.

Sawyer gasps when I land on the floor, my body loudly thumping into the linoleum. Her hands cover her red-painted lips as she steps back to assess the scene. My eyes blur from the hit, face stinging with pain that'll surely be a headache in a matter of hours.

Dawson falls too, the vodka bottle shattering on the

floor. Suddenly, there's blood mixed with the clear liquor, and I realize he must have landed on the glass.

Dixie appears out of nowhere, running over to Dawson, clearly having no idea what happened. Last I saw the girls, they were dancing with a few other people, including Lucy, in the living room. I didn't want to bother them when I went searching for the idiot now bleeding out on the kitchen floor. I wish I had.

Dixie lifts Dawson's cut hand. "Oh my God! What happened?"

I manage to stand, avoiding the vodka and glass littering the floor. "He fell."

Dixie pays me no attention as she coos over the drunken dickhead in front of her. She had enough liquid courage to flirt with Dawson earlier, but I'm not sure how much he was actually absorbing because his eyes were moving all over the room in search of something.

Or some*one*.

Whenever Dixie tried getting him to dance, he'd entertain her for a few seconds before grabbing another drink and glaring over to where I stood off to the side with a Corona. It makes sense now. He always wears his emotions when he's drunk, and they're obviously heightened.

Sawyer stares at Dawson from the hallway, her face flushed as she touches her lips. I'm about to ask if she's okay when people start flooding the room to see what happened. Some of the frat brothers I recognize are freaking out over the scene, but I don't stick around to see what they do about it.

Knowing Dixie will watch over Dawson until I get back, I follow Sawyer through the maze of students and out the front door.

"Wait," I call out to her.

She doesn't slow down, only tightens her jacket around her and picks up speed.

"Sawyer," I yell after her.

"Not now, Banks," she says over her shoulder. Her voice cracks, making my teeth grind. Dawson did that. "I'm fine. I just want to go home."

"If you wait, I'll drive you back."

She shakes her head, still unwilling to face me, before saying, "I'm fine."

It's a lie, and we both know it. I can hear it in the way her tone breaks.

"At least take the truck!" I yell.

Realizing I'm not going to catch up or convince her to wait for me to bring her home, I curse under my breath and stop halfway down the sidewalk. We're only a block away from our apartment, so I know she'll get there quickly. I see her out walking almost every day whenever it isn't raining, so I trust she can find her way back even though everything in me is screaming to follow her.

But I know her petite friend inside is hardly going to be able to handle Dawson on her own.

When I get back inside, Dawson is standing, leaning on Dixie as she holds a red-stained towel around his hand. "Come on," I tell her, helping her guide him when I see her struggling to support his weight. "I'll take him to the hospital and make sure he doesn't need stitches. I can drop you off at Sawyer's place since that's on the way."

Dixie's eyes widen as she keeps ahold of his other arm. "What? No! I'm coming with you."

"Dixie, I think you should—"

"Just let her come," Dawson cuts me off. "At least then I'll know I have one person in my corner who likes me."

Jesus. "Stop being dramatic and keep pressure on your hand." I look at Dixie. "Fine, but at least call Sawyer and make sure she got back okay."

She nods, texting her friend as soon as the three of us get into my truck. Once I hear that Sawyer is back in her apartment, I mentally remind myself to check on her later if we don't get back too late.

After a few minutes down the road, with Dawson already passed out in the back, I hear Dixie's quiet voice. "Who is Desiree? He was murmuring her name inside when you went after Sawyer."

Jaw grinding, I grip the steering wheel tighter. "She was somebody Dawson and I used to know. She transferred out to go to some school in California."

The only sound that fills the truck cab is Dawson's snores. Then, "Did he love her?"

Christ. I asked myself that too once when I saw how mad he was, so I can't blame her for wondering. "I don't know. I didn't think so until…"

Until she came onto me when I was hammered at that party. Was letting her make a move that night smart? At the time, I didn't think much of it. But I'd drank at least half a bottle of Seagram's 7 by myself on top of a couple beers, so reason was out the door by then. I always found her cute, and I liked the attention she gave me. We hooked up at the party and went our separate ways by the end of the night.

Dawson is right. I was a shitty friend.

I used alcohol and sex to get through a lot of shit I kept hidden from him and everybody else. And I hurt him.

There's nothing I can do about it now. I've managed to let it go. I thought he had too.

"Desiree is old news" is the only thing I can offer her.

The rest of the ride to the hospital is full of silence, and I know it's because she obviously doesn't believe me. When I turn the radio on to drown it out, an old eighties country song starts playing.

"You like country music?" Dixie asks to fill the silence.

My fingers twitch around the wheel. "No."

"Oh." She watches me for a moment.

Clearing my throat, I flick the radio dial to turn it to a different station. "Sawyer does."

I feel her eyes on me, but she doesn't reply.

But I see a small smile from my peripheral.

A few minutes later, Dawson fights me as I get him out of the back seat and into the emergency room. I don't care if he's going to get into trouble for whatever he's on because I'm more concerned about his hand. Hell, maybe getting into trouble will do him some good. That's what had to happen last time for him to get his act together.

Dixie volunteers to stay with him since only one of us is allowed back until he can get fixed up, so I let her follow the nurse when she takes him back to one of the rooms.

I'm walking over to the waiting room seating when I see one of the desk clerks staring at me with a frown. "That's going to be a shiner," she tells me. She glanced between Dawson and me when we brought him in like she knew exactly what happened. Working in a college town, I'm sure she's seen a lot. "Need some ice while you wait?"

I shake my head, willing to bask in the pain throbbing in my face.

I deserve it.

Enabler.

Knee bouncing when I sit, I realize that I'm in deeper than I want to be. Because instead of worrying about the person behind the closed doors probably getting stitched up as we speak, I'm thinking about Sawyer.

Frankly, I'm glad he fell when he hit me.

Because if he hadn't, then I would have returned the favor for grabbing Sawyer, and I'm not sure I would have stopped as easily as he did after I saw her body lock up from the invasion.

Who knows where my friendship with Dawson would have gone if that had happened.

An ice pack appears in front of my face.

When I look up, the woman from the desk is standing in front of me. "It'll help."

I blink at the offering, slowly wrapping my fingers around the bag of wrapped ice, not that I think I deserve it.

"You look like you have the weight of the world on your shoulders for such a young man," she notes, studying me. "Hopefully it gets better."

Her kind smile has me staring in disbelief as she walks back over to her desk and keeps working.

Sometime later, long after my phone dies and my patience thins to nothing, Dixie appears and tells me I can come back. As we're walking to Dawson's room, I say, "Speaking as a friend, you can do a lot better than him."

It's not a dick thing to say if it's the truth. She seems like a sweet girl with a promising future. I don't know how deep whatever Dawson got himself into is this time, but I know it's going to take a lot to get back out of. I'd hate to see him drag anybody down with him.

Dixie seems contemplative, hearing me out with a wariness to her sullen eyes. "Is he like this a lot?"

I know she's heard about his past from people around campus, so all I can say is "He struggles."

She looks down at the linoleum, absorbing my answer. After a few quiet seconds, she responds, "He could be worth it."

My chin dips, doubt curling my mouth. "He could be," I agree, knowing what she does with this information is solely up to her.

"Sawyer feels bad," she tells me, wiggling her phone. "She told me what happened."

I stare dubiously at her. How could she blame herself for something she had no control over? "It wasn't her fault. And I hope you don't get upset with her over Dawson's idiocy. I provoked him."

"I'm not mad. At her, at least." Dixie looks down again, rubbing her arm. "She wanted to go to a party so she could cross it off her list. If we hadn't gone, maybe you guys wouldn't have fought. He wouldn't have…kissed her." She cringes. "We wouldn't be here."

Chances are we would have gotten into it one way or another. In our friendship, I'm the voice of reason. Which is fucking scary.

"Dawson can be hard to be around sometimes," I admit. "That's why he doesn't have a lot of people in his life. But that doesn't mean you have to be one of them, especially if he's not going to respect you how you deserve."

"Speaking as a friend," she repeats.

"And as someone who knows Dawson."

She frowns, not saying anything. It's her decision at the end of the day. I'll still be his friend, even if I'm tempted to punch him in the face sometimes. I just hope she doesn't feel as obligated.

"So. A list, huh?" I remark, choosing to change topics in hopes of lightening the mood. "Tell me about it."

I don't bother being quiet in the morning despite the six-foot-six idiot passed out on my couch. It was a long night at the ER, and they wouldn't let him out until he sobered up. It was almost four when I dropped Dixie off at the dorms and brought Dawson back to my place to keep an eye on him.

Shaking my head when I see the way his long legs hang off the end of the couch, I make myself a pot of coffee with the intent of drinking the whole thing. But as soon as it finishes brewing and I see the way Dawson is still knocked out, I pour a second cup and walk across the hall.

It's almost noon, so I don't feel bad knocking on the door, especially when I have caffeinated reinforcements. But when a few minutes go by and nobody answers, I try again.

Nothing.

I wait for good measure, hoping to check in to see if she's okay, but when the door opens, it's not her who answers.

"Can I help you?" the older man asks, his eyes piercing down at me. He's not much taller than me, but he stands like he is.

I lift the coffee at the man I can only assume is her father. "I was just bringing Sawyer over something to drink."

He looks at the cup and then at my face. His gaze narrows. "And you are?"

"Her neighbor," I answer, adding, "sir."

He studies me with his dark eyes, making me wonder if Sawyer got her blue ones and blond hair from her mother. "She's already got coffee."

I find myself staring down at the steaming cup in my hands and nodding.

"That's a hell of a bruise, son. What happened to your face?" he asks, studying the black-and-blue coloring on my cheek suspiciously.

"Nothing."

He chuckles. "I work with a lot of young men with pent-up emotions. That's not nothing."

Sawyer said her father was in the Navy, so I'm sure he deals with a lot of people ready to fight from their long stints away from home. "It was a misunderstanding."

Half his lips kick up in the corners. "Ah. I was young once too" is all he says. Then I see his hand extend out. "Christopher. Sawyer's father."

I shake his hand, meeting his firm grip with my own. "Banks."

One of his eyebrows pops up, his hand tightening briefly before letting go. His eyes cast over me and then to the door across the hall. "Do you make a habit of bringing my daughter coffee every day?"

He's protective. "No."

A thoughtful noise comes from him before he takes the cup from me and steps back. "I'll make sure she gets it. I suggest putting some ice on that. It'll help. Trust me."

I watch as he dips his chin once and grabs the door. "And, Banks?"

"Sir?"

"Try not to make it a habit to bring your misunderstandings around my daughter. She's been through enough."

He closes the door behind him, leaving me in the hallway wondering what exactly Sawyer has been through.

Heading back to my apartment, I grab my cup of coffee from the counter when Dawson startles awake and falls off the couch.

I look over to see him groaning as he rolls onto his back. He's lucky he didn't slam into the coffee table and make me drive him back to the hospital. Although he'd probably do more damage to the table than himself since it was a cheap piece of junk I found at a yard sale when I moved here.

"You good?" I ask, bringing him the cup I was about to drink.

I wait for him to get up and sit back down on the couch before passing him the steaming mug. I've been through this with him enough times to know he probably doesn't remember shit from last night.

The second he sees my face, it cements my suspicion. "What the fuck happened to you?"

When I saw my reflection in the bathroom mirror this morning, I cringed. The nurse was right. I have a shiner, and it makes me glad my split lip is healed, or else people are going to think I'm in some sort of underground fighting club.

I gesture. "You."

For the first time since he woke up, his eyes drop to his hand. The six stitches in his palm are hidden behind the gauze that he flexes. "I don't..." His brows pinch in confusion. "I don't remember what happened."

I'm not shocked. "You owe Sawyer an apology," I tell him first and foremost. I couldn't care less about what he did to me, but she didn't deserve to be treated that way. "You crossed a line with her."

He pales, rubbing his good hand along the side of his face. "What did I do?"

How much do I tell him? "You were tweaked on something," I start with, eyes piercing him knowingly, which he avoids. "And drunk. Not a great combination to begin with."

His eyes stay on the cup of coffee in his hand, hyper-focused on the steam billowing from the top. "It was a tough week."

That's all he has to say? "You could have died mixing shit, Dawson. We both know it. And I don't want you to be angry at me for pushing this, but it needs to be done. You fought this addiction once; you can do it again."

Before it's too late.

His shoulders hunch. "What did I do to Sawyer?" I can hear the concern in his voice. He feels bad, which is good.

"Nothing you can't fix," I reply easily.

Neither one of us truly knows Sawyer that well, but I think she's a forgiving person. She's got a softness to her that could make or break someone, but it works in her favor.

Dawson sighs, setting the cup down. "I'm sorry," he says, and I wonder if last night's events are coming back to him or he's apologizing for relapsing.

"I'm not the one who needs to hear that," I tell him simply, clasping his shoulder. "I'm sure Dixie wouldn't mind hearing it either though. Drink your coffee and then we'll go grab something greasy. I think you could use it."

The low groan coming from him is amusing. I hide my smirk behind my cup, walking into the kitchen.

After one heart-attack-stacked plate full of pancakes, eggs, and bacon later, it's like nothing ever happened between Dawson and me. He's shoving food into his mouth like usual, downing his orange juice, and talking about school. Not Marco. Not the drugs. Not Sawyer or Dixie.

I almost feel bad for calling his counselor and getting a meeting set up behind his back.

As he finishes his last bite, I lean back in my spot across from him. "Grab your things," I tell him, setting a few bills

179

onto the table for our food and sliding out of the booth. "We're going to a meeting."

His eyes bolt up to me. "I don't—"

"It's not up for discussion. Let's go."

Betrayal sets into his eyes.

"You need help," I tell him quietly.

He stays seated, staring at his empty plate.

"Can I at least go to the bathroom first?"

"Fine. I'll wait by the truck."

A few minutes go by.

No Dawson.

Another five.

After two more, I walk in and knock on the bathroom door.

It's empty.

"Son of a bitch," I growl under my breath.

I call Dawson.

He doesn't pick up.

I text him.

He doesn't answer.

Scrubbing a hand down my face, I start my truck up and decide if I want to try finding him.

But how much more time can I give to someone who just wants to waste it?

Chapter Seventeen

SAWYER

THE NEXT FEW DAYS go by seamlessly thanks to the mundane routine I've fallen into. Wake up at nine, drink an entire pot of coffee, go to classes, and avoid the two boys who live in my building.

It's easy to do when I've learned from observation, and a little nosiness, that Banks gets up at the butt crack of dawn to go God knows where and only returns in the evening when I've gotten back from classes. He's tried coming over a few times, but I never answer the door. The first time he tried, I was still in bed after a horrible night's sleep, wearing nothing but an oversize shirt and a silk scarf on my head. Dad came in after he brought me breakfast, setting down a mug of steaming coffee onto my nightstand and saying, *"Banks is a weird name for a kid."*

I stared at the coffee with a frown, wondering what Banks must have thought after I ran away like an inexperienced moron at the party. What college girl gets kissed by a guy and then bolts on the verge of tears? This one, apparently.

It wasn't even that big of a deal. Sure, I hadn't expected Dawson to kiss me, but he was drunk. I could look past that because I'd been there before. But considering Dixie had already been on the fence about coming, the last thing I wanted was to hurt her by having her see something like that. And Banks...

Well, if my lack of experience wasn't obvious before, it's blatant now. And I shouldn't care what he thinks about something as silly as that, but I do.

I care more than I wish I did.

The second time Banks tried getting me to open the door, it was with the allure of beignets. A weakness I learned I had after he took me out to lunch at Commanders Palace the day he showed me around the Garden District. He'd gotten us three huge fried treats from a local bakery to split. I'd made a mess of myself from the powdered sugar I'd accidentally breathed on as I took a bite, but it was worth it. He promised to buy me some from the famous Café de Monde the next time we went into New Orleans, which is where the white paper bag was from—the one he left outside my door after I ignored his knocks again.

He has my number but never reaches out.

I'm sure if I'm grateful or not.

"You're not listening at all," Dixie accuses, shaking a giant cup of soda at me. The ice cubes rattle against the plastic until I finally take it from her. "I asked if I look okay."

She looks cute. Sporty. I don't know why she doesn't wear more outfits like the ripped black jeans and high-tops she's in that she paired with her purple-and-yellow LSU jersey. When she asked me to come over before the basketball game, I was more than happy to help her get ready. It got me out of my apartment, where I'd been sulking, and reminded me that we were good after what happened this weekend.

She wasn't mad the way I was at myself.

For making Dawson think he had a chance.

For letting him assume it was okay to kiss me.

Banks had been right. I led him on.

"You look great, and your butt looks amazing in those jeans," I compliment, sipping the overpriced Coke she bought for me and trying to brush off the guilt settling into my chest.

Two pink dots appear on her cheeks. "Thank you. Let's hope Dawson notices."

"He'll be playing," I remind her. Wiggling my eyebrows, I say, "But after…"

When we get to our seats, I scope out the gymnasium where the game is being held. I'm met with a lot of unfamiliar faces, which makes me ease into my seat.

"He's not here," Dixie says, slurping her cherry slushie.

Playing coy, I set my purse down between my feet on the bleachers. "Who?"

Dixie smirks. "Dawson said that Banks never comes to these things."

I'm both relieved and oddly a little disappointed. "Huh."

She doesn't make a big deal out of it, just like she didn't make one out of the kiss. I'm not sure what happened the night at the hospital, but the time she spent with Dawson there must have bonded them enough for her to forgive him the way I had. After all, they'd been on *a* date. According to Dixie, that didn't mean they were exclusive. If I were in her shoes, I'm not sure I would feel the same though.

"You can't avoid him forever," she tells me, bumping my knee with hers.

I look at her, biting the inside of my cheek.

She shrugs. "Just saying."

I lean back in my spot, pushing the thought away. Glancing at the court, I realize I have no idea what I'm about to watch. "Do you know anything about basketball? Because I don't. I tried playing horse with my dad and brother once, and I never made a single basket."

She stares at the empty court below, studying all the lines painted onto the floor. "I know they don't score touchdowns," she replies.

We share a look before breaking out into clueless laughter.

"This will be interesting," I muse.

A few hours later, I realize that Dixie isn't the shy twenty-one-year-old I thought she was. I've never heard someone so little yell so loudly at the referees calling the shots when LSU loses. It was a close game, which makes me feel bad for Dawson, who only got to play for a few minutes.

As the crowd starts dispersing, I stand and drape my bag over my shoulder when I hear, "I guess he does come sometimes."

A tingling sensation shoots down my spine before I even look at where her eyes are. When I see Banks leaning against the doors on the floor of the gymnasium, my fingers twitch.

And he's looking right at me, as if we aren't surrounded by at least a hundred people trying to leave at the same time.

How long has he been here?

Dixie takes my hand. "Are you okay?"

"I'm fine," I whisper, voice weak.

She knows I haven't seen him since the party but has been encouraging me to talk to him. Every time I tell her I will, I find a reason not to.

She calls me a chicken.

I don't deny it.

The pit of my stomach clenches as we descend the bleachers, and I can feel one particular set of eyes on me the entire time. I'm suddenly hyperaware that my face is naked of makeup, save for the cherry Chapstick that's become a staple in my life. The pair of leggings I'm wearing has a mini hole in it from when Maggie's claw dug into it trying to give me a hug once, and the yellow jersey with a tiger on it that Dixie lent me is big enough to be a dress. To hide my frizzy hair, I threw it into a bun that started coming undone halfway through the game, and I look like I haven't slept in days.

Which isn't totally untrue.

Anxiety bubbles under my skin when we approach Banks, whose eye looks like it still hurts from the fight that I feel partly responsible for.

It's Dixie who squeezes my hand and says to him, "I bet Dawson will be happy you came."

Banks's eyes aren't on her but me, and they're stormy—like an angry surge that moved the muddy waters of the Mississippi River. The way he stared at me on the swamp tour reminded me of something. Maybe it was the river I loved seeing as a child when my father would take me on it in a rented fishing boat. But my gut said it was something else. Some*one*. "Yeah, I'm sure *Dawson* will."

If that's a dig at me, it's deserved. Heat blossoming on my cheek, I murmur, "Hi, Banks."

His lips press together.

Dixie clears her throat, awkwardly patting my hand.

"I'm going to wait for you guys out there so you can talk." She looks between us, wincing. "Or just stare silently at each other. Whichever you prefer."

She walks away, giving me no choice but to address the elephant in the room.

Banks doesn't hesitate. "You gave me shit for avoiding you, but you've been doing the same thing to me the second it was convenient for you. What gives?"

Swallowing nervously, I rub my arm. "I..." Words get stuck in my throat. I wish he'd let that night go and never speak of it again.

He watches me, jaw ticking at my silence. "Sawyer..."

Sawyer. Not Birdie. The way he says my name has me shifting on my feet.

"I thought we were friends," he says, adding onto the guilt already weighing on my shoulders.

My eyes dip to my feet. "We are."

"Then *talk* to me."

Kicking my shoe against the floor, I close my eyes for a second and take a silent, deep breath before allowing myself to speak. "Is Dawson okay?"

He blinks slowly. "You're really asking me about Dawson right now. Seriously?"

"He got hurt," I reply.

"He crossed a line he shouldn't have with you," he points out matter-of-factly. "As far as I'm concerned, he deserved what happened."

Aren't they friends? I'd never say that about Dixie, even if she did something to hurt my feelings. "It went too far, and instead of sticking around to talk about it, I ran away. Even if he shouldn't have done that, he didn't deserve to get hurt. Neither did you. I'm—"

"Don't you dare say you're sorry," he all but growls.

I quickly shut up.

Banks looks behind me, gently grabbing my arm and moving us aside to let people pass us. "Most girls would be ready to press charges for the shit he pulled, and you're over here defending him," he mumbles in astonishment.

"I'm not saying what he did was right," I relent softly. "But I can't waste my life being mad at people. Life is too short."

Banks clearly doesn't agree, but he chooses not to push it. "He's doing fine, as you saw tonight," he murmurs. "Although I wouldn't be shocked if he messed up his stitches playing. He was supposed to be on the bench for the next few games while he recovered."

"The tall redheaded guy got hurt, and the guy with the goatee got benched for picking a fight with the person who did it," I explain, unsure of how much he actually saw. "Somebody in the crowd said they didn't have a choice but to put Dawson in or they'd have to forfeit."

His expression is pinched, like he's not ready to let this go. "You looked scared that night."

Closing my eyes, I internally groan. I can count the number of boys I've kissed on one hand. *Less* than one full hand. It's not something I'm necessarily proud of and definitely nothing I want to admit to him.

His voice lowers. "Did something happen that made you react that way?"

What is he talking—*oh my God*. He thinks something bad happened to me. "No. *No.* Dawson startled me, that's all. I wasn't... I didn't expect it."

There's something shadowing his face as he stands there with stick-straight posture. The way he looks at me is as if he's attempting to see through a lie. "Nobody should ever feel the need to put their hands, or anything else, on you."

This again. "Banks, it wasn't that big of a deal. He was clearly drunk. I puked all over my high school crush once because I had too many tequila shots."

I prefer not thinking about that, like I prefer never thinking about my one and only college party experience. I'm starting to think parties just aren't for me.

He shakes his head. "It was enough to make you leave. If I didn't have to bring him to the hospital, I would have tried going after you."

I got home within ten minutes and didn't think twice about walking alone. I'm sure my parents would scold me for it, but there were a lot of people out and about party hopping. Some girls by themselves, some in groups of friends. I was fine.

"I want to know why," he presses.

"Why what?"

"Don't play."

"I'm not!" I counter in exasperation. I mimic his posture, trying to show him that I'm being serious. "Look, I don't like talking about this stuff. Shouldn't all that matters be that I'm okay?"

His jaw grinds. I'm not trying to make him upset. Frankly, I don't know why he's getting worked up. I stand by what I said—people do stupid things when they've had too much to drink. It wasn't cool, but it also wasn't the end of the world. Considering I was more worried about what Banks thought of me and my exit or what Dixie would assume, I'd say things are okay. Especially since Banks is here, at a game that he apparently doesn't normally go to, and so is Dixie.

"Why are you so angry?" I ask, hoping to dispel the

tension clearly coursing through his body. I appreciate that he cares, but I don't understand it.

Banks shakes his head, teeth clenching once, before he grumbles something so quietly under his breath that I can't hear it. There's no way to describe the intensity behind his stare when those eyes meet mine, but I feel it deep in my chest. It's penetrating.

His next words have my gaze going back to the bruising on his face. "Because I know what it's like to have people cross lines they shouldn't. I'm used to it, but I don't want you to be."

My heart reacts to those words as I scan the deep-colored injury before dropping to his lips where a scab used to be. What has he gone through that he's not telling me? "Nobody should be used to that, Banks. Whether they deserved it or not."

He knows I'm not referring to Dawson. "You're right, but sometimes those are the hands we're dealt in life."

I know that all too well, don't I?

If I ask about his past, I doubt he'd tell me. It's hypocritical, but if anybody understands the reasoning behind a secret, it's me.

"I'm not mad at Dawson," I tell him honestly.

"You're a better person than I am."

"You're the one who took care of him after he punched you in the face," I remind him. He doesn't give himself enough credit if he thinks that isn't being a good person.

Banks hums. "I suppose."

"Why'd you take the hit?" I question. It may have happened fast, but he could have at least blocked him. Dawson could barely stand straight. If Banks wanted to stop him, he wouldn't have had to try hard.

189

"Because I deserved it too."

The answer has me gaping at him.

"He likes you," he adds, lifting a shoulder.

Yeah, and because I didn't turn him down, it led to the utter chaos we're talking about now.

"Man has good taste," my neighbor adds, more as an afterthought to himself than something he meant to say aloud.

Eyes widening, I watch as Banks stuffs both hands into his pockets, like he doesn't trust that he'll keep them to himself.

"What does that mean, exactly?" I ask.

He doesn't need to spell it out for me. I know.

But it still gives my heart a little jump when he says, "There's something about you that I can't put my finger on, which makes me want to stick around and figure it out. I don't blame Dawson for being pissed at me for that. He wanted my help gauging your interest, and instead, I fed mine."

"I'm not his to claim" is my only logical response, voice a notch above a whisper because I don't trust the emotions crammed into each word. I'm too busy thinking about one little piece of that.

He's interested. In *me*.

A noise rumbles from deep in his chest as he looks away, sighing. "You aren't mine either."

For some reason, hurt inches its way into my chest cavity. I swear, it's always one step forward and five steps back with this boy, who's now sweeping his gaze along the crowd of people waiting in the lobby.

"I don't regret kissing you," I admit, hoping it's enough to spark something that will tell me how he feels. Because right now, all I feel is confusion.

"Good." Banks's eyes darken when they meet mine, pinning me. "I sure as hell don't regret it either."

Relief has me nodding, waiting for something more. "So what are we going to do about it?"

He hasn't made a single move on me, so it's hard to figure out what's going through his head. He's interested, but not enough to move forward. Is it because of me? Or because of Dawson?

"Tonight..." he murmurs, closing the distance between us. His hooded eyes spark something in my chest that makes me nervous and giddy, but not nearly as much as when he leans down.

Holy shit, holy shit, holy shit.

Just when I think he's going to kiss me, those lips subtly press against my cheek.

My *cheek*.

They linger only a moment before he straightens, looking down at me with that stupid half smirk on his face. "For tonight, I'm going home. Alone."

The skin where he kissed me tingles, which sends disappointment into the pit of my stomach.

"That's it?" I doubt, frowning.

One of his brows rises. "Did you expect more?"

What a tease. "With you, I'm not sure."

He winks. *Actually* winks at me.

"Good." Mischief dances on his face. "It'll keep things interesting."

I want to say something else, but he doesn't give me the time to before slipping away.

As he walks through the crowd of people, Dawson takes his place in front of me. "Can I talk to you for a minute?"

I look from him to where Dixie is talking to a group of girls all wearing the same jersey.

When I glance back at Dawson, I nod.

He rubs the back of his neck with his good hand, shifting from one foot to another. "I wanted to apologize for the other night."

"You don't—"

"I do," he insists. "It was screwed up of me. I wasn't… I'm not in my right mind lately. It's no excuse; it's just the truth."

Wetting my lips, I peek in Dixie's direction again. She's still occupied with the girls, laughing at something one of them says. I smile a little at how carefree she looks making friends with other people.

Good, a voice says inside my head. *That means she won't be alone.*

"Look, I think you're a good guy," I start, seeing him wince at the choice of words. "And I think Dixie is a good girl—good for you."

His eyes go to the floor and stay there. "And you're not?"

I answer honestly. "No." Smiling sadly when he meets my eyes, I admit, "I don't think I'm good for anybody."

His brows furrow. "That's not true."

It is though. And he'll never know why.

"I'm sorry if I made you think otherwise."

He tugs on the T-shirt he changed into after the game, clearing his throat. "Is there a reason?"

Involuntarily, my eyes go to where Banks disappeared, and Dawson's gaze follows them to the double doors his friend walked out of.

I say, "No."

But his eyes stay on the door, his hands clenching and unclenching before he gives me a tense nod.

When I look over at Dixie, she's watching Dawson and me. I offer her a small smile and wave, which she returns.

I turn back to Dawson. "Sorry about the loss," I tell him of the game.

His eyes are distant when they meet mine. It takes him a second to reply. "Yeah," he murmurs. "Me too."

Chapter Eighteen

BANKS

With only two weeks until a much-needed spring break, I was balls-to-the-wall busy with midterm assignments. Including my capstones project that got one round of edits already from Professor Laramie and had a second one in the works thanks to a few structural integrities he questioned during the initial project proposal. I'd been dreading having the conversation with my father about it because he kept pressing me on the feedback I was given each time I saw him. I could only use so many excuses before I had to tell him that it's still not approved.

The drive from my apartment to my childhood home should have been the first indication that tonight wasn't going to go well. Because the projected sunshine on the forecast turned into a pitch-gray sky and showers that made visibility shit as I pulled my truck up to the curb.

"Paxton," my father greets from where he's sitting at the kitchen table with three empty beer bottles to his right and a fresh one in his hand.

It's two in the afternoon on a Tuesday, but I guess it's five o'clock somewhere. "Dad."

"Glad you actually showed up this time," he states, voice gruff with disapproval as he studies my rain-soaked clothes. "You should change. You're getting water everywhere."

The first time I ditched our lunch plans was when I found Sawyer wandering the neighborhood aimlessly. I could have left her alone. Hell, I probably should have. Because it led to a blowout fight on the phone with the man currently across from me about how I didn't know how to be a "respectable man who honored plans." It didn't matter that I was making sure nothing happened to somebody who didn't know their way around; I couldn't get a word in edgewise to explain. He used some colorful choice language that people down the street could hear from my cell phone, while I sat in my apartment hoping that nobody was in the building to listen to me getting reamed out for being a decent human being.

I go to the fridge for a bottle of water and frown when I see how empty it is. "When was the last time you went grocery shopping?"

"I eat," he grumbles, the glass bottle sliding from the table before he downs half of it.

I can see that based on the garbage full of take-out containers. Some of them have flies circling them, and there's a horrible smell coming from the bin. When was the last time he took it out? Growing up, we used to eat a lot of home-cooked meals. It wasn't only Mom who spent time in the kitchen—Dad was a good cook too. He had the best scallops and could make a mean steak, which he usually paired for a surf-and-turf night every Saturday.

I don't remember the last time I had a home-cooked

meal with this man. I'm not even sure he could tell me the last time we sat down and ate something that wasn't delivered.

Going to the cupboard and grabbing a glass to fill with tap water, I take the seat across from him. The seconds go by, and nothing is said. He sips his beer; I trace the design on my cup.

I can hear the *tick, tick, tick* from the grandfather clock in the living room. He knows what he's doing. I've always hated sitting in silence. When I was a kid, they did this to me as punishment until I broke.

Sighing, I take a sip of my water and set the glass down. "I told you I was sorry."

"Which time?" he presses, an unimpressed look flattening his hard, wrinkled features. When did he start looking so...old? "The first time you bailed on me for something you thought was more important or the second time?"

Fuck. "Something came up," I murmur, eyes staying solely on the glass my fingers are tightly wrapped around.

"I raised you not to mumble under your breath and to look me in the eye when I'm talking to you, boy." Instantly, my gaze shifts to him. I know that tone. I've been afraid of it for half my life. Mom was too at one point, which is why she was smart enough to leave.

Why the hell did I choose to stay?

The answer is right in front of me.

The empty fridge.

All the scattered beer bottles.

The garbage full of takeout.

I'm using his last clean cup because all the others are piled in the sink.

Without me, this man wouldn't have survived on his own.

I knew it at ten when the judge asked me who I wanted to stay with, and I know it at twenty-two.

Too bad the man finishing his beer doesn't see it that way. "You want to explain to me why I had people on campus asking me what happened to my son? That you were showing up to classes looking like you'd gotten into a fight?"

I shouldn't be surprised he found out. LSU isn't that big, especially when your father is a professor there. "It wasn't a fight."

"You trying to tell me that it had nothing to do with why Dawson had his hand bandaged?" he doubts with raised brows. "I'm not stupid. I know boys fight, but you need to be smarter than that."

"I never said you were stupid," I grind out. At least Dawson is showing up to class again. I'll take that as a win even if it means dealing with this conversation. "We had a miscommunication about…something. Things got out of hand. It's over now."

Dad leans back, his dark eyes so cold it sends shivers down my spine. "I have a reputation to protect at the school."

That's what this is about? I guess the day my father is worried about my well-being is the day hell freezes over. Screw the black eye or the possibility that something seriously bad happened. He couldn't care less. "I'd hate for any of them to think you laid a hand on me," I reply tartly, standing to leave. "Because you'd *never* do that. Right, Dad?"

"Sit. Down," he growls.

I don't.

No matter how much that voice scares me.

Tossing my arms out, I ask, "What are you going to do? Hit me?"

His nostrils flare, and his hand tightens so tightly around his beer bottle that I think it might break.

I get the hell out of there before he can do anything, slamming the front door behind me and walking right back into the downpour.

I'm not sure why I'm knocking on the door across the hall, but it's the first place I go after leaving my father's house. Not to the gardens. Not to Dawson's downstairs. Here.

When the door opens, my eyes instantly take in the long hair flowing down Sawyer's shoulders that hides her perky chest in the tight tee she's wearing. My eyes drop to the shorts she's in, internally groaning at her exposed legs. They're the same pair she was wearing the first night I saw her, and "cute" doesn't quite describe the way I feel about those stupid cartoon birds plastered across the fabric.

"Birdie," I greet, forcing my gaze back to her face to see her cheeks stained pink. "Bad time?"

Sawyer shifts, one of her bare feet covering the other as she tugs on the hem of her shorts. "I was doing the assignment for Grey's class."

Her toes are painted pink, almost the same shade as her face when I called her that nickname. I like it. Never really liked nail polish before, but on her it's different.

"Have you started it?" she asks.

My eyes are still on her nails. "What?"

Her feet move again. "The assignment."

I finally look at her, unashamed to be caught staring. "No."

"It's due in three days," she says dubiously.

I grin. "Good. Then I have three days to do it. Can I come in?"

Her eyes go behind her, nibbling her lip. "It's a little messy."

What part of my life isn't? "I'm okay with messy."

It takes her a few moments before she steps aside and lets me in. I take note of the way she plays with her hair, which she's done before when she was nervous. She walks into the back bedroom and comes out a few seconds later, putting a sweatshirt on.

I point toward the take-out containers littering her kitchen counters. Lips twitching, I pick one of them up and examine the rice inside. "There's enough food here to feed an army."

Setting down one container and picking up another, I sniff whatever sweet-and-sour mixture is inside. Chicken, maybe?

"More like the Navy," she corrects, resting her hip against the counter.

"Your father was here?"

She nods, coming over and starting to get rid of some of the boxes. "He wanted to check in on me since I haven't been keeping up with my mom's calls lately. I'm trying to convince my mom to spend my spring break here—that way, the family can be together again—but she's not sure because our spring break doesn't match the week that Bentley's is."

I notice how empty her fridge is when she opens it to put the leftovers away. It reminds me too much of the house I just left. "You don't cook, do you?"

Sawyer pauses, her top two teeth digging into her bottom lip when she looks over her shoulder at me. "Not really. We're college kids. Isn't that normal? I doubt you cook every meal from scratch."

On the contrary. "I'm a good cook."

She closes the refrigerator with an eyebrow up. "You don't get any delivery?" The doubt in her voice is understandable.

I've eaten my fair share of takeout, and I bring her beignets and coffee once a week on my way back from the Botanic Gardens where I work on my sketches for school. I don't have to, but I like the look on her face when she opens the door and sees the weekly deliveries waiting for her. It's almost as rewarding as when I put a Pop-Tart on her desk every Wednesday before class starts.

She tries sharing it with me, but I never accept. Instead, I doodle in my notebook while she watches me and eats the snack.

I do a quick scan inside her kitchen cabinets and fridge to see what I'm working with before closing everything. "I'll be back in five," I call out, walking to the door.

"Where are you—"

"Trust me, Birdie. You'll like this."

Eight minutes later, I'm standing in the kitchen with a cast-iron skillet, store-made pizza dough, sauce, and various toppings.

Sawyer stares at me while I get comfortable in her kitchen. "Are you making pizza?"

Smirking as I butter the bottom of the pan before putting the dough in, I point toward the onion. "Want to chop that for me?"

Her eyes widen. "With, like, a knife?"

I snort. "I doubt a spoon will do it."

She looks comically worried. Has she never helped her parents in the kitchen before? I gave my mom a hand until the day she packed her bags.

Walking over to the onion, she stares at it before asking, "Why are you here, Banks?"

After I'm done pressing the dough into the pan, I grab the sauce. "I don't have anywhere else I'd rather be."

The admission has her staring at the profile of my face. From the corner of my eye, I see her rubbing her lips together as she studies me carefully. "I'm not sure if that's sad or flattering."

I pause in spreading the sauce. "Why would that be sad?"

She shrugs. "Because you should have plenty of places to go."

Half my lips curl up. "I said I'd rather be here because I want to be. Not because I have no other choice. There's a difference."

Sawyer starts playing with her hair again. "Why do I feel like you're hiding something?"

Maybe I'm not as great at masking my feelings as I thought I was. My mood suffers after leaving my dad's, and it never just goes away, as much as I wish it did. "Don't we all have secrets we like keeping under lock and key?" I tip my chin toward her bedroom. "I'm sure even you've got a few skeletons in your closet, Birdie."

Her eyes go to the back room before returning to the onion to evade the conversation. "So how do you want me to cut this?"

The way she drops it so easily makes me wonder how many secrets she's keeping, especially when I see the telltale sign of color creeping into her face.

What are you hiding, Birdie?

"Here," I offer when I see her holding the knife in a dangerous way. "I've watched enough Food Network to know that won't end well."

She doesn't object when I step behind her and position her hands exactly where they need to be so they're away from the blade. I help her chop the way I've seen it done before, taking my time.

I could let go. Let her do it herself.

But I don't.

I hear her shudder a breath.

My lips graze her ear. "You okay?"

A shiver racks down her spine, moving her against my front and waking up a very specific part of me. She freezes, and I wonder if she can feel it. And just when I'm about to move back and apologize, she uses her ass to put more pressure on the hardening length growing.

Groaning, I murmur a pained "Sawyer..."

I realize I'm white-knuckling her hand as we hold onto the knife handle, so I let go and take a deep breath to try calming the roaring fire building under my skin.

It hasn't been *that* long since I've sunk between a pretty pair of thighs, but my dick is acting like it's been years.

Slowly, Sawyer manages to turn in my arms until the bulge trapped behind thick denim is pressed against her front.

"Why do you prefer casual hookups?" she asks, her hands moving to my face and tracing the bruise that's slowly fading on my cheek.

I hate that her touch makes goose bumps rise on my arms, but it does. "It's easier," I answer, staring down at her. We have an entire apartment, but the space between us makes it feel like the walls are closing us in.

Her warm breath caresses my chin as she releases it, her fingertips dancing along my cheek and then down to my jawline. "Easier to handle or easier to end it?"

I swallow at the question. "Both."

For a moment, she only watches me. There's something in her eyes that clouds them, and I wonder if I should have lied. But it's better to be honest. I haven't had a serious relationship in...ever, really. Not unless you count high school. And how serious can teenage relationships be when you don't know shit about life or love?

The last thing I expect her to whisper is "Good" before lifting to close the distance between us and pressing her lips against mine.

They're firm and sure and confident, taking me by surprise. I pull back only a fraction, breaking the kiss to look at her. "What are you doing, Birdie?"

She only hesitates a moment, her skin feeling welcoming and warm when I put my hand on the small of her waist. "I think casual would be...good."

Fuck me. I can't be hearing this right. "You don't mean that."

She frowns. "Why not?"

"Because you deserve..." I shake my head, trying to explain this the best way I can, combing my fingers through some of her loose hair and moving it out of her face. "You deserve the kind of guy who's going to give you the world. A future."

Sawyer looks down, her hands trailing over my front before her fingers curl into the cotton of my shirt. "Not everybody wants that kind of future. Maybe I want..."

I wait for her to finish. "What?"

She lets out a sober breath. "Easy."

Closing my eyes, I soak that in.

Sawyer wants casual.

With me.

"What are you doing to me?" I all but groan. Normally, I wouldn't think twice about this sort of thing. If an attractive girl wants to have sex, I'm almost always down. But this isn't some random chick I met at a party or at the store.

It's Sawyer.

My neighbor.

My classmate.

"I told Dawson that it wasn't going to work," she says.

"You what?"

"I didn't want to lead him on," she explains, lashes fluttering. "It wasn't fair to him."

She turned him down.

For me.

My dick is still painfully hard from the simplest of touches, telling me not to shut this down. It's not the only organ that's begging me to go through with this either, which makes it a hell of a lot more dangerous.

Hesitantly, she puts her hands on my chest, her thumbs rubbing the skin above my pecs rhythmically.

The movements stop. "If you're not interested—"

I cut her off before she can say something stupid. "Trust me. I'm interested." I'm half tempted to press her body against me again so she can feel the truth behind the statement. "That's not why I'm hesitating."

"Then why?"

I continue. "Well, the biggest reason is the person who did this to me." I point at my face, watching her eyes drift back to the gnarly bruise. "He's my friend."

"I'm not interested in Dawson."

That doesn't change the fact he's called me out for going after the same girls as him in the past. Even if Sawyer told him to move on, that doesn't mean he will. He'll retaliate.

Use this as an excuse to dive deeper into the hole that he's gotten himself into. "I've hurt him once before."

She doesn't say anything right away. Then, "What was her name?"

I don't bother asking how she knows it's a she we're talking about. "Desiree. It was a mistake I regret to this day. But we were younger and dumber. I didn't love her."

She doesn't comment.

"After last time," I conclude, "this would seem like I'm doing it on purpose. The guy has his issues. I don't want to contribute to them."

I think she'll understand, maybe back off, make it so I don't have to choose, when she does the opposite. She makes it harder. Both the temptation and other things. "Casual doesn't have to mean anything. We can still be friends. Neighbors. Peers. We don't have to tell anybody."

She wants whatever this is to be a secret. I think she's underestimating how well people catch on to things.

"Why do you want this, Birdie?" I finally ask, not understanding. "Why not more?"

More than me.

More than something disposable.

I'm not a bad guy, but my track record with women is pathetic. I'll be the first to admit it. My daddy issues are the biggest reason why. The closer people get, the closer they are to seeing a part of my life that I barely let myself accept. I don't want them to get to know me—know the truth. It's my problem to bear, not theirs.

"Not everybody believes in happily ever after, Banks" is her quiet, thoughtful response. "Some people are realists."

All I can do is stare. I know my reasons for not wanting to get too close, but what are hers?

As if she can sense my curiosity, she subtly shakes her head. It's only fair that I keep out of her business the way she isn't pushing into mine. No matter how badly I want to.

"So?" she says instead, her hands moving down, down, down and stopping at the waistband of my pants. She knows exactly what she's doing.

My mind tells me again to turn her down.

For Dawson.

For her.

But that's not what I say.

In fact, I don't say anything. Not right away.

I pick her up and set her on the edge of the counter, careful not to hit the abandoned cutting board full of onions. Pushing them back, I step between her legs and curl my fingers around the nape of her neck.

Hovering my lips over hers, I let them barely graze as I murmur, "Are you sure you want this?"

Her hands find my sides, her fingertips burrowing into my skin just above the elastic of my jeans. She doesn't say anything, only nods.

That's when I get my first real taste of her.

I don't count the last kiss. Or the one in the truck. I never had the opportunity to really savor those moments because I forced myself to back off—to hold back.

Not this time.

This time, she's asking for it.

And I'm not about to say no.

This kiss is hardly friendly, and maybe later I'll worry that I was too rough, but it's exactly what I need after this shitty day. Soon, her mouth is helping me release all the pent-up frustration that tensed my shoulders, and the little drowned-out moans that I swallow are the beginning of my undoing.

As much as I want to take this further—and damn, do I want to get her out of these shorts—I know now isn't the time.

I don't know how long we kiss for before I break it, grinning at how swollen her lips are from all the nipping, biting, and sucking that I just did to them. Satisfaction soaks into me, mixed with a small amount of disappointment when I mentally will my boner to go down.

"We should stop," I tell her, squeezing her hips and staring down at all the creamy skin exposed to me.

She lets out a shaky breath, touching her lips. She's flushed, her eyes glazed with lust like I imagine mine are too. "We don't have to."

I chuckle, taking a step back to put distance between us when her hands wander. "I want to do this," I tell her. "But not today. Not like this. I'm... It's been a long day."

She frowns, concern quickly washing away the sated expression that was there. "I'm sorry if I—"

"No. Don't. Believe me when I say I'm not sorry at all. In fact, I know exactly what I want to do to you when I'm in a better headspace. That's just not today."

Sawyer gapes at me, and I'm a little disappointed she isn't asking for details. Because I'd happily tell her about what other parts of her I'd like to taste, if only once.

I stroll toward her and press a single kiss against the underside of her jaw. In a teasing tone, I say, "Try not to fall in love with me along the way, Birdie. I'd hate to break your heart."

Her body locks up for a brief second before she uses her hands trapped between us to grip the front of my shirt. "Funny. I was going to say the same to you."

I stare at her when I hear how off her tone is, noticing the fresh glaze in her eyes. "Are you okay?"

She pushes me away just far enough to slide off the counter, turning to give me her back as she swipes at her eyes. Then I hear, "I'm fine." Her voice breaks as she grabs the knife. "It's the onions."

Chapter Nineteen

SAWYER

Dumping my bag of Skittles out onto the library table, I sort the different colors into piles while Dixie jots down notes from her sociology textbook. "This may be the driest class I've ever taken," she complains. "I should have taken creative writing with you and Banks. It sounds way easier."

I thought it'd be a cakewalk, but when I got back my first short story and saw the comments marking the margins, I realized I was wrong. Very wrong. "It would be easier if the professor didn't have favorites."

Dixie looks up from her notebook, clearly amused by my grumbly tone. "Is this about Banks again?"

When I asked him at lunch the other day if he'd finished his assignment yet, he told me he *still* hadn't started. "He admitted to me that he wrote it *two hours* before class and still got an A. I spent a week on my story only for Professor Grey to tell me there's an emotional disconnect. What does that even mean?"

When he told us to write our short story based on something personal to us, I had no idea what to write about. The obvious choice was ruled out by pride, which left me at square one.

Making something up.

"Did you read his?" Dixie asks. "Maybe if you saw what he did, it can help you for the next assignment."

Ask to read it? Something tells me that would feed Banks's ego, knowing he did better than I did after I spent days on mine.

"No way," I reply, popping a red Skittle into my mouth. "Then he'll want to read mine, and that's out of the question."

"Why?"

"Because I made the whole thing up, but he doesn't know that," I admit. "When the professor told us to write something personal, I figured I could write about a relationship ending because everybody goes through that. Well… almost everybody."

Skepticism takes over her face. "You've never gone through a breakup? Even *I* have, and I barely talk to boys unless a copious amount of alcohol is consumed."

Biting down on the inside of my cheek, I slowly shake my head. "I've never really dated, unless you count that one time in middle school."

Dixie blanches. "I wouldn't."

I lean back in my chair. How can I explain the reason for my lack of experience without outing myself?

Don't we all have secrets?

Mine is a big one, and I don't think I'll ever be ready to write about it.

"Do you have your story?" she asks, pushing her book away and dropping the topic. "If I read another sentence in this textbook, my brain might explode. I need new reading material."

My nose scrunches. "It's obviously not very good. Your brain might still explode."

She laughs, reaching out her hand and making a gimme motion. "I'll take my chances."

Making a face, I dig out the assignment and pass it over. I don't bother watching her as she reads it, too afraid of what her face might say.

Distracting myself with the view of the quad out the window, I people watch until I see a familiar gentle giant.

Dawson is walking next to two guys who seem to be having an intense conversation with him, digging into their pockets and smacking whatever they pull out into his chest. One of them has a tattoo sleeve and biceps bigger than my head, making Dawson stumble backward with the force of whatever he's given. He captures it before it falls, quickly studying his surroundings before tucking it into his bag.

The tattooed guy steps up to him, getting in his face. Are they going to fight? I hope not, since Dixie said Dawson just got his stitches out.

They're talking, but I have no idea what they're saying before the men who approached him back off and point toward something in their waistbands. I see the way Dawson straightens, towering over them, but not in a threatening way.

He looks...scared.

Before I can say something to Dixie, the two strangers walk around him, bumping his shoulder and disappearing from view.

I grab another Skittle from the table and peel my eyes

away from the window. "Have you heard from Dawson lately? I don't see him around as much."

Dixie finishes scanning whatever line she's on and looks up from my story. "We went to dinner a couple of times." Nibbling her lip to suppress a smile, she leans her chin on her propped palm.

My eyes trail back to the window, but there's nobody in sight. "And you're happy?" I ask, a nagging feeling in my gut thinking about what Dawson has in his bag.

"I was a little upset after the party, but Banks told me that he provoked Dawson. I won't pretend like that didn't hurt, but I think we've managed to get past it."

I hadn't realized Banks talked to her about it, but it makes sense. They spent a lot of time together at the hospital that night. They had to talk about something.

"But I am," she adds. "Happy."

I play with another piece of candy before tossing it into my mouth. "Good. I think…" Glancing out the window again, I clear my throat. "I think you're good for him."

She smiles. "Thanks."

Her eyes go back down to the paper, skimming it before she releases a tiny breath. "I think Dawson might be hiding something from me though. And I don't know if it's something I should worry about or not. I'm not experienced in relationships, so I don't know how to navigate this."

After what I just saw, she might be right.

But I don't tell her that because I don't think it's my place to speculate what happens in Dawson's personal life. I make a mental note to keep an eye out just in case though.

I think back to what Banks said. "Somebody told me recently that we all have skeletons in our closets. I guess we just have to decide if those skeletons are worth sacrificing the people in our lives for."

Dixie watches me carefully, but she doesn't say anything. I play with my pile of Skittles and think about the brown-eyed boy who is always at the forefront of my mind. And I can't help but wonder if my skeletons are worth losing him over when he's brought something into my life that I haven't felt in forever.

Peace.

Excitement.

Moments to look forward to.

We haven't talked about our make-out session or had any repeats. But my body still buzzes with the memory of his mouth on mine and his hands trailing along my body, gripping, grabbing, and pulling at me like he wanted more.

Midterm week has put a damper on anything moving forward while we prepare for exams, but it hasn't stopped him from leaving treats at my door. From the silver-wrapped Pop-Tart packages to the white bags of beignets, he's letting me know he's still thinking of me.

The girl across from me shifts gears, going back to my assignment. "This is really good, but I can see what he means. You can tell this is from an outside perspective. Why didn't you write about the list you made? That's personal to you."

So is the reason behind it.

I think back to Banks's question. "I don't want people to think it's pathetic. I'd rather lie about some fictional breakup than admit to writing down random things I want to do with my life."

Dixie frowns. "What's so pathetic about that? I think it's cool. A lot of people have bucket lists."

"I'm not exactly putting things like 'travel to Paris' or 'hike

Machu Picchu' on there." If Banks saw it, would he laugh? Would others? Having sex, going to parties, and making friends should be part of everyday life. Not things people strive for on the level I am, working to check them off.

I've never been ashamed of it before, but I've also never had anybody outside my family judge me for what I've gone through. They understand the reasoning. I've made sure that nobody here can.

"If I wrote about it, I'd have to explain it," I add, voice quiet. Fingers tracing the indents left on the wooden table-top, I ignore the curious gaze she's giving me. "Some things are too personal to share with strangers."

For a long moment, Dixie is quiet. She sets the paper down and slides it back over to me, fiddling with her pen. "What about sharing them with friends?"

I lift my head up, biting down on the inside of my cheek.

When the silence stretches on, she slowly nods. I can't help but sense the hurt on her face when she drags her textbook back to her. "I guess those are the skeletons you were talking about."

Suddenly, my appetite is gone.

A bottle of water appears in front of me, shaking until I sit up from where I'm resting on the desk. I knew it was going to be a long day when I woke up this morning feeling like lead weighed my limbs down. I slept past two alarms and was barely able to peel myself out of bed. It's been a long time since I've felt this weight on my shoulders, and I know part of it has to do with the guilt of hurting Dixie's feelings. I haven't heard from her in two days.

I rub my eyes and look up at Banks. "What is this for?" I ask, voice hoarse from the slight cough I woke up with. I raided the medicine cabinet that my father stocked with cold medication before he left on move-in day. A few people from my classes have been fighting colds, so I knew it was only a matter of time before I caught one too.

Lack of sleep and a worn-down immune system will do that to a person.

"You need to drink," he tells me, setting the cold bottle onto my desk.

I frown at it. "I *need* coffee," I grumble, twisting the cap off and taking a sip.

From behind his back, he also produces a bottled cold brew. My *favorite* coffee. "I figured as much when I saw you drooling on your laptop."

I sit up and swipe the back of my hand along my mouth. "I don't drool!"

He chuckles, passing me the caffeine before taking his seat. "I don't know, Birdie. I'm pretty sure I saw your computer short-circuiting."

Birdie. The playful tone makes things feel normal between us.

Sniffling, I grab a tissue and wipe my nose as discreetly as I can. "I don't get how you're not sick. There are at least five people out in our class alone with whatever this is."

Banks stretches his legs out, studying me. I want to hide my red nose, flushed face, and glassy eyes, but he's been looking at me since I walked into the room. The second he kicked my chair out for me to sit, he knew I wasn't okay.

"I've always had an iron immune system," he answers. Crossing his arms over his chest, he shrugs. "Can't remember the last time I got sick."

Must be nice to be God's favorite.

"What about you?"

I look at him. "What?"

"Were you the sick kid?"

My stomach drops. "Why?"

His brows go up at the slight rise to my voice, which gives me away. "It was just a question. My mom would get sick any time someone around her did. I take after my dad." His lips twitch, eyes dimming. "When it comes to staying healthy, anyway."

Playing it off, I grip the coffee. "Out of my brother and me, I'm usually the one who gets stuck with all the problems."

He makes a thoughtful noise. "Bummer."

I simply nod, unwilling to elaborate on just how unlucky I really am.

"Is your family coming to see you over break?" he asks. I'm grateful for the subject change. "I know you were looking forward to seeing Bentley."

Smiling at the sound of my brother's name, I move a piece of hair behind my ear. "I think my mom is going to pull him out of school for the week to visit."

"Shit," Banks praises. "I wish my parents would have done that whenever I wanted to go on vacation."

It's hard to keep my smile when I know the reason why she's making the time to come out. But I choose not to tell him any of that either. Like he said, some secrets will always be under lock and key. "We're close," I tell him. "It'll be good to see them."

Fidgeting with my laptop so I evade his wandering gaze, I pull up a random page and scroll through the news articles.

Banks clearly wants to keep talking. "I have a family

216

recipe for chicken noodle soup. Maybe I can make it for you this weekend."

When I look at him, I can't help but shake my head. This is the same boy who stole my Taco Bell unapologetically. The same person who avoided me for almost two entire weeks. I can't help but smile again, knowing how far we've come.

"You want to make me soup?" I ask quietly.

He studies my face before his eyes go forward. "It's just soup," he murmurs.

But I don't buy that.

And I don't think he does either.

"It's a shame," he murmurs not long after we fall back into silence.

I look at him.

"I was going to suggest we pick up where we left off the last time I was over," he says nonchalantly. "To celebrate midterms coming to an end. Guess that'll have to wait."

No matter how crappy I'm feeling, it doesn't stop my heart from picking up. I squirm on my chair, muttering, "Tease."

All he does is chuckle, going back to the doodles in his notebook.

I know the second I answer the phone that I should have let it go to voicemail. When I woke up, I could barely talk. My throat hurt, and my neck was swollen. After downing half a bottle of NyQuil at six in the morning, I opted to go back to bed and ignore all other responsibilities.

Mom's voice is full of concern when she hears the

raspiness that I greet her with. "You never told me you were sick" is the first thing she says. "What have you taken? Are you drinking enough? Have you eaten anything today? I'll call your father."

Groaning, I force myself to sit up in bed. "It's just a cold," I tell her. I knew she'd freak out, but this was the risk I took by coming here. It shouldn't be a surprise that I caught whatever was going around. "You don't need to call Dad."

"I can look into getting a plane ticket sooner. I've got the paperwork printed out."

The paperwork? "Did you print the ticket information?" Who does that anymore?

"And the insurance information," she adds, papers rustling in the background. "Just in case. You can never be too safe."

Rubbing my tired eyes, I lean back against the headboard. "There's an app for that, you know. I showed you before I left for Louisiana. It's a lot easier than carrying around paperwork."

Mom sighs. "Old habits die hard. I'm too old for all that phone stuff. Your brother just tried to show me how to use that dancing app he's on all the time."

"Are you talking about TikTok? Why do you want to use that?"

I remember begging her to let me have a Facebook. She was against social media for a long time and only agreed if she made an account too. She promised not to stalk me online and then started using it more than I ever did, posting embarrassing photos of me from when I was a kid and tagging me in them.

It was a great way to make sure I didn't go online often.

"Bentley was just showing me how it worked. It's not

something I'd ever use. But enough about that. How are you feeling? What do you need? Your father can be there in an hour if I call him now."

I grab the glass of water that I put on the nightstand when I got up earlier and take a sip to relieve my achy throat. "Mom, I'm fine. I've been taking cold meds. It's nothing."

Mom's voice lowers. "Do you remember what happened the last time you said that?"

That isn't fair. "It's not like last time."

When I ignored the stomach bug that came after the party I'd snuck away to, it turned into a cold that medication didn't touch. I'd been sick for weeks when I finally went to the doctor and was prescribed antibiotics for bronchitis. But at the weeks passed, those hadn't helped either. Then came the chest X-rays when they sent me to check my lungs for pneumonia.

Except that's not what they found at all.

Nobody expected to see the lump that had closed off one of my lungs, much less suspected it was cancer. Within two months of seeing the first doctor, I started treatment. While other girls my age celebrated their sweet sixteen at parties full of close friends, I was hooked up to a machine in the treatment center with strangers.

My mom and aunt bought me a chocolate cake for when I got home.

I threw it up by bedtime.

Then I cried myself to sleep.

It was a low point in my life.

"It isn't like last time," I repeat, voice hoarse for an entirely different reason.

I hate this—hate feeling vulnerable. Remembering the times when I could barely function without my mom and aunt by my side. Or all the times Bentley had to run to get the puke bucket when I woke up in the middle of the night sick from my chemo. I'd always feel bad waking him up, but Mom reassured me that he wanted to help.

I didn't want help then, but I needed it.

And I loathed every second.

I'm determined not to need help now. "I'll be fine. Don't come sooner or you'll catch it too. Then you'll have to deal with sick Bentley, and he's a bigger baby than I am."

Mom is quiet for a second. "You were never a baby. Sometimes I wish you were because it would have been understandable. Seeing you fight everyday…" Her voice trails off. "I'm grateful for your strength. I always will be. But I never wanted to see you in a position where you had to be strong."

My throat tightens as I swallow down the emotion rising up. We've had this conversation before—the one where she feels like I was more of an adult than she was in the time when I needed her most. We'll never agree. Because I always thought she handled things ten times better than I ever could.

"But you're right," she adds reluctantly. "Man colds are no joke. One day you'll experience that for yourself."

There's her optimism again.

One day.

I don't want to make her sad, so I force a smile on my face as if she can see me and whisper, "Yeah. Maybe one day."

We hang up after I agree to do a virtual appointment with my primary care doctor in New York. Within ten minutes, I get an email confirmation for the appointment. It's the least I can do for her.

Peace of mind if nothing else.

I don't remember falling asleep after that, but I wake up to somebody knocking on the door.

Swinging my legs out of bed, I groan at the achy limbs that drag me across the living room. Everything hurts from my head to my toes, I'm groggy, and I can barely keep my eyes open. Right as I approach the door, I realize that I'm still wearing the silk scarf I sleep in. Hands touching my head, I glance out the peephole to see Banks standing on the other side.

"One second," I call out, voice cracking in panic.

I don't give him time to reply before I'm frantically rushing back to my room, searching for the wig he's used to seeing me in. My room is a disaster, clothes thrown everywhere, textbooks scattered, and my wig nowhere to be found.

I was too tired to care when I got home yesterday, so I tossed my belongings everywhere on my way to bed. Cringing when I see my dirty underwear on the floor, I kick it under the dresser.

It takes me under two minutes to hide the majority of my things, shoving wigs and clothes out of sight. Then another few minutes to secure a new wig to my head, cringing at the soreness of my scalp as I adjust it as best I can. Trying to be quick, I rush to the door before Banks can go away.

The movement has me swaying as I open it, my vision becoming blurry as everything around me spins.

I hear, "Whoa," before hands grab ahold of my upper arms. Blinking rapidly to regain my vision, I feel heat creep up my neck and into my cheeks as Banks carefully walks us inside and over to the couch. "Sit."

My body slowly becomes overheated, ears ringing and heart racing in my chest. I don't know what's happening, but

I don't like it. Within minutes, I feel something cool press against my head. Peeling my eyes open to Banks squatting in front of me, I watch him hold a cold cloth against my forehead. There's a glass of water on the coffee table that wasn't there before, capturing my attention when locking eyes with him is too much.

"I'd say you look like shit, but I'm pretty sure you already know that," he remarks with a small smile teasing his lips. He reaches out and touches a piece of my hair with his free hand. "You did something with your hair. It looks darker."

Glancing down at the ends, which are slightly longer than before, I frown.

The strands aren't that much darker than the sandy color I was sporting for the first couple months of school. I'm surprised he even recognized it. Most men don't notice the little things, like when Mom spent a lot of time and money at the salon changing her hair to a completely different color and cut only for dad to come home and bring up what was for supper instead of her new hairstyle.

She was mad.

"I like it," he tells me, dropping the strand between his fingers. "Did you dye it?"

I tell him the truth. At least part of it. "I've never dyed my hair a day in my life."

His eyes stay on my hair for a moment longer before dropping back down to my gaze. "Huh." That's all he says before, "It suits you."

If I wasn't already overheated, I'd probably be blushing. "You're going to get sick," I tell him. I don't buy the iron immune system bit, and I'd feel awful if he got sick right before spring break.

"I'll be fine," he says casually.

It hurts to talk, but I ask, "What are you doing here anyway?" It's not one of the normal days he brings over goodies or cooks for me. Not that he has to use those excuses to come over. I like being able to see him outside class.

"Nobody knew where you were," he explains, gently brushing the cloth over my face. "I texted you. So did Dixie."

"I think my phone died," I admit quietly. I don't remember plugging it in after getting off the phone with my mom this morning. "I didn't mean to worry you."

Banks shrugs. "I know where you live. Dixie offered to come check on you, but it was out of her way."

I'll have to remember to text her once my phone is charged. "What time is it?"

"Almost five."

I wet my dry lips. "You should be in class."

Maybe I should be embarrassed for knowing that, but I'm not.

But then he says, "So should you."

Swallowing past the pain in my throat, I nod. It's nice to know he keeps tabs too. "I didn't feel well."

His eyes wander around my face. God knows what he sees. Paleness. Glassy eyes. Chapped lips. I don't need a mirror to know I look horrible, but I'm too tired to care.

"I can see that, Birdie." He sets the washcloth down on the table and passes me the cold glass of water. "Drink," he directs.

I take it. "Bossy," I croak, wincing at the sound of my voice. Taking a long sip of water to relieve the ache, I lean back on the couch and close my eyes. "You don't have to stay here. I'm fine."

Banks is quick to reply. "Usually when women say they're fine, they're not."

223

I manage to look at him. "Speaking from personal experience?" I guess, jealousy nudging my stomach.

He hums. "My mother."

Oh. I cross my feet under me on the couch, watching as Banks pulls the throw blanket over my lap as if he's going to tuck me in. "Tell me about her," I say, knowing he's not going anywhere.

He's as stubborn as I am.

Banks stands, bringing the washcloth over to the sink and draping it over the middle of the basin. "Not much to tell. She and my stepdad live a couple hours away. I don't see them often, but I talk to her once in a while when we have time."

"Do you like him?"

"Joe? Yeah, he's a good dude. Good for her."

Was his father not? "Is your father remarried? You said he lives in the Garden District, right?"

He pauses with his back to me, shoulders tense. After what sounds like a long, drawn-out exhale, he says, "That miserable bastard will probably die single. I'm all he has."

My eyes widen at the cool tone of his voice, but I don't question it. I don't know his dad beyond what he does, but it makes me sad that Banks feels that way. "I'm sorry. I shouldn't have asked."

Eventually, Banks turns and leans his back against the edge of the counter. "You can ask me anything."

So I do. "Why do you call me Birdie instead of my name?"

It feels like it goes beyond the shorts he saw me in, even though he clearly liked them based on how long his eyes locked with them the first night.

"It's fitting. You're adventurous, even if I didn't know it the first time we met. You're unafraid, which not a lot of people can say they are. Hell, I'm not. You moved from New York on a whim to experience new things. I admire that about you. Birds learn how to fly by jumping out of the nest not knowing if they'll make it—not knowing where the flight will take them. Seems like you."

That's the last thing I expect him to say. I'm quiet as I take in his response, toying with the hem of my blanket as he watches me from across the room. "And here I thought it was just my shorts," I murmur, amusement in my tone.

He grins. "Trust me. Those were a big part of it." When he winks at me, it goes straight to my chest. Then that feeling intensifies when he adds, "I've always been a leg man."

Not knowing what to say, I stay silent.

Banks chuckles to himself. "I'll be right back." He leaves, keeping the front door cracked open, coming back five minutes later with a plastic container of something in one hand and his backpack hanging from his shoulder.

I watch as he sets his things down, making himself at home. His backpack beside me on the couch, the container on the kitchen counter. It doesn't take long to realize that he's pouring out soup into two different bowls before putting each in the microwave to heat up.

Sheepishly, he looks over his shoulder and admits, "I made this last night. Figured you could use it after seeing you in class. Guess I was right."

He really made me soup.

When he brings it over to me, I accept it with a small smile on my face, staring at the steam billowing from the top. "Thank you."

He sits with his bowl beside me, his small backpack in between us. We eat in comfortable silence; the only sound is our spoons clanking against the ceramic.

When we're done, he gets me more water and another cool cloth before sitting down again and pulling textbooks and notebooks out of his backpack.

"What are you doing?" I ask in confusion.

He props his feet up on the coffee table. "If I don't get my homework done, you'll keep pestering me about it."

I sniffle. "You're staying?"

Without looking up from his textbook, he says, "Somebody should."

And maybe it's the cold or the warm soup finally heating up my body. But I feel…tingly. Unlike my mother, I don't fight him.

As I close my eyes and settle in, I murmur, "It isn't just soup."

There are a few seconds of silence between us where I hear only his breathing before one of his hands grazes my leg and stays there.

Then, "Go to sleep, Birdie."

As much as I want to stay awake and enjoy the time with him, I can't fight the fatigue plaguing my body.

When I wake up in a dark apartment, I realize my head is nestled on the lap of my neighbor. The blanket is up over my shoulders, tucked carefully.

And the boy in question is sleeping soundly exactly where I left him.

For the first time since I met him, he looks…at peace. So I don't wake him up. I don't move to my bedroom. I simply lie back down and let his calm breathing lull me back to sleep.

Chapter Twenty

BANKS

A FEW DAYS AFTER I play nurse at Sawyer's apartment, I'm walking through the quad when Professor Laramie stops me. "Paxton," he greets, using the name that makes me wince. "I really appreciate the effort you've put into improving your project design. I was just talking to your father about it."

I grip the strap of my bag hanging haphazardly from my shoulder. "You spoke to my dad about it?"

Laramie nods innocently, a professional smile on his face. "We have lunch from time to time. He was asking how you were doing. I told him the same thing I told you when I handed you the first draft revisions. You've got a lot of potential in your future."

I never know what to say when people bring up my father here, and I don't want to press Laramie for what his response was. I can use my imagination to figure it out given the less-than-stellar conversations my father and I have had lately.

Especially after I stormed out of his house last time we

saw one another. He left a few voicemails that included some colorful curse words, which I never finished listening to before deleting.

He calls.

I don't answer, even though my fingers have twitched over the "accept" button every time his name pops up.

Professor Laramie doesn't sense my internal tension over the man he works with, not that I would expect him to. I've grown used to saving face when I'm on campus. "It's always nice to see parents involved in their kid's education. He seems impressed by what you've come up with."

Unless those are the words my father used, I don't believe it. "He's always made sure to keep track when it comes to my education," I answer carefully. "Not hard to do, given where we are."

My father's squeaky-clean reputation here has gotten him far. He's well liked among students and faculty, and that's in large part because they don't know who he is behind closed doors. The man they see in front of a classroom is a very different version than the one I see at the bottom of a liquor bottle.

I've accepted it. Reluctantly. Defeatedly.

Laramie offers a quiet laugh. "I suppose that's true," he replies. "I've seen plenty of students come and go without any type of support from home, so it's refreshing when I experience it firsthand. He's a good man with a good kid."

My father must have laid it on thick during their lunch. It takes everything in me not to react negatively, no matter how badly my eye wants to twitch from the false appreciation.

From the corner of my eye, I see Dawson stumbling toward the library. He can barely walk in a straight line, so I decide to cut my conversation with the professor short and go help the idiot before he gets hurt. "Tell my father I said hello if you see him before I do. I'll see you in class," I tell Laramie, walking away before he can reply.

Jogging over to my friend, who I haven't seen or heard from in days, I swat his arm as soon as I stop beside him. Dawson has always been skinny, but he looks like he's lost weight that he didn't have to begin with. When I get a glimpse of his face, I can't help but flinch. His eyes are sunken in, and there are bags under them like he hasn't slept in weeks.

"Dude. What the hell happened?"

He jerks his arm away from me. "Nothing." When he scratches his nose, I know he's bullshitting me. "What are you up to?" he asks as if everything is okay.

"I tried calling you last night." I've texted him almost every day with no response. It isn't unlike him to ignore messages, especially since our fight about Sawyer, so I didn't want to assume the worst. I hoped he was with Dixie or the guys on the team. Someone to distract him from the other people in his life who encourage his bad behavior. "Where have you been?"

Dawson stumbles back. "What are you, my mom?"

I deadpan. "If I were, I wouldn't be around or concerned."

His mother was upset that I risked her son's scholarship by talking to the campus police about Marco. I never pointed fingers or ratted Dawson out for using drugs because that would have gotten him kicked off the basketball team, but enough word spread that it got him on probation. Apparently, taking time to get sober and heal from a near-death experience wasn't what she wanted her son to be doing.

I've never particularly liked her since. As far as I'm concerned, she's as bad as my mother. Worse, even. I'd like

229

to think if I almost died, my mom would at least want me to take time off school to get better instead of encouraging me to finish my degree before I was ready.

"Fuck off, Banks. Don't talk about my mom."

Dawson goes to move around me and into the library, but I won't let him pass. "Come on, man. I just want to make sure everything is good. My dad asked about you the other day. Said you haven't been in class again."

The six-six twenty-one-year-old in front of me fidgets before rubbing his nose again and then scrubs a hand through grown-out hair that needs a trim. "Needed a break. I'll pass in the assignments that are due next week."

That's not what I'm worried about. "I thought we talked about this. The shit with Marco—"

"Don't worry about Marco," he cuts me off, eyes narrowing in anger. "I've got it under control."

His eyes dart around, unfocused. Wary. It doesn't sit well with me. "You'd tell me if you were in trouble, right? I don't want to see you hurt, man. I know you don't like going to meetings, but I'll go with you. I'll take time off from the store. Just tell me what you need."

Dawson looks down before shaking off the hand I put on his shoulder. "What I need is for you to leave me the hell alone for once."

His attitude has my nostrils flaring. "I'm just trying to help."

He starts backing up. "Help somebody who wants it. I'm fine."

He's not, and it's obvious to anybody with eyes. "Where are you headed, anyway?"

He gestures toward the library. "Gonna study for my chem class."

His backpack isn't even on him. "Where are your things then?"

"I left them inside to get some fresh air. Are we done with the third degree, or can I go now, *Mom*?"

Christ. I know it's not smart to let him go, but how much trouble can you get into at the library? If I didn't have a test today, I'd probably join him and get some work of my own done.

"If you change your mind about wanting to go to a meeting, you know where to find me," I say, relenting that he's never going to accept help from me when he's like this—pent-up and exhausted from however much sleep he's not getting.

He murmurs, "I won't."

Clicking my tongue, I rub the back of my neck and check my watch. I need to get going, but I'm still reluctant to leave him. "Dixie mentioned something about a list that Sawyer has, and going to a Mardi Gras parade is on it. I was thinking about taking them if you want to tag along."

After checking in on Sawyer last night with a package of Pop-Tarts in hand, I figured she'd be good enough to go out this weekend. I'd like to thank my chicken noodle soup for doing the trick. Or maybe it was all the cold medication that I constantly force-fed her along with the water I fetched nearly every two hours while I worked on homework in her living room and watched her sleep.

She told me I should have gone to medical school. Dad would have probably laughed at that.

"You in?" I ask, hoping he'll say yes. In hindsight, the last place he should be is near Bourbon Street where all the bars are. But at least I can keep an eye on him if he's with us. "We said we'd do more things this semester since we're

231

almost done with school. Who knows what comes next for us. We should enjoy the time here while it lasts."

Dawson rubs his lips together, eyes wandering to the library as if he's afraid somebody is watching. "First Sawyer and now Dixie?" he grumbles like a question.

"Don't start."

His mouth twists into a scowl. "You're the one always around the girls I like."

I'm not doing this again. "Do you ever think maybe we just both enjoy being around good people? It doesn't have to be more than that."

He finally meets my eyes, a distance in his that breaks way to reluctance. "I..." Pressing his lips together again, his focus goes back to the library.

Who is waiting for him in there?

"Sawyer said Dixie is good for me."

It isn't what I expect him to say, and I don't agree or disagree. It's not my place to.

Dawson's weight shifts from one foot to another. "I'll think about the parade. And..." His eyebrow twitches as he scrubs at his nose. "The other thing."

The other thing. The meeting.

It's as good as I'm going to get.

Once again, his eyes move from me to the building next to us.

"Are you sure you're good?" I ask one last time, knowing it's for nothing. "I've got a test in ten minutes, but I can skip and tell the prof—"

"I don't need a babysitter," he snaps, walking away from me.

I can't help but watch him disappear into the building. My gut is silently urging me to follow, but I go against it.

But he's in the back of my mind the entire test, an antsy feeling making it hard to sit still as I'm filling out multiple-choice questions.

By the time I rush through the test and make my way back to the library forty minutes later, there's no sign of Dawson anywhere. I recognize a few of his teammates sitting off to the side.

"You seen Dawson?" I ask the center for the team.

The guys all share a look before one of the point guards turns to me and says, "No, but if you see him, tell him to come to practice. Coach is pissed that he's been skipping for the past two weeks."

A few of them nod, making my eye twitch.

I know the rules just as well as Dawson does. If he misses more than three practices, he's out.

He used to love the game, even when he didn't see a lot of play time.

What the hell are you doing, Dawson?

———————

The next day, I walk across the hall, knock on the door, and wait for the blond to greet me like she always does. When she opens the door, I instantly offer her the steaming mug of coffee I just brewed and brush her shoulder as I walk inside.

"Please come in," she says sarcastically.

Her voice is back to normal, not hoarse or raspy, and her face has color again. "How are you feeling?"

"Human," she answers, closing the door. She brings the coffee over to the couch and sits down, crossing her legs under her. "Or as human as I can feel. You're up early."

"We've got places to be."

Her brows move to her hairline. "We?"

I tip my chin toward her cup. "Drink up and we'll go. We have to pick up two more people along the way."

Confusion furrows her brows. "What do you have in mind? I'm behind on schoolwork, and I need to catch up on the notes I missed."

I sit on the opposite end of the couch, draping my ankle over the opposite knee. "Trust me, this is better than homework. That can wait until you're back."

When she remains silent, I sigh, knowing she's not going to let it go until I give her some information. "You want to see a parade. There are four today, all along the same route in the French Quarter. There's going to be a lot of people, so we'll have to go early if you want to get a good spot."

Her eyes widen. "How do you know abo—"

"Dixie," I answer before she can finish. "She might have mentioned something about your little list."

Embarrassment heats her face, but I don't give her time to overthink. "As a local, I'm the perfect guy to help you cross some things off it. It's going to be a nice day out. And I hope you have a good arm because you'll need to catch some beads."

Her answering silence only lasts for a moment. "What exactly did Dixie tell you was on my list?"

The nervousness in her voice makes me grin. "She only brought up a couple things, but there must be some interesting stuff for you to blush that hard. Care to elaborate?"

The hitch to her voice rises. "N–No."

I chuckle. "Figured as much."

But I'll be damned if I'm not curious.

She traces the edge of the ceramic mug as if she's lost in thought.

"What's on your mind, Birdie?"

She rubs her lips together, shifting on the couch again uncomfortably. "What exactly…happens at these parades?"

Her expression is almost comical, and I know what she's really asking. "You mean, how are you expected to get the beads?" When her cheeks darken even more, I can't help but laugh. "Relax. You don't have to flash anybody if that's what you're worried about. That's a myth. Don't get me wrong, some parades get a little crazier than others, but they have become a lot more family friendly over the years."

She visibly relaxes into the cushions, making my lips curl higher at the corners in subtle amusement. "Okay, that's… good."

My eyes go to the framed picture of the golden retriever on her wall. "There's one in particular that I know you'll like. It's a dog parade. Hundreds of people come with their dogs to watch it."

She perks up at the sound of canine companions, which I can only assume she misses having here. "Who's coming with us?"

"Dawson and Dixie."

I'm not sure how to interpret the way her smile slackens at their names. "Have you seen Dawson lately?" she asks, her voice quieter than before. Her fingers wrap snugly around the mug. "He looks a little rough."

I hate that she's seen him that way, and I know he would too. "I don't think he's sleeping much these days."

Her tongue starts out, dragging slowly along her bottom lip. "Should I be worried? He passed by me yesterday out front but didn't say anything when I said hello. It was like I wasn't even there. He used to be so much livelier than that."

Does she miss the days he would flirt with her the second

he saw her? I certainly don't. But I get her point. That version of him is a hell of a lot better than the one walking around like he's auditioning for a role on *The Walking Dead*.

I wish I could reassure her that he's fine, but she'd see right through the lie. I give her the safest answer I can. "It's nothing you have to worry about."

After taking a sip of coffee, she slowly lowers it to her lap. "I'm not asking for me."

She's asking for Dixie. We both want to be good friends, but we're in two entirely different situations. I can't lie and say Dawson is fine or even tell her that he's on his way to getting better. He's not. But hopefully we can change that.

"I already told Dixie to be careful," I admit.

Sawyer only looks at me, saying nothing.

"He went through a lot of shit over a year ago. I had to learn the hard way that in order to help him, he needs to be willing to accept the help."

For a while, my neighbor says nothing as she stares down at the drink that she's barely touched. "I've been around a lot of sick people in my life, but it doesn't seem like it's the same kind of sickness."

Addiction is a disease in itself, but I don't tell her that. "I don't know who you've been around, Birdie, but there are a lot of different illnesses in this world. Dawson is just fighting one of them."

"And he's won before?"

I look away, unsure of how much to divulge. This isn't my story to tell, but she's part of the narrative now. "He has, and it wasn't easy. He needs to get there again."

I can't explain the look on Sawyer's face as she sets the coffee cup down on the table. Her voice is barely audible when she says, "I understand better than most."

I want to ask how, but Dawson yells up from downstairs asking where we're at.

"Speak of the devil," I remark, pushing up from the couch. I cup my hands over my mouth and yell back, "We're in Sawyer's apartment."

Sawyer peels herself off the couch before Dawson comes in. "Let me change. Give me five minutes."

She disappears behind her bedroom door as the front one opens and Dawson saunters in. He looks a hell of a lot better than he did yesterday, the bags under his eyes lighter and the redness gone.

"She not ready yet?" he asks, studying the place. He goes over to the kitchen and opens the refrigerator, pawing through the inside.

"Dude," I scold, grabbing the back of his shirt and pulling him away. "Quit it. You can grab something to eat when we get to the city."

He rolls his eyes. "Sawyer wouldn't mind."

But I do. "Doesn't matter."

His sigh is long and dramatic. "If you're going to be a buzzkill all day, I don't know if I want to go."

"You love Mardi Gras." He's been asking me to go to parades with him and his buddies for the past few years, but I always find a reason to turn him down. Last year was the easiest because he was in the middle of his program and without a license.

He gestures toward the bedroom where Sawyer is getting ready, a blank expression on his usually playful face. "And you don't. Guess it only takes a leggy blond to change your mind, huh?"

It probably isn't a dickish thing to say if it's the truth, but I thought we were past this. "She and I are friends," I

237

explain to him. "This is a group of *friends* going to see a parade together. She hasn't been to one yet. Don't make it into something it's not."

For a moment, Dawson stares at me with his arms crossed over his chest. Except his eyes, which are usually gleaming with mischief, are narrowed in silent accusation. "I may not be the smartest dude around, but I'm also not an idiot. You can't pretend like there's nothing going on between you and Sawyer."

My eyes go to the closed door where the girl in question is.

When I don't say anything, Dawson murmurs, "My point exactly."

When I look back at my best friend, I can't help but shake my head. "Not today."

He watches me for a long time, leaning against the countertop. "I know I haven't been the easiest person to deal with," he says, not looking me in the eyes. "I hold onto grudges. I make dumb choices. I get jealous. But I..."

I wait to hear what he has to say, seeing the old version of him—the laid-back, carefree one—peeking through. "I do appreciate everything you've done."

Why does this sound like some sort of goodbye? "We're friends," I remind him. "Brothers. Brothers fight."

His gaze remains on the floor. "She reminds me of you."

My brows pinch. "Who?"

"Sawyer," he says, tipping his head toward the door she disappeared through. "She doesn't think she's good for anyone. Sound familiar?"

Why would she think that?

"Just thought you should know," he adds as the door opens and Sawyer walks out.

She threw her hair up so it's out of her face and put something glossy on her lips that draws my attention directly to them. It isn't like the red lipstick she wore at the party, but I notice it all the same.

Dawson gives her a once-over in appreciation of the tight jeans and long-sleeved shirt that leave little to the imagination. "You look good," he tells her, voice more chipper than moments before. This version of Dawson is dangerous—the one who can flip a switch like he's got another personality on standby.

Sawyer flattens her hands along her shirt. "Thanks," she tells Dawson. After doing another quick scan of my best friend and me, she asks, "Are we ready?"

It's Dawson who answers. "Ready as I'll ever be." He turns to the door, walking out before anyone can say another word.

Sawyer's lips drop into a frown, but when she looks at me as if she wants to ask what's wrong, I simply shake my head.

Why don't you think you're good enough, Birdie?

As the three of us walk downstairs toward the front door of the apartment building, I notice Dawson darting swiftly into his apartment at the end of the hall before coming back with a backpack hanging from his shoulder.

Unease claws its way up my stomach. "Why do you need that?"

Sawyer watches Dawson with wary eyes that match my own. But all he says is "We'll need something to put all the shit we catch in, right?"

It seems to appease the blond beside me, but I'm a different story. I watch him carefully as he saunters out to the truck. Something in my gut tells me to be cautious.

And my gut is never wrong.

The sea of green, yellow, and purple makes it easy to spot Sawyer in her red top. She must notice the same thing when she stops in the middle of the sidewalk and turns to me. "You should have told me there was a color scheme. I could have probably found something in my closet that would fit in more."

Dixie, who's been arm in arm with Dawson since we got out of my truck, looks over her shoulder at us. She barely spoke to Sawyer on the drive, and I can tell there's a reason why that I haven't been clued in on.

Her distant eyes go to Sawyer. "You'll be fine. Nobody is going to call you out for it. They're too busy having fun."

I bump Sawyer's shoulder. "I like you in red anyway."

I've never had a favorite color, but I think red might be it. Although the dark pink that likes to creep into her cheeks when I compliment her is a close second.

Dawson stares at me, then at Sawyer, and I wonder if he notices the inches I've put between us. *See, Dawson? I'm doing this for you.*

We walk farther down to where the crowd is gathered along either side of the streetcar rails. Police line the streets, blocking off the side roads and doing crowd control as the music from the parade gets closer and louder.

I can't help but notice the death grip that Dawson has on his backpack, which stands out far more than Sawyer's red shirt does. He placed it between his feet the entire ride here, protecting it from something. Me? I was going to suggest he leave it inside when we found parking half a mile from where the parade route ended, but he grabbed it as soon as we parked, getting out of the truck and using Dixie as a way to divert the conversation.

"What about right here?" Dixie suggests, pointing to an area that doesn't have nearly as many people littering it. "We stand a better chance at catching a few things here than we do anywhere else."

She's not wrong. A lot of people get up early and arrive as soon as they can at the start of the parade route so they can get as many throwaways as possible. By the time parades end, there aren't as many items being tossed.

I smack Dawson's arm to get his attention, grinning when he turns his head. "Remember that time I finally agreed to come with you to one of these and you tried catching the Styrofoam football they were throwing off the float and you almost tackled that old woman?"

Dixie gasps. "Was she okay?"

Dawson's lips twitch upward, fighting a smirk that he doesn't want to give me. "I avoided her."

"Yeah," I snort. "And he ended up landing in somebody's rose garden. They weren't very happy."

Sawyer cringes. "That sounds painful."

Dawson's eyes brighten the way I hoped they would by bringing up the story. "It wasn't all bad. There were a few sorority girls who saw what happened and decided to play nurses. I spent a lot of time at their house getting thorns taken out of me while they served me alcohol."

He talked about that for *months*. It was the first thing that really got us past the Desiree situation because he finally had people paying attention to him who were completely separate from me. And I was happy for him, even if it looked like he'd gotten into a fight with a porcupine after.

"I still have that football," he reminisces.

Dixie elbows his rib cage playfully. "I'm surprised you didn't give it to the sorority girls for helping you."

He winks at her. "Don't worry. I gave them something else."

Sawyer rolls her eyes, and Dixie blanches at the crude remark. It's something I would never say in front of a girl who's obviously got it bad for me, but that's Dawson. He doesn't always think with the right head.

When the music starts getting louder, I see Sawyer's face light up. She leans forward, trying to see past other people nearby, her lips stretching upward as she sees the floats make their way toward us.

"They must have pretty good aim," she remarks, shaking her head. "I'd never be able to do that. I'd be hitting cars or windows."

I explain the parking bans they have leading up to the event. The businesses lining the streets are far enough away to be safe from the bigger items being thrown, but there have definitely been a few injuries over the years that the medics on standby have dealt with.

Fifteen minutes later, I'm laughing along with the bubbly blond, who's jumping as the last float goes by. The collection of colorful beads I've helped her catch is around her neck, bouncing right along with her chest. I peel my eyes away from her in time to catch another purple necklace before it smacks me in the face.

Sawyer turns to face me. I smile down at her as I put the new addition around her, my knuckles accidently grazing the swell of her breast. Her teeth bite down on her bottom lip as she looks up through her lashes at me.

Even with all the noise, I can hear the subtle intake of her breath that accompanies the rise of her chest.

The moment is broken when Dixie asks, "Where did Dawson go?"

I quickly look to the spot Dawson occupied only moments before.

He and his backpack are gone.

"Shit," I mumble under my breath, stepping away from Sawyer to search the area. "He couldn't have gotten far. Come on."

The girls follow me, calling out Dawson's name. I tell them to stick together while I go over to the group of people by the food vendors, hoping he's just grabbing something to eat since he's been bitching about being hungry for the past twenty minutes.

After a few moments of looking through the different crowds gathered by the food trucks, street vendors, and surrounding bars, I come up empty-handed.

"Where the hell did you go?" I ask under my breath, irritated that I took my eyes off him.

Suddenly, I hear a frantic, "Banks!"

Looking over my shoulder, I see Dixie lowering Sawyer to the ground.

I bolt over to them, quickly realizing that something is wrong. Wrapping an arm around Sawyer's waist, I take her from her struggling friend and rest her on my lap on the pavement.

I look up at Dixie. "What happened?"

Dixie is pale, shaking her head. "I don't know. She said she was feeling dizzy, and then all of a sudden she was falling."

Fuck. It's warm, and she's been jumping around trying to catch things. I should have gotten her a water before we settled in. "She's probably dehydrated." I reposition her as her eyelids start flickering.

There's barely any color on her face as she comes to, blinking until those striking eyes look up at me.

"Dixie, go find the EMTs—"

"No," Sawyer cuts me off, forcing herself to sit up. She holds her head, her body swaying slightly until she steadies herself. "No, I'm fine. I just got a little hot. That's all."

"You should get checked out. There are medics right over there. They won't make you go to the hospital unless they think it's serious."

If it's possible, she gets paler. "No hospitals. I don't need anybody to look at me. Please?" Her eyes fill with panic, making me wonder what she's so afraid of. "I need water. That's all."

Dixie is quick on her feet. "I'll go get you some."

When it's just us, I brush fallen hair out of her face and tuck it behind her ear. "You scared the hell out of me, Birdie."

She looks down. "I'm sorry. I..."

I frown when her words trail off. "What?"

Silently, she shakes her head.

Dixie approaches, holding out a bottle of water to me with a nervous expression. "Er, Banks?"

I uncap the bottle and give it to the girl still leaning on my lap, unfazed by the people walking by and staring. "What?"

Her voice is so quiet, I almost don't hear her say, "I found Dawson."

It takes a couple of seconds for that to sink in before my eyes dart over to her right, where my dumbass friend is standing with blood on his face and a swollen eye. "What the hell happened to you?"

"I got mugged. Someone stole my bag."

Since his eyes won't meet mine, I don't buy it for a second. "Mugged, huh?" I gesture toward one of the officers

244

standing by the blockade gate. "You should report it then. I'm sure they'll want to know what was in it."

I see his throat bob. "Banks…"

"Don't." I stop him, holding my hand up. "I don't want to hear it right now."

We fall into tense silence.

It's Sawyer who says, "I think it's time to go."

I nod, helping her up and not caring when Dawson watches me hold onto her hand. "I think you're right."

Dixie sticks by Dawson, whose attention is on Sawyer, not me.

"Unless you're going to wait for the *mugger* to come back, I suggest you come too," I tell Dawson.

Dawson swallows, finally looking at me. "I fucked up."

My nostrils flare. "I know."

Putting my arm around Sawyer, I guide us to where we parked.

It's a silent ride back.

Chapter Twenty-One

SAWYER

I WAKE UP IN a ball of sweat, groaning in confusion as I sit up on my elbows and let my eyes adjust to the pitch-dark room. Everything hurts—from the tightness in my neck down to the pinpricks of pain settled into my feet. Wiggling my toes, I rub the side of my neck and feel the inflammation nestled just below my jaw.

Closing my eyes, I take a deep breath and swallow past the emotion trying to rise from my chest. On nights like this, when sleep evades me and I don't feel well, I miss home. I miss my mother and my brother and my dad. I miss being around people who understand the reason I am the way I am.

Picking up my phone, I don't think about the time before hitting a favorited number in my contacts.

Bentley picks up after two rings. "Are you okay?"

He sounds wide awake at...*damn*. Almost two in the morning. "Were you gaming?"

I can hear something in the background before he mutters a quiet, "Maybe."

Smiling to myself, I curl into the blankets. "I know Mom isn't going to be happy if you fight her when she tries getting you up for church tomorrow."

"I'm about to go to bed."

Somehow, I doubt that.

"Are you... How are you feeling?" he asks, worry in his tone. Maybe it wasn't a good idea to call him. I don't want him to concern himself over me.

"I miss you," I start, nuzzling my cheek into the warm pillow, choosing not to tell him about yesterday's incident. If Mom finds out that we talked, she'll berate him until he admits what I've said. It's better they don't know about the days I struggle. "But I'm okay. I got to see a Mardi Gras parade, and I didn't even need to show anybody my boobs."

My little brother gags, which is exactly the response I hoped I'd get. "I'm sure Dad will be happy to hear that."

I giggle. "How's skiing going? Mom hasn't said anything about you wiping out yet."

The thirteen-year-old groans. "I'm terrible. I don't know why I signed up. I can't even get off the bunny slope."

It's hard to refrain from laughing. Would I be any better? I'm not so sure. "Why *did* you join?"

For a long moment, he's quiet. I hear rustling and then a door closing before he says, "I think Mom and Dad worry about me."

The answer makes me frown. "Why would you think that?"

"Because I don't have any friends," he murmurs, causing my frown to deepen. "I don't think they minded as much when you were around because we'd go out together. But since you left..."

Closing my eyes, I stifle a sigh. "I'm sure they're not worried

247

the way you think. They just want you to be happy. Why else would they have let me come all the way down here?"

Bentley doesn't answer right away, but when he does, my stomach dips. "It's not the same for us, and you know it. They feel bad because of what you went through. They know that you…" He doesn't finish his train of thought, but I have a feeling I know where it's going.

"For the record, I never wanted their sympathy."

"I know."

"I don't want yours either," I add. I've always preferred it when he gave me crap. It made me feel normal to banter with somebody who wasn't afraid to dish it back.

Maybe that's why I like Banks so much.

Bentley doesn't say anything right away. "I guess that's good because it'd probably kill me to be nice to you."

My grin returns. "Try not to eat shit during your next ski trip. It'd suck if you fell and made yourself uglier."

He snorts. "Then I'd look more like you."

"Goodnight, dweeb."

"Goodnight, loser."

When we hang up, I feel lighter.

As I plug my phone back into the charger, I stare up at the ceiling. The last thing I remember is Banks driving us to the apartment building and walking all of us in. Dixie followed me to my apartment while the boys stayed downstairs and murmured in quiet conversation among themselves. I'd fallen asleep watching reality TV with Dixie only hours after getting back.

I don't remember getting into bed.

A soft knock on the door has me sitting up in bed. Banks pokes his head in, stepping inside once he sees me awake. "I was hoping you'd still be sleeping, but I heard you talking."

He pushes his glasses up and leans his shoulder against the doorjamb. At some point after he was done talking to Dawson, he must have changed and came to check on me while Dixie was still here because he's in sweatpants that hug his lean legs and a T-shirt that showcases his broad shoulders instead of his usual jeans-and-flannel combo that hides his body.

When I realize I'm staring, I force my eyes away. "I was talking to my brother." A pause. "Did you put me in bed?"

"You didn't look comfortable on the couch," he explains, pushing off the wall before walking in. He tips his chin toward my bed. "Do you mind?"

I shake my head, pulling my knees up to my chest and hugging them. Banks sits down on the edge of the mattress, making sure he gives me space.

"I hope you don't mind that I came in," he says. "Dixie was leaving since you fell asleep, and I figured I'd hang out to make sure you were okay."

"It's fine. Did you talk to Dawson?" I ask.

Banks leans his elbows on his knees, rolling his neck. "Tried to. He wasn't very receptive. I let him take Dixie home because he seemed okay enough and I think she wanted to talk to him."

Nibbling my lip, I make a mental note to check on her in the morning since we didn't talk much when I invited her in. She said she needed to use the bathroom before she went back to the dorms, and by the time she came out, I'd already fallen asleep on the couch from the fatigue that took over from the day. I appreciated her help today, even though I can sense things are still a little tense between us.

"That backpack had something bad in it, didn't it?" I guess. My memories were a little fuzzy after waking up in Banks's lap. One second I was fine, and the next, everything around me was spinning. My ears were ringing, my body overheating as I reached out to Dixie and started going down.

Not one of my finer moments.

I remember the tension on the ride back though. You could have cut it with a knife. Dixie tried to relieve it with friendly conversation, but it didn't seem to last long.

"Yes," he admits, scratching the column of his neck. "And if it really was stolen, then Dawson is in some serious shit."

That doesn't sound good at all. "Should we do something?"

"I've tried helping him. He doesn't want it."

We're quiet for a tense second or two. "I'm sorry," I tell him. "For earlier."

His brows pinch. "You don't have to apologize. Or be embarrassed, for that matter. A lot of people are afraid of hospitals."

My lips part to respond, but I find myself stopping. It's kind of funny because I should be terrified of them. But oddly enough, so many good memories happened in them. The nurses in the oncology unit do everything in their power to make patients comfortable. On my seventeenth birthday, they threw me a little party. On my eighteenth, they collected money to give me as a present because I talked about getting my license and buying my own car, which inevitably never happened. I was in remission on my nineteenth birthday. Out of remission by my twentieth. And during the battle, I built a lot of beautiful friendships and lost some of those same friends to ugly, ugly illness.

"It's not like that," I say quietly, squeezing my arms around my bent knees. The motion hurts my biceps, which ache from a soreness that I know won't be going away anytime soon. "There are a lot of things to be afraid of in life. Hospitals are full of the type of people who help take away that fear."

I can feel Banks's eyes on me, but I won't meet them. "You said you've been around a lot of sick people. Is there someone in your family who was ill?"

Tell him, my conscience pushes.

Do it.

The words are right there on the tip of my tongue, but I find myself swallowing them. Despite the pain, I squeeze my arms tighter around myself. It grounds me. Reminds me how far I've come despite the odds.

"I know a few people who have struggled with a lot in their lives, and their strength is admirable to me." Wetting my dry lips, I finally meet his eyes. "I really hope Dawson gets better. Life is too short to be battling with yourself when you should be living."

Banks doesn't call me out for switching the conversation back to his friend. "Well said, Birdie."

Flattening out my legs, I readjust the blanket on my lap and glance at the time again. "It's late. You don't have to stay if you don't want to. I feel bad that you stuck around this long."

He shakes his head, his hand going to my shin and squeezing it once. "I didn't mind. Wanted to make sure you were okay."

I stare at his hand, watching his thumb lazily rub the inside of my calf. Does he know he's doing that? "You..." I pause, biting the inside of my cheek. "You can stay if you want. Like you said, the couch isn't very comfortable, but..."

His brows rise. "Are you asking me to spend the night?"

Is he really going to make me say it? "Only if you want. There's plenty of room in the bed." To prove my point, I scooch over and pat the empty spot next to me.

I'm not sure if he'll do it or if I'm crossing some sort of line. Just when I think he's interested, he pulls back. I have a feeling the reason is a six-foot-six boy who he's worried about, and I can respect that, even if I'm a little disappointed.

It feels like forever before he finally moves, standing and kicking off his shoes before reaching for his shirt. "I can't sleep with this on," he warns, pulling the hem up just enough for me to see a sliver of muscled skin beneath.

"O-Okay."

My nervous stutter has a small grin curling his lips as he peels his shirt off in one fluid movement and drops it somewhere on the floor. I watch as he moves the comforter back before crawling into bed beside me.

I'm not sure what he'll say or do, but nerves bubble in the pit of my stomach from how close we are. As he settles in, he extends his arm out and coaxes me to lie down. I only hesitate for a moment before lying on my side and curling into him, using his chest as a pillow. I shiver when he hooks his arm around me, hugging me into him and releasing a content sigh.

Goose bumps pebble my arms as I feel his fingers brush through my hair, and all I can do is pray that the wig stays in place. Too tired to worry about it and too comfortable to move, I let myself relax into his hold.

And for a moment, I think…this is it.

Happiness.

I remember what my mom told me once—that one day I'd find somebody who would make life worth living.

I just hope that I don't hurt him pretending like that's possible.

I wake up with one leg draped over a warm, hard body and the other outstretched along the mattress, a new kind of ache coiled tight in the pit of my stomach. When I start coming to, I realize the reason is Banks's leg nestled between my thighs and pressing against the warmest part of me.

I don't mean to move, but the unintentional fidgeting only deepens the desire spreading through my body as I press myself harder against him and get the kind of friction that ignites prickles of heat up my spine.

Glancing up at the boy I'm practically lying on, I see that he's still sleeping soundly. One of my arms is somehow trapped underneath him so I'm unable to move away, and every time I try to, it only makes the ache between my legs that much more intense.

And then it happens.

After another failed attempt to get away, a low moan escapes my lips when his leg presses against me and puts pressure on the nerves that jump-start my heart.

Suddenly, two muddy-brown eyes are looking down at me.

"That's a dangerous sound," he rasps, voice thick with sleep and something else. Using my free hand, I try pushing myself up, only to accidentally graze my palm along his tented sweatpants, quickly realizing that he's feeling the same exact way I am.

Except his groan is pained.

And the sound sparks something inside me that leaves my hand lingering, brushing the length of him and feeling him twitch.

He makes another noise, this one low in his chest—not quite a growl but close.

"Sawyer," he warns, eyes clouded.

Experimentally, I move my hips along his thigh to create friction that releases some of the tension coiling tight in my stomach.

One of Banks's hands moves up my back, linking with the ends of my hair and tightening around the strands as I grind against him again, moving my palm over the bulge in his pants. His jaw tightens, head rolling back on the pillow until I see the tendons in his neck.

Seeing his reaction to me makes me feel victorious, but it also makes me feel a lot more than that. And the need coursing through my body is hard to ignore the longer I move my hips against him.

"You asked me what was on my list," I whisper, lust encasing us. When his knee moves, I gasp out, "This. This is part of it."

"This?" he repeats, dipping down until his nose tickles my jaw. "What exactly do you want me to help you cross off, Birdie? I may need details so we can do it right."

Oh God. My body is on fire right now, nipples pebbling from his teasing words. "I want…"

His lips press against my neck. "What do you want?"

Breath shuddering, I swallow hard. "To feel good. I want to feel good. To have fun."

You, I don't say. *I want you.*

But I don't say that because I don't want to scare him the way I'm scaring myself for how much I actually like him.

So I say one word. "Please?"

I don't even know what I'm begging for.

Relief, mostly.

But Banks doesn't need me to clarify.

Somehow, he moves me up his body so he can get a

better grip on my butt, getting a handful and helping me use him to get off. I can feel it, the tingling sensation at the bottom of my spine. It's so close yet so far away.

I chase the feeling until Banks moves so quickly that it steals my breath. Then I'm on my back with him hovering over me, using one arm to prop himself up while the other slowly trails down the side of my body, getting closer and closer to the place I want him most.

I'm incapable of putting together a coherent sentence, but I'd like to think my eyes say plenty. His hand stops at the waistband of the leggings I changed into yesterday, the knuckle of his index finger running back and forth in such a featherlight touch that it drives me insane.

"Please," I whisper again, hoping that'll be all he needs to make the next move.

He leans down, his lips barely grazing mine before his fingers move inside the elastic of my pants. My hips arch when I feel him graze me, his breath heavy on my lips when he realizes I'm not wearing any panties.

His teeth nip my bottom lip, tugging the same moment his knuckles press against my clit. It invokes a sound that I've never heard myself make before, and I feel him grow in his pants as he moves against me.

Deep down, maybe for the first time ever, I feel sexy. Desired. Confident. Because *I* made him feel that way.

He releases my lip, his mouth moving along my jawline before dipping into the crevice of my neck. "You don't have to beg," he says against me, peppering kisses along the column of my throat. "You never have to beg."

Then I feel him gently coaxing me into opening my legs further as he teases me in all the right places. The next moment, I feel one of his fingers sliding inside me.

I let out a shaky breath, my thighs falling open as he works me with skilled hands. Not knowing what to do with my own, I grip his shoulders and soak up the sensations he's pulling from me.

"I can tell how good this feels for you," he says against me, his teeth nipping the sensitive spot of skin above my pulse. "How badly you wanted this. Were you thinking about this since the night we kissed?"

Oh God. If he expects an answer, he's not going to get one. Not a coherent one anyway.

"That's it," he praises when he feels me clench around him. "Let go. I've got you, Birdie."

I've got you.

Those three words do something to me that they've never done before, and paired with his dirty talk and the way he uses his fingers, I can't help but give in when his knuckles rub against the bundle of nerves that creates chaos throughout my body.

Suddenly, my hips arch off the bed, his fingers going deeper as the pad of his thumb works me until I'm spasming around him.

Part of me wants to be embarrassed, but I can't find the shame when the blissful, sated feeling eases my legs down until I'm lying against the bed again.

When reality creeps back in, I find myself meeting his eyes shyly. "Let me touch you," I say, one of the hands that vice-gripped his shoulder moving down his chest.

But he stops me as I reach his belly button, his hand wrapping around my wrist. "As much as I want that, not today. This was about you."

I blink, confusion curling my lips downward.

He releases my wrist and brings my hand up to his mouth

to kiss the center of my palm. The kiss is so gentle, yet I feel it in my chest.

"There are some things I have to figure out," he tells me, sitting up.

It's hard to find my voice after what just occurred. "Like what?"

I see him subtly trying to readjust himself in his sweat-pants, making me blush and look away.

"Don't worry about it. Just..." When his eyes study my face, they take their time looking at every single feature. My mouth. My nose. One eye, then the other. "I'll bring dinner over later tonight. Okay?"

It's Sunday, and I'm grateful he's still willing to cook for me after what happened. "We're still friends, right?"

The silence I'm greeted with makes me regret asking.

Then he says, "No."

Heart tightening in my chest before dropping to my stomach, I whisper, "Oh."

I guess that makes sense. We crossed a line that most friends wouldn't if it was that simple between them.

Just as I'm about to make some sort of excuse, maybe apologize for asking him to do that, he says, "I'd say we're a hell of a lot more now that I've been inside you, Sawyer."

Sawyer. Hearing him say my name in such a low tone does something funny to my heart.

"Oh," I repeat, this time a little quieter than before as I soak that in.

Banks's eyes go down to my lips, staring for a moment before he sighs and gets out of bed. Collecting his shirt from the floor, he puts it on swiftly and then sits on the edge of the mattress as he slides his shoes on.

When he stands, he turns to me and lets his eyes wander down my body, which is still draped in the bedding.

His throat bobs before he forces himself to look away. "I'll see you tonight," he says, walking to the door.

I listen to him make his exit, only releasing my breath when I hear the front door close behind him.

Then I think about what just happened.

And I realize I'm screwed.

Because I don't deserve Banks and he doesn't deserve the inevitable goodbye that comes with having me in his life.

Hours later, after a day of keeping to myself and reliving the moments of this morning in bed, I realize I have a choice to make.

Banks isn't the only one who has to figure things out, but when he knocks at dinnertime with an armful of ingredients, I don't hesitate to let him in.

Maybe that's fate's way of deciding for me.

Chapter Twenty-Two

BANKS

THE FIRST THING I'M greeted with when I open the door to my father's house is the strong stench of expensive tobacco. I've spent weeks avoiding him at all costs, hoping by the time I showed up for dinner with him again that he'd have cooled off.

"Paxton," he calls out when I close the door behind me.

I hesitate only a moment before walking into the living room to see him sitting in his favorite chair. The place looks clean—cleaner than normal. Minus the cigar smoke, there's a hint of Febreze in the air. When I glance into the open kitchen, I notice the garbage is empty and there aren't any plates or dirty dishes scattered on the countertops.

It's...strange. "Hey, Dad."

"It took it being spring break for you to come home," he comments, face void of any emotion.

As far as I'm concerned, he should feel lucky. I know a lot of people who fled Louisiana altogether for vacation, but I stayed. "I'm here now," I tell him, walking into the kitchen and pouring myself a glass of water from the tap. "Did Laramie share the good news?"

Dad lowers his cigar, tapping the end against his crystal ashtray. "I'm not going to apologize for prying about your education, considering I'm the reason you have one. So if you were expecting one, I wouldn't hold your breath."

That's typical of him. "He approved my final design, so I can start working on the physical concept. Apparently, I have potential."

Dad huffs, and I doubt it has anything to do with the abuse he's putting his lungs through right now. "I could have told you that."

I'm almost surprised he agrees with Laramie since he hasn't exactly verbalized a lot of praise in my life.

Before I can feel good about it, he ruins the moment. "As far as I'm concerned, anybody is *capable* of potential. It's raw talent that gets you places in life."

Teeth grinding, I force myself to nod. I don't bother asking him if he thinks I have the raw talent to make it. "That's one way to look at it."

"That's the only way to." He takes another puff of the stogie in his hand. "Life is far too easy without a little criticism given out. That's what makes Laramie a good professor."

I want to ask if that's what makes him a good father, but I smarten up and bite my tongue instead. Why start another fight on the brink of our last one? I don't have the energy for it today after spring cleaning and closing down the campus store for the next week. Most of the students who normally work there are gone, save for me, Lucy, and our manager. It makes for a lot more work and a lot less time on other things.

Namely, the girl across the hall.

Which is probably a good thing.

Because I can still feel her clenching around me, still hear the ghostly echoes of her moans as she comes apart. It took everything in me not to come in my pants or take up her offer to get me off the way I desperately needed to.

I feel a little less guilty now that Dawson seems resigned to the interest I have in Sawyer, but I don't know if that's enough to make me want to take things further with her. He's too vulnerable to test the waters I'm tempted to with my neighbor.

The problem is, how much do I want Sawyer to know? There always comes a time when the people in my life get too close to the truth. Dawson was always too focused on his own little world to think about what was going on in mine, and while I sometimes resented his aloofness, it made things easier.

Sawyer is smarter than that.

The closer she gets to me, the more she'll uncover. Namely, about the man smoking another cancer stick mere feet away.

I sip the water to quench my parched throat, staring at the liquid as it ripples in the glass.

Sawyer wanted to feel good.

That was all.

She never said anything about love.

I'm getting ahead of myself.

Clearing my throat, I roll my shoulders back. "After break, I'm going to start the test model. We have until the end of April to get it done and submitted for our final project."

"Don't you think you should start it sooner?"

"It's break," I reiterate. I've been swamped all semester.

261

The only class that hasn't completely drained me is creative writing, but I choose to keep that to myself since I know my father's feelings on it. "If I'm going to submit my best work, don't you think I should be able to rest up when the school gives us the opportunity to?"

He doesn't answer my question. Lifting his wrist, he looks at the time on his watch. "Dinner should be arriving any second. I ordered from Rocky's tonight. Make sure you give him a tip when he answers the door."

Dismissed. I'm okay with that as long as it doesn't lead to an argument. Truth is, I hate avoiding my dad. As unpredictable as he can be, I like coming around and checking in on him. I never know if I'm going to walk into something bad after the long stretches when I don't hear from them. One of the few upsides to him working at the school is that I hear people talking about him enough to know when he shows up and when he doesn't.

"Got it," I reply, about to turn toward the door and wait. I stop myself when I see an old photo of Dawson and me as awkward teens. We're grinning at the camera, covered in mud. My mother took that. Gripping the archway that separates the foyer from the open living room, I force my eyes away from the image collecting dust on the wall. "I know you can't tell me any details, but has Dawson been doing okay in class?"

My father's eyebrows rise at the same time his cigar does to his mouth. "That boy dropped my class weeks ago. I'm surprised he hasn't said so." Blowing out the plume of smoke, he settles into his chair. "You want to talk about failed potential, he's the poster child."

Son of a bitch. I've stopped by his apartment a few times, but he either is never home or refuses to answer.

Wasted potential. My father's words echo in my head, lingering there when the doorbell rings and the delivery man passes me our dinner. I absentmindedly hand him a few bills that I had stuffed in my pocket before closing the door.

Dinner is quiet, and I hate it.

It's nothing like Sunday nights with Sawyer. We could sit in a room of silence and I'd feel the same as if we were having a conversation or joking, but it's not like that here.

It never has been.

And it makes me want to ditch my father and knock on her door, ignoring the fact that her family arrived today from New York to see her for break.

It's probably a good thing we're spending some time apart. The more involved we are, the likelier Dawson would use it as an excuse to spiral. He's already at his breaking point. He's been sporadic and unpredictable, not sleeping, and moody. The old version of him never used to be so angry or paranoid. Now, I watch him look over his shoulder like he's waiting for somebody to pop out of the bushes at any second.

If he knew how badly the temptation to be with Sawyer fully is, would he jump off the deep end?

I'm not going to be the reason he falls off the edge. I won't let Sawyer be either. Nobody should feel responsible for somebody else's downfall the way I've felt for Dawson's and my father's.

Enabler.

The only time my father speaks to me during dinner is to say, "Pass the ketchup."

We don't talk about school or classes or Mom.

The unfortunate thing is that it leaves me to my own devices, which include thinking about my friend's drug problem and my neighbor's sexy moans.

I knew I was fucked the second I saw her in the hallway the night she moved in, and the feeling was only cemented when she called me out in class for being a dick.

Dawson could never handle a girl like Sawyer.

But that doesn't necessarily mean I can.

Even though I'd love to try.

After an awkward, thick silence that only the news on the television breaks, I grab my things to leave.

Only then does my father look at me. "Make yourself useful for once and grab me a beer on the way out."

My eye twitches.

For once.

I could point out all the times I've been useful in the past, but where would that leave us? In another fight.

So I get him the last beer in his fridge.

He doesn't thank me.

I don't want him to.

Neither of us says goodbye.

It's late, well after the sun goes down, when I see Dixie walking through downtown Baton Rouge by herself. I slow down a few houses ahead of her, pulling over to the curb and rolling the window down.

"You okay?" I call out, watching her body lock until she lifts her head.

Christ. Her eyes are glassy, and her face is damp. She's been crying. I've never done well with people who cry, especially women. I blame my mother for not sticking around to set an example because my father sure as shit didn't show me what comfort should be like.

Dixie uses the back of her hand to wipe at her cheek, hesitating only for a moment before she drags her feet over to my parked truck. "What are you doing out?"

I frown at her raspy tone and wonder if the dipshit I call a best friend is responsible for it. "I could ask you the same thing. It's not safe to be walking out here on your own at night."

Limply, her shoulders lift as her damp eyes move to the ground. "I needed some air."

Checking my watch, I debate my options. Draping my arm on the open window, I lean back in my seat and use my free hand to grip the back of my neck. "Did you talk to Sawyer about whatever is going on?"

She sniffles. "She's with her family. I didn't want to disturb her. And we've been a little...off lately."

I'm tempted to ask why, but I decide not to pry.

Looks like we're both having a shit night.

I think about what I used to like doing when I was upset growing up. "How do you feel about ice cream?"

"Ice cream?" she repeats, swiping a finger under her eyelashes to catch tears before they fall.

I climb out. "I know a place that's open late. They're good too. Only if you want. I don't want to go back yet, but I can drop you off at the dorm if you'd prefer going home."

Dixie nibbles her lip and rubs her arm. "I'm not ruining your night?"

The only thing I had planned was going home and watching TV, so I suppose ice cream is a better alternative. "Nah. Climb in. It's my treat."

I walk over and open the opposite door for her, waiting for her to get in. Before I close it, she whispers, "Dawson ended things today."

Ah, fuck. What am I supposed to say to that?

I know she liked him a lot. And maybe if Dawson was a little clearer headed, it could have been reciprocated, but I'm not sure he would have ever gotten there in his current state. Telling that to the sad girl beside me is definitely not going to be as comforting as I'd mean it to be.

So the only thing I can say is "I'm sorry."

I don't know if I should press for details unless she wants to tell me. And, frankly, I don't want to. It's not my place, and God only knows what she'd say.

Shifting on my feet, I cuss to myself when I see her bottom lip quiver. "Don't cry. Dawson is an idiot. He's not in the best mindset right now."

She nods, not meeting my eyes.

There's no defending whatever he did, so I won't bother. "My favorite ice cream growing up was cookies and cream. But when I was sad, my mom used to take me out to The Dairy Lounge and get me their special."

Dixie blinks past her glossy gaze. "What was their special?"

My smile comes easily, remembering all the times my mom and I would sneak away just the two of us and enjoy a sweet treat before my father got home. Those were the good days when I knew what peace felt like. "Mint choco-late chip."

Her face scrunches. "You honestly like that stuff? It tastes like toothpaste."

I chuckle. "Don't worry, I won't make you eat it. You can get whatever you want."

Her sniffle is a little less sad as she inhales and exhales one more deep breath. "I like cookies and cream."

I nudge her arm. "Cookies and cream it is."

The first ten minutes go by in silence, which isn't totally uncomfortable. Dixie stares out the window, her reflection contemplative. I give her the time to think, to process whatever she's feeling.

Five minutes from the parlor, she starts fidgeting. "Banks?"

I hum.

"Sawyer is a lucky girl."

My eyes dart to her, one eyebrow rising.

Her smile is small, knowing. When she rests her head back, she closes her eyes, the smile disappearing. "Hopefully you two smarten up and actually do something about it."

That's the last thing we say to one another the rest of the night.

I buy us two ice cream bowls—I get her cookies and cream and me mint chocolate chip. She tries mine despite hating the flavor and then gives me some of hers.

It's quiet, which I think we both need.

To think.

To figure out what to do next.

Hopefully you two smarten up and actually do something about it.

Chapter Twenty-Three

SAWYER

I GIVE MYSELF ONE last look in the mirror as my mother rambles from outside the bathroom door. Something about dust bunnies, I think. She's been here for less than twenty minutes and already did the dishes and told me I needed a vacuum because the one Dad bought me didn't have enough power for the thick carpet in the bedroom. I tuned her out a while ago when she told Bentley to try finding the duster in the closet I keep all my odds and ends in.

Running my hands along the sides of my throat, I feel the lumps that make it hard to swallow. They've gotten bigger. Harder to ignore. Sighing, I take my hair out of the messy bun I'd thrown it into before they arrived and let it fall over my shoulders, hiding the swelling that I'm sure Mom would notice if she gave me another look.

Scanning the makeup lining the sink, I think about covering the dark bags under my eyes or adding color to the sharp cheekbones that make my face look hollower than normal, but I decide against it.

My family are the only ones I don't have to pretend with.

I can tell from the look on my mother's face that I'm about to be scolded as she pulls back from the millionth hug she's given me since arriving. As much as I want to be annoyed by the clingy affection, I'm not at all. Even though her strong hold hurts my thin frame, which isn't padded nearly as much as it usually is.

"By the way, Dr. Ortiz's secretary called and said that you missed your last two appointments," she informs me, disapproval in her blue eyes.

My shoulders droop. It wasn't intentional, if that's what she thinks. At least, not the first one. "I'm sorry. Something came up and I got distracted. I didn't see the reminder email for the makeup appointment until the day after."

Mom's hand brushes my cheek before dropping to the ends of my hair. I left it down the way she loves it. "I knew I should have called and reminded you. Your memory isn't as strong as it was before your last round of chemo."

Cheeks burning, I stare at the floor.

Bentley, who's been messing around on his phone for the past hour, snorts. "Busted."

I stick my tongue out at him. "Shut up, twerp. Go back to texting your *girlfriend*."

His whole face turns red. "She's not my girlfriend!"

I laugh, and even Mom looks like she's trying to fight a smile. "Whatever you say. I'm sure your love for skiing has nothing to do with her being on the team."

He mumbles under his breath before going back to his phone, probably texting the cute brunette who I've seen tag him in photos on social media at least five different times. I'm no expert, but I'd say that means something.

Mom focuses on me again. "I know you're busy, and I want to respect your space. But it's still important to talk to the doctor. That's why they're willing to do virtual appointments for you while you're here."

I'm not trying to take advantage of my health-care team, who have been nothing but great to me since I said I was coming to Louisiana for college, so I feel a little bad. I told Mom I didn't want to fill my schedule with appointments and having to hear the same lectures and spiels I have on and off for half a decade, but I never said I refused. I know it means something to her that I'm trying to give her peace of mind when we're apart.

So I say, "It won't happen again."

My appeasement puts her smile back, although the worry in her gaze doesn't go away completely. "Is everything okay? It wasn't something serious that made you forget, was it?"

I'm not telling her the real reason my mind has been scattered because that involves explaining why there was a boy in my bed Sunday morning. And while I'm sure she'd still lecture me on safe sex practices, she definitely wouldn't brush over the fact I fainted the day before and needed somebody to check on me to begin with. I can picture her now, telling me it wasn't smart to let a boy increase my blood pressure when I already had one fainting spell.

"Like you said, I've been busy with school," I say.

And the boy across the hall.

Mom watches me for a second, her hands going down my arms before taking my own hands and squeezing them and then pulling me in for hug number God knows what.

I can't help but laugh softly as I wrap my arms around her back and squeeze her as tightly as she is squeezing me. "I love you," I tell her, resting my cheek on her shoulder.

Her arms tighten even more. "Oh, baby girl. I love you to the moon and back. I'll make sure to schedule another appointment soon."

I don't fight her as much as I want to.

Because I'm here.

In a different state.

Away from family.

Letting fate take charge.

I think that's scarier for her than it is for me because I've accepted my fate, a feat not many people can conquer.

But I know my mother isn't going to accept it as easily because she hasn't had to fight the same way I have. I just hope she can forgive me.

Someday.

Eventually, my brother groans from the couch, flopping around like a fish out of water. "I don't want to spend the rest of the day here if there are no video games. Can we get some food now? There was a Taco Bell down the road."

"Trust me," I muse, thinking back to my first night here back in January. "There's way better food around here than Taco Bell."

I can feel Mom's eyes on me, and who knows what she sees? I'm fairly certain mothers have some sort of super-power that children will never be able to understand. She can see right through me at times when I really wish she couldn't.

But instead of questioning me, she grabs the keys to the rental that she got from the airport and says, "Let's go before your brother starts gnawing on your couch then. I'll let you pick where we eat."

She and I walk out side by side, me tucked under one of her arms, with Bentley trailing behind us. My eyes go to the door across the hall briefly, not long enough to catch notice but long enough to know that Banks isn't home. I haven't heard from him since Sunday night dinner, and I haven't reached out either.

He needs time to figure something out, so I'll respect it.

I don't have time to feel sad about it when Bentley starts complaining about how hungry he is. I pull my attention to my family, who I've missed ten times more than I let myself believe.

"You're lucky Maggie isn't here," I tell the thirteen-year-old in the back seat. "Or else I'd give her your portion of food since she's not annoying."

"Then I'd let her puke in your bedroom and wouldn't clean it up," he dishes back with a grin. "It'd be like a welcome-home present."

I stick my tongue out.

He does the same.

Mom exhales dramatically. "Should have known it wouldn't take long before you two were at each other's throats."

I grin at her. "Did you expect any less?"

I'm sure some college students would hate having their family around for a week during their spring break, but after a few days, I realize how much family means to me. And not just because I have clean clothes that are folded and put away, a polished apartment, and food in the fridge. I can sleep in until eleven to rest my body, opt for silk scarves around my head instead of the wigs that sometimes itch my scalp, and not have to worry about cooking for myself.

I'd like to think that I stay true to who I am even when I'm hiding behind the mask—and inevitably under the wig. Maybe the physical stuff about me changes, but my personality has always been the same. Like how much love I have for the people who came all this way to spend time with me, to see the place I missed for half my life.

When I walk out of my bedroom, I rub my eyes and walk toward the smell of bacon. I stop and smile when I see Dad in front of the stove holding a sizzling pan.

Walking up behind him, I wrap my arms around his waist. "I thought we were meeting you tonight."

Dad wraps an arm around my shoulders, pulling me over and hugging me to his side. "I figured I'd surprise you early. Your mother and brother went to the store a while ago to grab a few more things because we didn't have the right ingredients." He gives me a skeptical look. "I told you to tell me when you needed groceries and didn't like seeing such an empty kitchen."

Sheepishly, I steal a piece of crispy bacon from the plate set aside. "I eat plenty."

I can see from the corner of my eye the way he studies my thin figure. "There were barely any take-out containers in the garbage when I took it out," he notes, one of his brows raised in question.

Do I tell him that my neighbor has been cooking for us and leaving me leftovers? It's innocent. Enough. But Dad already asked me how many personal coffee deliveries I got from Banks, so I'd rather not feed his suspicions. "A friend has been teaching me how to cook."

Now both his eyebrows are touching his receding hairline. "Somebody is teaching you how to cook?" he repeats.

I shrug, hoping it comes off as nonchalance.

Dad studies me but chooses not to press the way Mom would, although it looks like he wants to. "Your mother and Bentley should be back any second. Then we can eat."

My stomach rumbles when I see the assortment of chopped lettuce and tomato on the counter. "Are you making sandwiches?"

It's odd how something as simple as a BLT can create so much excitement, but there's something about him making them that reminds me of my childhood when we all used to live together. Mom might have spent most of the time in the kitchen, but Dad would help whenever he could. And nothing compared to his homemade mac and cheese or his BBQ chicken that he'd grill in the summertime.

Dad glances at his watch, reminding me of Banks's silver Citizen. "Surprised they're not back yet," he says in concern.

I walk over to the window facing the back parking lot, my eyes widening when I see Mom chatting with Banks. "Oh God," I groan, quickly darting to my bedroom to grab my wig.

I'm not sure I can trust Mom talking to anybody because she doesn't always have a filter. And since I haven't exactly mentioned my neighbor, who knows what she's told the virtual stranger?

Dad appears in my bedroom door. "What's the matter, pumpkin?"

I can feel him watching as I frantically try putting my hair in place. "Mom" is all I say, brushing the frizzy strands out of my face.

Shouldering past him, I jog over to the window to see if she's still trapping Banks in conversation. I dart away when I see her pointing in my direction.

Dad follows me, head tilting and a secretive smile gracing his face. "A friend, huh?"

I ignore Dad as I head out the door and speed walk to the back lot, where Bentley is holding two grocery bags beside my mother.

"There she is." Mom beams, holding her arm out for me as I approach them.

"Mom," I greet nervously, eyes moving from her to Banks. At least he looks amused. That means she couldn't have told him too much.

Hopefully.

"I just met your neighbor," she says, rubbing my arm. "You never told me you had cute neighbors. I told him he should join us for lunch. Your father certainly made enough."

Heat blossoming over my face, I shift from one foot to the other on the loose gravel, only then realizing that I came out in my socks.

Mom notices too. "Why on earth do you come out here without shoes?" She shakes her head, looking up to my neighbor. "I swear, this girl always keeps me on my feet. She's an adventurer. That's why we named her Sawyer. We both knew she was going to be a handful."

Banks's spine straightens. I'm not sure what the alarm in his muddy eyes is when they dart to me, but I simply shrug it off. "They named me after—"

"Tom Sawyer," we say simultaneously.

Mom perks up, happiness curving her lips. "Oh, how nice. Not many young people have heard of the character before. Such a shame they don't teach the same classics they did in my day, although I suppose Mark Twain is a bit controversial."

Banks's attention goes from me to my mom, studying her as if trying to figure something out. His eyes move up to her hair, then over to me, his brows furrowing.

He must be uncomfortable with the invite.

I clear my throat. "If you have plans, it's no big deal."

It's Bentley who says, "What, sis? You don't want your *boyfriend* to join us for lunch? Are you afraid we're going to embarrass you or something?"

Narrowing my eyes at my annoying little brother, I hiss, "He's not my boyfriend."

Banks is now shifting uneasily. I can't look him in the eye for fear of what I'll see. Is he mad he was called that? Does he assume I referred to him as that to my family? Or does he see it as harmless fun?

Wrapping my arm around my mother's, I pull her in the direction of the apartment building while nudging Bentley along. I look at Banks as I shuffle along the driveway. "I'll talk to you later, okay?"

I don't give him time to reply before I all but shove my family back inside.

As soon as the doors are closed behind us, Mom pulls her arm away from mine. "That was rude, Sawyer. Why don't you want him around? He seemed perfectly nice."

"He is," I agree, walking them back up to my apartment. "But he also doesn't know."

"Doesn't know what?" my brother asks.

Mom doesn't need me to explain. Her eyes are sad and sympathetic when they meet mine, a combination I hate seeing. "Honey..."

I shake my head, brushing off the hand she tries putting on my shoulder. All I want to do is get inside. "Let's just have a nice family lunch together. I'm starving."

I can tell Mom wants to say more, but she doesn't. She probably knows it's a lost cause. And she and Dad will probably have something to say about it later, but this can't be surprising to them. I never said I was going to tell people the truth about me.

Not long after settling in with the plates full of food, I hear the door across the hall open and close. I feel a little bad for not inviting him in, especially because I'll have to explain later. At least it'll give me time to come up with an excuse.

That doesn't stop my mother from bringing him up halfway into our lunch. "I still think that boy is cute. I don't know, Sawyer. Maybe he's understanding too."

With food in my mouth, I say, "I wouldn't get your hopes up."

It's something I've been telling myself for a long time now. The same thing I wish she would drive into her head. Hope is the only thing stronger than fear, which means it has the power to destroy.

Dad sets his plate down on the coffee table and scoots to the edge of the couch. "Your mother and I want to talk to you guys about something."

Bentley and I share a look before turning to our father.

Mom puts her hand on Dad's leg, and he puts his palm on top of hers. Considering how lovey-dovey they seem, it can't be anything bad.

Dad smiles. "I've decided to retire after this year. I won't be renewing my contract."

Bentley perks up on the couch beside me, almost dropping his food on the carpet. "Are you being serious?"

Dad nods. "It's time. I'm getting older, and I can't keep up with the new recruits. Plus, I've been missing out on valuable time with family. I want to make the most of it."

His eyes meet mine, and my stomach clenches when I hear the words he doesn't speak.

While I still can.

My smile isn't forced, but it's tight with emotion. "Does that mean you're moving back to New York?"

Mom and Dad look at one another, something in their eyes flashing as they silently communicate.

It's Mom who answers. "We're considering our options."

Bentley frowns. "What other options are there? My school's in New York. So are my friends."

When Dad looks at me, I know what the other option is. Bentley is right though. He's got a lot of time left before he graduates. Unlike me, he didn't have to move around a lot when he was younger. He's settled and happy where he is now.

I've already taken his peace away—the last thing I want to do is take his happiness too.

So, locking eyes with my father, I shake my head. It wouldn't be fair to my brother if they packed up their things and moved down here for me. It wouldn't be a permanent solution, only a temporary home.

Bentley deserves more than that.

Dad's eyes dull, but his chin dips in acknowledgment. Even if they haven't decided yet, they know my vote. And I hope it's enough for them to consider what even five years down the line looks like, the way I have.

He turns to Bentley and says, "We're only looking into other options. That's all."

Mom's smile wavers, one of the corners of her mouth tilting downward.

She knows why I don't want them to move.

So does Dad.

My eyes trail to the time on my phone.

Tick tock, tick tock.

I stand, grabbing my plate and refusing to dwell on the reality we're dealt with. Voice cracking, I walk to the kitchen and ask, "Who wants more food?"

Bentley is the only one who answers.

That night, I hear voices outside my door when I thought everyone left for their hotel.

I use the peephole to see my father shaking Banks's hand.

Dad speaks so quietly to my neighbor that I don't know what he says.

Banks turns to the door, staring as if he knows I'm spying.

Then he nods at my father.

Once.

Dad leaves.

Banks glances at my door one last time before disappearing into his apartment.

I step back and rub my arm, wondering what they could have been talking about.

Walking over to the couch, I sit where Bentley was all afternoon as we watched movies as a family.

My hand drags across the stain he left on the couch when he spilled his soda.

Mom freaked out about it more than I did. She sprang into action and started cleaning it.

It's so quiet here now without them.

I hug my knees to my chest and look at the door, unsure if I should knock on Banks's.

I pick up my phone, nibbling on my lip when I see the time.

Dialing a number, I wait as it rings a few times before it picks up. "I didn't know if you'd answer," I tell Dixie.

She hasn't spoken to me much since we studied at the library together. I know I hurt her feelings because she found reasons to avoid me. First it was tests she was stressed about. Then it was homework she was behind on. Once, she mentioned a group of girls she met at Dawson's basketball game had invited her out to a game LSU was playing against a nearby college.

I'm happy she's making friends, even if it means I get the boot. It's what I deserve anyway.

Dixie sighs. "I was upset," she admits, her voice still weighed with emotion that makes guilt wrap around my heart. "There's just been a lot..." She sighs. "Never mind."

We're quiet for a long time, neither of us knowing what to say.

"I'm sorry," I tell her, fidgeting with the throw blanket beside me. "I've never been very good about opening up. It's not just with you."

For a while, I don't think Dixie is going to reply. But then she sighs. "You don't owe me any explanation. I shouldn't have been ignoring you. It was stupid."

It's not though. "Friends should always be there for friends" is my response, as I rest my chin on top of my knees. "I'm sorry that I haven't been. When you get back from Pennsylvania, we should do something. I'll make it up to you."

There's a brief pause. "I'd like that."

I smile.

After another brief moment, she says, "I hope one day you'll be comfortable enough to share your skeletons with me."

One day.

I hate that saying.

My lips part.

Then close.

The words get stuck in my throat.

Taking a deep breath, I force myself to nod and get out, "Yeah. One day."

Chapter Twenty-Four

BANKS

I'M SAWYER. LIKE TOM Sawyer. *It's a book.*

It could be a coincidence. An unlikely one, but still a possibility. There are plenty of kids named after books. I went to school with a girl named Austen, spelled after the romance author Jane Austen. Her brother's name is Woolf after Virginia Woolf. It happens.

But Sawyer's mother's hair is red.

Not orange like Carrot Top, but dark auburn with highlights the same color as the copper wire I used to help my father with when he did his summer projects at the house. The same color hair as the eight-year-old girl I used to share snacks with under the aging oak.

The same oak I rarely visited for peace and quiet after Katrina because it seemed…emptier when Sawyer stopped showing up. I waited. And waited. And waited. But the day never came.

Sawyer said she's never dyed her hair before, which would be an odd thing to lie about. So is her name really a coincidence? It's a steep chance, but one I can't let my mind wander from because I miss those days when life was simpler.

Before my father's drinking got bad and my mother left.

Life wasn't perfect, but the days I spent in the shade eating fruit snacks under the tree with Sawyer the redheaded adventurer were close.

"There's no way," I tell myself, swiping my hand through my hair.

The last time I saw *my* Sawyer was right before Katrina hit. My family drove north and stayed at my uncle's house in Mississippi, still getting plastered with the storm but not nearly as bad as Louisiana. Sawyer said her family was leaving too, but I never knew where they went or if they even made it. I pestered my parents with questions trying to find out, but we didn't know their last name or anything that could possibly help get me answers.

Mom and Dad were going through their divorce anyway, so the last thing they wanted to deal with was some random little girl I'd grown attached to. I was upset with them at the time, but looking back, I can't blame them. They didn't understand how I could possibly grow to like somebody so quickly when I barely knew her.

But the truth is, it was easy to like Sawyer when I had nothing else that brought me peace.

Maybe she was the distraction I needed—the perfect person to help me get through all the arguments at home I never wanted to listen to. She came into my life at the right time, and when she left it…

"There's no way," I repeat, pacing in my apartment.

I've felt unsettled since the conversation outside yesterday. Between her mother's familiar red hair to the number her father slipped me in the hall last night, I've been all but burning holes in the carpet from the back-and-forth pacing.

When I hear the laughter coming from the people I want to press for answers, I decide to stop torturing myself.

Sawyer didn't want me around, which is a stab to the gut that I don't like admitting. But it didn't hurt as much as how quickly she corrected her brother when he called me her boyfriend. Normally, I would have appreciated it. Labels in the past made me feel suffocated, scared. I'd hear them and run the other way. In large part because of the skeletons I didn't want anybody uncovering in my closet, but also because I felt like there was something more out there.

Some*one*.

And it pisses me off.

Since when is a girl not wanting more than fun a problem? I used to live for those moments. Hell, I stopped putting myself out there completely after I hurt a few girls' feelings when they got a little too attached. I didn't want to be a prick, so I didn't bother giving anyone hope.

But Sawyer is different because she's hiding something that I want to find out.

Obsessing over it clearly won't get me anywhere, so I force myself out before I do something stupid. Like go to her apartment on her mother's invite when she clearly doesn't want me there.

And twenty minutes later, as if my brain is on autopilot, I pull up to the one place I haven't been in months. Not since the fall when things got a little too heated between Dad and me. He'd almost hit me, and I was so, so close to doing the same. The second I raised my hand, I knew I needed to get out.

Because I didn't want to be like my father.

I wanted to be the version of Paxton a redheaded little girl knew me as.

An entirely different entity.

Without cares.

Without problems.

Without a father who hit and a mother who left.

Pushing back the overgrown shrubs that my father let take over the once-well-kept area, I see the decrepit foot bridge that I accidentally damaged last year when I kicked one of the railing posts after a blowout at home. There's a hole in the center from rotting wood, three missing pieces of railing, and a dried-up stream my father himself man-made to flow to a small pond past the tree line.

Walking past the fallen twigs, leaves, and debris that litter the ground, I kneel down by the end post where four letters are carved into the wood.

SH + PB

Running my fingers over the letters clearly written by two children, I'm taken back to all the snacks and gossip and good times spent in the backyard of a home I haven't made decent memories at since.

The two acres my parents had attached to their house stretch far enough out that coming here felt like an escape without the risk of getting into trouble for going too far. Clearly nobody comes here anymore, but these days, it feels like a private park just for me. And, at one point, the redhead who somehow stumbled upon it in her explorations.

I smile to myself.

"This is my bridge," she says.

"Did you build it?"

Opening my palm, I take in the tiny white raised scar from where the nail went into my hand when I helped my father put this place together. He designed the entire thing around the oak tree that he said has been there for longer than he's been alive. The greenery, the bushes, the bridge: they were all his doing.

"Maybe one day you'll design something just like this," he tells me, eyeing our handiwork. "I know it would make your old man proud to see what you come up with. You've got an eye, kid."

I helped him pick out some of the landscaping and chose the expensive wood for the project after seeing his sketches for it. It was one of the few bonding moments we had when he didn't smell like booze or cigars and didn't seem on edge from whatever fight he and my mother were in. Out here, he could let his mind stay busy outside all his problems.

Back then, he used his hands to create, not destroy.

Standing, I study the space and close my eyes, trying to remember what it was like when I was nine. The air was crisper, cleaner. The oak wasn't half dead, with shedding limbs that come down with each rainstorm. It seems appropriate that the place I enjoyed escaping to is falling apart around me.

Unkept.

Unloved.

Forgotten.

My eyes go down to the carvings again before something hits me. Walking back to my truck, I grab my sketchpad from the back and study the design I've been working on aimlessly for months.

When I take it to the hidden spot, I realize I've been working on the very thing my father always wanted me to. A newer version of my favorite place—somewhere to go to. Something to rebuild what'd been broken a long time ago.

Maybe I always knew that was why I chose this design. It wasn't to remember the times I had with the mysterious girl I never got to see again, but all to do with my father.

"Fuck," I cuss, closing my sketchpad and shoving it into the back seat. Swiping a hand through my hair, I slam the door closed and...

Laugh.

Because I've been subconsciously trying my hardest to gain a man's approval whose only focus in life is if he has enough liquor to get him through to the next week.

I sit in my truck for what feels like forever before I decide where to go next. Being trapped inside seems dangerous right now. If I'm left to my own devices, my shaky palm may wind up in the drywall by the night's end. And I don't want to think about how many holes I've seen my father patch or hide in my lifetime.

White-knuckling the wheel, I go to the only safe place I have left.

LSU's Botanic Gardens have become the peace my mind needs when life becomes too much. I always find myself under one of the trees or shaded by the gazebo working on whatever latest sketch I'm trying to perfect. I people watch. Listen to nature—the wind rustling the tree limbs, the birds landing in the ponds, the distant laughter of kids in the gardens.

Sometimes I envy the happiness that surrounds me, as if everybody else has it so much easier. I know better than that, but it still eats at me when bitterness bubbles under my skin as couples walk hand in hand or kids run around laughing without a single care in the world.

Once upon a time, I was like that.

That seems like a lifetime ago though.

Hours pass, and the sketch in my lap barely grows from

its last conception. I realize reluctantly that my father may have been right about needing a lot more time to get a scaled model created, which isn't something I plan on admitting to him anytime soon.

Sometime later, a shadow casts over the book in my lap. "Thought I'd find you here," Dawson says, dropping into the spot on the bench beside me and stretching his long legs out.

"Surprised to see you here," I admit, abandoning the work I've been struggling with all day to focus on the gaunt boy beside me. "Where have *you* been?"

Dawson's leg bounces anxiously. "Around."

Around.

Scraping a hand down my face, I set my sketchbook down on the ground. "Look, I'm not in the mood for any more bullshit today. So why don't you tell me why you're here when you've gone out of your way to avoid me?"

His eyebrows arch as he looks at me, seemingly stunned by my withdrawn demeanor. I try to be reasonable, but my patience is limited, and my mind is already full of things beyond what my best friend is getting himself into when I'm not around.

"I tried your apartment," he answers, stuffing his hands into his hoodie pocket. "Sawyer said she heard you leave. Figured there weren't many places to look."

Sawyer was paying enough attention to hear me go. Interesting. "Was her family still there?"

He nods, slumping back. "Her dad answered. Pretty sure he wasn't happy I was standing there."

I don't know her father well, but I know a lot of military men. They're protective and observant. It doesn't exactly take a rocket scientist to see that there's something wrong with Dawson.

The bags under his eyes are back, and he's fidgety. Not to mention his skin tone is off. Not quite pale, but off-white. Yellow. Sickly. I've known him long enough to see the weight he's lost, but Sawyer's dad probably doesn't know the difference. All telltale signs of drug use if you know what to look for, and I have a feeling the naval officer does.

Instead of indulging him on Sawyer, I say, "My dad said you dropped his class."

I'm met with silence.

When I turn to him, I shake my head. "I heard you broke things off with Dixie too. Don't get me started on your teammates, who told me you don't go to practice anymore. Who are you, dude? You were doing so well in the fall. You had things to look forward to. What happened that made you fall off the ladder so fucking hard?"

Dawson straightens. "I didn't—"

"All you wanted was to do was play ball when you enrolled here," I cut him off, not willing to hear more lies. "That's what you worked for. Now, you don't show up to class, you don't put in a fraction of effort to keep your grades up, and you disappear for hours on end doing God only knows what. What *do* you have left here? Because it seems like you pushed away everybody and everything that matters to you for something I don't understand."

He starts to answer before he presses his lips together and looks down. Evasion is a sure sign of guilt, which tells me what I need to know.

I stand, collecting my sketchbook and backpack. "I don't know what to say to you anymore. We've been down this road before, but I sure as hell hope that it doesn't take you as long to get the help you need since you won't accept it from me. Not everybody gets a second chance at life. Why waste it?"

Dawson's expression becomes pleading. "Don't be like that." He stands. "I just…" Stopping himself, he kicks the ground with the top of his sneaker.

"You what?" I press impatiently.

"Dixie deserved better," he says to the ground. "Everybody knew that. I couldn't be the person she needed."

He won't find me arguing, but I respect that he finally acknowledged it.

His hand reaches behind him, grasping his neck and squeezing. "I do need help."

The admission has me standing a little taller, hope scratching the surface. "Then let's go. I'll take you wherever you need to go. Back to the clinic. To see your counselor—"

"No. Not…" His hands twitch. "I need to borrow some money."

I blink slowly, repeating those words in my head to make sure I heard him right.

"Unbelievable," I mumble under my breath.

"Banks, I—"

"Don't." I reach into my pocket and pull out the loose bills I stuffed in there after stopping at the café earlier. I don't even know how much money I throw at him, but I toss it all in his direction and watch it flutter to the ground. "You're not the only one who has problems, Dawson. But by all means, keep acting like you are. Hopefully you put that money to good use instead of giving it to Marco or his cronies."

Something black tucked into the elastic of his pants catches my eye when his shirt rises up as he tries catching the floating bills. I reach for it, but Dawson is quick to pull his shirt down and cover it.

"Is that a *fucking gun*?" I hiss, stepping toward him and looking around us. "Where the hell did you get that?"

He tugs at his shirt again, scanning the area nervously. "I needed it."

What twenty-one-year-old needs a gun? "I cannot believe you right now. Do you see yourself? You're a goddamn mess, Dawson. I don't know who you are anymore, but it sure as shit isn't my friend. If you've gotten yourself in so deep you need a—" I can't let myself say it again, so I dip my gaze down briefly. "Then you need help. Real help. This is the last time I'm offering. Come with me and I'll drop you off somewhere. But this isn't healthy."

His hand goes to where the deadly accessory is tucked away, not saying a word.

No explanation.

No admission.

"It's for protection" is all he gives me.

Protection.

There are other options.

People to talk to.

The goddamn cops, for one.

Maybe that's the moment I realize he's too far gone for help. So I throw my hands up. "I don't want any part of this. None."

I hear him call out after me, but I don't stop until I'm unlocking my truck and climbing in.

Once the door is shut behind me, I slam my hands against the steering wheel in frustration, the anger boiling over. "Fuck," I yell, hitting the top again.

People pass by, some clearly disturbed by my outburst, some completely ignoring me. I'd normally be embarrassed, but I'm too emotionally drained to care about what a lunatic I must look like.

Leaning back in my seat, I peel off my glasses and pinch

the bridge of my nose. A tension headache is forming in my temples, which means I can forget about doing any more homework.

Maybe a forced break is what I need.

So I make my way back to my apartment in silence, gripping the wheel with one hand and holding my forehead with the other.

As soon as I get upstairs and pull my keys out to unlock my door, the one across the hall opens.

All I say is "Not now, Sawyer."

She pauses, and from the corner of my eye, I see her frown. It only makes me feel a little bad when I hear her quiet "Okay."

Pausing halfway through my door, I sigh. "I have a headache and need to lie down. I'll talk to you later."

I don't wait for her to reply before shutting the door behind me. I only catch a flash of her confused expression before hearing the door click closed.

My phone goes off.

Dawson.

I ignore it.

A few minutes later, it goes off again.

Dawson.

I ditch it in the living room, hearing it go off once more before shutting myself in my bedroom to ignore whatever else he wants from me.

The last time he needed me, I put my life on hold for him and he promised he'd never go to that place again. I was dumb enough to believe him then, but I'm smarter now.

Still, the nagging pit in my stomach remains.

It's after dark when a timid knock comes at my door, making me pause from searching the refrigerator for something to eat.

I have a feeling I know who it is before I even open the door, so I'm not surprised when I see my five-foot-three neighbor standing there with her arms full.

"What's all this?" I ask in confusion.

She passes me a cup first. "Caffeine helps when I get headaches," she tells me, shifting on her bare feet covered only in knee-high socks.

I'm assuming her family left because she's changed into a pair of leggings and a T-shirt that has some cartoon character I've never seen before on it. "You brought me coffee?"

Sawyer nods. "And dinner if you haven't eaten. It's not much, but I googled some easy recipes using the ingredients my parents bought me."

I stand aside, gesturing for her to come in. I watch as she dumps the food onto the kitchen counter and looks around. She's never spent time here before because I always find my way across the hall.

"You didn't have to bring me anything," I say.

She shrugs, moving a strand of hair behind her ear. "You cooked for me when I was sick" is her simple reply.

I watch everything she does as she searches each cupboard and cabinet until she finds what she needs. Eventually I walk over and lean down until my elbows are resting on the edge of the counter farthest away from her.

Her hair looks different today. Brighter. Softer maybe. I try picturing her with red hair like her mother's, but the image is foggy at best. When she catches me staring, her cheeks tint the same color as her shirt.

"What?" she asks, splitting the chicken and rice she prepared onto two plates.

Wetting my lips, I shake my head. "Nothing."

Ask her, the voice inside me prods.

Her focus goes back down to the dinner in front of her. "I'm sorry if my mom made you uncomfortable earlier. She gets excited about me making...friends."

I find it hard to believe she didn't have any before. "You weren't popular in school?"

Rubbing her lips together as she forks a pile of green beans onto the plate, she clears her throat. "No," she murmurs. "I had a lot going on that people couldn't exactly relate to."

"I'm sorry." I know how that feels. My father made it difficult to bring people over. Dawson was the exception, but he was also clueless. Anybody else would have asked questions. "Is your family still here?"

Sawyer puts the first plate into the microwave and heats it up. "They went back to the hotel for the night. Mom and Bentley are leaving in the afternoon."

We're quiet.

She looks around, noticing the picture hanging on the wall above the small table I picked up at a thrift shop. Walking over to it, she runs her hands along the edge of the cheap frame.

"That's at the Botanic Gardens," I tell her of the photograph. It's a landscape picture I took with my phone right as the sun began to set. The lowering rays somehow illuminated the blooming myrtles I'd taken the image between.

Sawyer leans closer and points to something in the background. "Is that a little waterfall and footbridge?"

The microwave beeps, but we both ignore it. I step beside her. "It is. The waterfall is man-made—purely for decoration. A lot of local teenagers go there to take pictures on prom night because of the aesthetic."

Something shadows her face, her shoulders slumping slightly. "It's beautiful," she tells me, turning with only a sad smile in my direction as she redirects her attention to the food.

"I can take you there," I offer. "If you'd like."

She passes me a plate and a fork, her lips wavering at the corners. "I've never been, so that'd be nice."

"About what your mom said—"

Before I can ask the question taunting me, my phone goes off for the millionth time. When I woke up from my short-lived nap, Dawson had called a total of eight times and left me ten different texts, which I ignored. Then Dad called me to let me know Dawson had shown up at the house.

He wasn't happy.

Sighing when I see my father's name, I decide to answer, knowing that ignoring him again won't lead anywhere good. "Is he still there?" I ask in greeting.

"I asked you to come here and get him three and a half hours ago," my father informs me.

Technically, he asked my voicemail. "I wasn't feeling well, Dad. I told him earlier that he had to figure his shit out. I never told him to go there and bother you."

"You owe me a hundred dollars to pay me back for the money I gave him," he tells me.

I shift away from Sawyer's curious gaze, lowering my voice. "You gave him money?"

The nerve of this motherfuc—"What was I supposed to do? My son was being selfish, so I had to step in like I always do."

A cool laugh bubbles past my lips. "Like you always do?" I repeat in dry amusement. "That's classic. Who was the one cleaning up *your* messes growing up after Mom left? Who made sure you were okay whenever you'd have one of your stints?"

His voice lowers. "Paxton—"

"You can call me selfish all you want," I cut him off, walking to the other side of the room and pacing in front of the television. "But maybe look at yourself in the mirror and figure out where I got it from. They say kids' first role models are their parents. Guess that's unfortunate for me."

I hang up before he can start in on me like I can sense he's about to. Turning my phone off, I throw it onto the couch with more force than necessary. It bounces off and lands on the floor, the crack in the screen protector visible from here.

Raking my hands through my hair, I give my back to the girl standing silently in my kitchen.

After a few minutes, I feel a hand on my shoulder. "Banks?" she whispers.

Taking a deep breath, I turn around.

She's staring up at me. "I'm sorry."

It isn't her who should be saying those words to me. "He thinks I'm selfish." An angry laugh escapes me as I look down at her. "He thinks *I'm* selfish."

"You're not," she reassures, eyes sympathetic.

I grind my teeth. "Everybody else gets to do whatever they want without thinking of how it impacts the people around them," I say, jaw ticking at everything I've endured trying to be a good friend—the better person.

Dawson. Dad. How many times do I have to put other people before myself? Consider their feelings when they can't even consider mine?

I'm fucking *done*.

Sawyer steps forward, a frown curling her mouth. "Banks—"

I close the little distance between us, grab ahold of her face, and say, "It's my turn to be selfish for once."

The kiss is startling. Demanding. Angry. Wanting. A list of things that Sawyer's surprised gasp only feeds as I taste her.

At first, she's frozen, but it doesn't take her long to melt into me. I tease her tongue and nip her bottom lip, drawing out a noise from her that hardens me as I roll my hips involuntarily forward to press against her.

In that moment, when everything inside of me is cold, I need her to be the warmth that thaws the thick ice layered around my heart.

I pull back far enough to say, "If you don't want this, if you changed your mind about what you want, now is the time to tell me. Because I'm not sure I want to stop after that."

I wait. One second. Two. Five seconds go by.

When she doesn't say anything, my eyes flare with anticipation. The same moment my lips crash against hers, I grab her by her hips and lift her up. She wraps her arms around my neck for support, her legs doing the same around my waist as I walk her backward until her back meets the wall. Pressing myself harder into her front, I groan when a muffled cry comes from deep in her throat.

My body needs release. Needs a distraction. It needs *Sawyer*. This Sawyer. The Sawyer from my past. I need them both.

And she kisses me back, matching every little movement, albeit far more hesitantly. I'm getting lost in the moment, burying my fingers into her hair and pulling her head back when she locks up.

"N–Not the hair," she says, breaking the kiss and pushing my hand away from the silky locks.

I release it instantly, pressing a warm kiss to the exposed column of her throat and offering her a quiet, "Sorry."

She exhales a shaky breath. "Don't be. I...it's..."

I spin us around until she's draped across the couch. There are a million things I want to do to the girl whose hair is spread out around her, but I'm not sure I have the patience for it all.

"You don't need to explain," I promise, taking in her body. I'll never understand the pull that I've felt toward her since the day she opened the door and accused me of taking her food. I chalked it up to horniness at first, but it never went away. It's like a string: pulling, pulling, pulling until it's so tight it's threatening to break.

"You're beautiful," I murmur, more to myself than her. The color that warms her cheeks makes me grin as I kneel down beside her, trailing my palms up her legs and watching her lips part with a shaky exhale from the slow, subtle touches.

Stopping when my hands meet her thighs, I lean forward and press a kiss to the inside of her knee. Then another, higher. Then another farther up until my fingers hook into the waist of her leggings and pull them down.

When I see the thin material covering her underneath, I trail my lips along the same path as the cotton I'm peeling off her until both her leggings and panties are discarded on the living room floor.

Selfish. That's what I plan on being right now.

Because seeing her exposed to me this way with vulnerability shining in her eyes makes me realize one thing.

Sawyer trusts me.

And having that control nearly makes me forget the reasons I was angry to begin with.

I try forgetting about Dawson and any interest he had in the girl who's writhing under my touch. I try pushing away the trouble he's in and the more than likely illegal firearm he has on top of God knows how much money he's taken from people. And I sure as hell don't want a single thought of my father's cruel words to enter my brain as my mouth acquaints itself with the warmest part of her.

In this moment, I do more than exist in a world where I try my best to keep to myself without intervening in things I can't change. Because I want to take charge of this moment; I want to soak in every second. Every kiss, suck, and nip that draws noises from my neighbor drowns out the demons poking my conscience, reminding me that I'm here. That she's here.

Nothing besides us matters.

She claws at my shirt, so I take it off.

Her shirt follows.

There's a moment of hesitation before she unclasps her bra behind her, leaving her completely bare in front of me.

I stare, mesmerized.

"What's this?" I ask, reaching out to brush what looks like a bump with a scar just under her collarbone.

She stops me, her fingers quickly wrapping around my wrist before I make contact. "It's an old injury," she explains, squeezing me once. "I don't like people touching it."

I nod in understanding, bringing her hand to my mouth and kissing the back of it. "You really are beautiful. Do you know that?"

My eyes rake over every inch of skin until she squirms, her hands reaching out to undo the button of my jeans. They shake, and I wonder if she's nervous. I let her take her time, watching as she pops the button and slowly lowers the zipper before tugging on the waistband of the denim.

I'm painfully hard by the time she frees me, swallowing a moan when her soft palm wraps around me and gives an experimental stroke. "If you keep doing that, this is going to be over before it starts."

Her blush deepens as she withdraws her hand apologetically, but I capture it and put it back, squeezing our hands until another sound rumbles from my chest from the sensation we create.

Sawyer's eyes lock on the way I move our palms, helping her set a pace as she pumps me. When I twitch, pulsing in her hold, a spark grows in her eyes that does me in.

Suddenly, my mouth is on hers, earning me another startled gasp as I move her backward until she's splayed out beneath me. One of my knees knocks into hers, guiding her to spread her legs until I'm between them.

In the back of my mind, I hear that word.

Selfish.

Then I hear another.

Enabler.

They repeat, taunting, haunting, leaving me desperate to push them away. Maybe if I stopped focusing on them and paid attention to Sawyer instead, on the moment my conscience was taking from me, I would have known something was wrong. Could have tried harder to be the man that the soft, mysterious girl under me deserves.

Instead, she gets the shell of me that struggles to put myself back in the moment.

The version of me who enters her to feel and kisses her to distract and touches her so the demons can't touch me. I take no heed of her tight grip around my neck when I see the pleasure written across her face, and I lose myself in her warmth.

I see stars as I repeat the movement, feeling her around me, absorbing every sensation.

Again.

Again.

Again.

I kiss her throat, her jaw, her mouth, quieting the noises she makes every time I thrust forward, the subtle creak of the couch bringing me closer and closer to the brink.

I comfort her with soft murmurs, relax her with eased touches, stroke her with confidence as her muscles loosen and tighten around me all at once.

Her hands explore my back, shooting shock waves of familiarity down my spine. Every inch of skin she touches leaves a path of flames permanently scorched into my skin like a brand.

My heart races to a beat of a new drum that syncs with the heartbeat against me, and when I look down at the girl beneath me, something sparks inside my chest when we lock eyes.

I've definitely had moments when sex was a means to an end, an escape that I used to get in, get off, and get out. And despite how hard I tried fighting the demons off to let myself be here with her, I become consumed by them instead. They poke at me like a roaring in my blood that sends my heart racing as my body loses control entirely around her, in her. I bury my face in the crook of her neck as I stiffen and give her everything I have. Every tense moment, every argument, every raw emotion that was building and boiling over releases the moment I do, my demons going with them.

And for the first time in a long time, there's nothing but an overwhelming sense of calmness taking over.

She did that for me.

If there's one time since I was kid where I've felt at peace with someone, it's now, lying on her, kissing her, caressing her soft, dewy skin.

My forehead leans against the crook of her neck, my hand stroking her upper thigh still wrapped around me until I peel myself up and pull out. She flinches, her eyes glassy as they briefly meet mine before looking away.

When I take the condom off, I notice the smear of red on the latex. My eyes move to her thighs, where I see other streaks of blood.

She closes her legs, sitting up and using one of the couch pillows to cover herself. I stare at the blood, then her flushed cheeks, and the way she evades my eyes. "I...I've..."

"Why didn't you tell me?" I whisper. I wasn't as gentle as I could have been. There are red marks on her arms and thighs from my fingers that I pray don't bruise.

I was too consumed by my own problems to even realize I was hurting her all for that peace I chased.

Selfish.

Sawyer quickly collects her clothes. "Does it matter? I've only done it once before, and that barely counted."

She's embarrassed.

I put my hand on her shoulder as she haphazardly redresses. "Look at me."

She doesn't.

She pulls her shirt on, forgoing the bra.

"Sawyer," I say, standing without an ounce of shame that I'm still naked.

I move the hair she's using to block me away from her face. "There's nothing wrong with that. I just wish you would have told me. I wouldn't have been so rough with you. I would have..."

I would have done a lot more. Checked in more. Made sure she was okay. Shut out those voices better instead of letting them in. Anything.

Her eyes briefly lift to mine before they move back down to the floor. "It shouldn't matter."

But it does.

I find my boxer briefs and jeans and tug them on so she'll feel more comfortable and then stand in front of her and tilt her chin up. "Are you okay?"

Her throat bobs, but she nods.

Sighing, I pull her in for a hug, wrapping my arms around her and tugging her closer into my body so her hands are trapped between us. For a moment, she's tense. Then she releases a breath and relaxes into me, her palms moving to my hips and resting there.

Selfish.

The word echoes in my head, making my lips twitch. I push it away, as far away as I can, and focus on the girl in my arms. The one who probably feels how my heart is drumming wildly against her. How my fingers twitch as they rub her back. She does that to me, and she doesn't even know it.

My hand finds the underside of her jaw, stroking the skin underneath. I frown when I feel something hard under the pad of my thumb, moving her hair away to get a better look at the lump. "Did you get stung?"

She stiffens. "No. It's nothing."

"I have ice—"

"Banks," she says, putting her hand on mine and moving it away. "I promise it's nothing to worry about."

I find myself nodding, unsure whether I want to believe her. But I relent, not wanting to ruin the night. "You're an anomaly," I tell her, shaking my head.

"Why?"

"I don't think you realize how different you are than

most girls." I pull her into the kitchen, grabbing the plates she made for us.

When she takes hers, she stares at the food. "I know better than you think I do," she murmurs, toying with the chicken.

"That's not a bad thing," I reassure when I see the ghost of a frown lingering on her face.

It takes her a long moment to face me, as if she's lost in thought or misinterpreting the compliment. I've known a lot of women, dated quite a few of them, and none of them compared to the one standing in my kitchen.

She follows me into the living room after we finish eating, sitting on the couch that she looks differently at now. "I don't have to stay. I can go."

I'd be lying if I said I didn't usually part ways after hookups in the past, but the last place I want her to go is home, even if that's only feet away. I want her to stay. I want her to be around. To pester me to do my homework. To argue with me about good music and TV. Her friendship fills a void that Dawson never could and keeps me away from the problems I have to face when I step outside this space.

"You don't have to go either."

We stare at one another, her lip back between her teeth. Biting. Hesitant.

Scared.

Her question is soft-spoken, with caution in every sylla-ble. "Do you always ask the girls you sleep with to stay?"

"No."

Swallowing, she offers me a subtle nod. "I don't under-stand why you'd want me to then."

I answer the only way I can. "I'm not sure why either, Birdie."

There's no way I can describe my will for her to stick

around or the familiarity of her presence whenever she meets my eyes. I feel bad for taking over the moment we just shared and not being more present like she deserved. I want to be better than that—to give her the type of peace she gives me.

Her friendship and kindness offer me hope that I can be the man she deserves one day. Because she's still here giving me the chance to prove it.

"I'll never force you to stay, but I'm also not going to tell you to leave. I'd like the company. Today's been rough. And I wouldn't mind a..."

What do I call her that doesn't make what we did weird? I'm never in my head about this kind of shit.

"Friend?" she finishes for me.

I dip my chin. "If you're still willing to be."

She finds my hand, squeezing her fingers around mine. "I told you before that nothing has to change. That's what we said, wasn't it? What we agreed on?"

I wet my lips. "It is."

"Then we're friends." She lets go of my hand, draws her knees up to her chest, and hugs them close to herself.

Friends. I used to like the sound of that.

When did I stop?

We watch trash TV the rest of the night.

I go to the kitchen and pull out two packets of fruit snacks from my stash in the cupboard.

When I pass her one, she stares at it and says, "These have always been my favorite."

I swallow. "I know."

Her eyes meet mine.

Opening mine, I turn to the TV and quietly repeat, "I know, Birdie."

I can feel her burning gaze on mine.

I don't ask her about her mom.

Or her past.

I could, but it would ruin the moment.

And I wonder what would change if I knew for sure that this Sawyer was the same one from the past. I'd built her up in my head for years—the girl who saved me without realizing it. Who gave me peace without ever trying.

I don't want to change anything.

Eventually, she also turns back to the TV.

I stretch her legs out across my lap, absentmindedly stroking my thumb along her shin as we listen to the mindless show.

She falls asleep on the couch.

I carry her to my bed.

And instead of pushing my luck and curling up beside her like I want to, I close the door and crash in the living room.

Only then does Dawson slip back into my mind, and by the time I text him back when guilt crests for what I said, I hear nothing at all.

Chapter Twenty-Five

SAWYER

THE HALLWAY FLOOR CREAKS under the weight of my bare feet as I creep toward the kitchen. I can hear her crying again—Mom. Aunt Taylor's voice is quiet, trying to soothe her.

"You'll wake the kids up," my mom's sister says, pouring white wine into my mother's empty glass. "You've got to be strong for them. For Sawyer. It's the only way you'll all get through this, Michelle."

Even from here, I can see how red Mom's face is as she wipes it with a tissue. How long has she been crying for this time?

I frown, wanting to make my appearance known, but my feet stick to the floor like they're weighed down.

"I should have seen the signs," Mom tells her sister, voice raw as she grabs the glass and plays with the stem. "There were so many."

"You couldn't have known it would be this," Aunt Taylor counters, putting her hand on my mother's free one.

The doctors said the same thing. Kids get sick all the time. Nobody would have assumed it was cancer. No number of bruises or amount of fatigue could have led to someone thinking I had more *than a stubborn cold and love for adventure. I told her that. Dad did too.*

Mom stares at her drink. She loves wine, but she's barely touched it. Maybe she's sick too. "I have a horrible feeling in my stomach."

My ears start ringing.

Mom turns her head, looking directly at me.

Wait. I don't remember this part.

She says, "I have a horrible feeling."

Is she talking to me?

I try speaking, but it feels like there's something on my mouth preventing me from saying a word. Tape. Glue. A restraint.

I try saying her name, but nothing comes out.

She starts crying again, a suffocating feeling crushing my chest as I watch her. "I have a horrible feeling," she repeats, her piercing focus cutting holes into me.

I attempt to walk into the room and tell her I'll be okay, but I can't move. I'm frozen, forced to watch her break down. I try to move my arms, my mouth, anything.

Mom straightens while looking straight at me—through me, knocking into the wineglass.

It falls, shattering on the ground into pieces.

I jerk up, nearly toppling off the couch that I must have fallen asleep on.

A piece of paper is stuck to my face with drool pooling from the nap I accidentally took. Peeling the paper off, I use the back of my hand to wipe my face off and take a deep breath, only to see a smear of red.

"Not again," I whisper, rushing to the sink in time for droplets to fall into the basin.

Drip. Drip. Drip.

Grabbing paper towels, I tilt my head back and try

stopping it before it gets out of hand, my mind still on the dream that my heart aches from.

I have a horrible feeling.

"It was a dream," I tell myself, eyes flicking to the broken water glass on the floor. I must have knocked it down trying to get to the dream version of my mother.

But it wasn't just a dream.

It was fragments of memories taunting me. How many times did I sneak downstairs and hear Mom crying? Or Aunt Taylor trying to reassure her that it would be okay? Too many to count.

I never said a word.

Never told her I would be fine.

I simply listened, tearing up in the hallway, knowing *I* was the one responsible for how she felt. Before then, I'd never seen my mother cry once. She was always strong. Always the glue that held us all together.

Without Dad, she had no choice but to be. He was supportive from a thousand miles away, but that could only go so far with two kids in New York. Especially when one of them was sick.

Closing my eyes, I swipe at the dampness pooling under the lids.

After giving myself some time to calm down and clean up once the nosebleed stops, I glance at the last thing I worked on before drifting off.

The short story I started in my notebook is smudged, the ink probably smeared on my face. I run my hand over the first line and think about what Professor Grey told me about using personal experience to guide me.

I open my laptop and start a new document, titling it "Mama's Eyes."

I have a horrible feeling.

My stomach clenches at those haunting words, lingering for hours as my fingers dance along the keyboard. I write from the heart, feeling everything on the screen.

I have a horrible feeling.

"I'm sorry, Mom," I whisper aloud, staring at the end of the story before closing my laptop.

I look back down at the broken glass.

Swallowing the emotion cramming into my throat, I sweep up the mess and dump it into the trash can.

When I crawl into bed, I hug my knees to my chest and pray that another dream doesn't come when I close my eyes.

Dixie frowns the second she sees me. "Are you sure you're okay?" she asks for the fifth time since we got to the dining hall. My appetite is limited, and even though the food smells delicious, nausea nips at my stomach too much to eat anything.

I've been waking up in the middle of the night for the past three days, feeling anxious and sick. I brushed it off the first time, started getting uneasy the second, and woke irritated at two in the morning the third time. Some dreams I remembered vividly; other nights I only remembered bolting upright in bed with my heart racing and ears ringing, sweat making my pajamas stick to my body.

"Tired is all," I promise her, sipping my water. I couldn't even stomach my coffee this morning because the first sip tasted metallic, causing my stomach to grumble in protest. "What were you saying?"

She plays with her fruit bowl. "There's a party happening

this weekend that I got invited to by a guy in my history class. He plays baseball. I guess that's not relevant." Is she nervous? "Er, anyway, he told me I should come. It's at his place. He lives with a few guys on the team."

I blink, realizing I've missed something vital. Feeling like a bad friend again for being out of touch, I ask, "What about Dawson?"

It's hard to miss the frown that curls her lips as she shrugs. "He's..." She stops herself, sighing and dropping her fork. Looking up at me, there's sadness in her eyes. "I told him I wouldn't say anything to anybody, but it's been bothering me."

Concern has me almost forgetting to feel sick. "What?"

She licks her lips. "He started acting stranger than usual. It started with the backpack at the parade and then got worse. Then he started asking me out more, but it seemed like I was way more into him than he was me, so I didn't understand why. I guess I kept agreeing because he seemed like he needed somebody, and I knew I could be good for him. Plus, I figured he'd stay out of trouble if we hung out a lot."

Her shoulders slump. Groaning, she pushes the food away from her. "The last time we went out, he took me to a nice restaurant I'd never been to before. We were talking about school, and he shut down when I asked about classes. So I changed the subject to basketball because I hadn't seen him at the last home game, and his mood got worse. He kept getting up to use the bathroom and got upset when I asked if he wanted to leave. Then, right before our entrees came out, two guys who looked way too old to be in college came up to our table and started talking to him. Dawson looked freaked out when they asked why he was avoiding them."

Oh no. "Did he say who they were?"

Dixie shakes her head. "One of them was covered in tattoos and kept touching his pocket. The other one was staring at me with a creepy grin on his face. When they left, Dawson told me we had to go. He didn't wait for the food to get wrapped or the check. I told him we needed to pay, but he was in a rush, so he all but dragged me out to the car. The whole ride back to campus was silent and awkward, and when he dropped me off, he said it was better if we didn't see each other anymore. He wouldn't even look me in the eyes when he told me. He seemed so sketched out by what happened."

Her bottom lip quivers, and I feel awful. I haven't asked about them because I wanted to distance myself from whatever was blossoming between them. After what happened at the party and what I told Dawson at his basketball game, it felt like the best thing I could do. Maybe I was wrong.

"I'm so sorry, Dixie. Are you all right?"

She shrugs limply. "I feel pathetic. I basically got broken up with by somebody I wasn't even really dating. And I...I liked him. Or the *idea* of him, anyway. I thought I could fix him. Or, at the very least, help him. I know Banks told me that people could only change if they wanted to, but it seemed like he was trying."

As much as I hate that she went through that, I know it's easier this way. "You're better off without him and his issues. In fact, I don't think he and Banks are talking right now either. Whoever those guys are, they're probably people you don't want to be around."

It's true, but I can tell she still hurts. Nothing I can say right now will make that go away. Only time can.

"I'm sorry I wasn't there for you." *I'm a terrible friend.*

"You should have called me when it happened. We could have gone somewhere. Gotten drunk and then posted bad things about him anonymously online."

She shrugs defeatedly, my sense of humor doing little to lighten the mood. "You were busy with your family, and it wasn't like we were exactly talking."

That's no excuse. Friends should be there for each other no matter the circumstances. I told her that.

Dixie rubs her arm. "Banks was there for me after it happened."

What?

"He found me wandering around town crying," she enlightens when she sees my face. Her cheeks turn red. "Not one of my finer moments, but I didn't want to be cooped up in my dorm room listening to everybody else have fun. He took me out for ice cream at his favorite spot. The one on the edge of town."

Banks was there, and I wasn't.

I'm grateful.

"That's nice of him," I offer, rubbing my arm. I didn't even know Banks liked ice cream, but I was glad he could help her when she obviously needed it.

"Don't be like me," she says. Brows pinching, I shake my head in confusion. She doesn't make me ask. "Don't hold back when you like someone because you're afraid. And don't hold on if you're too scared to let go."

Truth is, I'm terrified. But not for the reasons she probably assumes. Starting something isn't nearly as scary as when it ends, knowing you've hurt people along the way.

"It's not like that anyway," I tell her softly.

"Something happened," she accuses, eyes narrowing into suspicious slits.

The blush heats my cheeks before I can stop it, giving me away. When I woke up the morning after we slept together, I felt…good. Sore, but good. He made us break-fast, kissed me, and then pointed out the bruises on my arms from where he'd held me on the couch.

"I bruise easily," I admit, breaking off a piece of the Pop-Tart he gave me.

Since then, things have been…fine. Not complicated or awkward, but stagnant thanks to me and the funny feeling in my chest that tells me to be careful. It's not my gut waving the checkered flag but my heart.

Because I like him. As a friend. As a neighbor. As a cute girl likes a cute boy. Our first time wasn't exactly how I imagined it would be because I could tell he was in his head, but he still took care of me when it mattered. I know better than most that we all have demons, so I would never judge him for it.

It doesn't change how I feel. How *he* makes me feel. I like how he kisses me, how he touches me, how he pays special attention to the noises I make when he brings me to release with his fingers, and that one time with his mouth. I especially like what he does to me when our clothes are off and he takes control of the situation.

But Banks is the type of boy girls fall for.

And I can't afford that.

So I do my best to avoid it instead—that funny, tingly feeling.

When he tries coming over, I insist on going to his place so he doesn't see the mess of things that are hidden in my apartment. When he wants me to stay over, I worry my wig won't stay on and he'll see my real hair in all its horror in the middle of the night when restlessness from bad dreams becomes too much.

He pushes, I pull, and I can't even tell him why—can't explain that it isn't him.

Dixie is still waiting for an answer when I come back to reality. "Let's say I crossed a few other things off my list," I tell her sheepishly, nibbling on the inside of my cheek.

She smacks her palms on the table. "Oh my God, you *slept* with him!"

The group of girls sitting at a nearby table starts giggling.

I hide my face, sure that one of them is in the journalism class that I'm brutally failing. "Yes, but keep it down. It's not that big of a deal."

"You like him. It's a big deal."

"Tell me about the baseball player," I insist, hoping the topic change will get me out of the current conversation. "What's his name?"

Thankfully, Dixie gives me a break, her excitement switching to Miles, the pitcher for LSU's team. It's a welcome distraction from anything going on in my life, including the taunting dream I haven't been able to shake.

I have a horrible feeling.

By the end of lunch, I have plans Saturday night to meet Dixie's newest crush at a party that will hopefully be the turning point I need to shift my mood.

I'm excited about it until later that night, when Banks knocks on my door and sees me with another cloth pressed against my nose, stained with red.

He doesn't say a word.

Doesn't seem upset that our previous plans that involved far less clothing have changed.

He simply cleans me up like he did the first time, except his touches are softer, lasting longer, like the familiarity he has with me is stronger than before.

315

And my heart reacts.

It races. And pleads. And drums a sound I'm sure only he can hear.

And I *hate* it.

I hate that my body comes alive when he's near, how the hair on my arms stands up and my legs squeeze as if they remember how he feels between them.

I hate that he's nice to me. That he takes care of me when he doesn't need to. I hate that he's so close, always tempting me, always there without question.

And when I wake up the next day to a dehumidifier waiting outside my door, next to the boy with an armful of cooking ingredients, I hate him even more.

Even when he says, "It's old. I found it in my closet."

And especially when I go over to his unlocked apartment when he asks me to grab the pot he forgot and see the receipt for one dehumidifier crumpled on the counter.

"Dammit, Banks," I whisper, staring angrily at it with a fresh glaze of tears in my eyes. I swipe at my lashes and take a deep breath, staring at the ceiling. "Don't you dare make me love you."

I hide the receipt, dry my eyes, and pretend I never saw a thing when I return.

But my feelings remain the same.

Chapter Twenty-Six

BANKS

THERE'S ONLY ONE LIGHT on in my childhood home as I pull up to the curb, which means Dad is watching the nightly news in the living room like he always does. The question is, is he sober or not?

A heavy feeling weighs down my gut as I unlock the door using the spare key and push it open. "Dad?" I call out, smelling the smoke from his cigar.

I haven't heard from him in a while, and he didn't answer the phone when I called to check in on him so I wouldn't need to come here. As much as I didn't want to, I knew I needed to make sure everything was okay.

"Dad?" I say again, walking into the living room.

The old man is fast asleep in his recliner with a lit cigar in his hand burning a hole into the arm of the chair. When I see it spark, I jump into action.

That was my first mistake.

The second was not noticing the empty bottle of scotch on the coffee table. Or the empty twelve-pack in the kitchen. There's no food around—no dirty plates or take-out containers. Nothing to soak up the alcohol that must have caused him to pass out with a lit cigar in his hand.

I grab the cigar from him before it burns a bigger hole into the upholstery, and he jerks awake. And for a second time in less than six months, he swings at me. Except this time, his fist knocks me off balance until I fall backward into the coffee table and crack the wood and glass.

My ass and back take the worst of the blow, glass shattering around me until piercing pain stabs me through my clothes.

And the man above me doesn't stop there.

In his alcohol-induced rage, he fights like I'm an intruder trying to take away his vices, and I have no time to see the foot coming down before it connects with my rib cage.

Once.

Twice.

"Dad," I gasp, voice barely more than a desperate rasp from the insufferable pain as his boot swings at me a third time.

Blood spurts from my mouth as I try to breathe, but it feels like somebody is suffocating me—squeezing my lungs as I curl into the fetal position to try protecting myself.

"D-Dad," I gasp. "It's m-me."

He stops, blinking, foot midway to another strike before snapping out of it. When he looks down, his face drains of color. Then he falls to his knees, reaching for me.

I flinch as his hand nears my face.

He frowns, lowering it slowly to his side.

Frowns like he doesn't understand the terror in my eyes as I struggle for air.

I cough, blood splattering onto his face.

"Paxton," he whispers, still blinking like this is all some nightmare.

My head drops to the ground, eyes closing from the energy it takes to keep them open.

The pain is numbing.

So numbing.

I think I groan.

Maybe even black out for a second or two.

He doesn't apologize.

Doesn't offer to take me to the hospital.

He simply kneels there in pale disbelief, staring as I bleed out on the floor. Under his voice, so quiet I almost don't hear it over the thundering pain I'm too focused on, he whispers, "Please don't leave me like her."

That's when I know my father is a broken man. More than the shards of glass on the floor or the splintered wood underneath me. He's been fractured for a long time since Mom left, but each year split him apart further and further until the void became too big.

It consumed him.

Consumed us.

He says, "I swear I've changed."

But he hasn't.

His hands shake as they clean me up with washcloths and paper towels, blood soaking everything he uses.

I want him to stop.

To not touch me.

But I can't speak.

Pain silences me, takes me hostage inside of myself.

"Don't leave me," he repeats, almost as if he's talking to himself and not me.

I black out.

Cussing under my breath when I lift the garbage bag out of the can, I wince from the pain shooting out of my ribs. "Fuck," I growl, dropping the bag and scattering the contents everywhere.

I close my eyes as the empty beer bottles roll across the dirty floor, mixing with the food scraps and bloody paper towels.

It's been almost a week since the incident.

Nearly seven days of being trapped here, unable to move, needing help from the very man who's responsible for the bruises and swelling covering my body.

I hate it here. Hate that I've let it get this bad—that I told myself I couldn't leave the city because he needed me more than I needed my sanity.

Enabler.

I didn't answer my phone or go to class. I'm sure my father wouldn't have wanted me to draw attention by showing up looking like...this. Bruised. Beaten. Hunched over from the pressure in my torso.

Defeated.

Professors emailed me with what I've missed, classmates have sent me notes, and my neighbor has left me a few messages that I didn't have the heart to answer because it would mean explaining.

I can barely explain to myself why I put up with this.

How could I ever explain it to her?

To anybody?

Ever since I gave her the dehumidifier, she's shut down. The way she stared at it would have made it seem like I'd given her a diamond, not a machine. She barely talked that night, except to say goodbye at the door when she walked me to it. Dismissed. That's what I felt.

And maybe I told myself that was the exact reason I didn't need to try harder to reach out or respond.

Carefully kneeling down, I break myself from the pitiful thoughts and begin collecting all the garbage that's been piling up at my father's house. The only good thing about the injuries is that he plays nice. For a while. He hasn't hounded me about school or touched a sip of alcohol. I haven't even seen him light a cigar since he took the one that burned a hole into one of my favorite shirts after it fell when I went down.

A hand comes down on my shoulder, locking my body up. "Let me," Dad says quietly.

I didn't even hear him come in.

"I've got it," I murmur, shaking off his touch and cringing at the movement.

He doesn't stop picking up the trash, his hand pausing over a beer bottle with a crack in it. After a moment, he tosses it into the bag and then does the same with the next one. Then the third. His posture stiffens and his frown settles deeper, as if he actually acknowledges the problem staring him dead in the face.

Not that it matters. He's seen it for years.

Let it fester. Grow.

He made it what it is.

"I spoke to Laramie today," he says, clearing his throat once the floor is cleaned. He takes the bag from me and ties it up. "He said he could give you an extension on your assignment if you need it. He hopes you feel better soon. I told him you got the flu."

The flu.

Of course.

"I don't need one."

I stand, feeling so much smaller next to him even though I've got a few inches on his five-feet-eleven height.

"Son…" He won't meet my eyes, but he stares at the garbage hanging from his hand.

I wait silently.

He clears his throat. "Your mother called this morning. She said she hasn't heard back from you about if you're visiting her this summer. You should call her. Let her know you're okay."

Let her know you're okay.

Am I though?

Rubbing my lips together, I nod. No words. No promise that I'll do exactly that.

He goes to the door to take the garbage out to the bin, stopping halfway out. "And don't…don't worry about the money you owe me for your friend. I'm not worried about it right now."

Closing the door behind him, all I can do is stare at the wood.

He's not worried about the money he thinks I owe him for Dawson? He thinks I *owe* him?

I stand in the middle of the room.

And I laugh.

Coldly.

Bitterly.

With exhaustion.

It fucking hurts. With each breath I try to draw, my ribs ache. Yet I can't stop myself. I laugh until tears form in their ducts.

He beat me.

Literally kicked me while I was down.

And he thinks I owe him.

I'm glad he doesn't come back to see me in the middle of an obvious breakdown because God only knows what he'd do. Would the nice streak end? Would he raise his hand? I don't know.

And I don't care.

God, I don't care at all.

I grab my truck keys and head to the door, walking, or more like limping, right past him to where I'm parked by the curb.

"Where are you going?" he calls after me.

I don't answer him as I pull open the door and climb in, flinching at the way my ribs bend on the way up. Dad starts walking toward me, but I start the engine and drive away before he can say another word.

My mother used to tell me to never come to a woman's house empty-handed, so I stop by two different gas stations until I find Sawyer's favorite flavor of Pop-Tarts.

As I'm leaving the store, I see Dawson get out of the passenger seat of a beat-up vehicle that some guy smoking a blunt is driving.

He stops when he sees me, his eyes bloodshot and his body reeking of pot.

I stand there silently, one hand gripping the edge of my truck door as he studies the bruises covering half of my face and disappearing into my clothing.

His eyes widen. "What hap—"

"Gable," the man behind the wheel calls out impatiently. "We don't have all day."

Dawson's eye twitches.

I don't say anything as I take him in.

Every bone is hollowed out, covered in skin that looks so frail and thin. His eyelid tremors. He's fidgety.

He rubs his nose. "I gotta go" is all he says, walking around me and into the store.

He doesn't bother asking if I'm okay.

I make eye contact with the man behind the wheel of the piece-of-shit SUV parked a few feet away.

He asks, "You got a fucking problem?"

Yeah. "I've got a lot of them," I say honestly.

He blows out a plume of smoke, grinning. "I can see that by the look on your face. Keep staring and I'll add another bruise to it."

My fingers clench the Pop-Tart tighter.

I could go inside and talk to Dawson.

But I know what he'd say.

I don't need your help.

"Run along now," his new friend encourages.

I look over my shoulder at the gas station before sighing. There's no point wasting my energy when I can barely function as is.

Climbing into my truck, I suck in a breath, my ribs getting pinched as I position myself behind the steering wheel.

Dawson made his choice.

This is me making mine.

Ten minutes later, I'm hobbling up to the door across the hall from mine. Right before I knock, I hear a fit of giggles coming from the other side. Caution stirs in the pit of my stomach that has nothing to do with the injuries I sustained.

When I finally rap my knuckles against the wood, I wince and step back, holding my breath as the lock turns.

Two soft faces greet me, both quickly shadowing with shock.

"Oh my God," Sawyer whispers, eyes raking down the front of me. From my swollen face to my hunched posture, she takes me in while Dixie stands behind her looking just as horrified.

Quickly, my neighbor takes the things from my hand and puts them on the counter. "Get in here. Do you need ice? Hold on."

She doesn't give me a chance to talk before I'm being tugged inside, flinching at the jerky movements as I'm led to the couch and sat down. Dixie closes the door while my neighbor-turned-nurse gets a washcloth from the kitchen and an ice pack from the freezer.

Dixie stands by the door, still gaping at my face.

I offer her a half-assed smile even though it hurts. "I'm okay," I tell her.

Neither of the girls believe that, not that I blame them. I could barely look at myself in the mirror the day after the misunderstanding. The bruises have gotten darker, the cut on my cheek looking worse as it's started healing. God forbid they see the discoloration on my side. They'd have nightmares.

Dixie swallows. "I think…" Her eyes go to Sawyer before she backs toward the door, unable to glance in my direction. "I'll let you two talk. I hope you feel better."

I'm about to tell her she can stay when she makes a swift escape.

Sawyer appears in front of me, the cloth wrapped around the ice pack that she carefully presses against my face. "What happened to you?"

This isn't why I came here, so I take the ice pack and lower it. "I came to apologize for ghosting you, not to make you take care of me."

She crosses her legs under her. "I should have known something was up, but I never thought..." Her tongue slowly drags across her bottom lip as she studies me, sadness masking her face. "Did Dawson do this?"

Dawson? We may have gotten into it that one time, but it's the first time we ever fought. I don't anticipate him doing it again. "No. He's avoiding me right now.

"Dixie said you helped her when he ended things. Thank you for being a friend to her when I wasn't."

"I barely did anything."

She shrugs. "It meant something to her."

I know what a handful Dawson can be, and Dixie seems sweet. Maybe too sweet to be the person my friend needs right now, as much as I wish she could be. But nobody should have that much responsibility on their shoulders.

I'd know.

Sawyer nervously takes my hand, tracing along one of my fingers. "If it wasn't Dawson, then who?"

She won't let this go. If I were in her shoes, I'd probably be the same way. Hell, when I first saw her with a bloody nose, I was ready to go after the person responsible without knowing her well at all.

But the truth is too damning.

She must know I'm trying to find an out when her fingers squeeze mine, pulling my attention to her wide blue eyes. "Please?"

That fucking word...

Nostrils flaring, I look down at our hands. Her touch is so light I almost don't feel it at all despite the warmth that soaks into my skin. It's calming, making me forget about the pain plaguing my body. Momentarily.

"Some things are too heavy to burden people with, Birdie. Because once you know..." I let my voice fade, shifting and sending pain shooting through my sides until it's hard sucking in the oxygen my lungs desperately need.

"You can't unknow," she finishes, as if she understands all too well. Her touch on me lightens, but I keep ahold of her, afraid that she'll let go. I need her to keep me grounded right now, not to pull away.

Her eyes go to our hands before they close.

"It was an accident," I tell her, hoping it's enough to placate her curiosity.

"What kind of accident leads to *this*?"

My free hand clenches tightly against my side where she can't see it. I'm careful when I lean back until I'm flush against the cushions. Blowing out a breath, I refrain from making a face. She's already worried. If she knew what happened...how bad it really is...

All I can manage to say is "He didn't mean it. Life happens sometimes."

Even with my eyes closed, I can feel her watching me intently. "Who? If it's not Dawson, then who could be responsible for this?"

"Let it go, Birdie. Please."

Her throat bobs as she studies me, her fingers reaching up to touch where my lip was split months ago. Her fingertip stills there, causing a shiver to creep up my spine. Then it moves to the eye that was discolored from my best friend and is now colored again from somebody different. Swollen. Red. Sore.

When she lets go, it's to tug the collar of her shirt down

327

to reveal the scar under her collarbone that I asked about before. "The skeletons I have in my closet have to do with this. It wasn't an accident. It wasn't anything I could control. But that doesn't mean I deserved it. I've held onto the burden of this for a long time, Banks. That weighs on a person. Drowns them. I'm here because I'm tired of swimming. I'm tired of fighting for life. I simply want to *live* it."

I stare at the bump silently, taken aback that she would share that with me. She's been close-lipped about a lot in her life. Some questions go unanswered, avoided, and evaded like a politician. Trained. Like she's used to doing it.

We're alike in that way—always pushing people from the truth when they get too close to it. Scared of what they'll do when they find out.

"We fight sometimes," I tell her, not meeting her eyes. I focus on some random object in the kitchen. "It's worse when he drinks. He's gotten...bad over the years. This is the worst it's—" I cringe when I move, sucking in a deep breath at the pain coursing through me. "This is the worst it's gotten."

She watches me; I can tell by the burning sensation on the side of my face that doesn't go away. It only grows. Becomes more intense as she soaks that in. Never naming. Never fully saying what's between us.

Gently, so gently, her palm cups my jawline, her thumb stroking my bottom lip. "You got into an argument with your father on the phone once. About Dawson. He seemed... mad."

All I can do is blink, hoping she doesn't connect the dots. But my Birdie is too smart for her own good.

"You don't talk about him. Ever." There's pain in her voice, asking the silent question that she can't seem to

328

verbalize. "You get a faraway look on your face whenever he's brought up."

I try to answer, to put into words anything that could justify what's been done. But how can I? She'd never understand. I barely do.

The only thing I can think to say is "He's sick." Her crestfallen expression is hard to absorb, so I put my hand on top of the one she still has on my face. "I've been surrounded by sick people my whole life, always trying to help them. Cure them. Never able to make a difference no matter how hard I try. My father. Dawson..."

Sawyer's eyes dim, her hand twitching underneath mine. Still, no words come.

"I'm the enabler. Letting them get away with whatever they want, and it destroys them. Destroys me. But with you, it's different. *You're* different. You're the peace that I need. A semblance of normalcy I didn't know I could have."

Glassiness fills her blue eyes as she shudders out a sharp breath, like she's struggling to breathe. I can imagine what I'm saying is a lot to process. I never want to burden her, or anybody, with the past I've endured.

I lean into her touch, my grip on her tightening to ground me. "I'll forever be grateful for you, Sawyer."

"Banks..." she whispers, voice broken.

"I know, Birdie," I murmur, moving her hand to my mouth and pressing a kiss against the center of her palm.

"I need to tell you..." She shakes her head, lips parting but not saying another word. I wish I could read her mind, but I don't think I need to.

All I can do is make a promise to the girl who I feel like I've known my whole life. I could ask her, try fitting the pieces together and see if they're one of the same.

But I don't want to.

Because I need this Sawyer more than the one I held onto in the past.

"We'll figure it out," I tell her. A single tear trails down her cheek, and I swipe it away with my thumb. "Don't be sad for me. That's the last thing I want."

"What *do* you want then?" she finally asks, voice cracking from the emotion I put there.

Nobody has ever asked me that.

Neither of my parents.

Not Dawson.

What do you want?

I swallow, trying to push past the pain still thrumming through my body.

As much as I want to help my father, I know there's nothing I can do for him.

I want to escape.

Him. This place.

I want to get my degree and find a job that can appreciate my designs the way my father never could.

Maybe I want what Sawyer wants.

I want to *live*.

But that takes time.

Day by day.

Choice by choice.

"This," I finally say, pulling her close and biting back the pain that comes from another person's weight against my side. "This is what I want."

Her eyes peek up at me once, studying me, her lips tilting downward at what she sees, before she nods.

We spend the rest of the night curled into each other on the couch, silence blanketing us. I endure the pain as she falls asleep, the air thick with the truth that I can tell she hasn't swallowed fully yet.

Putting an arm around her, I settle in as best as I can until sleep finds me too.

It's dreamless.

When I wake up on the couch, she's not there.

Chapter Twenty-Seven

SAWYER

DRAWING MY KNEES UP to my chest in the dewy grass I've been sitting in for two hours, I wrap my arms around my legs and let the gaping hole in my chest take over. I don't know which park I wandered to or how long it took to get here, but the sun was in full force by the time I found a shady spot under a tree off the walking trail with few to no people around.

The entire time, I can only think of one thing.

He says I'm his peace.

But he has no idea how wrong he is.

I'll be his devastation.

Swallowing, I suddenly feel hatred rise from the deepest pits of my stomach. When I came here, it was for me. To find happiness. To find freedom. To find my *own* peace.

My bridge.

Myself.

I never wanted to drag anybody else into the hurricane of chaos that I'm in the center of. All because of a list. All to feel like I'd accomplished something before…

Tears well at the backs of my eyes, burning them until hotness sweeps over my skin. "I'm sorry," I whisper aloud, not sure who it is I'm talking to.

In this moment, I wish my mother were here.

I wish I'd never left New York.

I wish I'd never needed to come on this journey to begin with.

Those hot tears spring from my eyes, and I grab my phone, hands shaking as I pull up my contacts.

Sniffling, I stare at my father's name and think about Banks and his heartbreaking admission. I've been so lucky to have such amazing parents, but not everybody is as lucky.

The people who are most deserving of happiness in life seem to be the ones who suffer the most trying to obtain it.

My father picks up on the first ring. "What's wrong, Sawyer? Do you need something? Are you okay?"

For a moment, my words get stuck in my throat, choking me. Lip quivering, I suck in a harsh breath and force out, "N–No. I need you. And I d–don't know where I am."

I hear his keys in the background. "Make sure your location is on and I'll come to you. Stay right where you are."

He's here in fifteen minutes, pulling me into his arms as soon as he sees me tucked against the tree like a little girl separated from her family.

And in the moment, I am.

I feel lost.

And hopeless.

And empty.

"It's not fair," I cry into his shirt, soaking the button-up that he'll have to change.

He doesn't need to ask what. Life. Life isn't fair. *This*

isn't. The pain. The circumstances. It all weighs on me little by little, building until the crushing weight caves in.

"I know, baby girl. I know."

"All I wanted was to be happy."

He wipes my face, his own eyes growing glassy as he watches the walls I built come crumbling down around me. "Tell me about it."

So I do.

I tell him everything because I know he would never judge me. Every detail I've withheld from the people I've grown attached to. Every relationship that has developed since January. Every secret I've held onto for my own benefit, finally releasing some of the tension coiled around my heart. I tell him about what a bad friend I am to Dixie and how much I like Banks even though I don't know his first name. I tell him about the classes I'm barely passing and how itchy my wigs are and how tired I am all the time.

It all comes out as if there's nothing holding it back. Every tiny inconvenience bubbles past my quivering lips, begging to be heard after months of suppression.

And when it's all out in the open in the quiet of his car, my father wraps me up in the throw blanket he brought me and pulls me into his side. "I wish there was something I could do to make this better for you. I would trade places in a heartbeat if it were allowed. Life will never be easy, no matter who you are or what you're going through. But you know what? You've always wanted to be like everybody else. The girl with friends and boy problems, even if the latter kills me a little inside. So I'd say you're finally doing it, kiddo."

I blink up at him, his image blurry as I wrap the blanket tighter around me. "It hurts this bad?"

He pecks the top of my head. "Sometimes." His voice is raw, raspy as though he's trying his hardest to fight his own tears. "I suppose that's how you know you're truly living. When you find things that you love, it's not always easy letting them go because they become a part of you. Your mother and I, all of us, have wanted nothing more than for you to experience that."

If I knew this is what it felt like, I wouldn't have wished for it at all. "What do I do, Dad?"

He strokes my arm, the friction keeping me warm against him. "You need to be honest. Not only with your friends, but with yourself."

Be honest.

Such simple advice, but it's not simple at all.

"They're going to hate me."

"No, they won't. Nobody ever could."

Another set of tears begins flowing, but these are silent. It's only when my father can feel them against his shirt that he tries comforting me. "It's going to be okay, Sawyer." His arm tightens around me as he loosens a sigh. "It's going to be fine."

I'm not entirely sure who he's talking to.

Himself or me.

And when he drives me home after buying me something to eat, I feel ten times worse that Banks doesn't have a father as good as mine.

When the elevator doors slide open to the third floor of Julian T. White Hall, I stand taller and take a deep breath. My confidence has wavered since I made the decision to come here after a sleepless night once my father left, but it's not going to stop me from coming here to say what I need to.

After giving up on sleep at almost four in the morning, I did some research on the college faculty website and found the office belonging to one Terry Banks. I debated my options, weighing them carefully because I didn't want to make matters worse for the boy across the hall, who dropped off his usual treat for me in front of my door before his first class of the day.

I couldn't face him knowing what I was going to do because I had a feeling he'd talk me out of it. Maybe for good reason, but I'd like to think reason was out the door the second I read between the lines after seeing what his father had done to him.

Life is never easy, no matter who you are.

Banks proved that I'm not the only one with problems that are hard. We've both been dealt a shitty hand in life. But his could be fixed.

Nerves bubble under my skin as I approach the open door at the end of the hall, glancing at the piece of paper I wrote his information down on this morning.

Before I knock, I take in the middle-aged man who looks harmless. Graying hair with speckles of the same dark brown Banks has. Clean-shaven. Glasses sitting on a fair-skinned face as he reads over something on the computer. When I make my presence known, I'm struck by the familiarity in his facial features when he looks up at me.

Banks looks just like him.

Their eyes are the same color brown, yet this man's seem deeper, darker. Like there is a case of secrets hidden beneath the surface. A madness masked by false professionalism. An abyss that seems so...cold.

"Are you Professor Banks?" I ask, refraining from fidgeting as badly as I want to at his doorway. If I show my discomfort, he'll feed off it. People like him always do.

He leans back. "I am. Can I help you with something?"

His voice is lower than Banks's is, aged with experience and something that scrapes against my soul like nails on a chalkboard.

Swallowing, I force a smile. "I'm friends with your son. We're neighbors, actually."

Banks's father sits silently behind his desk, a stoic expression making it hard to get a read on him. "Is there a point to this visit, Miss…?"

"Sawyer. Sawyer Hawkins."

If my name has come up before, it doesn't register on his face. He leans forward, "Well, Miss Hawkins, this time of day is reserved for office hours with my students should they need me. Unless you plan on signing up for one of my future classes, I ask that you make this visit brief."

Maybe if he was even the slightest bit nice, I'd consider being cordial. But screw that. Banks is my friend. More than that, if I'm truly being honest with myself, if I could let him be.

If his father is willing to talk to a stranger like this, God only knows what his son has had to endure.

"Your son is one of the kindest people I know," I start, walking into his office. "Which I'm assuming must come from his mother because I'd hardly say his manners are from your influence."

Professor Banks sits straighter in his chair, his lips pressing into a firm line at the blatant insult that I throw at him unabashedly.

I ignore the way his eyes narrow as he peels his glasses off. I continue, "Nobody should have to endure the horrible things I've seen him go through, least of all from the people who are supposed to protect him."

The second realization dawns on him, Banks's father sets his glasses down onto the desk and tries condescending his way out of it. "I don't know what you're talking about, Ms. Hawkins, nor do I like the tone you're taking with me."

I cross my arms over my chest. "Well, I don't like having to clean your son's wounds when you're done with him, so I suppose we're both going to be leaving here unsatisfied."

For the first time since I walked in, the man in front of me pales.

"Nothing to say now?" I press, nostrils flaring with disgust as he stares at me. "I don't know what could possibly make you think hurting another person is okay, much less your son. My father would go to the ends of the earth for me. He would rather hurt himself a million times over than cause my brother or me any type of suffering. And if you knew what I've put him and my mother through, you'd know what wanting to take my place would entail. But he'd do it. If it were a choice, he would. And Banks..." My voice cracks from anger. From sadness. "Banks is miserable because he puts everybody first. Including you. And this is how you repay him?"

"Ms. Hawkins—"

"He could barely walk," I cut him off. I only saw what Banks wanted me to, but I could tell by how he was moving that he was hurt far worse than the eye could see. Standing straight was impossible. Every little movement caused him to flinch. Whatever was done to him went deeper than one angry strike. "Since I've known him, he's been covered in injuries that he refuses to talk about. But he still puts you first, even after everything."

The aging professor grips the edge of the desk, his

338

jaw ticking. "I would be very, *very* careful about what you say next, girl. These kinds of accusations are how people's reputations get ruined."

That's what he's worried about? His *reputation*? My heart hurts for the boy who cooks me dinner and cuddles me to sleep. Who is willing to give me casual and put up with the brick wall I built between us to prevent us from being more. How could somebody who receives so little love be capable of offering so much of it?

"You should be ashamed of yourself," I whisper, shaking my head slowly. "We all get one chance at life, and you've decided to be a miserable, abusive asshole. And you don't even care an ounce about what it's doing to your son."

Slowly, he stands, remaining behind his desk with his palms flat against the top. "I highly suggest you stop while you're ahead. There's a lot to lose for you as well. One day, that mouth is going to get you into trouble."

Suddenly, and maybe surprisingly, I start laughing in disbelief. It's maniacal, causing the man to look even angrier than before. But I can't stop. Can't help myself.

Swiping at a tear, I give him an empty, distant smile. "That's the thing, professor. I have nothing left to lose because life has already taken so much from me. Your son... He still has the world at his fingertips. It's not too late for him. Not like it is for me. If speaking up gets me into trouble, at least it'll have been worth it."

All he does is stare, not grasping the reason my chest deflates.

I'm not being completely honest. Banks is someone in my life I have to lose, and he doesn't even know it.

I loosely lift my shoulders, letting them drop heavily, and tell him the same thing my conscience has been saying to me. "If you can't love him the way he deserves, the best thing you can do is let him go."

Those words sink in, sinking, sinking, sinking until they land in the bottom of my heart.

Instead of sticking around to hear him cuss me out, blackmail me, or deny the obvious, I walk away with my head held high but my heart in the pit of my stomach with the realization of what I have to do.

I don't go to class the rest of the day.

I go to the college store to find the boy behind the counter. When he sees me, he rounds the corner and walks to me. "What's wrong, Birdie?"

I'm careful when I curl my arms around his middle, not squeezing but feeling his body heat soak into me.

I don't say a word as I rest my cheek on his chest and listen to his heart drum against my ear, its pace picking up as I loosen a sigh.

One last time.

I want this one last time.

Eventually, he wraps his arms around me and pulls me closer, ignoring the bite of pain he must be feeling.

When I look to my right, I see Lucy smiling at us before she disappears into the back to give us some space.

"Talk to me," he murmurs, brushing hair away from my face to get a better look at my somber expression.

I think about the sage advice I gave to his father, knowing I should listen to it myself.

For Banks's sake.

But in this moment, I don't.

Because he tilts my chin up, stroking my jaw with the pad of his thumb as those muddy eyes do a once-over across my face that I feel deep inside my chest.

"Nothing is wrong," I lie, swallowing the truth when his thumb lands on my bottom lip.

Banks is smarter than that. "I don't buy that for a second. But I know what might help you feel better."

My eyebrows jump as he reaches into his pocket and pulls out his truck keys.

The confusion makes him chuckle. "Don't be mad, but I looked at your list when you were sleeping the other day. It was on the nightstand."

That stupid list.

He wiggles his keys. "What do you say? I think everybody should know how to drive, and it looks like you could use the distraction."

"You want to teach me how to drive?"

A small grin curls half his lips. "If my Birdie wants some freedom, that's what I'll give her."

I'm struck speechless, staring at him like an idiot. Then, ever so slowly, a smile returns, and I almost forget about my encounter with his father.

Almost.

"There she is," he says, tweaking my lips.

"You're working," I point out.

Lucy pops her head out of the back, clearly eavesdropping on us. "I'll cover. You two get out of here."

Banks winks at me, grabbing ahold of my hand and walking us out of the store, but not before grabbing a Pop-Tart and passing me the silver-wrapped treat.

I can't focus on that though.

All I can do is look at our conjoined hands.

It's mundane.

Probably mindless for him.

But nobody has ever held my hand before.

341

A lump reappears in my throat, sticking to the back of it and making it hard to swallow.

In the sea of faces that we pass, nobody seems to pay us any attention. For all they know, we're just another couple on campus. Nothing special or out of the ordinary.

And it's...nice to blend in. For once.

Then I see Dawson, who's walking from the west side of campus.

His eyes go from me to Banks and then down to where we're joined.

He's too far away to say anything to, and I can tell Banks doesn't notice him at all as he guides us to the student parking lot.

I raise my free hand to wave.

Dawson doesn't return it.

That's when I realize he's just another one of the victims I've hurt.

Let him go.

Let him go.

Let him go.

Banks was called selfish once, but the only person that truly describes is me.

Chapter Twenty-Eight

BANKS

"BRAKE. BRAKE. *BRAKE.*" BANKS slams his foot down on the imaginary pedal on the passenger side the same time I hit the actual one, gripping the handle above his window.

Stopping in the middle of the dead-end road, I white-knuckle the steering wheel and let out a shaky breath. We're inches away from a ditch that drops deep enough that a tow would have probably been necessary if I went in.

"I'm horrible," I state.

Banks takes a minute to collect himself before shaking his head. "No. You're learning. There's a difference."

I bet he was way better at driving when he started. Putting the truck into park with a shaky hand, I lean back into the bench seat.

"I got my learner's permit when I was sixteen," I tell him, closing my eyes and willing my heart rate to calm down. What I don't admit is that I technically failed the first exam because I panicked and started answering the questions randomly. I've always had test anxiety, but my brain was still fuzzy from the chemo I'd been undergoing. Mom told me to wait to take it until I was done with my first round of treatment when I could process things easier, but I didn't want to be behind my friends.

Ironic, considering I barely had any of those by the end of the year.

I blame the toxins for making me forget everything I studied in the manual before going in. Maybe the people behind the counter felt bad for the girl who looked as sick as she was because they simply went over the answers one by one and passed me when I should have never walked out of there with a permit.

I hate pity. Always have. Always will.

What I hated more were the looks on their faces when I had to fill out the information that would appear on my future license. Their eyes went to my hair when they read what I'd put for my natural hair color because the wig, which cost more than my mother's monthly car payment, wasn't anywhere near the tone I'd been born with, and my eyes, which Dad used to say reminded him of the ocean, were so dull from the drugs that they looked gray.

I could feel their questions—their doubts—but they never came. The day that I'd been looking forward to for sixteen years was nothing like I'd expected at all. It was ruined, along with every other big milestone teenagers should experience.

I don't want Banks to look at me like that—like the broken girl I am. I want him to like me, to judge me, to be here with me in the moment even when I almost kill us or total his truck.

"Where'd you go?" he asks, his hand coming down on mine to bring me back to earth.

I simply shake my head. "Nowhere. I'm here." Curling my hand around his, I caress his skin with my thumb and think back to the look on his best friend's face earlier. "I think Dawson saw us holding hands."

Banks's gaze drops, his fingers involuntarily squeezing mine. "Screw Dawson."

I give him a sad smile. "You don't mean that. That's what makes you a good person."

The scoff that comes from him has me frowning. "Maybe I don't want to be."

I don't believe that for a second, but the way his eyes flash has me unbuckling and sliding over to him. He watches each movement carefully, his eyes darkening as I find the courage to climb into his lap and straddle him.

His hands find my hips. "Hi, Birdie."

I smile innocently. "Hi."

Cupping his face with my hands, I lean my forehead against his.

"What are you doing?" he asks, voice a notch lower than normal as I feel him harden underneath me.

Taking a deep breath, I move my hips experimentally and hear him groan. I shake my head and whisper, "I don't know yet."

I stop the conversation with a kiss, silencing any other questions he has. He meets my lips, his fingers digging into my hips before moving upward to cup the back of my head.

It's a sea of sadness and passion all mixed together, and he doesn't even know it as the kiss grows deeper and more demanding. The ball in my chest tightens, expanding, consuming me as I undo the button of his jeans and pull the zipper down.

"Birdie," he rasps, catching my wrist.

"You will always be a good person," I tell him. "Who deserves so much better than what he's gotten. One day, I hope you see that."

His throat bobs with a thick swallow.

Peeking at him through my lashes, I dare to close the distance between us, wrapping my hand around him until he jerks. I let him watch me as I stroke him through his boxers, fascinated by how he grows in my palm.

Leaning forward, I press a tentative kiss against one side of his mouth, then the other. My lips trail downward, nipping his jaw and then the column of his throat as I keep moving my hand.

A breath stirs when I slide to the truck floor, nervously peeking up at him as I free him. One palm wrapped around his base, I lean forward and hear him suck in a breath right before my lips experimentally cover the tip.

One of his hands goes to the back of my head as I take my time with him, not guiding me, simply resting there as if he needs to be grounded. I can feel his eyes on me, so I angle my head up while still keeping him in my mouth.

Banks cusses, shaking his head before pulling me away and tugging at my jeans.

"Did I do something wro—"

"Don't even finish that sentence," he cuts me off, somehow undressing the bottom half of me quicker than I ever could.

I gasp when he pulls me back onto his lap and crushes his lips against mine before his fingers do a dance of their own between my thighs until I'm panting into his mouth.

From there, it's a frenzy.

Everything is clouded by lust, and everything that happened today gets pushed to the side the second I feel him nudge against me before slowly, torturously, sliding in.

He helps me set a pace, showing me what to do from the position I'm new to. Not controlling but giving me everything I need to take the moment.

And I take it. Because I need it. Need him. Need this. I need this to last. To savor it. To enjoy it, knowing it's bound to end. Every touch sets me on fire, and every murmured word between hungry kisses fuels it.

When I lean down to kiss him, he presses me against his chest and meets my hips to go deeper. The full feeling still offers a bite of pain, but nothing that his gentle touches along my body can't distract me from. His tongue grazes mine, tasting me, testing me the same way his fingers are as they tease the sensitive spot above the apex of my thighs.

My stomach tightens as he plays with me, causing my movements to become jerky and uneven above him, which Banks doesn't seem to mind at all. He simply holds me against him with one arm around my waist and pumps his hips up again and again and again until—

The noise he makes as he buries his head into the crook of my neck causes stars to burst in my eyes. Head tilting back, I can feel him twitching inside me as our harsh breathing mixes in the otherwise silence of the steamy truck cab.

I stay like that for what feels like forever, not wanting to move. Not wanting to let go.

Let go, let go, let go.

My heart starts thundering for reasons outside what we've just done, remembering what I told his father, the words echoing like I yelled them into a tunnel until they're deafening.

Eventually, I pull away to see him staring at where we're still connected. "I didn't use protection."

I stroke his face, hoping to comfort him. The last thing

we have to worry about is a child, but I don't bother with that reassurance. "It's fine."

"You're on…?"

I nod, suddenly grateful for all those talks Mom forced me to have.

At least it doesn't make me a liar.

This time.

"If driving lessons end like this every time, we should schedule one again soon," he muses as the two of us put ourselves back together.

Biting my lip, I buckle into the passenger seat as he opens the windows to clear the steam. I'm lost in thought, leaning against the glass when he says, "Go out with me."

My ears ring as I keep my face turned away.

If you can't love him the way he deserves, the best thing you can do is let him go.

Slowly, I turn to him and say the only thing that I can. The only thing that's fair to him.

I say, "No."

"Birdie?"

"Take me home," I whisper, unable to meet his eyes. It's the choked "Please" that makes him put the truck into drive after a long, tense moment.

We're a few minutes down the road when he breaks the tense silence. "Whatever it is, we can figure it out."

That's the thing. We can't. "You're going to ruin everything," I whisper.

The truck slows. "What are you talking about?"

I can't look at him. Not if I'm going to get through this. "We said casual. That was all I wanted."

He's quiet. Too quiet. Then, "You're serious."

Did he think I was kidding? "You said you liked the

simplicity of casual. There were no expectations. It was easy. I need easy."

"Why?"

"Because."

He stops the truck in the middle of the road, not caring about whom he may block. "Because *why*? *Talk to me,* Sawyer."

"I don't want to talk. I don't want…" It hurts to swallow, my fingers going up to brush the swollen lymph nodes that remind me why I have to do this. "I didn't want feelings or complications. That's why I wanted this. That's why I wanted *you*." My voice breaks on the last word, and I hope he chalks it up to anger and nothing more—not the lie that it tastes like.

"If you didn't want conversations or feelings, then maybe you should have entertained Dawson when you had the chance," he replies coolly.

"Maybe I should have," I agree emptily, my eyes going back to the window. "It would have been easier than this."

"You would have been miserable."

Aren't I miserable now?

"Misery loves company," I answer.

"And Dixie? What about her?"

I never would have intentionally hurt her, which is why Dawson was never an option. Even if he was the easiest one. He could have offered me the mindless fun I needed because I would have never fallen. If Dixie wasn't a part of my life, maybe I *would* have thought of him as a choice.

Banks doesn't need to know any of that.

"None of that matters, does it?" I say.

You don't matter is what he hears.

He tries to talk. To argue.

But I shut down.

Shut him out.

My hand rests under my jaw, the swollen lymph nodes pressing on my throat.

In my head, I hear the clock.

Tick tock, tick tock, tick tock.

It's better this way.

For him.

Only him.

Chapter Twenty-Nine

SAWYER

EXAMINING HERSELF IN THE little compact mirror, Dixie runs her finger along the bottom edge of her lip and turns to me as the Uber rolls to a stop in front of the busy house. "Do I have any lipstick on my teeth?"

I shake my head, having to force myself to really look. It took everything in me to still come out tonight when my physical and mental energy was spent. "You're good."

We get out of the car, saying our goodbyes to the woman who may have been judging us for the obvious party going on, and straighten our outfits. Dixie took hours figuring out the perfect look, which makes me think she either really likes Miles or really wants Dawson—who I'm not even sure will be here—to regret his choice. I don't know the last time I saw her leave a cardigan behind, but tonight she's wearing a short denim skirt that I'm pretty sure she bought specifically for the party, a tight long-sleeved shirt that she borrowed from my closet and looks way better with her boobs, and heeled boots that make her look taller than she is.

"You look hot," I admire, giving her an impressed once-over. Compared to her, I look as frumpy as I feel. Even though I attempted to put effort into the braided hairstyle and makeup, I can still see the bags under my eyes from the string of nightmares that had me up at three in the morning. It's always the same one, with my mother looking through me and relaying the same message, and I find myself reacting the same whenever I'm woken from it.

My jeans and sweatshirt are a far cry from the clothes Dixie's wearing, which I knew must have looked rough when she asked if I wanted to borrow something the second I showed up to her dorm holding the shirt she wanted from me.

But I don't care how I look.

I don't want to impress anybody.

Especially not after letting go of the one person I would have dressed up for.

Dixie blushes, moving a curled piece of hair behind her ear, which I spent over an hour on because of how much she was fidgeting on her bed. "I hope Miles thinks the same thing." Her eyes go to the crowd gathering around the house. "Are you sure you're okay being here? I understand if you want to go. We can eat ice cream and sulk."

After Banks dropped me off at the apartment building yesterday, we went our separate ways. He stayed in the truck as I walked inside, and I felt his eyes on me the entire time. I watched from my window as he sat in the parking lot for ten minutes, slammed his palms against the steering wheel, and drove away to who knows where.

I laid in the dark for three hours before Dixie called me about the party. I didn't have it in me to lie when she asked me to ask Banks to tag along. I simply said I couldn't do that. My tone apparently said it all because she came over with two milkshakes, two fries, and three sappy movie options that she said she loved watching when she was sad.

Banks never came home that night.

I didn't want to think about where he was.

Or whom he was with.

"I'm sure," I promise now, stomach dipping at the thought of Banks showing up. What would I do if he did? What would I say to him to make him understand?

I want to be there for him, especially after he confided in me about his father. But if I agreed to go out with him, it would make ending things later on so much harder. It could only last so long before it had to end. Before feelings complicated it.

I didn't have time for feelings.

Or for complications.

"This will be good," Dixie states, but I don't know if it's her or me she's trying to convince. "I think it'll be a distraction for the both of us. You can meet Miles, and maybe one of his friends—"

"No. No boys. It's the last thing I need."

She peeks at me with a subtle frown. "Maybe you and Banks can fix things."

Pressing my lips together, I stare at the house. I wait a moment before shaking my head. "He deserves better than me, Dixie. I said some... I wasn't nice to him. I said some awful stuff." She's about to argue, be the kind of good friend I can't be, but I stop her. "Let's just go inside and find Miles. Okay?"

Reluctantly, she starts walking with me toward the house with our elbows linked. "Thank you for coming with me," she says under her breath. "I don't think I would have worked the nerve up if you didn't tag along."

"You don't have to thank me." Isn't this the least I can

do? I want to be her friend, to offer her what little of myself I can. Since I wasn't around for Dawson thanks to my own selfishness, I wanted to be for Miles.

She sighs. "I know, but you haven't been feeling well lately, and now with B—er, well, you know who, I felt bad asking you to come."

"I'm fine," I reassure her, although it takes everything in me to accompany the statement with a smile. One I'm sure she sees right through because she's seen what my real smile looks like.

The music drowns out our conversation when we walk inside and get pushed together by the packed bodies. I've never seen so many people in one place before.

"Whoa," I faintly hear Dixie say, looking around at the crammed people dancing and drinking among friends.

I nod silently, cringing when I see a couple in the corner putting on quite the show for everybody. The last party we went to seemed so tame compared to this one.

Tightening my arm around her, I say, "We should stick together. Do you see Miles?"

She gets on her tippy toes and starts searching the crowd, frowning. "No. Let's go find some drinks and then we'll look for him."

It doesn't take long to get to where two giant kegs are set up in the corner of what I'm assuming is the living room. There are two boys pouring drinks and passing them out to everybody who comes up.

Dixie leans into one of them. "Do either of you know where Miles is?"

The boys flash each other a grin before the one with moppy brown hair points behind him. "I think he went into the kitchen."

My eyes narrow at the glimmer in his eyes, which look like my brother's when he's up to no good.

Tugging on Dixie's arm to get her away from the table, I suggest staying put. "Let him come to you." I gesture toward a small opening on the opposite end of the room. Something about those boys doesn't sit well with me, and Dixie is way too excited about Miles to think rationally.

She looks down at her drink. "What if he doesn't find me?"

With the amount of people here, it'll be hard, but not impossible. "If he knows you're coming, then he will."

At least I hope.

I'm not sure how long we stay in that spot for, but it's clear that Dixie's anxiety is getting the better of her when she finishes her drink and takes mine. I watch as the petite five-foot-nothing brunette guzzles it down, earning a few appreciative glances from the guys dancing around us. She's oblivious, the worry in her eyes growing as she gazes over the various faces.

Taking the empty cups and putting them down on the nearest table, I pull her into the middle of the room that people are using as a dance floor. "Let's dance! You love this song."

She nibbles her lip, letting me get her into the center of the crowd despite her hesitancy.

"Relax your arms," I direct, showing her what I mean. "And smile. You look miserable right now. At least try pretending like you're having fun."

She feigns a smile that resembles more of a flinch, making me snort. I'm hardly the expert on how to get a guy, considering the one I like isn't even here thanks to our circumstances, but Dixie has a lot going for her that Miles would be stupid to miss out on. If it takes a little encouragement to get her there, I'll be her wing woman for the evening.

Three drinks later, which we've been fetching every few songs, Dixie is spinning around and dancing with guys who are most definitely not Miles. But she's happy and having fun, so I choose not to point it out as the popular pop song plays.

When the guy who came up behind me spins me around, I stop facing the window to see a familiar truck pulling up outside. Stomach clenching, I grab Dixie's arm. "I think Banks just got here."

Dixie stumbles, giggling as one of her dance partners catches her. "Ooooh. What are we going to do?"

My feet stay planted where they are, trying to weigh my options. Nausea balls up in my stomach. "I'm not sure."

"We could go out there and talk to him," she suggests. "But then we need to find Miles."

The guy still holding onto her arm speaks up for the first time since coming over to us. "Miles is with his girlfriend upstairs."

Dixie freezes, her eyes widening as she looks between me and him. "What?"

He nods, having the decency to look apologetic for being the bearer of bad news. "They're on and off, but she showed up earlier and we haven't seen either of them since. That usually means that they're, uh…preoccupied."

I reach out for Dixie's hand the second I see her crestfallen expression. "I'm sorry, Dixie."

She looks down, her cheeks darkening.

I squeeze. "We can ditch if you want. I'm not sure I'm ready to talk to Banks anyway."

The guy she was dancing with says, "I'm single."

Dixie locks up, stepping toward me.

"Me too," my dance partner says with a wink.

I cringe at the opportunists. "Maybe another time."

Before he can reply, I pull Dixie after me toward the front door. I can hear her sniffling, which means we have a matter of minutes before the tear ducts open.

Once we manage to weave our way outside, the cool air blasts into us and dries the sweat that was sticking to our skin.

I look around. "Do you see him?"

Dixie sidles up beside me. "No."

Her voice is weak. I turn to block her from everybody else's sight. "Do you want ice cream? Soda? I heard about this one place that makes the best ice cream floa—"

"Oh God," she groans, looking at something past me. "As if this night can't get any worse."

Confused, I look over my shoulder to see what she's talking about. It isn't Banks who gets out of the pickup truck I almost put into a ditch but Dawson. He stumbles around the front and toward a group of guys standing off to the side on the front lawn.

"I'll go talk to him," I offer. As much as I would hate to ask Banks a favor, it may be needed based on how Dawson is acting. "Maybe Banks is with him. We can get a ride with the—"

"I am *not* getting into a truck with him."

Nodding slowly, I let out a breath. "I get that. I don't really want to ask Banks for much right now either, but it's our best shot at getting home. Let me just go make sure Dawson's okay, and then we'll figure it out from there. Deal?"

Reluctantly, she nods, crossing her arms and staring down at the ground.

When I turn toward Dawson, he's already walking away

from the guys who call out to him with profanity. He tucks something into his pocket as he makes his way back to the truck, nearly tripping over his feet.

Right before he reaches the side door, one of the guys says, "Marco is always watching."

A nervous look crosses Dawson's face as he nods bleakly at them, touching his pocket and whatever he put inside it.

Jogging over, I call out to him. "Wait up, Dawson." He stops, nearly toppling over again but catching himself on the bed of the pickup. When I get a better view of his face, I gape. "Are you okay?"

His eyes are sunken in and red, his lips are chapped, and his face is a strange pale color that not even mine got at my very worst. "What are you doing here, Sawyer?"

I point behind me. "Dixie and I were invited by someone. We were actually just leaving. Is Banks with you?"

Dawson straightens, his eyes moving to my friend in the distance, and then he hunches over. "No. I borrowed his truck for the night."

He borrowed...? There's no way Banks would have let him drive in this condition. "Does Banks know you took it?"

His words are barely understandable when he replies. "I know where *Paxton* keeps the keys. It's the least he could do for me."

My brows pinch, the name stirring something in my chest. "Paxton?" Then I realize the other tidbit of information is a little more important than the name I haven't heard in a long, long time. "Wait. You *stole* his truck?"

He snorts, a dark look twisting his face. "Is it stealing if you're friends?" he questions. "And you don't even know the first name of the guy you're fucking, do you?"

I cringe at the hostility in his tone. "That's not..."

Choosing to brush off his crudeness, I sigh. "You shouldn't be driving. Why don't you let Dixie drive us back?"

His eyes go back to the brunette, softening a moment before he shakes his head. "I don't want her to see me like this."

I look to Dixie, who's doing her best not to pay us any attention. "Dawson, I don't know how to drive. I never got my license."

Thankfully, he's too high to look judgy. Only surprised, which is reasonable. Most twenty-one-year-olds can drive.

Putting my hand on him, I lift a finger. "Give me one second. Please don't go anywhere."

Jogging back over to Dixie, I say, "He can't drive himself. He's going to need us. He took Banks's truck without permission anyway, so I don't want anything to happen to it."

Dixie stands straighter, her eyes moving over to Dawson to study him. Whatever she sees, she doesn't like. "No," she says, to my surprise. "I don't want to keep doing this. He needs to figure things out himself without one of us saving him."

Normally, I'd understand. But I can tell he's in a particularly bad state of mind tonight. "You know I can't drive. It'd be safer if you took the truck—"

"No," she repeats, standing her ground. "I'm sorry, Sawyer, but I'm not doing it. Maybe he needs something to happen for a reality check."

"You don't mean that."

She pulls out her phone. "I'm getting an Uber. Are you coming with me or not?"

Nervously, I bite my nail as I look at Dawson, who's walking around to the driver's side. It doesn't give me a lot of opportunity to think about my choices.

"Shit," I curse. I have seconds to decide, and based on

the determination on Dixie's face, she's not going to break. "I can't let him go alone."

Dawson gets into the truck.

Quickly reaching into my pocket where I tucked some money, I pass it to her for a ride home. "Please, please, please let me know when you get back to your dorm. I'm sorry, Dixie. But I can't let him drive."

Dixie gapes at me and calls out, "You can't drive, either!"

Not knowing what else to do, I run over and open the passenger door as Dawson starts the truck up. I know Dixie is upset, so she doesn't mean any harm. She'd never wish ill will on anybody. And I feel horrible for leaving her here alone, but Dawson is clearly not in his right mind.

He seems surprised as he puts the truck into drive and takes off right as I close the door behind me.

"You shouldn't be driving," I tell him, voice pleading. "Pull over and we can call Banks. Then we can get an Uber and come back for the truck tomorrow."

Whatever logic I throw at him doesn't seem to work. He keeps driving, making my nerves soar. In a grumbly tone and slurring words, he says, "You shouldn't have gotten in if you didn't want to come, Sawyer. I don't know why you bothered."

He doesn't? "Because we're friends."

Dawson has the audacity to snort. "Are we?"

I frown, grabbing the seat belt and buckling myself in, keeping a firm grip on the part that goes across my chest. "We've never *not* been. You're the one who started distancing yourself from everybody."

His eyes snap to me. "Because *you* started fucking my best friend."

"Dawson!" I squeak when the truck veers off the road.

He barely corrects it before we hit a parked car. Letting out a shaky breath, I ease into the seat. "You're right. I do like Banks. I'm sorry if that upsets you. He's just…" I shrug, not knowing what to say to make this better. "I guess he was what I thought I needed at the time. I never meant to hurt you or lead you on. Banks didn't either. He cares about you. No matter what fight you two are going through, he'd want you to get home safe."

He white-knuckles the steering wheel, his jaw grinding. "He said he wouldn't do this again. Desiree chose him too. He doesn't care."

Scrubbing my eyes, I try redirecting the conversation to one less hostile. "I'm the one who pushed for this," I reason. "If you're going to be mad at somebody, be mad at me. I deserve it. Not him."

For a moment, he seems contemplative. "If he didn't want to, he wouldn't have. I'm never picked first. I'm too fucked up."

"It's not too late to fix things."

His murmured words hit me all too well: "For some of us, it is."

It's a sad truth, but I choose not to press him on it. "Who were those guys back there?"

"None of your business."

I heard one of them mention Marco, who was the person responsible for Dawson's initial use. "I want to help you. Let me help you."

"I don't want your help. I don't want B-Banks's help. I don't want *anybody*." His voice rises. "Can't you fucking see that, Sawyer? Some of us are in too deep for help!"

His driving becomes more erratic as his head starts bobbing. When I see his nose bleeding, panic seeps in. "Fine.

You don't need me or anybody else. But can you pull over now? Your nose is bleeding, and you're starting to scare me."

"I'm f-fine." His eyes get heavy.

"Dawson?"

Once again, his eyes go to mine. "I told y-you that you s-shouldn't have gotten in if you didn't want to—"

Suddenly, headlights flash into the windshield, blinding me as I feel the truck move into the opposite lane. "Dawson, watch—"

The loud screech of bending metal is all I can hear. Not Dawson. Not my own screams as we start to slide and roll.

There's chaos as my body gets tossed brutally until something heavy crashes into me. It feels like it goes on forever before everything stops.

And then there's nothing but my ears ringing.

My eyes get heavy.

Then I hear a voice.

My mother's.

I have a horrible feeling.

My world goes black.

Chapter Thirty

SAWYER

THERE'S A CRUSHING WEIGHT on my chest and throat as I try drawing a breath.

Breathe, I tell myself. *You have to breathe.*

I try but feel like I'm suffocating.

Breathe. Scream. Something.

I muster everything I possibly can from the deepest pit of my stomach and let go, screaming through the blackness in my vision that feels like a nightmare.

Keep screaming.

Keep breathing.

I do it again, the darkness settling in.

Encasing me.

Trapping me.

Luring me to it.

Then, through blurry vision, I see lights.

Red ones.

Blue ones.

Yellow ones.

From a distance, such a far, far distance, I hear voices.
And I scream again.
Scream until my voice cuts out.

Chapter Thirty-One

BANKS

I'M GOING TO KILL him.

Dialing his number for a third time, I pace where my truck *should* be. There's only one person who knows where the spare key is, and I saw him leave the apartment over an hour and a half ago looking sketchy as hell.

He's lost his damn mind.

"Pick up the fucking phone, Dawson," I growl into the voicemail as soon as the recorded message finishes playing. "I'm not playing games. You crossed a line. If you're not back in twenty minutes, I'm calling the goddamn police and getting your ass arrested."

A lie, although tempting. So tempting.

And as if fate is taunting me for being such a pushover, I hear sirens blaring in the distance.

"What the…?" I hang up the phone and walk out toward the road, listening as multiple emergency vehicles roar by in the distance after the first siren sounds.

A few students who are walking from that direction

look drunken and stirred as they head to some of the other student housing nearby, all looking behind them.

"What happened?" I ask one of the girls, who smiles at me.

She shrugs. "Somebody said there was an accident. I don't know."

One of the guys walking behind her stops beside me as his friends keep going. "My buddy said there was a head-on collision over on North."

Ice coats every inch of me. "North Street or North Boulevard?"

The guy makes a face. "Uh...I don't know, dude. Does it matter?"

Yes. Because the party Dixie told me she and Sawyer were going to is on North Street. I step closer, all but grabbing his shirt to stop him from walking away. "What did your friend tell you? Was it near a party? Did he say what vehicle? Who was involved?"

The group is clearly uncomfortable with my prying, and the guy I'm grilling holds his hands up when he sees the look on my face. "I think it was North Street, but I doubt you can get over there easily. If what Trevor said was true, they probably blocked it off."

This time, I do grab his shirt. "*What did he say?*"

He winces, trying to get away from where my firm grip wrinkles his tee. "There are two people dead. Supposedly. Supposedly! But that may not even be true. You know how people get fired up. Rumors spread all the time about this stuff when it turns out to be nothing."

Based on the sirens howling, I doubt it's nothing.

I release him, letting him stumble backward until he almost falls into the road. One of his other friends catches him, cussing me out as I run into my apartment and grab my things.

The next twenty minutes are a blur.

I don't know how I get across town or how I manage to avoid all the police officers who have multiple roads blocked as EMS and firefighters work on the scene.

But suddenly I'm there, along with a massive crowd of onlookers trying to get a better picture of the mangled mess of metal and debris of two overturned cars that's destroyed the road.

From here, I can tell one thing for sure.

That's my truck that's upside down.

Or what's left of it.

Elbowing my way to the front of the line that officers have taped off, I say, "I need to get through." I'm unapologetic as I shove people to the side, working my way to the front until a police officer stops me.

"Whoa," she says, holding her hands out to prevent me from going farther. "I can't let you pass this line. You need to stand back, sir."

I ignore her, grabbing ahold of the tape anyway. "I need to get through. That's my truck. My friends are there."

"Sir," she repeats, blocking me with her body. She barely comes up to my chest, so I could easily overpower her if I needed to. "If those are your friends, you need to let my colleagues do their jobs without getting in the way."

I can't keep my eyes off the ambulance putting somebody into the back. It's too far away to see. Moving my gaze down to the stern-faced blond in front of me, I ask, "Are they okay?"

Something crosses over her face before her expression neutralizes. "I'm not allowed to say, but..." Lowering her voice, she says, "If they are your friends, I'm sorry."

I'm sorry.

My legs suddenly feel weak. "Sorry?" I whisper.

From the radio attached to her uniform, I hear a male say, "Two confirmed dead. Caucasian male, twenty-one years of age. Caucasian female, twenty-one years of age."

Somebody beside me gasps.

I drop to the ground.

"Sir," the officer says, trying to help me up.

Not willing to believe my ears, I use the advantage to dart under the tape and run faster than I ever have toward the accident site. There are tons of people in uniforms working around the mangled vehicles blocking the street, the car partially under my totaled truck smoking as firefighters work on it.

"Sir," a male officer calls out from somewhere to my right.

I search frantically until I see blond hair on the opposite side of the street, the body small and curled into itself on the edge of the sidewalk.

Holy shit. I know before I can even process the features of the person on the curb that it's Sawyer.

My Sawyer.

Swallowing down the realization that somebody else died, I manage to break free from the officers attempting to restrain me, and I run to her.

"Sawyer," I scream.

She keeps rocking, mumbling words to herself that I can't understand until I'm dropping to my knees in front of her.

"Sawyer," I repeat, examining the blood caked to her face and hair.

She's saying something under her breath.

I try tilting her chin up, but her body is frozen.

In shock.

As she continues to rock, I try listening to the words she's saying over and over again. "I'm sorry. I'm sorry. I'm sorry."

I shake my head, moving hair out of her face and trying to get her to look at me. "Sawyer, I don't know why you're saying you're sorry. If it's about the truck, I don't give a fuck."

"I'm sorry. I'm so sorry."

When I swipe my hand along the hair framing her face, I stare wide-eyed when I see slivers of red underneath. Suddenly, the blond disappears, falling behind her until short strands of youthful red are revealed beneath my fingertips. "Sawyer—"

Two hands grab ahold of me from behind, pulling me away from the girl who looks so much like the one I knew.

Red hair.

Blue eyes.

Tom Sawyer. *It's a book.*

"Sir, you need to move away, or we'll be forced to arrest you for obstruction. We can't have anybody else back here right now."

I jerk out of his hold, uncaring of what happens to me. Kneeling back down, I cup Sawyer's face until she finally meets my eyes. I look at her. *Really* look.

I'm Sawyer. Like Tom Sawyer. *It's a book.*

Her lips are moving, but nothing is coming out. Over and over, they form silent words. Her arms are wrapped around herself. "What are you saying, Birdie?"

Her head shakes slowly, her blue eyes glazed and distant until they finally *see* me. A shallow breath escapes her. "It should have been me."

It's the last thing she says before two officers haul me away, one of them handcuffing me and another talking into his radio.

But all I can hear are those five words.

It should have been me.

They haunt me as I'm guided into the back of the cop car.

It should have been me.

They echo in my head as I'm driven away from the redhead who's being looked over by the paramedics that take my place.

Chapter Thirty-Two

SAWYER

THE SOUNDS SURROUNDING ME are all too familiar—beeps from expensive machinery, quiet mumblings of nurses and doctors talking to patients, and wheels on linoleum as transport moves people in and out of rooms.

When I peel my eyes open, I'm met with dimmed fluorescent lighting. It takes a few moments before I adjust to it, blinking as reality creeps in. And the pain.

God, the pain.

There's a heart monitor attached to my finger, an IV in my vein, and a thin gown on me I know I didn't put on myself. Wiggling my toes, which are oddly as stiff as the rest of me, the warm blanket falls off to reveal a pair of purple socks that I know from personal experience have white grips on the bottom.

Beep.

Beep.

Beep.

Beep.

It takes a few minutes staring at my body under the blanket to finally remember what happened.

"Oh God," I whisper, nausea bubbling in my stomach as the crash comes back.

My heart rate on the monitor starts increasing as my brain replays the sound of crushing metal and glass shattering, the beeping erratic until the door opens and a petite nurse jogs in.

I'm able to get out, "Sick," just in time for her to lunge for a garbage bin and stick it under my mouth before I empty the contents of my stomach into it.

It's only after the kind middle-aged woman is wiping off my mouth that I realize I didn't get any in my hair like I used to in the past when chemo got the better of me. The nurses in the oncology unit used to tell me it was a safe space—that I didn't need the wig. But I felt far too naked, too vulnerable, without it.

Hesitantly, I reach up and brush my shaky fingertips along the short pieces of red hair attached to my scalp. It's thin, fragile, but growing slowly day by day.

The nurse pulls the computer over to her and scans her badge to access it. "I'll get you some anti-nausea medication in a moment. How is the pain on a scale from one to ten?"

Even though she's right beside me, she sounds so far away. So distant. I have to blink a few times as she smiles softly at me to really find my words. "Six."

Her eyebrows go up. "You're strong," she says with a shake of her head. "Can you tell me your name and date of birth, sweetie? I need to verify your information before I can order you medicine."

"Sawyer Hawkins." I swallow, my throat raw. "May 20, 1997."

The nurse nods, scrolling on the screen, her eyebrows staying up as she scans something. "I need to go over some questions with you now that you're awake, and then we can get you some more pain meds. Okay?"

I try finding a clock but can barely move my head without cringing at the stiffness settled into it. "What time is it?"

"Try not to move, honey," she directs, placing a hand on my arm. "From the initial CT scan you went through when you first arrived, you don't have any broken bones, but that doesn't rule out sprains. The doctor thinks you have whiplash from impact. Your ribs are bruised too. Do you remember going through the tests and talking to our staff when you came in?"

The last thing I remember is Banks. Somebody took him away, and I couldn't do anything but sit there. Frozen. In disbelief. People were yelling. Men in uniforms pointed toward other men in uniforms, rushing around. The lights flashing were so bright. My head hurt. My ears hurt. Everything hurt.

Then everything went black. Until now.

I don't even remember getting out of the truck. Did I do it myself or did somebody free me? Was it Dawson or—

Dawson. A harsh feeling punches my stomach, but I don't have time to think about it as the nurse starts explaining what happened after I got here.

"You were in and out of it. The doctor wants to redo a CT scan to double-check a few things after your bloodwork came back with some questionable results. You have a minor concussion, which is incredibly impressive considering how serious the accident was. You are very lucky, Sawyer. If you didn't have a seat belt on, it would have been a different story."

My ears ring, body shaking as I recall how many times my body was tossed around as the truck flipped. "Dawson," I breathe, frantically looking at her. "I need to know if my friend Dawson is okay."

There were so many people at the scene, but the pain made it hard to focus on what was going on. I couldn't figure out what the first responders were saying. Somebody came and talked to me there. I think. I don't know what I said. I don't know if I said anything.

The nurse clears her throat. "I don't have any information on your friend. The best thing we can do is work on you and go from there. Since you're a new patient here, maybe you can help us get some of your medical history sorted. It could help clear up the markers we found in the initial blood panel."

I close my eyes, knowing what the bloodwork shows has little to do with the accident.

"Dawson," I repeat, voice frail as I lean back onto the pillow somebody placed behind me to keep my body propped up. "I need to know what happened to him."

She sighs. I know she knows something. I'm too familiar with how hospitals work. Everybody gossips. If one trauma patient comes in, there are bound to be questions about where the others are—*if* there are others. "Honey, what's important right now is you. Your labs—"

"Show that I have cancer," I cut her off, voice distant as I stare at the door. I can feel her eyes on the profile of my face, but I don't need to look to know there's sympathy, and maybe shock, in them. "Advanced non-Hodgkin's lymphoma. Stage four. I know what the labs show."

For once, she doesn't say anything.

What can she say?

That she's sorry?

I've been told that too many times to count.

I came all this way because I was done being sorry, done being sick. I was here to live.

Live.

That word rocks me to the core as I think about hanging upside down in that truck.

It should have been me.

That's what I told Banks.

Because it's true.

I was damned if I was going to believe whatever God is out there would let me survive and take somebody else when I was on borrowed time already.

It should have been me.

When I finally look at her, there's a fresh glaze of angry tears in my eyes that blurs the deep frown settled into her face.

I don't want pain medicine.

I want answers.

"Now tell me where Dawson is."

Chapter Thirty-Three

BANKS

WHEN I SEE MY father follow the officer back to where I'm being held in the small cell, the fear that cemented into my chest intensifies because I have no idea what he's going to do. He won't cause a scene. Not here. After is a different question.

When the door is unlocked and my father steps in, I don't expect the crushing hug he pulls me into before either of us can say a word. Even though my ribs still hurt like a bitch, it's a pain I don't mind in the moment.

Because I needed it more than I knew after being stuck here for the past fourteen hours.

And when he pulls back, I definitely don't expect the tears in his bloodshot eyes. "They said..." He chokes, throat bobbing as he runs his hands over my face to make sure I'm real. "I heard that your truck was involved in a fatal accident. They said the driver died. I thought..."

He stops himself again, pulling me back in and hugging me harder than he ever has before. I almost forget the physical pain because of all the emotional pain that envelops me.

"God, Paxton. If I lost you…" His voice is hoarse, cutting off and forcing him to clear his throat.

Don't leave me like her.

"I don't know what I would do," he admits. "I thought you were gone. Just like your—"

He stops himself short of saying my mother, the look in his eyes full of the dread that my soul understands all too well.

Except Mom isn't dead.

She's alive and well and living a happy life away from us and all of the bullshit that comes with being stuck here.

This time, it's me who pulls back.

My jaw trembles.

I didn't cry when they brought me in.

I didn't even shed a tear when I heard the radio scanner talk about the two people who were taken by the coroner from the accident, knowing one of them was my best friend.

Physically, I couldn't let it out, even though I felt the desperation and sadness boiling over.

But here, in front of the father I've never let see me cry once in my lifetime, no matter the arguments or the beatings or anything in between, I break down and say the words I haven't been able to aloud. "Dawson is dead."

He doesn't respond.

His throat bobs.

His hand comes out.

I flinch.

Then he pats my arm, as if he already gave me all the comfort he possibly could have.

Chapter Thirty-Four

SAWYER

THE IV POLE THAT I drag along with me from the bathroom across the hall is the only thing keeping me upright after the last twenty-four hours.

According to the doctor on call, it's a miracle I didn't sustain worse injuries outside the scratches, scrapes, and bruises marring my body.

A miracle.

Two people are dead, and I'm still here.

How is that a miracle?

My body is still stiff and sore, but I've refused pain medication. It makes me too groggy, and I prefer feeling the weight of reality. Drowning it out will only make the comeback ten times worse when I remember what I'll be walking into once the hospital releases me.

When I get back to my room, the new shift nurse, Melody, offers to help me back into bed. I shake my head, determined to show them I'm perfectly fine on my own.

After all, I'm a walking *miracle*.

I snort to myself, making Melody's brows pinch in confusion. Once I'm seated, she helps me get the blanket over me. "Have you reconsidered?"

She's asking about my parents.

I'm legally an adult, so nobody needs to tell them I'm here. "They would freak out," I whisper.

Melody gives me a small smile. She can't be much older than me, but it seems maternal somehow. Not sympathetic, but something close to it. "Wouldn't they feel the same way if they found out after the fact? You've gone through so much, Sawyer. They should be here for you."

They've been through enough because of me.

My recklessness.

Everybody who's dealt with me knows the circumstances of my health. My scans all lit up like a glow stick. I was all but a Christmas tree that the medical students are probably sad they missed out on. "Would it matter?" I doubt, not bothering to shrug as I settle into the bed.

She doesn't answer, but I can tell she wants to argue with me. We both know that's not her job, though, even if it's frustrating for her. "Do you need anything?"

To get out of here.

To go back to that night.

To stop Dawson from getting into that truck.

I close my eyes. "No."

A hand comes down and touches my shoulder. "The oncologist will be in shortly to speak with you. Then we can discuss your departure. Okay?"

I say nothing, closing my eyes before the nurse leaves sometime later. When I open them, I'm greeted by the darkness in the room.

The *tick tock, tick tock, tick tock* seems so much louder than it actually is, and nothing I do can quiet it.

Then the door reopens, and an older man in a white lab coat enters, introducing himself as the head oncologist. I don't hear his name. I barely even hear the first half of what he says.

He's patient but stoic. I suppose in his profession he has to be. Not cold, but not overly friendly. Why put effort into people it won't make a difference to? He can't grow attached to the types of people he sees, or he'll never survive his own life.

"Do you understand?" I hear him ask.

It's only then that I finally look at him. He's older than my father, if I had to guess. There are age speckles on his face. Wrinkles on his forehead. He's well kept. Groomed. Clean shaven. Nothing about him sticks out. He's not wearing bright colors but neutral tones. Even his socks are white. There's nothing special about him.

Or about this conversation.

He must know I haven't been listening, so he says, "The survival rate for people with your type of stage-four cancer is fifty-seven percent over the course of ten years with treatment. I don't need to tell you what that entails, from what I've heard. But a decade is a long time, especially for somebody so young."

Ten years is also a long time to slowly wither away, losing all that youth and letting the people you love watch it drain from you no matter the money they sink into medications or the hope people offer in their prayers.

A decade's worth of pain and suffering and watching people crumble around you is not what I want to be put through.

Not again.

I choose silence, letting him have a one-man conversation to tell me what he came here to.

"But," he adds, the word a scratch to my soul. There's always a "but," and it always leads to bad news.

At least my mother isn't here to witness it.

"Dr. Miranda noticed the start of discoloration on your skin and in your eyes when he examined you earlier, and your labs are showing significant damage to the liver. All of this to say that the cancer has spread since you stopped your treatment."

It's the first time anybody has said those words—that I *stopped* treatment.

Not finished.

Not won.

Ended it.

I never got to ring the bell.

Never got a farewell send off with claps and cheers from the oncology team.

After five years of battling, of broken hopes, of sickness and weakness and mental and emotional debilitation, I was done.

Mom begged me to reconsider. *"One more, baby. Try it one more time."*

But I had tried.

I tried over and over and over.

I tried for her.

I tried for me.

I tried for Dad and Bentley and my grandparents and aunt. I gave everything I had until I had nothing left to give.

Maybe she finally saw that, finally realized I couldn't keep going on the blind hope that a miracle would happen.

So I stopped. Told the doctors no more.

I told them it was time for me to live my life.

What time I had left, anyway.

"There are tests we can do to figure out a better timeline—"

"No," I finally say, voice small. "No tests."

He pauses, clearing his throat. "Miss Hawkins—"

"You've seen firsthand what we go through," I cut him off, looking him straight in the eyes for the first time since he walked in. "I've been doing this for five years. For *five years*. I've seen people get their hopes up that this treatment will be the last. And then the treatment after that. It never ends. I don't want to live like that anymore. I don't want to live..." I stop myself when my voice becomes hoarse, shaking my head and staring down at my hands fidgeting over the blankets.

The doctor nods once, standing and flattening his palm along his shirt before pulling a card from his front and holding it out. "You've had to make a lot of tough decisions at such a young age. For that, I'll never envy you or any of my patients who've had to do the same. If you change your mind, call my office."

I take the business card and stare at it, not saying a word as he leaves the room.

I'm grateful he doesn't apologize.

I'm sick of people saying they're sorry.

It doesn't change anything.

A single tear falls on the rectangular piece of cardstock in my hand.

Then another.

Then another.

I'm stuck in my head, reliving the final moments of the boy that the police officer who came in two days ago said was dead on arrival.

Partially ejected were his exact words.

The questions they asked were hard to digest, knowing what I knew. I didn't want to tell them anything that would make Dawson out to be a troubled person, even if he was. He was gone. Why make his memory into something it didn't deserve to be?

Somebody else died, Officer Pedler reminded me when I was stuck in my own grief. *If you know anything to help us put her family at ease, now would be the time to tell us.*

Dawson was a good person with bad habits.

Addiction.

He should have never gotten behind the wheel or looked away from the road. Maybe if I wasn't there…wasn't arguing with him…

Swallowing, I squeeze my eyes closed.

I know it wasn't my fault, but I can't help but feel the gripping weight of guilt on my conscience anyway. How could I not? It was bad enough Dawson was de—

The word gets stuck, causing the nausea to come back. I was suspended upside down by my seat belt while Dawson lay somewhere half in the vehicle and half out of it, through the windshield because he hadn't had his seat belt on.

I don't know how I got out, but I did.

All I can hope is that it was quick for him.

That he didn't suffer.

Sniffling back tears, I clear my throat.

I've had three days to think about what it must have been like for him while I slipped in and out of consciousness before the firefighters finished pulling me out of the vehicle.

I have no idea who the second person was, the one driving the other vehicle—couldn't gather the courage to ask for a name. It was another student from LSU from what I heard. I wonder if the school will have a vigil and if it'll be for only her or for both of them.

Not wanting to think about it anymore, I swallow down the emotions crammed into my throat and take a deep breath.

Despite not wanting to tell my parents what happened, I wish they were here—wish Mom could run her fingers through my stubbly hair and tell me everything will be okay. I'm sure she'd say she's glad that I'm still here.

Maybe that's what I want to avoid.

I don't need to hear that.

It should have been me.

I'm stirred awake sometime later by the nurse knocking and letting me know that my sister is here to see me. I don't have the energy to point out that I don't have one or to bother with my appearance, knowing I look as bad as I feel.

Dixie walks in, stopping short when she sees me. The real me, not the version I've been hiding for almost three months. Nobody knows what happened to my wig, and I haven't cared enough to worry about how much money is gone with its disappearance.

Her lower lip wiggles, but she doesn't cry. If her red, puffy eyes are any indication, she's been doing that enough as it is.

She has to have heard about Dawson by now.

"I'm sorry," she whispers once the nurse leaves us. She stays by the door, fiddling with her hands. "I should have stayed. I should have driven you two h-home. I could have. If I'd stopped thinking about my feelings, if I had thought rationally…"

I'm not mad.

Dawson isn't her responsibility.

Neither am I.

Her eyes go to my head, walking in hesitantly to take a better look. "Your hair..." She shakes her head. "It doesn't look bad. You didn't have to wear a wig if you were uncomfortable with it."

I wish vanity was the only illness that plagued me. Living life would have been a hell of a lot easier if that's all I had to worry about.

Still feeling numb, I curl into the blankets.

How much money is this going to cost? Another hospital bill stacked up and weighing on my conscience. Will Mom and Dad have to pay for this one too?

"Sawyer," Dixie pleads. "Talk to me."

I blink, my eyes finally meeting hers. She looks so far away even from beside my bed, somehow seeming so much more fragile than I do. She knows how this accident impacted people, unlike me, who's locked far away from the people I started integrating with regularly.

Dixie looks at me with glassy eyes, waiting for me to say something. Anything. Then she looks around, seeing the notes on the patient board hanging on the wall.

I know the second she sees the two words in red under the specialty notes.

Cancer patient.

Her breath catches as she stares, as if she read it wrong somehow. When she turns back to me, her eyes go to my hair, then down to my face.

Then she says, "Your skeletons."

I release a breath before closing my eyes and fighting back the tears. "We all have them. Some of ours are just bigger."

She starts sniffling, so I reach out until she takes my hand. We hold on so tight that I can't feel my fingers, but I don't care. It's what we both need.

I don't know how long we stay like that before I whisper, "I'm sorry about Dawson. I know you...cared. I did too."

Her lip quivers.

Then I say, "I told Banks I should have chosen Dawson. But I...I didn't mean it."

She stares at me.

"He deserves more than me."

She swallows.

"You all deserve more than me," I whisper.

Dixie shakes her head, her mouth starting to open.

But I don't let her argue. "He's going to need you."

Her mouth parts again and then closes.

All I whisper is "Someday."

Chapter Thirty-Five

BANKS

IT'S BEEN DAYS SINCE the accident, and the apartment building is too quiet—void of the people who made it so lively. I wish I'd taken my father's invitation to stay at his place, but I couldn't risk his mood shifting when we're finally, and maybe sadly given the circumstances, in a better place. Not a healthy one but…better.

It's always temporary, anyway.

Walking past the second door on the first floor has been painful knowing that there's nobody behind it. I've been tempted to break in. Dawson showed me how to pick a lock once, but I was never as good as he was. The more I thought about seeing the things he hid behind that door, though, the less I wanted to see.

People are already talking.

The school sent out emails for grief counseling if anybody needed it, along with numbers for those who might need *other* kinds of help. The help that Dawson needed.

But I didn't want to think about that pointed dig or

think about how the girl across the hall hasn't been back since the day I was arrested.

I waited.

And waited.

And waited.

Then I went to the hospital, where I was told the same thing each time I asked where Sawyer Hawkins was, whose last name I finally learned when I asked the professor to give me any assignments that I could pass along when she was better.

The hospital turned me away three days in a row.

It doesn't stop me from going a fourth time.

The same nurse from the first two days is sitting behind the desk in the inpatient unit. She smiles when she sees me, her eyes a mixture of sadness and sympathy as I walk toward her with a cup of coffee from my favorite café. It's the same one I used to get for Sawyer, so I figured it was leverage.

"You're persistent," Faye comments, eyeing the cup I slide over to her. After looking around, she takes the offering. "And creative."

I do my best to smile, even though it takes every ounce of energy possible because it's the last thing I want to do. "I was coming by to see Sawyer, so I figured you could use some."

She blinks, her eyes going to the older woman sitting on the opposite side of the desk with a headset on as she talks on the phone. When she looks back at me, she says, "I can't allow anybody but family to see her."

It's the same response every day. But today, I'm not turning around or going home. Not after seeing the redheaded girl rocking helplessly alone on the side of that road. My stomach has been in knots ever since.

Faye must know that. "Only family," she repeats, eyebrows going up as she stares at me.

I nod slowly. "I'm her...brother."

Faye sips her coffee as if she can't see the blatant lie, her eyes brightening. "Why didn't you say that before? I just need you to sign right there in the log, and then I'll have somebody come get you to bring you back."

Quietly, I say, "Thank you."

Her smile is softer, understanding. "From what I hear," she murmurs, eyes shooting to her coworker again, "she needs somebody. Her sister has been visiting her, but she barely talks."

Sawyer doesn't have a sister, unless that's another lie she told. I'm starting to wonder what exactly she's been honest about. I can't get her red hair out of my head, wondering why she would have kept it a secret all this time. She's not a vain person, at least not the version I used to know.

But who is the real Sawyer?

It doesn't take long before I'm following a nurse with a firm face back through narrow hallways with flickering fluorescent lights. I don't say a word or ask the questions balancing on the tip of my tongue.

How is she? Is she doing okay? How is she taking the news? Does she know about Dawson?

The nurse turns to me as we stop in front of a door at the end of the hall. "Somebody out there is looking down on her. None of us can believe how she walked away. After all she's gone through in life..." Her head shakes. "Your sister is very lucky."

Your sister.

Lucky.

I press my lips together and nod, not trusting myself to

389

speak. Given the circumstances, I bet she's used to a lot of different reactions from people when she delivers them to patients.

"She's been…" Her voice lowers, her eyes moving to the door and back. "She's closed down since she spoke to the police. Your sister could barely get her to eat anything, so it's a good thing you're here. I think she needs somebody now more than ever. Maybe a brother's reassurance that everything will be okay."

I should have known the police would have been here. I had to go and talk to them when they ran the registration on my truck. Dad dropped me off and waited for me in the lobby of the station while I gave them my statement. They hounded me with questions I wish I had the answers to, about the second I found out my truck was gone to the moment I was hauled away in the back of a cop car after breaking past the police tape on scene.

I wasn't sorry for getting in the way.

Not when I saw Sawyer sitting there helpless while the world moved in slow motion around us.

She needs somebody now more than ever.

She's not the only one.

My heart picks up when the nurse twists the knob on the door, her knuckles gently rapping on the wood. "I have another visitor for you, Sawyer," she says gently, gesturing for me to follow her in.

I stop in the doorjamb when I see her.

Birdie.

Sawyer.

Tucked under two layers of blankets, looking so small in a room no larger than my tiny apartment bathroom, lies a pale girl with short, red hair. Her eyes aren't shining with blue mischief like usual but drained of life and light. Dull. Almost gray from here.

The person lying on her side, curled into herself, can barely meet my eyes when I step in.

But when she does...

I swallow.

Red hair.

Blue eyes.

I'm Sawyer. Like Tom Sawyer. *It's a book.*

My eyes stay locked on her hair, the same color I remember from thirteen years ago. Except it looks like somebody cut it all off. Did somebody do that to her, or did she do it herself?

It's hard to process how different she looks compared to what I'm used to, no matter how long I take her in.

Sawyer doesn't make a move, doesn't say a word as I soak up her fragile image.

The nurse puts a hand on my arm, as if she's trying to understand what I must be feeling. She has no idea though.

Because thirteen years ago, I said goodbye to the only person who offered me a semblance of peace when my life was falling apart.

And now, all this time later, I'm meeting her for a second time after saying goodbye to the only other person who helped me get through the cruel fate dealt to me after Hurricane Katrina.

Sawyer left.

Then Mom.

And now Dawson.

The nurse squeezes my arm, bringing me back to reality. "Sawyer is one of the most stubborn patients I've had in quite some time. But that kind of strength is exactly what cancer patients like her need to get through it."

My ears start ringing as the world stops around me. I'm not sure when the nurse drops her hand or when my eyes peel from Sawyer's short red hair down to her unblinking eyes.

She just lays there. Staring. Distant. Like she's not even here at all.

Cancer.

Suddenly, I forget about the short memories we created together when we were kids. The fruit snacks and the chips and the tree climbing and the gossiping. I forget about missing her and wondering what ever happened to her and her family and focus on what's right in front of me. Because none of that matters now.

Not when we're here, two adults trying to figure out life, both grieving the same person, dealing with our own traumas.

What happened to us?

"I'll leave you two be," the nurse tells me softly, her eyes drifting to Sawyer. "If you need me, you know what button to push."

Once the door closes behind her, Sawyer finally blinks. It's slow. Tired. Her eyelids heavy with exhaustion.

"How long?" I ask, still standing by the door.

I'm too afraid to walk farther in, to get closer.

Sawyer pulls the blankets up to her chin. "I've known for a long time."

I stare, unable to speak.

She's known she's sick for a long time, but she's never gone to the doctor while she's been here. Never told me about any appointment. Any treatment. My aunt died from breast cancer. My mom took her to every appointment, every scan. I remember it all. How the life drained from her eyes the longer she fought.

That's not Sawyer.

Her eyes have always been so…lively.

So hopeful.

"Your list," I murmur, the pieces slowly coming together as the last few months resurface in my head. I never understood why there were so many items on it that any twenty-something could easily do, but I also never would have judged her.

Sawyer's eyes close, her head seemingly too heavy to stay up as it settles into the pillow. "I spent so much time fighting to live that I only ever had the energy to exist. So I made a list and enrolled in college."

There's a lump in my chest that rises up into my throat and lodges there. "A bucket list," I rasp.

Her eyes crack open. "A *live* list."

My body feels weak as it leans against the door for support. All this time…

She watches me. My Birdie. The girl who used to look ready to fly anywhere if it meant having an adventure. Now I know why.

"All this time…" My words fade as I drag my fingers through my hair. All this time, she knew she was sick. All this time, Sawyer—*my* Sawyer—was fighting a battle all by herself.

All by herself.

Fists tightening at my sides, I peel my eyes away from her. She lets me have my moment, lying in silence, nothing but hospital machines sounding around us.

Then I stand up, my spine straightening as I open the door and walk out of the room.

The nurse who left me only moments ago watches with wide eyes as I approach her desk with a whole new expression on my face. It's probably a mixture of fury and determination. "I want to sign her out."

Her eyebrows go up, but a small smile curls the corner of her lips. "We would need to see an ID to make sure you're eighteen or older and to go over a few things with you about where you two will be staying, but—"

I toss my ID at her, my eyes going back toward the hallway with the door that I left ajar.

Nobody should be stuck here.

No matter how much they're used to it.

"She doesn't deserve this," I murmur.

The nurse passes me my ID back and says, ever so quietly, "No, she doesn't." Her smile saddens, making me think she knows exactly how bad it is.

Cancer.

My stomach drops.

Sawyer's words from the night of the accident haunt me.

It should have been me.

When I go back to her room, Sawyer is watching the door. I don't ask her any of the things that I want to know. All I say is "You're coming home with me."

She blinks.

Once.

Twice.

Three times.

We stare at one another, our eyes never breaking even when the nurse comes in with discharge papers and care instructions.

The only time I look away is when a curtain separates us as Sawyer changes out of the gown and into a spare set of clothes Dixie dropped off.

A swarm of memories comes back to me, hitting me as hard as the news did, and I wonder if Sawyer will ever be honest with me.

Maybe that's why I don't ask the questions I should know the answers to. Because I don't want to know. They say ignorance is bliss.

So I embrace it and add it to the list of my own secrets that fester under my skin for another day.

"I didn't mean it," she whispers.

I can only stare at her.

"What I said that day in the truck."

My stomach dips.

I should have chosen Dawson.

Her voice is broken when she says, "He's gone."

It should have been me.

"I know." My voice cracks. "Let's not talk about it right now. We have…time."

I stare at her, wondering how true that is.

Time.

She's said time is relative.

I guess now I know why.

Chapter Thirty-Six

SAWYER

A WARM BODY ENCOMPASSES my frame, making it impossible to move from under the blanket wrapped snugly around me.

The last twenty-four hours have been a bigger blur than the days I spent at the hospital. I barely acknowledged the nursing staff who wished me the best as I was wheeled out of the building. I tried fighting them, but I still found myself sitting in the pathetic chair, being wheeled to where Banks was waiting at the curb beside an unfamiliar car. I didn't know until later that it was his father's, but I didn't let myself ask why he'd let him take it or if they'd talked about what I'd said to the older professor when I'd stormed into his office.

"I won't fall apart if you let go of me," I murmur tiredly now, blinking past the grogginess that weighs down my eyelids.

Banks has been stuck to me like glue since we got back, worrying the same way my mother used to when we first found out I was sick. I'm not sure which I would prefer—someone who caters to my every need or somebody who runs from them.

I know from experience that there's never an in between.

Banks's arm tightens once before I feel a pair of lips against my shoulder. He pulls back, sitting up and letting me turn onto my back to look up at the ceiling of my bedroom.

"Is there treatment?" he asks, voice far too awake for the time of day. I'd bet money on him having been up for hours—I could feel his eyes on me as I slept, like he was afraid I'd stop breathing in the night.

That's what my mother did until Aunt Taylor had to tell her to give me space.

"Yes," I say.

A long pause silences the room.

"Good. That's…" He's struggling.

"Banks…I endured those treatments for five years," I tell him, turning my head to meet a pair of wide, muddy eyes. "I can't do them anymore."

He pales. "What do you mean you can't do them? Have they stopped working? There's medicine for everything these days; there has to be a—"

"I said I can't," I repeat, clenching the top of the blanket when I see his brows furrow. "Not that they can't."

He shakes his head, giving it time to soak in. I see the moment it clicks for him because his eyes bug before he sits straighter. "Are you really saying what I think you're saying? You're only twenty-one, Sawyer. You can't just *give up*."

Is that what he thinks I'm doing?

"Almost six years," I tell him, pulling the blanket up to my chin. "That's how long I've been fighting this endless battle, Banks."

He gets out of bed, gripping the back of his neck. "So you're just not going to fight it anymore?"

I force myself to sit up, my ribs aching the way I'm sure he can relate to, and I lean my back against the headboard. "Do you know how bad the treatments made me feel? I spent years hoping the remission would stick, and it never did. So they'd pump me with more toxic chemicals and radiation, hoping that would finally do the job. And just when you start to feel a little human again, after days of vomiting, sleeping, and barely being able to function from the last dose, you have to go back in for another round. It's a cycle of torture that puts your body through so much. It's not meant to be a long-term treatment. It physically can't be. At some point, it has to end."

His fingers rake through his unruly hair as he begins pacing. His silence is deafening. Not that I can blame him. Only the people who go through it can understand the bone-deep exhaustion that comes with the grueling routine of treatments and follow-up appointments.

When he finally speaks, his voice is thick and raw. "Why did you come here?"

Swallowing, I wet my lips. "Thirteen years ago, I fell in love with this place. I figured, what better way to live my life with the time I have left than to come back and explore it as an adult? You can't experience life if you're afraid to live it. I don't want there to be any regrets when my time comes."

I don't want you to regret me.

But I see his eyes.

I can tell.

He already does.

Isn't that what I wanted though?

I should have chosen Dawson.

His eyes roam my face, moving toward my patchy red hair, which I've found pointless to hide, and then back down until he meets my gaze. "I can't believe you didn't tell me."

Drawing my legs up, I hug them to my chest as tightly as I can for comfort. "There's a lot we didn't tell each other."

His nostrils flare in irritation. "I'd hardly say our secrets are comparable. You have fucking *cancer*, Sawyer. Not telling you about my father doesn't even come close to what you've been keeping from all of us. Me. Dixie. Daw—" He stops himself, swallowing the name.

I answer with the only truth I have left. "Our skeletons have never been a competition. But maybe they're the reason why we were drawn to each other in the first place. We're both a little broken inside but still trying to make something of our lives."

Banks's jaw grinds. "Yet all that effort you put into yours is for nothing."

I don't believe that for a second.

Secretly, I don't think he does either.

"Did you think of anybody but yourself when you chose to come here?" he asks, anger shooting from his eyes.

The icy words pierce my skin, and I realize it's a valid question.

So I answer it honestly. "No. I didn't."

All he does is nod, dropping his hands to his sides, where they turn into fists.

Clenching. Unclenching. Clenching.

Then he turns on his heel and walks out of my apartment.

The door slamming echoes, making me cringe.

I deserve it.

Loneliness.
Because I'm selfish.
It should have been me.

Chapter Thirty-Seven

BANKS

THERE WAS SO MUCH I wanted to say to Sawyer when I walked into her hospital room, but all of those things—that I was glad she was okay, that we were going to get through this together despite her hesitations—went out the window the second I realized she was dealing with this alone.

But the difference is, she *has* people.

Not everybody is that lucky.

I've been driving for hours when I decide to stop at the Botanic Gardens and walk around. It only seems fitting when it starts raining, drenching me as I walk the trails aimlessly. I guess I'd feel cheated if it were sunny because that'd hardly match my mood. Ever since the night of the accident, everything has been dark. Cold.

When my phone goes off in my pocket, I pull it out, having the pathetic reaction of thinking it could be Dawson since we haven't spoken in days. Then it hits me all over again that it couldn't be.

One of the last conversations Dawson and I had ended

in a fight. Harsh words were said. Things I can't take back. I hold on to a lot of regret because I can't apologize or tell him I didn't mean it.

Scrubbing at the dampness on my face that I'm not sure is rain or angry tears, I ignore the call and slide my cell back into my pocket to protect it from the rain.

Sawyer doesn't want to live life with any regrets, but I don't see how she wouldn't have any. She's close with her family, and her decision left them behind. Led her to *me*.

On my way back to the car, when my clothes are sopping wet and sticking to my skin, I stop by the little footbridge that a chipmunk scurries under for cover.

Then I think about the last item on Sawyer's list.

Grabbing my keys, I get back into the car and stare at the bridge a little longer.

I didn't get a chance to make things right with Dawson, so I'll be damned if I mess up with Sawyer, even if she doesn't feel the same way.

So I come up with a plan and then find the number her father gave me that day in the hallway.

"If anything ever comes up," he tells me, slipping the paper with the phone number into my hand with a solid shake, "I trust that you'll let me know."

He could tell I cared.

I stare at the number.

And hit call.

I change into dry clothes before knocking on the door across the hall, not willing to push my boundaries and welcome myself in after my exit earlier.

When Sawyer opens it, I take my hands out of my pockets and say, "Go on a date with me."

She blinks. "W-What?"

"Go on a date with me," I repeat. In hindsight, I should have brought flowers or chocolates or pastries, but I wasn't thinking about that. "I know you told me before that I was ruining everything for you, but I have somewhere I want to take you. Somewhere you're going to want to see. So just one date. That's all I ask of you. Give me today."

She's still wearing the same clothes that she was in when I left—the same ones that she wore yesterday. Fidgeting with the sweatshirt, she shakes her head. "I don't think that's a good idea."

"We've been through hell, Birdie. I promise it'll be worth it. I just need you to trust me. If this is the last thing you give me, then so be it."

Her eyes are sad as they meet mine.

"*Do* you trust me?" I ask, afraid of how she may answer. "We were friends once."

I wouldn't be upset if she told me no, so I'm patient as she stares at me in heavy contemplation. I'm not giving her much to go on except instinct. Hopefully, her gut is on my side.

"We still are," she tells me.

My eyebrows go up.

So when she says, "Yes," I feel the pressure on my chest lift. "But it doesn't change anything, Banks. There's nothing you can do. My family has already tried. I need this for me, and I don't expect you to understand."

I know. Swallowing those words, I force a nod. If she's set her mind on it, I doubt there's anything to be done. "Get dressed. I'll wait for you here."

403

It's my way of saying, *I know it won't change anything, but I wish it did.*

———————————

Sawyer keeps her body angled toward the passenger window and her hands tucked under her thighs as she takes in the setting sun that paints the sky in yellow, orange, and pink as we drive down the interstate.

I know I'm the reason her walls are up.

It doesn't change anything.

It's a harsh truth that I don't want to think about as I pull off the New Orleans exit and weave through the slow traffic with out-of-state plates piling up the lanes.

"I'm sorry," I say to break the silence.

She still won't look at me. "I don't need an apology," she replies, staring at the scenery rolling by. Her shoulders rise with the deep breath she takes before they slowly release with her exhale. "You have every right to be mad."

I don't though. "It's your life."

I may not ever understand exactly what it's like to go through what she has, but I've seen it with my aunt. I know it isn't easy. My aunt had children, my three cousins, whom she fought for. A husband who loved her. Two dogs that she adopted from a shelter. She'd built a life for herself long before she was diagnosed with cancer.

It's different for the girl beside me.

We drive another twenty minutes in silence until I slow down, nearing a side road outside of the Garden District. If we keep driving, we'll stop in front of my father's house, which is the last place I want to be.

"Where are we?" Sawyer asks, finally turning to me.

I open my door and slip out, bending down to look at her still sitting inside. "Come on."

Closing the driver's-side door, I open the one behind me to grab the little basket I put together before knocking on her door.

Sawyer hesitantly steps out, looking curiously at the wicker basket hanging from my hand. I walk around the front and put a hand on her lower back to guide her toward the thick magnolia bushes that were replanted a few years after Katrina hit. The hurricane wiped out a lot of the landscaping, but money donations to the gardening clubs eventually helped bring life back to the area when civilization slowly started rebuilding. But Dad and I redid this. It was the last project we ever did together. "Follow me."

She bites her lip, looking around as we take the path that very few people ever have. It's grown in, barely visible unless you know what to look for. Once upon a time, this private area used to be beautiful. The abandoned spot is still well kept on the outside but closed off to the public, thanks to the faded private-property signs hanging on the large oaks surrounding it, so very few people know that if you push back two of the bushes right behind the crape myrtles—

Sawyer freezes when I move the shrubs aside. The only sound around us is the slow trickle of water coming from the tiny stream behind the greenery, which only runs if there's a lot of rain.

I step through the bushes and keep them back for her to do the same.

She steps back, snapping a twig and almost losing her balance before I manage to catch her wrist with my free hand.

Disbelief lifts her gaze to mine. "Your father called you Paxton."

My heart gallops hearing her say that name.

The pad of my thumb rubs the back of her forearm. "He's the only one who does. It's why I prefer going by Banks."

Her eyes dip to where I'm holding her.

"Come on," I urge, tugging on her arm until she's stepping past the bushes and into the cozy environment that I've managed to keep up despite the damage inflicted all those years ago.

I let go of Sawyer, letting her spin as she takes in what's left of the oak that used to shade the area. It was so damaged by the storm that a majority of the branches had to be cut down before they became a hazard. Most of the shrubs were crushed by the thick branches that had fallen during Katrina, and one of the original crape myrtles snapped and fell too, damaging the other bushes that surrounded it.

Then she stops, her lips parting as she stares at the wooden footbridge. Or what's left of it.

It's still standing despite the rotting and missing wood.

Broken but beautiful.

"The bridge," she whispers.

I walk over to it, kneeling down and setting the basket beside me. "I always thought you felt familiar," I tell her, looking over my shoulder at where her feet are glued to the ground. "I couldn't figure out why until your mom said you were named after Tom Sawyer."

"Like the book," we say simultaneously.

The smile comes easily. "I tried picturing you with red hair but couldn't. You said you never dyed it before."

Her hands go to her head, her face turning a similar shade to the strands she touches. "I...I haven't."

"I know that now."

She never had to dye it.

She lost it and hid what came back.

Wetting my lips, I run my fingers over the inner post, where two sets of initials in messy handwriting are carved.

Finally, Sawyer walks over and stares at the initials she put into the wood. She told me she used a butter knife and then brought the same one a few weeks after we met so I could do the same.

"I didn't think..." Her head shakes back and forth as she lowers herself to the ground. "I had no idea if it'd still be here."

"It almost didn't survive."

The broken structure is made of thick pieces of wood that probably shouldn't still be here after the abuse they were put through, but the bridge fought its own battles to remain standing.

I look to Sawyer, whose hair looks exactly as I remember it in the sunshine. Right here, standing beside the bridge, she looks so similar to how she did back then. Just older. Frailer.

"You told me back then that this was your happy place," I comment, sitting down and patting the grass beside me. "When I realized who you were, I understood what the last item on your list was."

She joins me, pulling her knees up to her chest and staring at our initials still. "I couldn't remember where it was. The chemo..." Her throat bobs. "Chemo brain makes it hard to recall details. I wanted to come back and try finding it because I wanted to feel how I did back then. Normal. Just...just one more time."

Her eyes are wet when they turn to me. "I'm sorry," she whispers, resting her chin on top of her bent knees. "You were right. I never thought I'd ever see you again. I was only thinking about me when I chose to come here. I was thinking about closing a chapter I didn't get to thirteen years ago, and I wanted to do it my way. I wanted to say I was a college kid. Reckless. Dumb. I wanted everything to be..."

"Easy," I finish for her.

That's what she wanted from me. Easy.

"Paxton," she says again, but it's clear she's not trying to talk to me. Not this version of me, anyway. Her eyes close, and a small smile tilts the corners of her lips. "You were my favorite memory."

Wetting my lips, I reach over and take her hand. "You were mine too, Birdie. Always."

When her eyes open, they glisten with a fondness that I haven't seen in a long time.

"There were days when things at home were bad," I tell her, fingers tightening around her. "I'd come here to get fresh air. I used to come with my dad, but when things started getting rough with my mom, he stopped coming out. It's like he forgot it existed. But I was glad."

It meant more for me.

More time alone.

More time with Sawyer.

"This is on the property I grew up on," I say, watching her eyes widen. My foot taps the closest post. "I built this with my dad. Before the alcohol took over, when things were normal. Or as normal as they could have been. I always wondered how you found it, but I never cared enough to ask."

Sawyer stares at the bridge. "You built...?" Her head moves back and forth in disbelief. "You never told me back then. I found it when I went out adventuring. I was hot, needed a place to rest, and this place seemed so..."

"Safe."

She nods. "Safe," she agrees.

"Maybe we were meant to meet," I remark, leaning back and thinking about us as children, sitting in this very spot. "We both needed somebody back then, and we both need someone now. Especially since Dawson..."

We fall to silence.

Then I pull out the two bags of fruit snacks that I snagged from the campus store, and she lets out a watery laugh and accepts one just like we did as kids.

I play with the gummies poured out into my palm, not eating any of them. "Is there really nothing the hospital can do? If you changed your mind..."

It's not going to change anything.

Sawyer picks one of the fruit snacks out and squeezes it between her fingers. "The oncologist came to see me after I was brought in. Even if I did change my mind, it wouldn't matter. It's spread. They told me it would."

Emotion crams into my throat, making it hard to swallow.

"I can feel it," she whispers, a tear sliding down her face that she wipes off with the back of her hand. "I think I've been feeling it for a while. Since I got here. Maybe even before."

My nose burns as I fight off the tears prickling the backs of my own eyes. What can I say to her? There are no words that would make it better. Nothing I could say to comfort her.

So all I do is hold her hand.

She squeezes it.

I squeeze back.

Her voice is nearly inaudible when she speaks again. "I never wanted to hurt you. I never wanted to hurt anybody."

She tried warning me. Tried pushing me away. But I wouldn't let her. "I know you didn't, Birdie."

We sit with the quiet swirling around us as the sun begins to set. Then I look up, hearing a faint chirp before a red bird lands on a twig above us.

I point. "Look."

Sawyer's head moves up toward the cardinal staring down at her. Its head cocks to the side as if studying her. Then to the other.

"They say cardinals are spiritual birds," I murmur, transfixed by its fascination in Sawyer. It flies off the branch and onto the ground a few feet away from her. "I've read about how they're believed to be people we've lost checking in on us. I took out a book on birds not long after coming back to see what Katrina had done. It reminded me of you."

We watch as the bird hesitates before bouncing over to her feet, stopping by her shoe. It pecks her once, twice, then flaps its wings and takes off.

"Maybe that will be me someday," Sawyer says.

The lump in my throat returns, and I can't find the words to answer her.

It's well after dark when we finally pull into the parking lot of the apartment building, her hand tucked into mine the entire way. I don't even know if she realizes it's there, but she hasn't let go.

Sawyer turns to me. "Thank you."

A single tear rolls down her face that I swipe away with my thumb. "You don't have to thank me, Birdie. I'm just glad I could help you finish your list."

Her eyes close for a moment, eyelids clenching to fight the flow of tears as she nestles her cheek into my palm. "Still...it means the world to me. I never thought I'd see it again. Didn't know if it still existed. After everything, I didn't think you'd even want to be around me."

If she'd gotten her way, maybe I wouldn't have. But there's a tug in my chest that always leads me to her whether I want it to or not.

When I see somebody walking toward the car I'm borrowing from my father, I take a deep breath and say, "Just remember that, okay?"

She opens her eyes with confusion twisting her features before knuckles rap on her side of the window.

As soon as she sees her father standing on the other side of the glass, she locks up.

"They love you as much as if not more than you love them," I tell her, hoping she'll forgive me. "More than I...I could have loved you. Don't you think they deserve to be part of your life no matter how hard it gets?"

Her jaw quivers. "You called him?"

I turn off the engine. "My father and I may never see eye to eye, but you still tried for me. This is me trying for you. Be with your family, Sawyer."

Be with your family.

Forget about me.

"Close the chapter."

Her breath catches as she stares at me.

I squeeze her hand once before letting go.

Chapter Thirty-Eight

SAWYER

MY FATHER TOOK A leave of absence from work, which is the last thing I wanted him to do. But between him and the daily calls from my mother since Banks—*Paxton*—contacted him, I stopped fighting them on anything.

I haven't been to school in almost two weeks, and Dad gave up encouraging me to after the first one came and went. It was clear I'd made up my mind. It took everything he had to convince my mother to stay in New York with Bentley, and I could hear how tired he was from their conversations at night, which usually led to intense fights.

All because of me.

Always because of me.

On Thursday, my father knocks on my bedroom door and cracks it open. "Can I come in, baby girl?"

He will anyway, so I simply nod.

My eyes follow his shoes as they near me before he turns and sits on the edge of the bed. "I know it's hard, but you can't stay in here forever."

His hand comes down on top of my head, playing with my hair the way he and my mother used to do when I was little. It doesn't feel as good as it did then—doesn't comfort me the way I wish it could.

"I'm tired" is my only response.

I've been tired for days. Weeks. Months. But the kind of fatigue plaguing my body now feels so heavy, it's like somebody tied two anchors to my ankles and expected me to walk. My limbs ache and drag and hurt. Despite barely eating, I'm bloated and uncomfortable. And based on the way my rib cage stuck out when my father forced me to shower yesterday, I'm losing weight.

I want to chalk it up to sadness.

To the non-breakup that still did something funny to my heart.

But I know what it really is.

I stare at his watch, watching the hands move.

Tick tock, tick tock.

"If you got up and ate something, it'd help," he suggests, though it's pointless. I've entertained the meals he's given me because I know it'll make him feel better, but I've gotten sick the last three nights in a row. Even toast doesn't stay down long enough to matter.

I shake my head, closing my eyes again.

Dad sighs, his hand stilling. "I know this might not mean much, but if it makes you feel any better, I like him."

Him. Paxton. Banks. Whoever he is.

"He went behind my back."

"He cares about you." His voice is thick. "I don't know any other reason he would have called me when he could have let things go and had time with you to himself. Kept your secret. Not a lot of people would sacrifice what he did, but he did it for you. That says something, kiddo."

It's better he pawned me off. We couldn't stay in a fantasy world forever. What would happen when the lymph nodes became so swollen they collapsed a lung? Or made it impossible to eat? What would he do when I was in my apartment hunched over a toilet while he was supposed to be in class? I didn't need a caregiver, nor did I want one. If I did, I would have stayed home.

I needed a friend. A companion. A distraction.

Somebody I could have feigned happiness with for a little while longer.

Selfish, selfish, selfish.

I'm certain there are no more tears left to cry because despite the prickle of emotion rising up my throat, my eyes don't water. "If he cared, then where is he?"

He hasn't come to my apartment.

Hasn't dropped off any Pop-Tarts or coffee.

There have been no texts. No calls. Nothing.

You were my favorite memory.

Maybe that's the only thing he will ever be.

"Tonight is the service," he tells me quietly.

I crack an eye open. "How did you—"

"I went to the school. Don't make that face, Sawyer." My father gives me *the look* that has me swallowing my reply. "They needed to know what was happening. Your adviser told me where Dawson Gable's service was in case you were able to attend."

I can't believe he would go to campus. I should have known he wasn't just going to let me stay here. He's too logical.

"Banks will be there," he adds.

Finally, I meet his eyes.

"They were friends, right?" he asks, brows drawn up.

"There's no doubt that he'll be there to say goodbye. I wish I was there for you when the accident happened, and I wish I was there when you were in the hospital, but I can be here for you through this."

"Dad, I don't know if—"

"Was Dawson your friend?"

He already knows that answer. "Yes."

"You tried to save him," he points out. "You cared enough to get into that truck to try to make sure he was safe. I'll be honest with you, sweetie. I'm not a fan of his, and I hate speaking ill of the dead. He put you at risk, and I'll never be okay with that. But it says a lot more about your character than it does his. I know you, Sawyer. You'll regret not going. You'll regret not being able to gain some closure from this."

Closure.

Isn't that what this whole journey has been about?

My bottom lip quivers. "I didn't save him, Dad. I failed him. And I lied to a lot of people."

He pulls me into him for a hug. "You did what you could. That's what matters."

I clench my eyes closed, burying my face into his chest and breathing in his signature scent that has always calmed me—laundry detergent and Irish Spring soap.

Running his hands over my back, he presses a kiss on top of my head. "What do you say?"

I force myself to sit up, letting the blankets pool at my waist. "Why?"

"Why what?"

Shame coats my heart. "Why aren't you yelling at me? Why aren't you mad? I keep messing up, Dad. And now somebody is *dead*. Somebody who had a whole life ahead of them. There's another hospital bill for thousands of dollars in my name. I've hurt people, even though I tried so hard not to get too close. I..." I can't finish, my voice becoming too weak from the mistakes weighing on my vocal cords.

The weight on my chest is crushing.

Pulling me under.

Squeezing out what little air I have left in me.

For a moment, he's quiet as he soothes me by rubbing my arm. "Breathe. Just breathe."

When I manage to take a long, deep breath, he pats my hand gently once.

"There's a lot I wish you had been honest about," he admits, disappointment in his eyes. "But you never meant for any of this to happen. Sometimes bad things happen to good people. And none of that is important right now. Today is about grieving. It's about saying goodbye. We'll figure out the other stuff later. Together. Okay?"

Saying goodbye. To Dawson.

To Banks.

To Louisiana?

He stands. "Why don't you take a shower and find something to wear. We'll get something light to eat before the service. I'll drive us."

Sometimes, I wish he'd tell me how disappointed he is in me. That he's upset at how I've acted. They gave me freedom, and this is what I've done with it.

He loves me too much to let any of that change his perception of me.

Before he leaves, I say, "I love you."

His smile brightens his eyes when he smiles at me, but there's still a dullness to them that I know I've caused. "I love you too, baby girl."

The service is somber, the funeral home only half-full of people I mostly don't recognize. Dad and I walked in fifteen minutes before it started and took a seat toward the back. Being next to the casket...

I couldn't do it.

For somebody who has been surrounded by terminal illness, I've gone twenty-one years without attending a funeral. I never thought the first one would be under these circumstances.

Dixie showed up five minutes before it started, looked at the casket, and walked out. I wanted to follow her, but Banks...Paxton beat me to it. Neither of them saw me hidden next to my dad in the back pew. I asked Dixie if she was going, and she never replied.

She was upset with me, and I understood.

I lied time and time again.

I didn't tell her about the biggest part of me.

That would hurt anyone.

I spend the first thirty minutes staring at Paxton, who's sitting beside a crying woman in the front row after coming back without Dixie. When she gets up to speak to the crowd, I see how much Dawson looked like the older woman. His mother. A man walks up beside her. Tall. Maybe as tall as Dawson was, if not taller. His father.

I wonder if he's looking down on this moment to see how his parents have come together for him. And I can't help but wonder how my family will act the day of mine. Will they share embarrassing stories about me? Talk about their favorite memories? I wouldn't be happy to see them torn up. I'd want them to be happy to know I was okay.

Finally okay.

Done fighting and finally at peace.

An hour in, Paxton turns to study the crowd, and I wonder who he's looking for. His eyes find their way to me and then to my father, who tips his head in acknowledgment the way he does when he's greeting other men.

It's simple. Respectful.

My father *does* like him.

If things were different, would my father choose him for me the way I would choose him in another lifetime?

The spell of thoughts is broken when Paxton shifts his focus to somebody else, sitting straighter in his seat. From here, the only way to describe his expression is shock.

Leaning forward subtly, I try finding who's captured his attention. There are a few people lining the seats three rows ahead of me, but his eyes look like they're locked on a tan brunette whom I've never seen before.

My father gently clears his throat at me.

Blushing, I sit back and turn my focus back to what the officiant says as he wraps up the service. Nobody shared their stories of Dawson the way I expected. Did somebody ask them not to in fear of what they'd say? I find it hard to believe that the people here weren't touched by him at some point. He had his troubles, but he was kind. Funny. Charming, even.

When the night ends, my father waits by the car to give me space to talk to whom I need to. He nods in encouragement when I look to him, so I stand taller and remind myself that I've been through worse than a conversation.

Walking over to where Paxton is standing by the mysterious brunette, I can't help but listen in while his back is to me.

"Desiree, don't you think it's a little pathetic to attend the funeral of somebody whom you treated like shit? This isn't a church. I'd hardly consider it the place to confess your sins."

"I apologized to him *and* to you for what I did," she hisses, looking offended. "Just because things didn't end well doesn't mean I didn't care. And you guys made up, even after you were a willing participant in us getting together. So why are you being an asshole to me?"

Paxton snorts. "If you cared, you wouldn't have gone after both of us knowing we were friends."

The girl, Desiree, sees me standing behind Paxton and turns red. She looks back to our mutual friend and says, "I came here for Dawson, not to prove anything to you. It's nice to know you haven't changed, Paxton."

She called him Paxton. Not Banks.

A crack forms in my heart.

I thought his father was the only one who called him that—and me, a long, long time ago.

Paxton turns. "Sawyer."

"Banks," I say, unsure of what to call him. "I—" Wetting my lips, I look between him and Desiree. She watches me curiously before scoffing and leaving us alone, disappearing to God only knows where. "I didn't mean to interrupt."

"You didn't."

I'm not sure I believe him.

He clearly sees that. His tone softens. "I mean it. Talking to her is the last thing I want to do tonight. Ever, if I'm being honest."

I wet my lips. "Not me?"

His brows furrow. "You?"

"You've been avoiding me."

"I've been giving you *space*."

Space. Is it really that simple? "What if I don't want space?"

His eyes roam over my face before a frown settles onto his. "But what about what you *need*?"

This time, I don't answer him.

Paxton glances in the direction of my father before looking at the ground. "How are things with your family?"

That's what he wants to talk about? "We're friends, aren't we?"

His gaze lifts. "Yes."

"At one point, it seemed like we were more," I press, swallowing down the embarrassment of the non-question. "And I know I messed that up, and I know you know why I had to. But you can be honest with me."

If I have to ask, isn't that answer enough?

Paxton closes his eyes. "Sawyer..."

"She called you Paxton."

He closes his eyes and pushes his glasses up with a long exhale. "Desiree has always done whatever she's wanted. She knows what buttons to push to get a reaction. But she doesn't matter. She hasn't mattered in a long time. I don't think she ever did, if I'm being real with you."

All I can do is nod, feeling embarrassed that I'm jealous when I have no right to be.

"You chose this," he reminds me.

"I know." I swallow. "Friends. Friends is good. Friends is what I...I need."

Friends is all it should be.

I start backing up.

"Birdie," he says, trying to stop me. "Thank you for being here. It would have meant a lot to Dawson."

His eyes are pleading like he wants to say so much more, but he refrains.

So he settles with "It means a lot to me. Dixie...she wanted to stay. But she couldn't handle it. You should check on her."

"She hasn't been talking to me," I admit.

"She's upset about a lot of things," he tells me quietly. "But regardless of that, she needs a friend. You can push me away all you want, but don't push her away. Even if she lets you."

I stare down at the ground. He cares about her. That's... good, I decide. Really good.

I told Dixie he'd need her someday.

"I'll try," I say.

"Good."

I peek up at him. "Good."

As I start walking away, I see his face pale at somebody lingering off to the side.

"Banks?" I ask.

His nostrils flare, and I swear I see his jaw grind the way it did when he got into an argument with his father on the phone the first night we ever slept together.

Selfish.

That's what he was upset about.

But he's the least selfish person I know.

"Banks?" I repeat, putting my hand on his arm to snap him away from whoever has his attention.

"I can't believe he had the nerve to show up here," he says, so low that it sounds like a cold growl and feels like ice over my skin.

I turn. "Who?"

"Don't." He pulls my attention away from the person I'm trying to see. "Marco. The person responsible for Dawson's habit. And more than likely his relapse."

Marco is *here*? I turn again despite Banks's warning, scoping out the lawn until I see somebody staring in our direction. He's by himself, half hidden by the shadows of the side of the building with his arms crossed. But I can see one arm covered in a sleeve of tattoos, just like the guy who approached Dawson on campus. And he's...smiling?

"I've seen him before," I tell him. "At school."

Banks's eyes snap to me. "He's not allowed on campus."

Well, that didn't stop him. "He went up to Dawson and gave him something. Dawson looked a little scared."

Banks steps forward. "That son of a—"

"Don't," I plead, grabbing ahold of his arm to stop him from approaching Marco. "That's what he wants. A reaction. Don't give it to him. It won't change what happened."

His eyes stay on Marco. "He doesn't deserve to be here. Somebody needs to do something about him before he ruins more lives. To stand up to him."

"Somebody will," I promise him. "But it doesn't have to be you. He's already gotten into trouble once. He'll get into it again, especially if they find out he was associated with the drugs that caused Dawson to..." I can't say the word.

Overdose.

Nobody talks about it.

Nobody acknowledges it.

It's the elephant in the room.

Before he crashed, he started overdosing on whatever he'd been given. My guess is he took what he got from the guys at the party, but he took too much. I'm not sure what would have happened if he didn't get behind the wheel. Would be still be alive? Or would the drugs have taken him on the side of the road? In an Uber?

I don't like thinking about it.

Because he's gone.

What–ifs don't matter.

Eventually, Banks stands down, his eyes dipping to where I hold on to his arm. When they lift to meet mine, I say, "Let it be somebody else's problem."

It takes him a few deep breaths before he nods, only once, with his lips pressed into a reluctant straight line.

When I know he's not going to approach Marco, I let go of him. "Thank you."

He wets his lips. "Paxton."

My brows pinch.

His throat bobs. "You're the only one who I want to call me that. You were the only one I ever liked calling me that. Not my father. Not Desiree. You."

You were my favorite memory.

Heart swelling in my chest, I nod. "Okay."

"Okay," he repeats.

We stare at one another for what feels like an eternity before I realize my father is still waiting.

"I should go."

"Okay," he says again.

"Bye." I pause. "Paxton."

He parts his lips and then closes them.

He doesn't want to say goodbye.

So I don't let him.

I walk away and let my father help me into the car without looking back. I'm afraid of what I'll see if I do.

"Your mother called again," he tells me as soon as we're driving. "You should know that we talked about it, and I've chosen to take an early retirement. Your mother and I feel it's for the best to spend as much time together as a family since…"

I close my eyes and lean my head against the cool window, saying nothing at all.

Since my cancer progressed.

Since we're on borrowed time.

Tick tock, tick tock.

That night, I ask Dad to drop me off at the dorms after stopping by the closest gas station. I knock on Dixie's door and hold up a plastic bag. "I know ice cream is you and Banks's thing, but I think we both could use it."

She stares at the bag and then at me.

Tears form in her eyes.

I hug her. She hugs me back.

We cry until we fall asleep in her twin bed.

The ice cream melts.

Chapter Thirty-Nine

SAWYER

I'M STARTLED AWAKE BY the annoying sound of my ringtone. Jerking up, I absentmindedly search for my phone on my nightstand, which is full of water, pills, and other junk that my father put there per my mother's commands.

When I finally find it, I slide my finger over the green button and don't even get a chance to see who it is before I hear my brother say, "You *promised*. When you left, you said you wouldn't let them change anything."

It's hard to break past the grogginess as I sit up slowly, with a pain in my ribs that has me cringing, and rub my eyes. "Bentley, I don't under—"

"I have friends here. A girl I like," he cuts me off angrily, his voice getting louder even though it's—*God*. Two thirty in the morning. "I thought you had my back, but they're making me give it all up for you. You *promised*."

It takes longer than I want to admit letting everything he's saying soak in before I finally get what this is about. "They haven't said anything to me about this. I swear it. The last time I heard them talk about moving was over spring break."

That doesn't appease my little brother. "It's always been about you," he accuses, voice breaking. "For once, I wanted it to be about me. I did everything I could to make life easier for them. *I* did. Not you. *I* tried to make things better knowing you were going to wreck it. Wreck *them*."

I swallow past the lump in my throat.

The dig is well deserved.

I am going to wreck them.

I already have.

"Bent—"

"I hate you," he hisses before hanging up.

I stare at my phone, fully awake now. If I call him back and try to talk to him, will he answer? I doubt it. I know Bentley. He holds on to grudges.

Swinging my legs over the side of the bed, I trudge over to the door and wake up my father, who's been sleeping on the couch since getting here. "You can't uproot Bentley's life."

If he's surprised by the statement, he doesn't act it. He sits up, wincing as he massages his neck and rolls his shoulders. "Sawyer, your mother and I think it's what's best."

I cross my arms. "For whom? He's mad at me because you guys are taking away the only stability he's ever had. I don't want to be responsible for that. I've already caused enough damage to the family for one lifetime."

His eyes widen. "Sawyer, how could you say that? Nothing you've done is your fault."

I may not have asked for cancer, but I made plenty of decisions since stopping treatment. "If you take him out of New York, he may never forgive me. I promised him I wouldn't do that to him."

Dad swipes a palm down the front of his face and sighs. "Can we talk about this in the morning? I think this conversation needs coffee, and I can tell you're upset."

"Bentley is more upset," I argue.

He watches me for a moment, lips pressing together in contemplation before he eventually nods. "No matter what choice we make, somebody is going to be upset. But your mother and I aren't comfortable leaving you here alone given the circumstances."

It's always about you.

Selfish.

Whom are you trying to fool?

I hate you.

Closing my eyes, I squeeze my fists together where they're tucked under my arms. "Give me a month. I'll be finished with the semester, and then I'll go back to New York. Just don't..." I take a deep breath. "Don't make Bentley leave. That's the only home he's ever known."

In that moment, I realize what Paxton must have been thinking when he chose to call my father.

Life is all about sacrifices for the people you care about. The people you love.

"Sawyer," Dad says softly.

"I'm going to bed."

I close the door behind me, curl into the blankets, and think about how to make the most of my time left.

But when sleep evades me and I find myself too pent-up to relax, I creep out of my bedroom, past my sleeping father, and out the front door.

It smells exactly how I remember it did, the blooming flowers tickling my nose as I settle against the remaining trunk of the oak. I can tell how much effort it took for Paxton, or whomever, to maintain this little slice of heaven.

Using my foot to nudge the one of the bridge's wooden posts, I frown as it teeters out of place. Despite Paxton's work, I doubt it'll last much longer without some major TLC. And who has the money for that? I guess it's good that I won't be around long enough to see it completely destroyed.

I hear footsteps near me. I scooch closer to the stump, hugging my legs into my body and hoping what little remains of the darkness from sunrise can shield me from whoever is coming.

I see a flashlight enter the little alcove before a body does, and past the bright glare, I see Paxton. Relief eases my tense muscles as he walks over. "Thought you might be here."

"How did you know I left?" I ask, relaxing into the stump. "My dad didn't even wake up when I snuck out."

My neighbor chuckles. "Are you sure?" he remarks with a secretive smile.

"Why?"

He grins, turning the flashlight off and tucking it into his front pocket. "Who do you think came to my apartment asking if I knew where you might go?"

I sit up straighter, looking toward the set of bushes hiding us. "Is he here?"

Paxton settles beside me, stretching his long legs out in front of him and holding out a silver-foiled wrapper for me to take. "Nah, he let us have a moment. I think he knows you need it now more than ever."

I rest my chin back down on my knees, staring at the Pop-Tart. "Did he tell you?"

There's a pause. "Yes."

"I'm doing it for my brother."

"I know, Birdie."

"I don't want to be selfish anymore."

His throat bobs. "You never were."

What a lie.

"Bentley hates me," I tell him, nibbling my bottom lip and closing my eyes. "Going back is the only way."

Paxton rubs my arm. "No, he doesn't. He's thirteen and upset. I can't tell you how many times I told my family I hated them when I was his age."

But the difference is, he had a reason to. "You didn't mean it though? If I were you, I would have."

He stares at our bridge quietly, thinking about his answer. Clicking his tongue, he shakes his head. "I heard once that life is too short to be at war with yourself. If I spent my whole life hating my family for the choices they made, wouldn't I regret the decisions I was making for me?"

I consider it, realizing our mindsets aren't that different after all. Neither one of us wants to waste our time existing with the cards we were dealt when we could reshuffle the deck.

"Paxton?"

His eyes flicker to me, sparking when he hears me speak that name. Long before he was Banks, the boy who shared my bed, he was Paxton, the boy who shared my fruit snacks.

My happy place.

I let out a tiny breath. "You were never just an item to cross off the list."

He looks away, face overcome with emotion. I don't

think I needed to tell him that, but I can tell he appreciated it anyway.

Eventually, in such a quiet voice, he says, "I always saw you as more than my neighbor, more than a friend." He pauses, still not looking at me but at the wooden bridge. "Maybe in another life, we could have explored that."

That crack in my heart deepens, making my chest threaten to cave in. "Yeah. Maybe."

We sit in silence, his hand sliding toward mine until our pinkies wrap around one another. I don't know how long we sit like that, but it doesn't seem like long enough when I choose to break the silence.

"I'm grateful for you and what you've given me," I tell him, squeezing his pinky. "I always will be. And I hope one day you can find the kind of friendship we had in somebody who can truly make you happy."

His grip on my hand tightens until it's almost painful, but I know that's not his intent. Paxton Banks would never hurt me.

Not the way I'm hurting him.

His voice is raspy when he says, "I hope so too, Birdie. I hope so too."

Chapter Forty

SAWYER

IF THERE'S ONE THING I hate more than walking into a room late, it's being stared at when people know your secret. There's always pity in their eyes. Empty sympathy. They know, but they can't relate. Most people are only sad because they feel like they should be. There's nothing personal about the emotion they feel, no reason for them to lose sleep the way I know my family has. The way Paxton and Dixie have. They feel obligated to, like they'd be bad people if they didn't act like they cared.

Professor Grey is the only one who treats me normally when I come back on my father's and Paxton's recommendations to finish the last few weeks of school. There's no special treatment, no after-class talks of encouragement like I get from my other professors. He's smart enough to know there's nothing that can be done except to move forward.

At the end of class, he hands me back my graded short story with his notes jotted into the margins. He pats my shoulder and in a low voice says, "That's what I meant when I said to channel something personal. Good job."

When he moves on, I read the comment he made on the last page.

A beautiful story that will forever haunt me. One day, you should consider publishing this.

One day...

I flatten the stapled papers down and sink into my seat. My parents would love his optimism, but all I can think is... *how appropriate.*

I can add another nickname to my arsenal.

Sawyer Hawkins.

Tom Sawyer.

Birdie.

Ghost.

Maybe that should go on my gravestone.

Here lies the haunted Sawyer Hawkins. Daughter. Sister. Ghost.

Paxton leans over. "That's awesome. You got an A." When I drag my eyes over to him, he pales. "Sawyer?"

A droplet of blood lands on the paper.

Then another.

My stomach drops as I run my hand under my nose and see the smear of bright red on my skin.

I stand abruptly, drawing attention from everybody in the room. Then I run out, barely able to grab my bag before I launch myself into the bathroom.

When I see my reflection in the mirror, I see sunken, sad eyes dulled to a stormy blue-gray. The sink quickly fills with blood, reminding me why I'm there. I grab as many paper towels as I can and tip my head back to stop the bleeding.

A few minutes later, I hear a hesitant "Sawyer?" at the cracked door.

"Go away, Paxton."

The door opens farther, his head poking in. "Are you alone in here?"

"This is the girls' bathroom," I point out.

He sighs, pauses, and then walks in to where I'm standing by the sink. "I should have figured it out sooner."

Feeling lightheaded, I sink to the floor, not caring what may be on it. Paxton watches me lean back against the wall before joining me.

"The nosebleeds, when you passed out, the bruises..." He lets his words fade.

How could he have guessed? "I didn't want you to," I murmur, pinching my nose harder. "I wanted you to like me."

"I still like you."

From the corner of my eye, I see him studying me. His jaw ticks before he looks away and mimics my body language, leaning his head against the wall and staring up at the ceiling.

In another lifetime.

"Fate is a cruel bitch," I murmur.

Paxton is quiet for a second.

Then he starts laughing, and it sounds like it comes from deep inside him. The rumbling sound shakes his shoulders and his chest, and eventually, I can't help but join him.

Only when he catches his breath does he say, "It really is."

After I get the bleeding to stop, Paxton helps me dispose of the soaked paper towels and guides me up. "Come on," he says. "I'll take you home. Unless your dad is coming to get you."

I shake my head, watching as he puts my bag over his shoulder. "He went back to his apartment for a few days. I think he's finally giving me some space now that he knows I'm not going to randomly drop dead."

He swallows, the light mood from before quickly darkening. "That's not funny."

All I can do is shrug.

Putting his hand on my lower back, he holds open the bathroom door for me and ignores the skeptical expressions that we get from passersby. I don't care what they think, and he obviously doesn't either.

"Can we go to our bridge?"

He wets his lips. "I don't know..."

He's worried. I get it. "Please?"

His eyes close briefly before he loosens a sigh, his fingers moving away from my back for a moment before putting pressure there again. "I can't say no to you when you say that."

I wonder if he wishes he could.

An hour later, we're sitting by the broken bridge that looks like it lost another plank. "It won't last much longer."

Paxton walks over and examines it, testing the posts and carefully balancing on a few pieces to get to the other side. He almost falls into the tiny stream below but catches himself on the railing, which creaks and groans under his body weight. "It has a chance. It's strong."

Is he talking about the bridge still?

I stand on the opposite end and watch him kneel to study the integrity of the structure. "Your sketch," I start. "Was it inspired by this?"

Paxton looks up at me through his lashes, two little pink dots on his cheeks. "You noticed that, huh?"

"I should have realized sooner."

He stands, leaning on the post. "How could you have? There was so much we couldn't have known about each other months ago."

I don't say anything.

"My father designed this whole hideaway," he explains, looking around. "He taught me everything I know about landscaping and architecture. He helped me win science fairs with bridge models we'd build together in his shop. He taught me how to draw. How to make my own designs to scale. I wouldn't be here, not at the college or as far into my degree, without him. Sometimes I have to remind myself of that when..."

He stops himself from finishing. "When what?" I ask.

His eyes go to the sky, his shoulders rising and falling with a deep breath. "I saw Marco yesterday. I was *this close*"—he moves his two fingers together—"to confronting him. To telling him off. To making him regret putting Dawson and God knows who else in the position he did. How many deaths is he responsible for? Overdoses? He's walking around like he hasn't impacted anybody. Like he's innocent."

"I thought you were going to let it go." After the service, it seemed like he heard me. Like he understood that Marco would be caught. "What could you have done if you confronted him? What if he's dangerous?"

Paxton doesn't speak for a tense moment. "Dawson had a gun." My eyes widen, but before I can say anything, he adds, "He was afraid of Marco and whoever else he was involved with. I don't know what I would have done. But I would have risked it. I thought about risking it."

"Why?"

"Because..." His eyes evade mine. "Because I don't know

435

what I have to lose anymore. My father will never change. We'll never be okay. Dawson is gone. You're..."

Once again, his words fade away, and the empty expression on his face makes my heart sink. "The future," I tell him.

He finally looks up at me, those brown eyes distant through the lenses of his glasses.

"You have the future to lose. Trust me, Paxton. That's everything." I nod, almost to myself more than to him. "I don't like what your father has done to you, but he's set you up for a future that not all of us are going to get. And I'm sorry... I'm sorry that I lied. That I kept secrets. I don't know what I expected to happen, but my intention was never to hurt more people than I already have. You're a good person. The kind of person who doesn't deserve what life has handed you. But it's not too late. To change it. To take control of it. Sometimes a risk isn't worth taking if it means giving up what you haven't even discovered yet."

His throat bobs as he watches me, his nostrils flaring open and closed before he turns away. I see him wet his lips, swallow, and take a deep breath. Then he asks, "And what about you and your risks? What about the things you haven't been able to discover?"

I inhale slowly, exhaling as I make eye contact with him. "My biggest risk was coming here. Leaving my family behind. And you know what I discovered?"

He stares at me.

"You."

His jaw ticks.

"Dixie."

He swallows again.

"Dawson," I whisper.

His eyes close.

"I discovered what it's like to be part of something outside me," I tell him, hugging my legs to my chest. "I learned what it's like to have friends. To have...more."

We fall to silence while he soaks that in.

Then, ever so quietly, I say, "In another lifetime, right?"

He opens his eyes to reveal a glassy gaze pointed in my direction.

I smile. It's small. But it's genuine. "You don't have to stay here, you know."

He watches me.

Taking a deep breath, I say, "You could go somewhere far, far away and never look back if you wanted to. Away from your father. Away from...all of this."

The memories.

The pain.

"I do want that, but I don't know how to get there. This is all I know," he whispers.

My smile wavers. "Is it? Or it all you've allowed yourself to accept?"

Paxton is quiet, his eyes dropping to the ground.

"I read a book once and remember a quote in it about how we accept the love we think we deserve," I murmur, my chin resting on my bent knees. "But you deserve more than what your father can offer you. More than what I could. Than what even Dawson could. This life"—I gesture around us—"that you've made yourself used to can be changed. You don't need your father. He needs you. That's the difference."

He doesn't look at me.

"You have the ability to do amazing things in life, Paxton," I say softly, finally getting him to lift his head. "And

437

I'll be living vicariously through you from wherever I go after this."

He blinks.

I blink.

Taking a deep breath, he looks up to the sky.

I give him the time he needs.

One minute.

Two.

After three, he meets my eyes. Then he holds out his hand. "Come here."

Biting my lip, I look down at the planks.

"I won't let you get hurt. I promise. I just need..."

You is the unspoken word I let myself believe he was going to say.

My steps are slow and careful as I try mimicking the moves he made to avoid the weak spots. The second I put my hand in his, a spark shoots up my arm as he pulls me into him as the board underneath my foot gives out.

We fall, me landing on top of him on the ground. Heart racing as I look down at his panicked face, he's quickly examining me, frantically about to ask, "Are you—" when I stop him with my mouth.

The kiss drowns out his question as I position myself over him so my knees dig into the soft grass on either side of his waist.

His hands go to my hips, my shirt rising slightly until a sliver of discolored skin appears. He gently runs a finger over it, his brows furrowing. When he lifts the material, he sucks in a breath when he sees the other bruises along my abdomen.

They started showing up days ago. Each spot a horrible shade of purple and blue. There are other patches that are yellow. My ribs show in ways they haven't in a long time, making me look ten times worse than I feel. If my mother had a say, she would be force-feeding me every two hours.

I can only imagine what being back home will be like once she sees me. It'll kill her. All of those memories of her crying in the kitchen over me will become another reality.

But I don't want to think about that.

I don't want to think about anything.

I return his hands to my bare skin, trailing them up to my chest until I make him cup me above my bra. "Help me forget."

"Sawyer—"

"I won't break."

Doubt clouds his eyes.

"I won't," I whisper in assurance.

I lean forward, kissing him once, twice, three times until he finally kisses me back. Gently, so gently, he explores my mouth and my body under my clothes. When it's clear that he won't take the lead, I do.

And he lets me.

Not turning me down.

Not rejecting me.

Giving me control.

Letting me set the pace.

To take what I need.

His hands explore every marred inch of me.

Every bruise.

Every scar.

Every piece of exposed skin that shows the state of my health that's ripping us apart.

And in that moment, he's mine, and I'm his, and we're the only two people who matter.

What comes next doesn't cross our minds.

Not until our shuddered breaths catch at the release we both find in each other.

And as we collect ourselves, bodies sated, eyes mirrored with sadness as we stare at the tattered bridge, I realize how full circle we've come to pass the broken bridge to be with each other again.

One last time.

"In another lifetime," he finally repeats.

Chapter Forty-One

SAWYER

STARING AT MY NAKED body in the mirror, I frown at the way my rib cage tapers in. I trace my fingers along each bone that sticks out under the skin and then move my attention down to the yellow, purple, and blue discoloration lining my torso.

Moving my hands up, I press them under my jaw and feel the bumps hidden beneath the surface. The swelling has gotten worse. Every time I swallow, I can feel it. Every time I breathe, I struggle. I didn't need the doctors to tell me that the cancer has spread. I can sense it in the way I move, the way I sleep, the way I live.

Blinking, I drop my hands to my sides and study the patchy hair on my head that's slightly thicker than it was when I moved here. But it's still short. Still ugly. I can't style it. Don't want to shave it. Wearing a wig is starting to hurt, like my skin is far too sensitive to hide under it. I've given up caring what people think.

It doesn't matter anyway.

Once upon a time, I considered myself pretty.

I had the potential to get back to that place.

But I know the odds. Fifty-seven percent is a generous survival rate for my type of cancer. There is nothing I can do that would make it any better at this point.

Rubbing my yellowing eyes, I grab a towel and wrap it around my tiny body. I'm done seeing what's been done to me.

Done feeling sorry for myself.

I don't remember dressing.

Don't remember leaving the building.

I know Paxton is at work. He dropped Pop-Tarts and coffee at my door before he left. I had no appetite, so they're still sitting on the counter.

My body goes on autopilot as I walk through the city, my feet hurting, my lungs aching when I go up even the slightest incline.

I have no real destination in mind.

The bridge is too far, and I don't want to cloud the last memory I have of it, of being there with Paxton. I'm okay with walking away from it.

Just one more time.

That was all I wanted.

To see it one more time.

And I got so much more.

As I near the edge of campus, I see a group of guys huddled around somebody smaller than them by a solid foot, and I can tell they aren't playing around the way friends do. I stop halfway down the sidewalk, debating what to do. I could cross the street and pay them no mind. That's what my parents would tell me to do. What I *should* do.

But I know what it feels like to be beaten down by life. I know what Paxton must have felt getting treated poorly by somebody who should have never laid a hand on him. Maybe that's why I walk over with feigned confidence.

"Leave him alone," I call out.

Two of them turn to see who's talking, looking uninterested when they see me. The other three surrounding their prey stand taller, the wild-eyed one in the middle giving me a curious once-over as I stop a few feet from them.

"Leave him alone," I say again, looking at the shaken boy behind them. "Are you okay?"

He's silent, eyes darting to one of the guys still hovering over him. I don't believe him at all when he stammers, "Y-Yes."

The boy with wild eyes walks over to me, shooting me a slimy smile. He looks familiar, but I can't place him up close. "You're brave." His eyes go up to my hair. "And not only for that haircut. It's…daring. Butting into people's business though…" He whistles.

"Yo, Marco," one of the guys behind him says. "What do you want us to do with this dude?"

Marco?

Marco.

The person standing in front of me shifts his focus behind him. "I expect my payment by the end of the week. You know what will happen if I don't get it."

Whoever the smaller boy is quickly nods, not hesitating to run the second he gets the advantage.

Payment. It this some sort of deal that I walked into?

"Damn, baby," Marco whistles, giving me another once-over with raised brows. "I'd offer you something good, but it looks like you're already on it. Haven't seen somebody this skinny since my ex started shooting up heroin."

I have no doubt this is the same Marco I've seen based

on the tattoos that peek out from the edge of his long-sleeved shirt—the same one Paxton has been willing to risk everything to get revenge on. My gut is telling me to walk away and pretend like I saw nothing. But I can't. Because Paxton is right.

Somebody should stand up to him.

For Dawson.

"You got my friend killed," I say.

His eyebrows go up, and his friends go silent behind him. "Come again, sweetheart?"

My shoulders go back, ignoring the pet name. "You killed Dawson."

He looks over his shoulder at his friends with a slick grin before turning back and chuckling. "Were you sweet on Gable? I thought his type would be more...put together. His last girl was. Then again, I always had a sweet spot for brunettes."

Dixie.

"Real shame about him," he coos. "He still owes me, you know. He screwed me out of my legacy and then he screwed me out of a lot of cash."

That's all he has to say? Somebody is dead because of him and he's worried about money? "Do you have any conscience at all?"

The smile remaining tells me he doesn't. "When you're in my position, you can't afford to have a conscience." His eyes rake over me for a second time, landing on my chest, which has flattened considerably over the past month. "Shame about you too. Bet you were hot once."

I swallow at the words that feel like a knife to the heart. "Fuck you."

His eyes spark. "You're a spicy one, huh? I guess I could

look past the body with a face like that. You willing to pay back your boyfriend's debts on his behalf? I can think of some ideas on how to make things right."

He's disgusting. "If you think I would ever touch somebody as slimy as you, you're mistaken. Dawson had his problems, but he was obviously ten times the man you will ever be."

The guys behind him stand taller as Marco walks up to me and grabs my arm. His grip is painful, and I know it'll be another bruise. I'll deal with that when the time comes. In the meantime, I swallow the surprised yelp and try acting unfazed, even though my heart is beating so fast in my chest I'd be shocked if he didn't hear it. "You better watch your fucking mouth, bitch."

I was told once to be careful what I say.

That it could lead to trouble.

But I also said I didn't care, if what I had to say was worth it.

And Dawson was my friend.

He *is* worth it.

Paxton is worth it.

I don't know what I have to lose anymore, Paxton said.

Unlike him, my future doesn't matter.

"Or what?" I challenge Marco.

Something digs into my stomach.

When I look down, my body freezes.

"Scared yet?" he taunts, jabbing the barrel of the gun farther into me. His shirt sleeve rises up, revealing the edge of the tattoo I've seen before. "Dawson Gable was just as much of a scumbag as me; he just hid it better. It's not my fault that you were too dick-blind to it. So how about an apology, hmm?"

He drags the barrel upward, keeping it between my breasts and hidden from plain sight if anybody were to pass us.

Don't do it, a voice pleads in my head. *Be smart with your next words.*

Professor Banks's words echo in the back of my head. *That mouth is going to get you into trouble someday.*

I don't know what I have to lose anymore.

I take a deep breath. "Did Dawson get an apology?"

Marco's eyes narrow. "Do you have a death wish?"

I lean into the gun to show him I'm not afraid.

I am not afraid.

"He didn't deserve to die," I tell him. I know I speak for a lot of people when I say that. "There's nothing you can say that will change my perspective on him. He was my friend. He was a lot of people's friends. And you took that away from all of us. I will not apologize to you because you don't deserve it. I can only hope you get what's coming to you in the end, the way we all will. So do it. Pull the trigger."

I put my hand over the barrel.

Not moving it.

Not trying to push it away.

"Do it," I taunt, voice breaking.

"Marco," one of the guys calls out. "Come on. She ain't worth it."

I stare Marco straight in the eyes. "Do. It."

His eyes get dark, darker than they were before. "You psycho little—"

One loud *bang* cracks, so loud it's deafening.

But I barely hear it at all before I'm falling.

Falling.

Falling.

I see the horrified look on Marco's face above me before

he and his friends all bolt, scattering as darkness blankets over me.

I think I hear somebody say, "I didn't pull it. I didn't do it."

The voices are getting farther and farther away.

There's pain.

So much pain.

Everything gets fuzzy.

Grows warm. Comfortably warm.

Then there's somebody above me. The boy who ran away from Marco. He's kneeling above me, frantic. I think he's saying something. Touching me. Trying to comfort me.

But he sounds so far away.

He's got dark hair.

And dark eyes.

He doesn't look like Paxton, but I pretend he is. Just for a moment. Just enough to say, "In a–another l–lifetime."

The boy shakes his head, his mouth moving but nothing coming out. Nothing I hear anyway.

My eyelids get heavy.

Heavy.

Heavy.

Suddenly, the pain subsides altogether.

Until there's nothing but...

Peace.

And when I close my eyes, I see Dawson.

Healthy. Happy. Himself.

He reaches out to me and says, "Thank you."

Chapter Forty-Two

BANKS

AN ALARM GOES OFF on campus that I've never heard before, so loud it makes my ears ring.

Suddenly, Teddy is running out from the back room and lowering the cage door that locks the store up from the rest of the building. "Get in the back now," he directs me and Lucy. "There's an active shooter. A shot was heard fired somewhere on campus."

I pale, doing what he says and pulling out my phone as soon as we're both secured in the back.

Me: Don't come to campus. It's not safe

I want for her to text me back.

To see the bubbles.

She's been sleeping a lot lately, so her silence isn't that unusual. Her class doesn't start for another couple of hours, which means she wouldn't have a reason to be on campus until later.

Me: I'll see you later

My gut tightens, a feeling I rarely get.

Stress. Anxiety. Given the circumstances, it makes sense why I'd feel uneasy.

I wish I hadn't written it off so quickly.

My knocks on Sawyer's door go unanswered for two hours by the time the campus is cleared and everybody is allowed to go home. Classes are canceled for the rest of the day, so I wanted to check on Sawyer. I call out to her every time I knock.

Nothing.

Anxiety bubbles up to the surface again.

Entering my apartment, I dig through the shit piled onto the counter until I find the sticky note with a name and number written across it.

"Pick up," I murmur as it rings.

And rings.

And rings.

And rings.

"The caller you have dialed is not available at this time. At the tone, please record your message."

"Fuck," I growl as it beeps. Gripping the back of my neck, I start pacing. "Mr. Hawkins, it's Paxton Banks. I, uh, was just wondering if you and Sawyer were out. If you could call me back, I'd really appreciate it."

I don't bother mentioning the school shooting because I don't want to alarm him. If it's not all over the news, I'm sure it will be soon enough anyway. When Teddy gave us the all clear to unlock the store, they were saying that there was a shooting just outside campus related to drugs. An altercation, the cops called it.

That was all they said.

I didn't stick around once we closed early to get more details because there was only one person I wanted to see.

Ten minutes go by agonizingly slowly.

Then thirty minutes.

An hour.

I don't stop moving, biting my nails, and pacing the entire time. The person who lives below me is probably sick of the back-and-forth creaks of the wood groaning under my feet, but I don't give a shit.

She wasn't at the bridge when I stopped by earlier like I thought she'd be. I walked inside our little private happy place and stared at the spot where we were the last time we visited, hoping she'd be sitting there thinking about it too, but she wasn't.

And she's not at home.

I look at the clock again.

An hour and forty-five minutes go by.

Nothing.

After sundown, when the silence is too much to bear, I grab the keys to my father's car and storm toward the door. I open it to see the stricken face of Sawyer's father.

His eyes are red.

His face pale.

I drop the keys when I see him shake his head and start shaking mine. "No."

"Son…" His voice cracks.

"I just saw her. She was fine."

He walks in, grabbing my arm when I nearly trip backing up. "I think you need to sit down."

"No" is all I can say as he guides me to the couch anyway.

When I'm finally sitting and looking up at him, he takes a deep breath, his eyes a level of sad I've never seen on a grown man before, before saying only one thing. "Yes."

And there, in the middle of my apartment, I break down in front of a father who is not my own, and he comforts me in ways mine never could.

"I just saw her," I repeat.

Her father is white, silent, nodding absently.

"I just..." I choke on the words.

He puts a hand on my shoulder, clenching it once. "They caught the person who did it. He was identified this afternoon by a witness."

I stare at him.

"Marco Hastings."

I sit straighter.

"Does the name mean anything to you?"

It's hard to swallow.

She wouldn't.

"Son," her father says. "Talk to me."

I blink.

Blink again.

Processing.

Understanding.

You have your future to lose.

She already wrote hers off.

"Yes," I whisper. "I know Marco."

And I tell him everything.

Chapter Forty-Three

BANKS

THE VIEWING IS HELD in Louisiana because it was her favorite place, at a funeral home near the house she lived in when she was eight years old.

She would have loved it.

It's close to the water.

Close to our bridge.

Besides her family, the only person I recognize is Dixie, although she barely looks like the same girl I met at the beginning of the year. She looks like she's seen a ghost. She's lost weight. Barely speaks. Looks like she hasn't slept for as long as I haven't.

We sit together in silence, staring at the closed casket at the front of the room with the picture of a glowing redheaded girl above it.

Sawyer looked so much younger.

So much healthier.

A different person.

"I regret not staying at Dawson's funeral," Dixie tells

me, taking my hand. I don't even know if she realizes she's holding it, but I don't let it go. I'm not sure I'm physically capable. "I don't want to regret this."

We sit like that for what feels like forever.

"She chose her fate," she eventually whispers, leaning her head against my shoulder.

I blink, stuck staring at the blown-up picture of what used to be my neighbor. She refused to let life take her down without a fight.

She took control.

One last time.

I rest my cheek on the top of her head. "I guess we couldn't have expected any less from her, could we?"

All she does is hum.

When everybody files out of the building, I see my father standing in the corner. I stop in disbelief, waiting for him to come to me.

Dixie is still holding my hand, standing behind me as he stops in front of us.

All Dad says is "You cared about her the same way she did you. I...I've failed you a lot in life, so I wanted to be here for you now."

He didn't show up to Dawson's funeral, and he knew him for over a decade. Why now? Guilt? Shame? I can't trust it. Can't be sure it's honorable.

He's had his whole life to make up for his failures. It's too late now. The same is true for Dawson and Sawyer.

"I don't need you," I inform him, voice void of any emotion. It's all crammed in my chest, the tight ball growing and growing and ready to burst.

I pull Dixie along with me, ignoring his gaping expression.

"Are you okay?" she asks.

"No."

Her hand squeezes mine and I know it's her way of saying, *Me neither.*

My father calls out to me, but I don't stop.

Sawyer lived her life the way she wanted. She chose her fate—chose the people she wanted in her life.

It was time I did the same.

Maybe one day I would consider letting him back in, if he proved he deserved it.

But I would only cross that bridge when, and if, I got there.

Epilogue

BANKS

IT TOOK THREE YEARS after graduating from LSU to raise enough money and gather the building materials for the reconstruction based on my senior project. After the model was approved by the city, a process that stretched far longer than my patience could tolerate, it took another six months to bring to life.

But staring at the red ribbon tied to the freshly planted oak on one side and a wooden post on the other, I can breathe easier knowing all that wait was worth it.

A small hand grazes my bicep, pulling my attention away from where the cameras are setting up by the memorial. "Hey, you," I greet, draping an arm around the person who's made the last four years tolerable.

Not easier, but...better.

Dixie smiles up at me. "It's almost time."

"Are they here?" I glance at my watch, a new stainless-steel Citizen that she bought me for Christmas two years ago when my grandfather's stopped working for the final time.

She nods, softness in her eyes. "They just pulled up."

If it hadn't been for her suggestion to put on a string of charity shows across the East Coast, I'm not sure we would have been able to make today possible. Her music raised the money we needed and then some, giving us the opportunity to immortalize the person we both mutually respected.

Not to mention she was the voice of reason when the city council kept holding back the approval because of the ridiculous bullshit they needed to do per policy.

Fuck the policy.

Dixie went to every single meeting—every planning board and every public hearing—to make sure I didn't jump over the dumbass tables and punch the council members in their uptight faces.

It was a memorial for a sick girl.

For a girl who sacrificed herself for others.

And they couldn't make one simple request happen?

"Let's go get them," I say, turning us with my arm still around her shoulder.

A space between the magnolia bushes is open now after we removed and relocated one of the flourishing shrubs in order to create a pathway into the quiet alcove that's no longer a secret to the public.

First I see Bentley Hawkins , who towers over his mother by a good foot and a half. He shot up since the last time he was in Louisiana. Gone is the boyish fat on the seventeen-year-old's face, where instead there are mature teenage features.

When his father turns to me, I'm struck by the same emotions I was when he showed up to my apartment the day Sawyer died. He holds out a hand for me to shake, which I do as soon as Dixie and I stop in front of him.

"It's good to see you, sir," I say.

Dixie hugs Sawyer's mom. They've become fast friends over the years, talking a few times a month to see how the other is. There's never going to be a replacement for what Sawyer meant to her family, but I think Dixie offers them comfort with every step she takes in life.

They watch her live because they couldn't see their daughter prosper. It's not what they wanted, but I think it's as close as they can get. So Dixie indulges them the way she indulges me.

"Follow me," I tell them, leading the small group into the revamped garden.

When they see the new bridge where the old one stood, they stop short.

Sawyer's mother lets out a shaky breath.

I walk over and grab the framed piece that I preserved from the original structure. "This is for you," I say, handing them the wood with our initials in it. "We made those when we were kids. I didn't want it to get lost or taken if we left it hanging here, so I thought the safest place would be with you."

Bentley is the one who takes it when his mother gets stuck frozen in place, staring at the gift that I hope isn't too much.

I selfishly thought about keeping it for myself, but I know where it belongs. Which is why hidden under my shirt, right above my heart, is an identical tattoo that I had an artist trace and ink on me permanently.

A personal memorial of my own.

"Thank you," Mrs. Hawkins whispers, eyes glistening as she stares at her daughter's initials.

Her husband turns to the ribbon. "I know she would

have loved this. The days she ran away to meet you were some of her favorites."

You were my favorite memory.

Dixie rubs my back in silent comfort.

I clear my throat. "They were mine too."

The photographer from the paper comes over and interrupts. "We're ready for you."

Nodding, I turn to Sawyer's family. "I was wondering if you'd like to do the honors at the ribbon cutting. They're going to do an article on the memorial. You don't have to talk to them if you don't want to, but it'll highlight Sawyer's time here and why this is important."

The three of them share a look before Mr. Hawkins finally answers. "We'd be honored to do anything to share the love Sawyer had."

Bentley, who's been standing silently the entire time, tucks the frame under his arm. "If it's all right, I think I'll sit out on the ribbon cutting."

His mother looks heartbroken. "Bentley..."

He shakes his head. "I can't," he whispers.

I grasp his shoulders. "That's fine."

Ten minutes later, the photographer takes the photo of Sawyer's parents cutting the ribbon for the official Sawyer Hawkins memorial and starts the interview.

Hours later, after everybody leaves for their hotels for the night, I'm standing by the end of the bridge when I notice something silver reflecting off the streetlight overhead.

Kneeling down, I graze my fingers over the package of chocolate fudge Pop-Tarts resting by the tree, along with the flowers, stuffed animals, and other mementos left behind.

Bentley.

"I apologized to her," a voice says from behind me,

causing me to dart up and spin to see the seventeen-year-old standing there with his hands in his pockets. He's looking at his sister's favorite treat, a permanent frown settled on his face.

"Do your parents know you're here?" I ask.

He shakes his head.

In that moment, I recognize so much of Sawyer in him. I gesture toward the bench Dixie helped me build and sit, waiting for him to join me before saying, "It doesn't get easier right away, but it will. Eventually."

He toys with his fingers, keeping his eyes on his lap. "Is it easier for you?"

If I lie, how will that help him? "I'm getting there. It doesn't happen overnight."

We fall to silence, save for the passing vehicles and insects in the background.

"I apologized to her for what I said," he tells me quietly, voice barely more than a murmur. "It doesn't feel like that matters though."

I knock his knee with mine until he looks at me. "Sawyer loved you and knew you didn't mean what you said. She was willing to come back to New York because of that love. That's what you should focus on."

"She wasn't mad?"

I lean back and stretch my legs out. "No. Sawyer had a lot of things to be mad about, but she never let them consume her. If she wasn't mad about those things, there was no way she was going to stay angry with you."

I don't know if that helps or if it even can. It was hard enough losing a friend, a neighbor, a woman who could have possibly been the person for me. But a sister? That break is deeper—harder to heal. I'd know. Dawson was like a brother to me, and his absence is still one I feel wedged into my soul.

"Did you love her?" Bentley asks.

"Sawyer?"

He nods.

Wetting my lips, I stare into the night. It's not a conversation I've had with anybody and definitely not one I planned on having with her little brother. "I loved who she was as a person. I loved a lot of things about her. I could have..." I clear my throat. "If things were different, I could have."

"And do you love who Dixie is as a person?"

The question raises my brows.

"I like her," he says, shrugging.

Me too. "Dixie..." Dixie got me through a tough time. We mourned together. Grieved together. Slowly tried healing together. She became one of my closest allies, and for that I'll forever be grateful. "Dixie has been a good friend to me."

She grounded me when I needed it most, no matter how much I fought her. Helped me make this memorial come to life. I'll be grateful for her for life.

"Nobody can compare to Sawyer," I tell him, if that's why he's asking. "I think we love people in different ways based on how they fit into our lives. As friends. As family. Sometimes as more."

Contemplation has him nodding along slowly. "I guess so."

One day, I think he'll understand.

Hell, maybe one day I will.

I think about Dixie, who was going to meet up with a group of friends she met at the music store she works at part-time when she's here in the summers. Between her travel schedule for the mini tour she's been doing at concert halls with her family and the help she's given me to make today possible, she's busier than normal.

And I...I miss her. Watching TV is boring without her commentary. Music doesn't interest me the same way when she's not here giving me her explanation of the beat changes and what she thinks the lyrics mean. Her friendship fills the hole in my heart that's been there since Sawyer passed.

I knew being apart was bound to happen eventually, especially since I accepted a job in New York working for an architectural firm. I start in two weeks, move into my small, overpriced studio apartment next week, and bring Louisiana to a close once and for all.

You could leave here, Sawyer told me.

I knew I couldn't until I finished this.

But now that it's done...

It's time for me to start a new chapter instead of rereading the last one.

Bentley sighs. "Today meant a lot to my parents. They needed this. Thank you for making it happen."

"You don't have to thank me."

He lifts his shoulders and stands. "It made them happy to be part of something that involved her again. I miss them being that way."

I watch him quietly as his eyes move over the bridge, then to the tree covered in memorial gifts, and then back down to the Pop-Tarts.

Before we can say anything else, a bright-red bird lands on the tree branch directly in front of Bentley and squawks once. Its head tilts as it studies the teenager before making another noise.

"I called her Birdie," I note, staring at the bird watching him just as intently as he is watching it.

The bird turns to me, squawking again.

A case of déjà vu hits me. "That's a cardinal."

Bentley doesn't look away from it.

The bird flies over, landing on his shoulder and squawking once more, as if trying to talk to him. Then it flies over to me, and I swear it rubs its head against my jaw once.

"Birdie," I whisper.

It spreads its wings and does a loop around us before landing on the railing of the bridge.

"You don't really think…?" Bentley's voice fades, shaking his head in disbelief.

"I think anything is possible at this point."

The bird watches us for a little while longer before taking off, its fleeting squawks fading into the distance as it soars up, up, up until we can't see it at all.

But its lasting effect remains.

"Paxton?" Bentley says, turning to me.

I look at him.

"She'd want you to be happy."

All I can do is stare at him.

"Dixie seems nice."

I'm silent.

He gestures to where the bird was watching us. "I think that's probably as good of a sign as you'll ever get to move on. She clearly has. Maybe we should too."

That's all he says before tucking his hands into his pockets and walking away.

Later that night, I find myself at the apartment Dixie rents on a month-to-month basis. When she answers the door, I say, "I'm moving to New York."

She blinks at the news, which she's asked me about since

I admitted to submitting a few applications up north. "You got the job."

"I got the job."

She smiles, stepping into me for a hug. "I'm happy for you, Paxton."

Paxton.

I'm still not used to hearing that name.

When she steps back, I lift my car keys. "Ice cream to celebrate?"

She smiles, grabbing a jacket and following me out. "I thought you'd never ask."

She gets mint chocolate chip.

I get cookies and cream.

And another little piece of the hole in my chest closes, stitched up by the hope of someday.

Whatever someday brings.

Prologue

RAINE

THE UNIVERSITY FOOTBALL FIELD looks different set up for the graduation ceremony. Instead of the bleachers being full of fans sporting Lindon's bright red team colors, it's a crowd of people in formal wear supporting their loved ones, spread in rows of folding chairs across the turf.

A pressure builds in the pit of my stomach when I hear *Raine Joanna Copelin* announced through the microphone. On wobbly legs, I look to the crowd and see a blur of faces cheering me on. Mom and Dad are there beside each other with big smiles on their faces despite the divorce drama they've been going through for the past few months, and Mom's sister, Aunt Tiffany, is perched on her other side, holding up her phone to take a billion pictures that she'll undoubtedly tag me in later.

Skin tightening as I shake the long line of hands before accepting my diploma, I turn to face the front of the stage and roll my shoulders back to stand taller. There's a warm buzz creeping along my skin as I hear one voice in particular cheering me on louder than anybody.

From the corner of my eye, I see Caleb Anders clapping the loudest, along with half the school's football team cheering right alongside him.

Normally, the former running back whistling at me is the one everybody has their eyes on when he's standing on this field. There isn't one game of his that I missed during the season. I'd sit beside every other fan watching the Dragons take on their opponents, feeling the anxiety of every chase, tackle, and touchdown that came with the intense game.

I keep reminding myself that this very moment has been one I've been dreaming of for years. The start of something new—a big future with *Dr. Copelin* printed on an office door in bold lettering to a practice that is solely mine.

But I know the future is murky when it comes to other people's plans for me.

Namely, Caleb's.

My ears ring when the ceremony ends and everybody tosses their caps into the air. I barely register callused hands pulling me to the side when our class disperses with a newfound freedom tied to four years of steep debt.

Caleb wraps me in a big hug, which I instantly return despite the *thump, thump, thump* of my pounding heart. Can he feel it drumming against his chest? When he pulls back, there's a glossy look to his eyes that sets off alarm bells.

Because I know that the future Caleb wants is about to be thrown into my face in front of all these people.

A future I can't give him.

My stomach drops at the same moment as he does onto one knee. I hear a collective gasp come from the people around us as they watch the scene unfold.

The panic seeps in as he looks up at me with those warm

chocolate eyes that have always made me feel so loved and taken care of.

When he pulls out a small black velvet box, I know exactly what's resting inside before he even opens it to reveal the beautiful white-gold ring sitting in the holder. The sun hits the small diamond, making it shimmer like the hope on Caleb's face as he asks me those four words.

"Will you marry me?"

The ringing in my ears intensifies, drowning out the crowd waiting for my response. My eyes lift to graze the eager bystanders and lock with Mom's and Tiffany's stricken faces, then Dad's blank one as he stares at the ring my boyfriend of seven years is holding.

Thump, thump, thump, thump.

When I finally look back down at the twenty-two-year-old with a boyish smile, I know without a single doubt in my mind that I love him. I've loved him for a long time— long before he gave me that little stuffed polar bear holding a heart that had *I love you* stitched into it.

It was our thing. *His* thing. When the verbal words were too much, he'd gift them to me, and I'd felt them all the same.

I love you.

Be mine.

Happily ever after.

I'd fallen in love with his wit and how much he cared for his family. The boy kneeling in front of me with wavering lips as he awaits my answer is a family man to his core. He's going to take over the hardware store in Lindon, a legacy his father has built for many generations to come.

Which is the problem.

Legacies like that will leave a mark on the world along with huge expectations that I can't live up to.

467

But Caleb can't know about the reason why.

Because then he'd know the truth about what happened that summer back in 2015.

Inhaling deeply, I let out an unstable breath and slowly start shaking my head. "I'm sorry. I'm so sorry, Caleb."

No matter what, I'm going to break his heart. Whether it's now or ten years into the future.

With a glassy gaze that I fight, I stare down at the gorgeous ring that I want so badly to be wearing on my finger right now.

Despite the crack that becomes bigger and bigger in my own heart, I whisper, "I can't."

ACKNOWLEDGMENTS

This book wouldn't have existed if it hadn't been for my father's own battle with non-Hodgkin's lymphoma. I saw firsthand how hard it was for him to go through treatment—how much it took from him every single day to beat cancer. And I'm so grateful he was able to do just that and be here to cheer me on today. From day one, he's been my biggest supporter.

I also want to thank the BookTok community for helping my books get the attention of Bloom. Without you talking about *Underneath the Sycamore Tree*, I'm not sure I would have ever gotten a chance to tell this story. You've opened doors I wouldn't have otherwise been able to explore as an indie author, so thank you!

To my family and friends who I ignored so I could write this...sorry. I'll make it up to you now that this book is out!

As always, the Bloom team have polished this book into the beautiful creation it is today. Thank you for giving me the chance to share my words with the world. I'll forever be grateful for the opportunity you've given me.

Until next time.

Xx B

ABOUT THE AUTHOR

B. Celeste is a new adult and contemporary romance author who gives voices to raw, realistic characters with emotional storylines that tug on the heartstrings. She was born and raised in upstate New York, where she still resides with her four-legged feline sidekick, Oliver "Ollie" Queen. Her love for reading and writing began at an early age and only grew stronger after getting a BA in English and an MFA in English and creative writing. When she's not writing, she's working out, binge-watching reality game shows, and spending time with her friends and family.